EVERYTHING
ABRIDGED

EVERYTHING ABRIDGED

----→ STORIE$ ←----

DENNARD DAYLE

THE OVERLOOK PRESS, NEW YORK

"Recent Activity" was first published in *Matchbook* in 2016.
"Comments" was first published in *McSweeney's Internet Tendency* in 2018.
"Hell in an Inkwell" was first published in *No. 2 Literary Mag* in 2019.
"Question" and "Urban Market" were first published in *Points in Case* in 2019.
"Own Goal" was first published in *Clarkesworld* in 2020.
"Liberty Points" was previously published in the New Book Bay Science Fiction contest.

Library of Congress Control Number: 2021947024

ISBN: 978–1–4197–6096–9
eISBN: 978–1–64700–636–5

Printed and bound in the United States
1 3 5 7 9 10 8 6 4 2

Abrams books are available at special discounts when purchased in quantity for premiums and
promotions as well as fundraising or educational use. Special editions can also be created to
specification. For details, contact specialsales@abramsbooks.com or the address below.

ABRAMS The Art of Books
195 Broadway, New York, NY 10007
abramsbooks.com

For Eugeny Higgins.

Contents

What's Happening?

If you're alive today, you're either confused or too deluded to be confused. *Everything Abridged* is the cure. A comprehensive guide to what the world is, was, and will be. My handmade gift to everyone navigating the Anthropocene. If you can't define "Anthropocene," you're welcome.

Like any proper reference, it's been researched, written, and reviewed by a leading expert. To complement current attention spans, most entries have been kept short. Longer entries indicate areas of particular interest. They include letters, records, histories, and hallucinations for your education. While technically untrue, they reflect reality.

Get ready to change. You might absorb *Everything Abridged* in one linear burst or slowly pick through random sections. Either way, you'll be marked as a leader by your community and intelligence agencies. The daily bombardment of information will start to make sense, and you'll gain a working definition of "Anthropocene." You'll be more than you were.

All you need to know is that this is all you need to know. Good luck.

Best,
Dennard Dayle, Expertise Specialist

A

abolition: An early invasion of property rights by left-wing extremists.

advertising: 1. A combination of art and business. Specifically, the profit of art and creativity of business.
2. The easiest way for a writer to live with a semblance of comfort and dignity.
3. When a talking beach ball asks you to buy insurance.

Africa: Home to enduring, storied, and diverse natural resources.

age: Decline in thought, vigor, and ability in exchange for wealth and authority. The wealth and authority are not guaranteed.

agnosticism: Uncertainty about your willingness to argue on holidays.

Alexander the Great: The tone-setter for violent sociopathy's role in history.

aliens: 1. Fungi found on a rock orbiting Alpha Centauri.
2. Talking bugs currently engaged in their version of the Napoleonic Wars.
3. Rubber suits used to haze new CIA recruits.
4. Your future masters.

alimony: Love's hangover.

allegory: Literary passive-aggression.

American Dream, the: An industry-defining ad campaign by Horatio Alger.

Americas, the: An exciting Early Modern opportunity for everyone but the residents.

analysis: The journey back to your established opinion.

anarchism: A brick-based martial art.
Author's note: I tried joining a local group, but the guy in charge was the worst.

anger: Overexposure to education, current events, family, romance, unemployment, employment, or a neighbor's taste in music.

anime: The ongoing memoirs of Karl Ove Anime, a high school sophomore with a unique power.

Annotations

I. Admiral Titania Largo opened every victory speech with this sitcom-grade lemon of a joke. While her grasp of field tactics and statecraft are undeniable, the same cannot be said of comedy.[A]

   A. Nonetheless, survivors of the battle likely appreciated it.

II. This is slightly misleading. Three out of every five drafted citizens died. Titania's statistic only references mech pilots, who enjoyed a gentler 50 percent survival rate.

III. At this point, the admiral paused to allow applause to die down. Few Free Dominion factions had more enthusiasm for the end of the Senate than the Senate itself.

IV. Widely debunked.

V. "The Final War" refers to World War III, reflecting a postwar optimism that would be violently dispelled over the next fifty years.

VI. "ACT" is shorthand for "anti-civilian tactics," a field developed and perfected by the admiral.[A]

    A. Some scholars, including myself, credit ACT with the overall decline in terrorism in the twenty-second century. Largo's innovations rendered terror obsolete.

VII. Later retracted. Sadly, many well-read people still believe this, thanks to the populist and inflammatory hackwork of C. T. Thompson. There was, just to be clear, no "neo-Jihadist android cartel" behind the Houston firebombing.

VIII. Video edition viewers might note that this is the last speech with Titania's once-signature stutter. C. T. Thompson famously wrote: "The crown may be heavy, but power is a palliative."[A]

    A. Thompson is an imbecile. As I wrote in *Rise of the Valkyrie*, Admiral Largo stopped stuttering two days after the passing of Fleet Admiral Arnold Baldur, her only serious rival for First Citizen. Titania was left with no reason to feign weakness and adjusted accordingly.

IX. A poor way to die.

X. A not-so-subtle reference to losses incurred during Baldur's Charge. Fleet Admiral Baldur believed the Divine Alliance would be unwilling to use atomic weaponry within their own cities.[A] A platoon of Justiciar[B] mechs were lost in the conflagration.

    A. A similarly pigheaded attitude is common among editors of academic journals, who consider a few simple explanations a "self-indulgent waste of the reader's time and yours." I'd like to thank the Dominion Archives for showing more respect for the spirit of intellectual endeavor.

    B. The first mech produced by the Free Dominion Navy. Considerably less refined than later models, the Justiciar required two pilots, used a nonatomic power core, and had a surprising dearth of chemical weapons. The unit compensated for these flaws with enough armored mass to crush a two-story refugee shelter under a single foot.

XI. There were no survivors.

XII. There were no survivors.

XIII. There were three survivors.

XIV. The model for the memorial statue was Sergeant Roderick Liao, the only pilot to survive a direct hit from an orbital rail rifle.[A] From the waist up, at least: the sergeant's lower half was permanently fused to his mech. His spouse claimed that he smiled more often than you'd expect.

    A. Sadly, the most credible book on this subject is *Big Guns and Big Mechs: Rough Riders of the Final War* by C. T. Thompson. It's thorough work, if one is willing to overlook the prosaic style, rampant grammatical errors, and complete absence of intellectual value.

XV. A reference to the "Die on Your Feet" recruitment poster, which featured a portrait view of the admiral.[A,B] Titania was chosen for her subtly judgmental glare, which seemed to follow the viewer long after they'd turned away.

    A. This remains the iconic image of Titania Largo's early career: a wiry woman in a winter infantry jacket, standing in the shadow of a burning city. A popular apocryphal story claims she responded to a photographer's request to cover her braids by having him beaten and imprisoned.[1]

    1. This is, of course, nonsense. He was merely beaten.

  B. Shortly before his accident, Fleet Admiral Baldur expressed regret for "Putting that witch's face on every street sign in the country."

XVI. Deliberate misquote. V. F. Ali referred to mid-war famines as the "wages of hubris," not the "wrath of heaven."

XVII. The less said about the state of North Africa in the aftermath of the war, the better.[A]

  A. As the center of Divine Alliance mech production, North African cities were natural targets for strikes[1] by Dominion pilots. In this context, ACT thrived. To quote the Admiral: "Without noncombatants to supply, support, and inspire an army, there is no army."[2]

    1. My grandfather was the lead engineer behind the 87-VV "Widowmaker," the anti-civilian mech seen in most films about the period. He reminded us of this during every phone call, visit, family reunion, and wedding reception.[a] We did not get along.

      a) During my wedding, he entertained himself with an obsolete cell phone game about arranging colorful gems. He saw no issue with playing at full volume, an incident I consider solid proof that people now live for far too long.

    2. Sampled from Titania's Christmas Day address, found later in the volume.

XVIII. Despite extensive training, Divine Alliance guerrillas were unpaid, underequipped, and casually sacrificed for minor strategic gains. Much like the contemporary adjunct professor.

XIX. A "war crime" was a twenty-first-century neologism for "anti-civilian tactics."

XX. Another reference to a famous soldier. Much like Sergeant Liao, Private Jose Farrell fell into narcotics after the war. However, enthusiastic drug abuse propelled his life instead of truncating it. Stimulants fueled Farrell's journey through a "post-gonzo" journalistic career in which he covered traumatized veterans, bureaucratic corruption, and the cities rendered uninhabitable by ACT. The third topic won him the Dominion Journalism Award despite his continued presence on the Dominion blacklist. Farrell remains the most acclaimed author you're not allowed to read.

XXI. Dubious.

XXII. Subtle pandering. The admiral showed some favoritism to the navy, whose pilots adopted ACT with far more speed and fervor than other branches of the military. However, every military wing would fare better than the Senate during postwar reorganization.[A]

    A. See figure 3: Gulag Population by Occupation.

XXIII. Overt pandering.

XXIV. In the aftermath of the war, postapocalyptic films suffered a tragic drop in sales and critical interest. Blighted, radioactive hellscapes lacked intrigue. The genre's share of public attention was reclaimed by a new wave of romantic comedies. Stories of dull couples unconcerned with cobalt bomb fallout, sixteen-story mechs, and seven-digit daily death tolls offered an imaginative break from daily life.

XXV. Radiation defects are still common among the region's children.

XXVI. Slightly misleading. Toronto could sustain plant life by the end of the decade and is currently scheduled for resettlement within the next five years.

XXVII. Brigadier Elia Menendez was widely considered the best rail-rifle operator of her time,[A] especially after downing sixteen enemy mechs within one hour during the Battle of Mumbai.

    A. Jose Farrell later asked her the secret to her success. Her answer: "The enemy assumed I wouldn't fire through population centers to hit them. I'm sure the survivors are wiser today."

XXVIII. This concept would define much of Titania's administration. Post-Maynardism called for capitalism as a state's core project rather than a neglected companion to government.[A,B]

    A. The resulting economy was extremely rigidly centralized. In *Titania and the Treasury*, I argue that the postwar Free Dominion economy was far closer to the command economy in early twenty-first-century China than any libertarian ideal.[1]

        1. An idea later plagiarized by C. T. Thompson.

    B. This would become a core point of contention during the Fourth World War.

XXIX. Apocryphal.

XXX. Apocryphal.

XXXI. Complete fabrication.

XXXII. Admiral Largo was fond of referring to a bygone golden age. In all of my studies[A] of her speeches, writing, and surprisingly mundane personal life, I've never been able to peg the specific time period described here. I'm of the opinion that it's the same opaque era praised by every conservative in history.

    A. And they've been *long* studies. I spent my early twenties moving from cramped box to cramped box, sifting through videos of a dead woman. The best years of my life, according to most media.[1] Hopefully the "leading expert" tag is worth it.[2]

1. Said media advertises a life ill-suited to producing great thinkers. Modern leisure has produced multiple generations of somnambulant mental vegetables.

2. I can't really know Titania Largo. I know her construct. I know the image she left behind better than my ex-wife, two or so friends, and ever-growing circle of undergraduate sycophants. My longest relationship, in a sense.

XXXIII. There were no survivors.

XXXIV. There was one survivor.

XXXV. The assassinations created a logistical problem: while the Divine Alliance leadership desired to surrender, there was no one left alive with the authority to do so. The conflict continued for two more months, until V. F. Ali seized power and begged Admiral Largo for a cease-fire.

XXXVI. This received deafening applause.

XXXVII. Three months after this address, Admiral Titania Largo became First Citizen Titania Largo. She held the position for the final thirty years of her life, carving out a towering legacy of energetic border expansion, shrewd statecraft, and unprecedented public admiration.[A]

A. She died alone and heirless in her parents' manor. All her friends had been replaced by rivals and admirers— a privilege reserved for leaders in their field.

anodyne: 1. A word keeping SAT tutors in business.
2. A pill taken after a standardized test.

anomaly: A talking dog, dancing statue, or innocent billionaire.

anonymity: 1. The internet's best feature.
2. The internet's main design flaw.

anthrax: A nostalgic memento of a better time in America.

Antietam: The bloodiest day in United States history until next spring.

Antigone: The oldest surviving parenting guide.

antiracism: Racism's most popular villain, introduced in volume 2, issue 14. Set to appear in the film *Racism Rising: Dawn of the Real American.*

Anthropocene: History's thrilling climax.

Apex Competitor

Adrian believed in consistency. Eight months ago, he'd committed to an hour of daily sketching. Now he could draw a nearly photorealistic gold medal at will. Other subjects might have been possible, but nothing else held his attention.

He kept dozens of medal references on his phone. Sketches based on flukes like Caribbean bobsled teams tended to miss the mark. His best work adapted vintage photos of Muhammad Ali (then Cassius Clay), particularly the group photo from the 1960 Olympic games. Adrian had sketched McClure, Ali, and Crook's medals enough times to reproduce them from memory. They looked identical to laymen, but Adrian knew every distinction in shine and texture. Hopefully his own gold would have the fullness of an Ali, or at least the glimmer of a McClure.

Adrian sketched his first medal of the day during lunch. He'd chewed through 760 of the 2,800 calories a day his frame demanded. The fried shrimp cubes microwaved by his manager were a reliable

40 calories apiece. When Adrian had first asked if the cubes met his protein and carbohydrate macros, Trianna shrugged and said, "Sure." They tasted like dry rubber, which let him focus on ratios. He preferred drawing his medals slightly longer than wide. If a sketch was too circular, it lost the power of caricature.

He paid for multitasking by missing half his chopstick strokes, and now a stray shrimp cube bobbed idly inside his cup of meldonium milk. Adrian had invented the cocktail, but Trianna perfected it by adding vanilla flavoring and a second, sourer performance enhancer. It wouldn't mix well with shrimp. After failing to spear the cube, Adrian reached for it with his left index finger and thumb. This left his fingers wet and scalded.

"What are you doing?" asked Trianna, more curious than reproachful. Adrian was proud to have attracted management that truly cared. Her oversight of his training walks, press bookings, and personal finances made his career. She'd even suggested trying art as an outlet outside of training. No one was better suited to keep track of his credit cards.

"Getting into frame," answered Adrian. He gave up on his chopsticks for the third time and scooped five cubes with a spoon: 960 calories.

"Again with the pickup artist slang. I told you to stay off the internet; it's bad for your concentration."

"Sorry," he said earnestly. "It helps with the stress. We're only three hours away from the event."

"You need to be more careful. Strentovia is counting on you," she reminded him without looking away from her phone.

Adrian nodded, realized that she couldn't see this, and then grunted. As the first and last athlete representing Strentovia in Tokyo, it fell to him to represent over one hundred thousand men and women. Every eye in Strentovia City—Strentovia's only city—would be on him.

Moreover, he was part of the first Olympic do-over. The original Tokyo Olympics had filled stadiums, hospitals, and funeral homes with activity. Lawsuits followed. To save the soul of the games, the IOC announced a "grand reset." The Japanese public remained unconvinced, while the Japanese government remained eager. The new prime minister called the event a "living tribute to the dead." Adrian's performance needed to live up to that ideal.

"Don't forget to finish your milk," she added. Adrian complied without hesitation, draining 250 mL of meldonium milk in fifteen seconds.

Marrying Trianna was a secondary, more closely guarded fantasy. Her refusal to make extended eye contact stirred his champion's passion. It took a genius to manage the affairs of an internationally ranked racewalker. Moreover, she looked like a heavily made-up version of his mother. Adrian knew his Freud too well to deny the appeal.

He depleted the rest of his plate, bringing the total to an even 1,280 calories—1,350 if he counted the meldonium milk—but if there was ever a time to treat himself, it was now. A positive mindset was a racewalker's best tool. Along with his feet.

"Want to go on a warm-up lap? You might be a layman, but I can teach you a few tricks."

"I don't do sports." Trianna cleared another row of colored gems on-screen.

He'd have to ask the dating reactionaries for more advice later. Adrian retreated to his sparse bedroom and took stock. There were eleven duffel bags left, meaning the Olympic Village staff had stolen only one last night. At this rate, he would have at least six of his bags left when the games ended. A reasonable sacrifice for his country.

He saluted his flag without the irony of his countrymen. Medieval records marked Strentovia as a "kingdom of little import," a label they had internalized throughout the ages. Charlemagne marched around it as he forged the Holy Roman Empire, and his successors never bothered threatening them into the young nation. Strentovia was subsequently forgotten during the unification of Austria and ignored by design during the unification of Germany. Their participation in both world wars amounted to sitting in the basement and waiting for the loud noises to stop. They were still waiting for an invitation to the European Union. The new millennium offered a chance for a new start, with something like dignity.

Adrian was less interested in contributing to Strentovia's athletic legacy and more interested in defying it. The nation's history of athletic failure went back to the 1970s, when their three-man delegation limped through the Munich Olympics. The delegation consisted of two reporters and one competitor, a sharpshooter named Kirk Hansi. Kirk sat out all five of his events, citing psychological trauma following the Israeli team massacre. This story might have held up if the reporters hadn't released graphic images of Kirk's adventures in the Olympic Village. The sharpshooter had made diplomatic contact with at least four European sprinters, one Ethiopian long jumper, and a pair of North Korean weight lifters. The cultural exchange did not involve clothing. From then on, Strentovia engaged the Olympics with the enthusiasm of a semiannual polyp check.

Throughout the next four decades of competition, Strentovia earned four silver and seven bronze medals. These happy accidents were invariably leveraged into starter positions on overseas teams. Once their new citizenships became official, the athletes discovered hitherto unseen senses of patriotism for their adopted homelands.

Adrian wanted to show the children of Strentovia something different. He would win, and he would stay. The Strentovian dream didn't have to mean leaving Strentovia.

Especially if he was the *last* winner. Weaker souls wanted the 50km gone, for "humanitarian reasons." Adrian could live with that, once he brought the final medal home.

He finished humming the last four bars of the national anthem, which was composed with quarter tones. Humming it properly typically required a semester of music theory, but Adrian was a patriot.

"Are you changed yet? The last ten years of your life are going to be pointless if we're late," chided Trianna. Adrian slid into his uniform and followed the call of love. He took care to walk: running was a habit that could cost him his dreams.

On his first day in Tokyo, Adrian had taken the obligatory tour of tourist traps. The experience left him with an enduring sense of guilt. Most of Shinjuku had the clean gloss twenty years of television had led him to expect. He could walk around at night without fear, dropping high-value coins every time he used a vending machine. But his dorm sat on the edge of Kabukicho, the former red-light district. And current red-light district. An army of pimps had offered him drinks, good food, local highlights, and bareback. The streetwalkers didn't even mention the first three. Adrian had politely rejected all of them, since all this and more waited in the Olympic Village. But the brush with the edge had reminded him of how sheltered his world was. The streets the shuttle flitted by and the resort he lived in weren't one city. They were barely one world. The Village cleaning staff's quiet robberies were the one thing that let him feel human. As long as he paid his tithe to the gods of poverty that ruled outside the Village's pastel-colored bubble, he could focus on his own struggle.

The journey to the marathon course took twenty minutes. Trianna intermittently jogged ahead, realized she was alone, and glared angrily over her shoulder. Adrian walked steadfastly, putting his nation ahead of romance.

He took a moment to appreciate the sun. Normally, Adrian made a vampire's effort to avoid getting burnt. Strentovia's finest indoor athletic track sheltered his training, exhibitions, and cell phone self-portraits. But the nature of the race made roasting a foregone conclusion. There simply was no way for a human of any complexion to complete a fifty-kilometer racewalk under the uncompromising summer sun without a mark. The SPF 125 glazing his skin simply served as a respectful nod toward the power and influence of skin cancer.

He felt the early tingles of a burn when they reached the starting line. Security held them for seven minutes; an enterprising guard felt the need to make sure Strentovia was a real country, going as far as asking Adrian to point it out on a map while they waited for word from management. Throughout the ordeal, Adrian kept his eyes on the stands. He'd never seen a racewalk crowd this size in his life.

"How big's the course?" asked Trianna.

"It's a two-kilometer loop," answered Adrian. He tossed his visor behind him. His face might as well share the same color of burn as the rest of his body. "Relatively small. I'll only have to complete it twenty-five times."

"Remember to walk fast."

"I can't walk too fast. That would be running, which would shame the sport of racewalking and Strentovia itself." Adrian waved to the crowd as he spoke.

A pained expression flashed on Trianna's face and disappeared just as swiftly. Remembering Strentovia's Olympic record tended to have that effect. He moved her up the list of names he had to represent today.

"Fucking sad," she mumbled, returning to her cell phone.

"Only if we lose," Adrian countered. Trianna considered something caustic, squinted, and finally nodded. Then she moved on to the rest stops with the other handlers, managers, and confused members of the press.

Adrian's slot was in the third row from the front, a comfortable distance from the established walkers. The media favorites to win hailed from America, China, and Russia, with betting odds that corresponded loosely with their homelands' spheres of influence.

Unlike the others, Adrian held no loud resentment for the great powers. He carried his resentment quietly, like a proper Olympian. While Adrian was stuck using outdated gutter enhancers like meldonium, the Americans had moved on to more sophisticated methods of cheating. The Russian and Chinese teams still flirted with meldonium, but only as a cost-cutting measure in events deemed expendable.

Grumbling on this topic dominated the lunches and orgies of the Olympic Village. Yesterday morning, a South African pole vaulter had almost ruined the simple joys of cunnilingus with a rant about her Texan rival, who espoused the joys of clean competition with needle-pockmarked triceps. Adrian had expressed nonverbal commiseration to the best of his ability.

The referee fired the warm-up shot, and the walkers began stretching as one. Adrian watched the American's movement with a technical eye. The universe granted Matthias Harding expansive thighs and powerful calves. Adrian could only hope to match their force through superior training and unflinching effort. As the first hints of sweat pooled above Adrian's eyes, Matthias showed no sign of exertion.

To his right, Trianna unfolded a plastic reclining chair and unhooked the Velcro straps on a six-foot-long golf umbrella. Her prudence lifted his spirit: a racewalker lived and died by his support staff. Adrian's childhood hero, Elias Peralta, never properly recovered from the 1996 Games, when his water boy took a bathroom break during the thirty-second kilometer. Peralta's coma lasted for three years, and his performance was never the same. When he'd only earned a bronze during the Sydney Games, Adrian knew the legend of the Brazilian Blur had come to an end.

"This is for Elias," Adrian muttered.

"What about Strentovia?" asked Trianna. She'd moved on from her cell phone to a bulky hardcover novel. The cover featured a shirtless man without the quiet dignity of a racewalking champion.

"That goes without saying," said Adrian.

The referee fired a second shot, warning the athletes to prepare for the third, starting gunshot. Adrian rolled his right ankle one more time before adopting his pre-race pose. It looked like standing to lay observers, but he applied twice the pressure to his left heel for a more energetic launch.

The third gunshot cut through his doubts. Adrian's legs moved before his brain processed the sound, and he took his first step as an Olympian.

Adrian walked the first lap at half speed. It was a chance to feel out the resistance of the course and strength of the competition. Adrian slipped into the fourth row of walkers, confident in his ability to upset the formation over the next forty-eight kilometers.

Six kilometers in, a Canadian racer to Adrian's left bent his forward leg. Adrian averted his eyes as the man fell to his knees and crawled off the course. The rules of the game were as unforgiving as they were simple. Straight leading legs, with at least one foot on the ground at all times. He hoped that his rival would find glory in the next race, or at least the next life.

At eleven kilometers, Adrian rejoined the third cluster of walkers without an increase in speed. Raw, foolhardy walkers had already wasted their energy on a starting lead and fallen victim to exhaustion. The Peruvian walker to his right had the glazed eyes, red skin, shallow breathing, erratic stride, and extreme sweat indicative of mid-race heatstroke. Adrian's moderation had only earned him two of these symptoms.

At twelve kilometers, he surged to his maximum walking speed, taking advantage of the spiderlike limbs that made him king of the Strentovian circuit. Matthias wasn't the only athlete with gifts.

Then the cull began in earnest.

Adrian wished to succeed, but it hurt to see others fall. Each walker that collapsed on the track held the same dream. The sun and stride took four victims during the twenty-second kilometer and showed no sign of slowing. He joined the second row of walkers with a leaden heart. Each ambulance speeding away from the race carried a brother.

He pumped his legs through three more laps and slowly left pity behind. His breath was steady when the South Korean walker passed out. His pace was unchanged as the Latvian walker started foaming at the mouth. His heart was unmoved when the rest of his row voided themselves, pushed to the limit of human endurance. They knew what it meant to step onto the field of honor.

Adrian's own body finally began to complain. His heels screamed for mercy and went ignored. His eyes were sieged by sweat and sunlight, but the pain kept him sharp. He reminded himself that a comfortable walk could easily slip into a jog, and that would cost him everything. With a body temperature far past the point of fever, Adrian focused on the vision of gold.

He made it to the water stop. A cool stream of liquid hit him in his right eye, blinding it. Trianna fired three more shots from her water pistol, dousing the rest of his face with ice water. He gave her a thumbs-up that went unnoticed as she returned to her novel and reclining chair.

"Get going."

He got going. The muscles in his thighs had torn open, but Adrian made it to the leading row of walkers. The German, Russian, and American front-runners were in a dead heat.

His soul swelled as he passed Germany's walker. Each step erased centuries of half-smiling Strentovian impotence; Adrian's people now had a chance to trade irony for pride. The German didn't seem to recognize Adrian or his flag but smiled politely. Adrian ignored this gesture and pushed forward. Such was the privilege of the conqueror over the conquered.

Then the Russian walker threw up his hands and decelerated. Adrian glanced over his shoulder and found Antonov occupying the space between himself and the second row at a leisurely stride. The defection shocked Adrian more than any of the casualties. How could anyone leave at the edge of history? He couldn't remember the name of a single bronze medalist.

Adrian felt his large intestine cave in. Mercifully, the chunks were solid and stayed sealed in his athletic shorts. There would be stains, but anyone could survive that level of humiliation. It was the liquid that tested his soul. Even now, preoccupied with the race, he could feel the stream trickling toward the earth.

Matthias glanced to the left, meeting Adrian's eyes. The American's shorts were chestnut brown, hiding any signs of digestive strife. But fashion couldn't hide the smell.

"I'm impressed. Not every man can walk beside God," wheezed Matthias.

"There is no God," wheezed Adrian. After a pious lifetime, the truth stood clear.

They walked for some time. Behind him, Adrian heard cursing in every language he knew. He filtered it out. There was only one opponent worth watching, and Adrian had already memorized the intricacies of his walk. The countless hours of racewalking footage branded onto his brain told him enough.

In the semifinal lap, Adrian forgot Matthias. He forgot the audience, and the pain, and Trianna. Strentovia faded into memory. He simply walked. There was nothing else. The human story began crawling out of the tar pits and ended walking down the track. Everything else was an indulgent lie. Adrian's legs moved freely, coated in enlightenment and urine. The smell of enlightenment was overpowering.

He heard a dull popping noise and then found his face against the ground. He turned upright and discovered his left shin spurting prodigious amounts of blood through the vertex of its mortifying new V shape. The other walkers tramped over and around him, providing mocking smiles and vicious glares as they limped past the finish line.

There wasn't enough moisture left in his body to cry. Before blacking out from the pain, Adrian cursed the heroes of every country he could remember. He called Usain Bolt a fast monkey, Jesse Owens a slow monkey, Larisa Latynina a flexible whore, and Derek Redmond a codependent monkey. Once the cameras turned his way, he lambasted the IOC as a cabal of cocaine-addled inbreds and announced his excitement for the third world war. The blood had soaked into his jersey by the time paramedics arrived to drag him off the world stage.

Two days later he awoke in a hospital bed. His cell phone was missing from his personal effects, meaning he was still in the Village. Trianna arrived to check on him, whistling an overplayed Vangelis movie composition. She made direct eye contact, which meant she wanted something.

"The Paralympics are in two weeks, and Strentovia could use a racewalker."

Apocalypse, the: An event hotly anticipated by evangelicals, survivalists, and debtors.

arson: Amateur urban remodeling.

art: Anything that lacks utility or popular appeal.
Author's note: Anyone can be an artist. Half of marriages end in art.

Asia: Contains the majority of Earth's land, people, and atomic standoffs.

austerity: The poor's punishment for hoarding half the planet's wealth.

authenticity: A resource mass-produced by branding agencies.

B

banter: Replacing conversational depth with one-liners.

barrio: Any community untouched by the gentle healing hand of gentrification.

baseball: An impossibly slow farm game popularized by America's biggest and fastest metropolis.

Bastille, the: A glorified day camp for wayward nobles elevated to a symbol of tyranny.

Batman: The modern American's main father figure.

bayonet charge: The innovative post-gunpowder tactic of running screaming across the battlefield with a big knife.

bile: An alkaline fluid that aids in digestion and op-ed writing.

billionaires: Local representatives of the king's authority, given free reign over serfs in their territory.

Bipolar Tendencies

Prince Roland Nor prepared to meet the new president of the United States. Diplomacy was traditionally the queen's domain, but an unforeseen and dangerous surplus of royal wine demanded executive attention. Roland's mother risked life and liver to fight the threat, leaving him to greet their honored guest.

The prince stood before the palace steps and adjusted his bow tie. By his understanding, he was a year too young to vote in America, let alone hold any kind of office. If he didn't know better, he'd think that his mother was using him as some kind of insult. But her wisdom put her above suspicion. In fact, considering the idea at all almost amounted to treason. He cursed his flimsy loyalty and vowed to repent in private.

The queen spread her wisdom through memorable, pocket-sized maxims. This year she'd become fond of "Never trust a sober adult" and "A short memory means a long life." Leather-bound books of her musings were a popular gift on Thorn Island, allowing citizens to carry the royal family's presence with them. For similar reasons, the royal family's used clothing and utensils were black market mainstays. Roland preferred not to dwell on that for too long. The Caribbean was full of wonders that spared him the need to reflect on human absurdity. Including the survival of a monarchy in the twenty-first century.

The royal palace was at the bottom of an ancient, revered mountain. During Thorn Island's warring states period, the palace's indefensible location made a statement: the Nor family—"Nor" loosely translated to "the Grim Reaper's Chosen"—feared nothing from their rivals. Today, the Nors embraced a softer approach to governing, largely enabled by the long-past extermination of every competing noble family on the island. Spanish sailors had observed one of these purges in the eighteenth century and decided to sail on toward saner prey.

Roland enjoyed exterminating sandwiches. He finished off a tuna melt as the president's motorcade made its way down the mountain.

The flavor helped mute his fear of disappointing his mother. She wasn't the type to reprimand him or even make a passive-aggressive comment. Her eyes would simply radiate disappointment until he slunk out of court.

The most impressive limousine drove past the prince, stopping three car lengths to his right. Six hypertrophic men in black suits (one rogue wore navy blue) and matching glasses stepped out, nodded at each other, and waved at the stragglers. A second limousine pulled in and five more hypertrophic men emerged. Followed by the president.

President McDowell had a poster-friendly face. He looked like he was in his mid-fifties, which Roland recalled as the ideal age for the white men standing behind podiums in American films and newsreels. In person, the black roots under his dye-gray hair were visible.

"Greetings, Mr. President." The prince extended his hand.

"Greetings, Your Highness," said President McDowell. He bowed. This wasn't a Thorn Island tradition, so the prince assumed it was an American pastime and followed suit.

"We're honored to have you."

"I'm honored to be here. And now I have to go."

"What?"

"I have a lot of ground to cover. But I hope we can do this again sometime."

"Of course. I'm, er, glad we could get to know each other."

The president bowed again, pivoted, and darted back into his limousine. The vehicle backed out of the palace driveway at a mildly dangerous speed and then sped up the mountain road at a pointedly dangerous speed. The rest of the motorcade struggled to follow suit. Prince Roland waved as they fled.

On March 12, Year X + 4, Prince Roland prepared to meet the new president of the United States. After years of reflecting on his first diplomatic outing, the prince decided that the Secret Service lent the president his mystique. The well-dressed killers had captured Roland's imagination, and he'd prepared his own guard for today. Ideally the extra gravitas would lead to a longer meeting.

The new motorcade was made of black vans. Peculiarly, the president emerged from the first van to park, stepping out of the driver's seat. He looked behind him and smiled as the rest of the motorcade struggled to catch up to their charge. Then he turned toward the royal palace and snorted. Roland coughed to make himself (and his guards) known.

"Greetings, Mr. President." Roland bowed, recalling the last visit.

President Leon handed Roland his suitcase, coughed, and drew a cigarette. It took him three tries to light it, and he looked more frustrated with each attempt. He took two deep drags, and then put the tip out on the hood of his van. The area was full of small circular scorch marks.

"God, look at this dirt pile," grumbled President Leon. The prince's briefing said the man was forty, an infant in American political years. Roland chalked the layered insults up to inexperience.

"We're honored to have you."

"Honor my dick."

"What?"

"Just messing with you. Don't you people tell jokes here? Please tell me you do. I started this goddamn diplomacy tour in Russia, and we just glared at each other for half an hour. Stodgy pricks."

"I know a few jokes," Roland volunteered. He was off-balance but remained eager.

"Maybe later. I've got some American jokes for ya."

"That sounds—"

"How many pinkos does it take to lose an election?"

"Let's see. I'll guess—"

"Doesn't matter. They're too stoned to vote. Let's go inside, I hear your momma's got a nice ass."

"She's the wisdom of our people."

"I'm not hearing a no."

The president adjusted his collar, popped a small white mint into his mouth, and marched up the palace steps. Roland weighed ordering his guards to open fire, but the president's own security detail had emerged. They outnumbered Roland's retinue two to one, and the bored glaze in their expressions said they'd consider a firefight a welcome diversion.

On December 2, Year X + 12, Prince Roland prepared to meet the new president of the United States. He looked forward to a diplomatic reset after President Leon. Over time, the queen had honored him with more responsibility. Said honor included dealing with any and all letters, phone calls, and handshakes exchanged with President Leon. It had been trying.

That said, he'd rather have tended to his sagging love life. Dating meant sorting through relentless gold diggers, foreign intelligence assets, and heirs to monarchies with flightier stances on inbreeding.

This time the motorcade descended the mountain at a leisurely place and arrived forty minutes late. The stretch limos entered in pairs instead of the standard single winding line. President Hobbes stepped out of the left car in the third row wearing a pair of red-tinted reflective sunglasses above his eyes. Before he approached, he put a hand on his forehead to block out the sun.

"Greetings, Mr. President."

"Nice digs. Hey, Roland, can I call you Rolex?"

"What?"

"Like the watch. You're a rich guy, it fits."

"I don't think I like that."

"That's fine. I plan on being rich too once my four years are up." President Hobbes adopted the inspired dreamer's expression that defined his campaign posters.

"A noble goal. I think."

"Maybe, who knows. I try not to get caught up in that shit. I leave it for the academic types. You got any wine? I love wine."

"We keep the palace dry. Mother is trying to quit."

"I respect that. I tried to quit once, until I got bored of it. I find that three or so drinks help me get in the mood to look over bills. Otherwise, all that legalese starts running together."

A question about the wisdom of drunk leadership almost reached Roland's lips. Almost. But no other visit had gone this smoothly. This was, for all its warts, a leap forward for international relations.

"Actually, 'Rolex' is fine. And there's some tequila in my quarters, if that's your taste."

"Sounds great, Rolex. Hey, you ever joined a coalition invasion? Because I've got this idea . . ."

Roland only paid cursory attention to the proposal and quickly moved the conversation back toward drinking. He had six bottles of imported SpiderHead tequila, a now-banned Arizona specialty that mixed traditional tequila with a drop of tarantula venom. Its logo was an eight-legged skeleton, ignoring biological fact in favor of making a statement. The prince and president drank out of the same bottle, hurling insults at the mountain from the roof of the royal palace.

By dawn, Roland had committed two thousand soldiers to invading a country he'd never thought about before. He hoped that most of them would make it back.

On March 16, Year X + 20, King Roland prepared to meet the new president of the United States. He missed the novelty that waiting on the palace steps once held. Now it felt too serious. There was no one above him to untangle any mistakes he might make. He could only rely on the echoes of his mother's maxims.

Roland wore a black suit paired with a black shirt and black tie. He usually preferred more eccentric colors, but the grim cloud of his mother's funeral still hung over him. Dignitaries from nations great and small had come to pay their respects, or at least be seen next to people paying their respects. A state funeral, if nothing else, was a good opportunity to show a solidarity transcending regional alliances. The new president had been absent.

Roland would have been insulted, but he'd come to respect a head of state's schedule. His personal desk was coated in proposals from Parliament. He'd shredded the more obvious cash grabs and planned to review the others for subtler forms of graft. This process was, until now, his main distraction from grieving. The endless pattern had a calming, Zen garden quality.

President Tarth stepped out of the last car in his motorcade. Two of Roland's guards exchanged small sums of cash. They'd taken to placing bets on how visiting heads of state would make their appearance. The king knew he should disapprove, but their levity had helped him get through the last three months.

"Greetings, Mr. President."

"I know you've been trading with the Russians, goat-fucker. Give me one reason not to nuke this hole into next Tuesday."

King Roland's tongue hung limp inside his mouth. Then he recovered, steeled himself, and found a sane reaction to an insane world.

"People live here."

"You're going to have to do better than that, goat-fucker."

"We don't even have goats here."

"Whatever, goat-fucker. I'm just here to warn you, in person. Straighten up or I'm carpet-bombing this hole and renaming it 'Guam 2.'"

"I won't stand for this."

"Stand for my dick, goat-fucker."

"What is it with you people and your dicks?"

President Tarth grabbed his crotch with one hand and flipped the king off with the other. He maintained both gestures as he reentered his van, which played a cartoonish march (which Roland later learned was called "Stars and Stripes Forever") at painful volume while pulling out of the royal driveway. The king imagined a long four years and then corrected himself. The Americans would definitely keep this one around for eight.

On January 29, Year X + 28, King Roland prepared to meet the new president of the United States. After his last experience, he toyed with the idea of an assassination. But the maxims of his dearly departed mother were still with him. She believed in forgiveness, especially when the alternative was inconvenient. To that end, the king had to maintain peace with the nuclear monkey to the northwest.

News networks praised President Kei as the first female head of the American Empire, effectively vaulting two glass ceilings at once. This was, by and large, made possible by the immense personal and global failures of her predecessor. While watching him blunder brought Roland no small amount of pleasure, the threat of global thermonuclear war lost him no small amount of sleep. As he occupied his usual spot before the steps, Roland quietly prayed for someone stable to come down the mountain.

President Kei emerged from a single, tanklike vehicle. Like Roland, she had the round figure that came with pairing a civilian's desire for food with a statesman's authority. The king inhaled and extended his arm.

"Greetings, Madam President." The king followed habit and bowed.

"I am so, so sorry," said the president.

"What?"

"That's how I'm starting all my trips. My predecessor was . . . temperamental. But I'd like you to know that we're sorry. From now on, things are going to be different."

"That's good to hear."

"I mean it. This is a fresh start for us—and everyone that comes after us. I promise you a golden future between our people."

"We don't fuck goats."

"I know you don't fuck goats. And if you did, we'd be fine with it, because we respect you and your culture."

"We don't fuck goats."

"You don't. I am so, so sorry."

A beat passed between them.

"One of your predecessors called me Rolex."

"Is that a slur? I'm sorry for that."

The king laughed. He could have a decent time with this one. Her stress-induced-early-coronary attitude recalled his old friends at Thorn University. Admission required brilliance, amphetamines, or membership in the royal family. Back then, Roland liked to think he possessed all three. Today he simply considered himself blessed with patience.

On February 21, Year X + 32, King Roland prepared to meet the new president of the United States. He thought Eden Kei deserved a second term—she was the only U.S. citizen invited to his wedding—but American pundits considered failing to grow a penis a severe political blunder. The new president had shown more foresight.

This time Roland had brought out a folding chair. His ankles had been bothering him lately, and he'd come to realize that decorum did little to change how a given president treated him. They'd chosen long ago. He still maintained his guard out of habit, and the minor chance that a new president might try to bite his nose off.

Despite keeping an eye on politics around the hemisphere, the king couldn't put a pin on any of President Torres's political positions. Few people could. Torres had coasted through the election without putting forward much of a political platform at all. Roland wondered if it would be fun to throw an election sometime. The rules got more unclear as he got older (evidently you didn't need the majority of votes?), but the constant novelty seemed to capture the world's attention.

President Torres emerged from the dead center of three identical gray limousines. He approached the king with blank eyes and an unshifting smile.

"Greetings, Mr. President," said the king.

"Hello, citizen," said the president.

"Citizen? That's technically true, I guess."

"I believe in revitalizing the middle class."

"That sounds like a quality goal. Welcome to Thorn Island."

"I hear that Thorn Island has a thriving middle class. If not, I'm sure we can work to revitalize it."

". . . Right."

"Yes, secure paths to retirement are a right of the middle class. Which I, personally, am dedicated to revitalizing."

"Are you a robot?" The king took a step behind his guard.

"That's a great question! I believe that revitalizing the middle class will bring us closer to an answer."

"Well, it could be worse. Why don't you come inside?"

"Will it—"

"Yes. Coming inside the palace is integral to revitalizing the middle class."

President Torres beamed and followed Roland inside. After posturing for the press, the king tested how many shots the president would take in the name of revitalizing the middle class. The experiment ended with Torres passing out beneath a portrait of the dearly departed queen. Roland noted that the president mumbled sweet nothings about revitalizing the middle class in his sleep.

On February 3, Year X + 36, King Roland prepared to meet the new president of the United States. He no longer held positive or negative expectations. He simply waited to find out who the universe decided he had to work with. Hopefully, they liked to drink. The good ones usually liked to drink.

Four black Italian supercars descended the mountain. Two guards emerged from the front car and laid out a red carpet that stretched from the palace gates to King Roland's feet. They took positions on opposite sides of the carpet and saluted as President Kincaid marched past them.

This flamboyance extended to President Kincaid's fashion sense. He wore a bronze armlet on his right, engraved with the image of a bald eagle chopping down a cherry tree. His left armlet was made of gold and had an engraving of his own face. The engraving looked far less gaunt but was an otherwise faithful rendition of the sixty-seven-year-old former senator.

"Greetings, Mr. President."

"Who stands before a god but does not kneel?" President Kincaid extended a gloved hand and waited. It took the king several moments to realize he was expected to kiss the large red-white-and-blue ring on his finger.

"King Roland. The leader of the sovereign nation you're standing in."

"You will be the king of ashes."

"A sovereign nation with nukes," the king added. They were new.

"Ahem. Sorry for the attitude earlier. Jet lag, you know how it is. Want to get some coffee?"

"Please leave."

"Fine, mortal. But know that there are consequences for testing a god's patience. You will find your political opponents much better funded—and far more heavily armed."

"If you come back here, I'll have you shot. I don't care what happens afterward, I'll have you fucking shot."

"Why would I grace this pit twice? This is a kingdom of goat-fucking—"

"You have three minutes."

President Kincaid jogged down the red carpet. King Roland was impressed to note that both of the guards flanking the president had drawn their sidearms and one standing by the gates had discreetly produced a compact assault rifle. Threatening Kincaid had been a risk, but Roland had read one too many goat jokes online. Some had even found their way into news articles.

On January 23, Year X + 44, King Roland prepared to meet the new president of the United States. He'd upgraded the folding chair to a full-blown lounge chair, complete with a small plastic stand holding a bowl of fresh fruit. A veteran bodyguard cut a pomegranate into fourths as the presidential motorcade rolled in. The luxury cars had been replaced with Japanese motorcycles, for reasons that probably made sense to the Americans. The king didn't worry himself about that kind of thing these days.

President Cameron was a Democrat, or a Republican, or something else. According to the news, his platform had excited some people and angered others. Judging by his presence, more people were excited. Roland was more focused on the man's baldness. After the relative vigor of the last president, it was odd to see the electorate pivot to a geriatric.

"Gree—"

"I'm so fucking sorry."

"Hmm. Been a while since they elected your type." Roland flicked a chunk of pomegranate toward the president, who caught it with surprising dexterity.

"Just . . . we were . . . I'm so fucking sorry."

"I accept your apology. But I'll also need you to apologize again."

"Pardon?"

"Let me clarify: I want you to apologize for your successors. It will make their insults easier to ignore."

To his credit, the president pushed past the confusion etched onto his face, clasped his hands together, and bowed. Roland suppressed a groan. Years of watching dignitaries in the news had convinced his own people it was a Thorn Island tradition.

"I'm sorry for any insults my successors might make. But since we're turning a new page in history, I'm confident that there's nothing to worry about."

"There's always something to worry about," said Roland. "But let's forget about it for now. We've got a whole bowl of fruit to get through. Once we're done with the strawberries, you can fly off to a larger, angrier country."

On April 4, Year X + 48, King Roland prepared to meet the new president of the United States. He approached this burden with a positive, floaty mood. His first granddaughter had been born two days earlier. That was a positive omen that even the American executive branch couldn't ruin. The king sat upright on his lounge chair, scrolling through pictures of his grandchild on a waterproof smartphone. Focusing on this task kept him from noticing the entrance of the presidential motorcade or the arrival of the president.

President Nolan was a skinny man that took deep breaths. The unseemly noise brought the president's presence to the king's attention. Roland glanced up from his cell phone and found an open-mouthed scarecrow in an expensive white suit. The opening was slight, closer to a model's fly-catching expression than a look of constant shock.

"Greetings, Mr. President," he said warmly. "I hope you're ready for a feast. Tonight we're throwing the party of a lifetime, in honor of a healthy heir's birth."

"Do you hear them? The spiders?"

"Oh, Lord."

"Of course not. The spiders are everywhere. In our eyes, in our mouths, in our souls."

"Please tell me you're fucking with me."

"The spiders come from the niggers. That's why I have to punish them. I have to stop the spiders."

"The people of Thorn Island are black."

"Yes, but you're not niggers. You didn't come on the spider boats to spin webs around our women. Why do they take the women? Help me get the women back."

Two of President Nolan's handlers gently grabbed their charge's shoulders. "The president appreciates you taking the time to meet him," said one of the men in black. "He deeply respects the people of Thorn Island and the Caribbean at large, and apologizes for anything that may have been misconstrued as an insult."

The speaker introduced himself as the newest director of the Central Intelligence Agency. Roland recognized the name; his appointment had grabbed headlines as a conflict of interest, which Congress subsequently ignored. He looked accustomed to interrupting the president.

"Hmm. I can understand a president needing management. Lord knows, a few of the last batch could have used more. But isn't that typically the vice president's purview? Or at least the secretary of state's?"

"I like to think that I wear many hats," said the CIA director. He started steering President Nolan back toward the motorcade.

"Don't trust the hats," suggested the president. "They're made of spider silk."

"That's right, Mr. President. Good job telling him. Now why don't we take a little nap?"

King Roland watched the president and shadow president enter the first of six black vans. He thought he saw a pair of triangle-shaped cuff links on the shadow president's sleeve, but the implications of this were too stupid to consider.

On February 17, Year X + 56, King Roland prepared to deal with his regular diplomatic enema. He sat on the railing of the palace steps and swirled a half-empty mug of SpiderHead tequila. It was a beautiful day, marred only by the descent of his guests down the mountain. The presidential motorcade moved with the self-conscious sloth that marked the duller commanders in chief. Roland hoped that if he glared intently enough, the vehicles would explode, or implode, or fly into space. Instead, they crawled to the royal palace.

The president emerged from a black hovercraft. It was the first time the king had seen President Such-and-such's face. Roland had abandoned tracking American politics two years before—watching humanity's worst specimens claw their way ahead was stressful, and he had resolved to spend his golden years savoring life. At a glance, he hadn't missed much. The new president fit the same dull pale template as most of his forebears, down to the plastic smile.

"Greetings," said the president. "I'm honored to be here."

King Roland continued glaring.

"Greetings," repeated the president. He bowed.

The king's glare intensified.

"Did I say something impolite?" asked the president.

"What the blue fuck is wrong with you people? You change philosophies the way I change shoes. I never know if you're going to hug me, insult me, or ask me to help you blow up the fucking world!"

The president gave a bobblehead nod. "Not blowing up the world was the center of my platform. It resonated with the youth."

"America isn't the only country that sends me madmen. But the others at least have the decency to send a consistent *type* of madman. Why should I talk to you? Your successor might resent me for even making eye contact with you, let alone making any deals. Leave. Fly away. Go home. I'm sure your people have already invented a new crisis to handle."

The president stalled by wiping his sunglasses on his shirt. Roland's mother had frequently abused the same gesture. A new cliché-filled maxim typically followed. He missed those clichés.

"I was hoping we could have a productive talk."

"What could we *possibly* talk about?"

"Well, lowering tariffs. On both sides."

"If I lower the damn tariffs, will you leave?"

"Sure."

"And tell your successors to stay home?"

"I can't promise that."

"Then the tariffs stay."

"That might lead to a police action."

The king contemplated the Secret Service. They were the only American visitors he consistently respected, representing the brightest killers in their empire. His guards wouldn't stand a chance. Nonetheless, he slammed his fist into the president's throat.

His old, fat fingers ached from the effort. He had never been athletic, or even particularly mobile, and the consequences had wreaked havoc on his body. This was the first time he had regretted it. If he'd spent more of his life running and jumping, his blow might have killed the president. As things stood, he'd merely knocked the man to the floor, where he clutched his neck and wheezed.

"Do your worst. I've enjoyed sixty years of harems, two years of Illuminati membership, and forty years of unlimited access to the state treasury. Feel free to invade and deal with the rebels your predecessors funded. In fact, I *invite* you."

Roland looked down. Ten distinct laser sights formed a near-perfect circle around his heart. His own guards stood still, frozen in understandable terror. The young men had hometowns that they likely didn't want to see burned by drones, ravaged by mercenaries, and occupied by brutes. That same fear had paralyzed the king—until now. The whims of the great powers usually had nothing to do with his actions. Dying as a direct result of his choices would be a refreshing change.

"Hold on!" The president stumbled to his feet and gave two more violent coughs. "You're about to shoot a valuable regional ally."

"What?" said Roland. The dots faded, save one near the center of his chest.

"He hit back, which makes him perfect. We need more global partners with a penchant for violence. Thorn Island is a perfect staging area for operations over the entire Caribbean."

King Roland Nor groaned and trudged back to his perch on the palace steps. For him, the visit was over. After his best attempt at courting death and ruin, the status quo had shrugged and marched on. He drained the rest of his SpiderHead and imagined how much simpler life would have been with an older brother.

black lung: Early proof that coal is the ideal fuel for an ideal society.

Black Panther: Hotep Batman.

blue: 1. The favorite color of people without a favorite color.
2. Staring at the ceiling for longer than sixty seconds at a time.

bomb: A ballot variant popular in close races.

bombing: The bridge between comedy and office management.

boson: One of many particles introduced in secondary education and promptly forgotten.

Boston: Defender of the Founding Fathers' ideals, drinking habits, and racial attitudes.

bowling: A drinking game interrupted by pins.

Brave New World: A somewhat dry documentary.

buffalo soldiers: Black regiments adding vital diversity to tribal repression.

burnouts: Existentialist philosophers sans graduate school.

Byronic: Preindustrial slang for "emotionally stunted."

C

Cain: The first human to give his brother an honest opinion.

Canada: A thriving community leader chained to an alcoholic with a revolver.

capoeira: The most stylish way to lose a fight.

carat: The scientific shininess of your shiny rock.

Carter, Jimmy: The only U.S. president to be attacked by a swamp rabbit.

Cassandra: A Trojan epidemiologist.

censorship: The last bipartisan effort in America.

children: Overrated.

China: [Redacted.]

chivalry: A common side effect of the fungus found in medieval bread.

Christianity: The religion of universal love, occasionally.

cicadas: God's punishment for light sleepers.

cinema: Superhero comics with sound.

Civil War, the: 1. A struggle between de facto slavery and de jure slavery.
2. The only civil war fought in any country at any point in history.

classic: A cliché in a dress.

climate change: 1. Your gift to your children.
2. Based on new data, your gift to yourself.

coal: Our most reliable weapon in the war against air.

codependence: 1. Where babies come from.
2. Diet love.

Cold War, the: 1. An experimental World War franchise spinoff, originally announced and marketed as the third entry.
2. An international game of "I'm not touching you."

college: Facilities dedicated to molding the skills and character of debt slaves.

Columbia: Harlem's deer tick.

comedy: Moderately funny.

comics: The only print genre where fun is allowed.

Comments

As a black man, I agree.

As a white woman from Florida, I disagree.

As an East Asian woman from Milwaukee that plays electric bass, I agree.

As a Hispanic man from Oregon that plays standing cello and likes professional wrestling, I disagree.

As a white man from Texas that plays steel drums, dislikes professional wrestling, and can take ten shots before passing out, I agree.

As a black man from Nevada that plays the flute, likes professional wrestling, can take twelve shots, and hates *The Last Jedi*, I agree.

As a Native American woman from South Dakota that plays the harpsichord, likes professional wrestling, can take eight shots, likes *The Last Jedi*, and believes Ted Cruz is the Zodiac Killer, I disagree.

As a half–South Asian, half-Ukrainian woman from New Jersey that doesn't play an instrument, dislikes professional wrestling, can take nine shots, likes *The Last Jedi*, believes Ted Cruz is the Zodiac Killer, and can't remember what we were originally talking about, I agree.

As a Madagascan-American man from an air base in Guam that plays one of those recorders they give you in kindergarten, loves professional wrestling, can take three shots, dislikes *The Last Jedi*, believes Ted Cruz is the Zodiac Killer, can't remember what we were originally talking about, and rides Disneyland's Tower of Terror once a year, I agree.

As a Jamaican-American man from the Bronx that plays a down-tuned eight-string guitar to imitate Meshuggah, thinks *Lucha Underground* is the best show on television, can take ten shots of overproof rum, enjoys *The Last Jedi* but found the gambling planet extraneous, is absolutely certain Ted Cruz is the Zodiac Killer, cannot for the life of him remember what we were originally talking about, and hasn't been to Disneyland since everyone's mind snapped sometime halfway through 2015, I don't see the point.

communism: Everything left of *The Fountainhead.*

Confederacy, the: Bold defenders of states' rights to bet on slaves fighting to death in filth-covered pits.

conservatism: Nostalgia for a simpler time with fewer eligible voters.

contra: 1. The root of tired cheat code jokes.
2. The root of fresh CIA jokes.

coronavirus: Single-stranded RNA viruses spread by birds, mammals, and "rugged individualism."

COVID-19: Something one typically reads humor to forget.

crack: Working as intended.

cults: Future tax-free organizations.

D

Damocles: 1. A Sicilian courtier subjected to ruthless workplace bullying. 2. The namesake of roughly half the doomsday weapons in speculative fiction.

Darkseid: Is.

Dark Souls: The reason this book didn't come out in 2017.

dating: Information warfare.

dating apps: The sole topic of open mics worldwide.

death: The end of your relationship with the IRS.

Death Comedy Jam

I can't believe I'm doing a gig on Earth.

It's an honor, really. Back home, everyone talks about coming here after striking it rich. I'm not rich, but I have a great prop gag. It'll be my last joke tonight.

I wanted to look decent for this, so I'm wearing my only suit. It was a gift from my ex, Jana. My other shirts are covered in band logos and skulls.

Smoking indoors isn't popular here, but I'll need a cigarette to keep you laughing. Is that fair? Thanks. Where I'm from, everywhere's indoors. So I have some bad habits.

I'm from Mars. The *colony* Mars, not the *planet*. No need to rush the stage.

Trust me, it's just as confusing for us. The planet still gets half my mail.

Besides, you guys named both. I would've gone with something more descriptive. Like "Big Tin Can." Or "Poverty Storage." Or "Neo Compton."

My solution? Add "New" to the title. "New Mars" has a better ring to it. There's just one problem: they settled the *planet* after we built the *tin can*. If they like the name, we'll be at war with Mars. Like everyone else.

Let's be real. If I were a Red Martian, I'd have pulled out a gun by now.

That said, you don't have to wait for gunshots. There's an easy way to tell what kind of Martian you're talking to: sleep with them. Afterward, colony Martians talk about their feelings. Red Martians salute.

Any couples here tonight?

Wow, almost all of you. Well, I just got dumped.

She was a Red Martian, and brilliant. She moved off-planet before things went all *Sieg Heil*. Which makes her smarter than their entire legislative branch.

But I couldn't stop staring at the barcode.

I tried to be sneaky about it, but Red Martians know when they're being watched. Main benefit of a surveillance state education. The first time, she laughed it off. The second time, she stormed out of the apartment. The third time, she stormed off the colony.

That one hurt. Anyone ever given up their civil rights to leave you?

In my defense: it was a *barcode*. On a *person*. The same black-and-white stripes you see on a can of tuna. I knew autocracy made people disposable, but I didn't think it made them refundable.

I miss her. She'd hate that joke.

I crossed the line at the supermarket. We were price checking some imported food, when I pointed the scanner right at her forehead. She wasn't on sale.

That stunt's the closest I've come to dying. You haven't seen mad until you've seen Red Martian mad. I don't know how they lost the war.

And I've burned a lot of time on the question. You see, I play a lot of strategy games. You know, toy tanks for grown-ups. So I try to look at war analytically. And I wonder: What was Earth's advantage?

It's easy to blame manufacturing, but I think there's something deeper: steaks.

No one throws their life away for synthetic meat. It's like marrying a sex toy. If I'm going to get mulched by androids, my last meal should have a soul.

That's why you didn't send much livestock up with us. Or medicine. Smart.

Any veterans here? Round of applause for the veterans.

I'm sure the front lines were terrifying. But so were the sidelines. I've never been more conscious of living in a big metal egg. Either of you could have stepped on us without noticing.

No one's blaming you. It's just that Mars is a lot smaller than Mars. And every time a missile drifted off course, we risked taking another bar fight's knockout. You know, if knockouts were banned by interplanetary law.

Another round of applause for the veterans.

I don't get much romantic attention here. It's either my face or the fact girls have something to lose. Stakes are low on a colony, so dating a professional clown sounds fun. Here, where you can have a yard? I'm a liability.

Still, I managed to get one date. A friend of my agent's friend. She looked disappointed from the start, which I'm used to. The reason still caught me by surprise. She said, "I thought you'd have a barcode."

Karma's real.

Still, I've kept myself busy. There's a jar in my hotel room. I'm going to fill it with clean air and pinecones. Selling it should cover my rent for a year.

I also have a set of Little Picasso colored pencils, from home. One says "sky blue." After a week here, I can safely say that Little Picasso is full of shit.

You know what "sky blue" looks like? The ocean. I've spent thirty-two years thinking the ocean looked like the sky and the sky looked like the ocean. And then there's "grass red."

That's why our movies about Earth suck. The directors are working off secondhand stories. It's like telling a joke you heard when you were five.

Once, I took Jana's kid to see a movie called *Baxter the Bat*. It's fine that the bat talks. Kids have to learn about friendship and drugs somehow. I'm even fine with it having thumbs. But Baxter spends half the movie underwater and lives. I'm not local, so let me double-check: Do bats have gills?

Jana's kid probably thought so. He was great. Everyone needs one friend with terrible taste. That way you never miss a movie.

Hey there. Yes, with the drug dealer sunglasses on indoors. Would you call this a big venue?

"Sort of?" Very decisive. You can't all be General Clark, I guess.

This is the biggest room I've ever played. I've done bigger *crowds*, but they were packed elbow-to-elbow like crates. You guys have *space*. That kid in the front is *stretching*.

Kicking the poor people off the planet probably helped.

Kidding! Kidding! We make fun of everyone here. You can't just laugh at the Mars jokes.

You were nice about it, in a way. Instead of rounding everyone up, you made rockets cheaper than rent. That's a gentleman's eviction.

And you had to save the planet somehow, right? Either kick people off or stop using plastic sandwich swords. I love those things. Any lunch can be a duel.

I've got this friend, Robin, who Jana never trusted. Robin says we shouldn't call our tin can a *colony* because it's not self-sustaining. Technically it's a space station made of a million little shipwrecks welded together. I don't know why Jana felt threatened. I'd cheat with someone less pedantic.

But it really is crammed up there. My apartment's like a coffin with a laptop, and the walls are thin. I hear all of my neighbor's breakdowns, arguments, and breakup sex. He has the kind of boyfriend you write bad poems about.

Sometimes I give him some advice. I don't even have to shout.

"He didn't look for a job. He's been fiddling with your guitar all day."

"He's not going to change! His only hobbies are pills and selling your stuff for pills."

"You're overcooking your food. It smells like charcoal briquettes in here."

I think I'm helping. My neighbor's still with the junkie, but his cooking smells *much* better.

Still, it's good to get away. I only had one near-death experience on the way here.

I saw space junk up close. Have you heard about this? The giant balls of compressed trash floating through neutral space? Specifically, *your* trash? I call them "trashteroids."

One missed my ship by inches. I thought it was the end. I was up at five a.m., sober, waiting to see if I'd be crushed by old campaign T-shirts. My personal nightmare. The whole point of smoking is choosing how I'll die.

Half my life passed before my eyes. I skipped all the sleeping, drinking, and erotic cinema analysis. I mostly saw myself doing crowd work, and it wasn't pretty. I looked like the king of Martian hacks.

"What's your name? What do you do? Can you teach me how to write a joke?"

Then I fell on one knee and humbled myself. "God, if you get me past this, I'll never ask anyone where they're from again."

And then I died. Okay, I didn't, but I still do crowd work. It pulls people in.

Anyway, I'll speak on behalf of your neighbors. Details show us that you care. Things like not leaving trash on our lawn, or not naming us after planets that already exist. Be more thoughtful in the future. Or cut taxes. I'd overlook a few trashteroids to get that four percent back.

Four percent. I guess that's what textbooks will say all the shooting was about. As if three would've been fine.

I'll break a soft rule of stand-up and give you a peek behind the curtain: I lied to you earlier. Sometimes, when the moon is full, comics lie for a punchline.

I never scanned Jana's barcode. She left to look after her parents on Red Mars. I didn't have the stones to follow because of all the nukes flying around. The barcode story's just less embarrassing. And "idiot" sounds better than "coward."

I felt guilty, so I tried reconnecting. I'm not good at apologizing, but I've gotten semi-famous. Which tends to work better.

I sent six messages, with no response. Just like old times. I cleaned up my place in case she brought her parents back with her. Optimism tends to race ahead of my common sense. That's why I like comedy: it gives my inner cynic a fighting chance.

Then I found out she'd moved to Haven City. Which doesn't exist anymore, in the legal sense. Or the literal sense. It was the first city bio-bombed after the armistice.

Games didn't help me figure that choice out. So I tried sports. A war crime makes perfect sense in boxing. Why not sneak a punch in after the bell? It could make the next round easier.

General Clark received a medal for "distinction in character." Jana got a low-res photo on my fridge, printed in black-and-white. Ink's hard to come by right now. Wartime supply chains and all that.

Man, it's *quiet* in here. Let's go back to fun comparisons between Earth, Mars, and Mars! That's what the poster advertised, right? "Ever notice Martians walk like this?"

Now, tell me if I'm nuts. If I'm off the mark. If I'm gently rocking back and forth in a padded room. But is it just me, or are you guys a *little paler* than me? Or my manager, or mother, or anyone I've spoken to in my life?

It's strange, because my colony's *much* farther from the sun. It's part of our energy problem, in fact. So I can't *imagine* why the descendants of the migration would be so much *darker* than the people that got to stay! It's a puzzle! A real brain tickler. It sounds like the Middle Passage, without the jobs waiting.

Not much heckling culture here, is there? You guys just sit there and *glower*. I love it. I thought everyone would've left by now.

When I was a kid—I started as one, despite the rumors—I read that half the people in the migration didn't make it. Half. It blew my mind. More people survive suicide.

That same textbook came up in the news last year. The publisher apologized for downplaying the fatalities, and that's as far as I read. *Half* was enough to turn me into this. More would put me in the hospital. Or improv.

Dirty secret? The colonies don't like you any more than the Red Martians did. The Reds just had enough uranium to express themselves.

Last cigarette. Time to get out of here. I'm sure I'll be invited back soon. Right after Haven City grows back.

But first, I promised you a prop gag. Ready?

What's the difference between this cigarette and Earth?

This cigarette doesn't deserve to burn.

democracy: The perfect system for communities of two hundred or less.

Democrats: A loose alliance between doomed idealists and Republicans with black friends.

depression: A rising phenomenon in black teens, despite all they have to look forward to.

diamonds: Subject of a fiery debate between abject human misery and shininess.

Diceman, the: A naturally gifted comedian dedicated to variations of "Bitches, amirite?"

dilation: A feature of Hugo-winning doors.

Disney: Copyright holders for the human imagination.

diversity, equity, and inclusion: Meetings for subalterns to enjoy while not getting promoted.

divorce: Highly underrated.

dogs: Servants created by providing wolves unlimited food, shelter, and toys.
Author's note: Many Americans now enjoy unlimited food, shelter, and toys. Expect collars in the near future.

Domme: Professional recipient of specific, loud, and pointed instructions on how to dominate others.

doom: 1. The onomatopoeia for melting ice.
2. Digital anger management.

Dr. Seuss: A rebronged roogle fond of zoogling nonsense words.

Dune: A testament to the literary power of mescaline.

Dust Bowl, the: The total failure of topsoil to pick itself up by its bootstraps.

dyscalculia: The inability to understand the ending of *1984*.

dyslexia: Disorders adding difficulty to reading.

E

Earth: 1. A hot planet with some cool lizards.
2. Home of a large game of *Risk*.
3. The uninhabitable homeworld of the Tyrannus Empire.

economic inequality: A force ready to accomplish what the British Empire, civil warfare, Spanish flu, the Axis Powers, the Soviet Union, and Ronald Reagan couldn't.

editors: Society's last line of defense against an interesting idea.
Author's note: An editor asked me to make my book blacker. I cut out two-fifths of it.

elders: 1. Children without humility.
2. Children without bladder control.

elections: Warfare without the fun part.

empire: Democracy's flirtatious older sister.

"Entry of the Gladiators": The national anthem of the United States.

epidemic: An opportunity to catch up on reading, exercise, and panicked sobbing.

epidemiology: The science of screaming too loudly to be heard.

eternity: 1. Incomprehensible infinite time.
2. The estimated length of the average first date.

Europe: Winners of the global sprint to invent the rifle.

euthanasia: The right to cut the boring part of your biography.

evangelicals: The holy union between twelfth-century politics and twenty-first-century media.

Eve: Pandora's plagiarist.

Evola: Fascism's Velvet Underground.

existentialism: Starting every sentence with "I," "me," or "my."

extinction: Around September 23, 2064.

extraversion: The ability to hold eye contact without writing a personal essay about the experience.

extremism: The most reliable fuel for voter participation.

eye contact: Best saved for marriage.

F

Facebook: The place a forgotten version of you lives.

faith: The belief that belief is sufficient reason to believe.

famine: A universally condemned human tragedy preventable at marginal collective expense.

Fantastic Four: The characters you skim over to get to Doctor Doom.

fantasy: Imaginative tales of dragons, wizardry, and moral justice.

farce: Every human project since the wheel.

***Fast and the Furious, The*:** An American cultural renaissance peaking with the masterpiece *Furious 7*.
Author's note: Furious 7 is the triumph of minimalism: every frame is a fist, butt, or car. The totality of the human experience, from love to the march toward the singularity, is seen through these three filters. And a car jumps between skyscrapers.

father: The bass player of parenting. Good to have, but nonessential.

fatwa: A career goal of any writer worth reading.

festival: A celebration of youth, music, and hepatitis.

fiction: Lawsuit-proof nonfiction.

fire: The first mistake.

football: Compelling gladiatorial action arbitrarily yoked to a leather ball.

four: Either luck or death, depending on your mood and time zone.

fractions: The last easy math before the pain begins.

Free Panels

To: diversitystarz@gammacomics.com
From: J.Ruvola@gmail.com
Subject: Get Ready for Radiotron!

Dear Ms. Luna,
Nothing draws dreamers like a Gamma Comics contest, and I'm sure you've seen countless pitches. Mine might stand out among all the manga imitations. *Radiotron* (twelve twenty-three-page issues) recalls the idealist glow of classic superhero comics, where anything felt possible. Hence the title cyborg's catchphrase: "Justice never changes."

He's based in no small way on my father. I've never met anyone with a clearer picture of right and wrong. I suspect, after his passing, that I never will. We need that nobility to transcend hate today.

I'm biased, but I think Radiotron could stand shoulder to shoulder with the best of the GammaVerse. He has the same core that made Alpha Man great: humble roots, indomitable inner strength, and faith in the people. Today's stands lack true adventurers, and Radiotron could help Gamma Comics fill that void.

The *Diversity Starz* contest brief asks: "What perspective do you bring to the table?" Personally, I'd say an eye for history. As Gamma Comics forges ahead, creators that remember the medium's past will prove invaluable. Mental diversity is an important intersectionality, and with it we can elevate our praxis. I'd love to help Gamma stay on top of the game.

I've attached three sample script pages, per guidelines. They're from *Radiotron Rising*, the first six-issue Radiotron story arc. *Radiotron Rising* explores his origins, enemies, and unkillable dream.

Sincerely,

Jeremy Ruvola

Jeremy Ruvola is a Queens-based writer. His fiction has appeared in Pocket Galaxy, Yuck-Yucks, *and* Southern Lights. *His cat Nebula is his biggest fan and harshest critic.*

[Attachment: The Future.odt]

PAGE 41 (3 PANELS)

Excerpt: Radiotron Rising

PANEL 1

RADIOTRON tugs at the energy field holding his limbs in place. Is this the end? Even if he survives, can he save his love?

　　1. RADIOTRON: Where is she, demon?

PANEL 2

Close on VEXUS as he gloats. With RADIOTRON bound and SEDUCTRA slain, nothing can stop the Abraxas Drive from charging.

　　1. VEXUS: Dead, Radiotron. Just like your meddling mother.

PANEL 3

Close on RADIOTRON's eyes. They glow with a hero's strength. And delta radiation. The glow is both literal and figurative.

    1. RADIOTRON: Just like you!

PAGE 42 (4 PANELS)

PANEL 1

Driven by mingled fury and grief, RADIOTRON tears through his bonds. SEDUCTRA's gone, just like his mother, sister, neighbor, and wife. Thanks to their sacrifices, he can strike the next blow.

    1. VEXUS: Impossible!

PANEL 2

RADIOTRON strikes the next blow, punching through VEXUS's stomach.

    1. VEXUS: Impossible!

PANEL 3

VEXUS stares down at the hole in his stomach. There's no robot, clone, or hologram this time; he's suffered a mortal wound.

    1. VEXUS: Impossible!

PANEL 4

VEXUS goes limp. RADIOTRON holds his oldest foe in his arms. Taking a life, even one as twisted as VEXUS, weighs heavily on him.

    1. VEXUS (weakly): Impossible!

PAGE 43 (2 PANELS)

PANEL 1

Close on the fading VEXUS, who smirks.

PANEL 2

With his last wisp of spite, VEXUS presses a hidden button on his collar.

    1. VEXUS: I may die . . . but you'll never defeat . . . Radiotron Dark!

    2. SFX: Doot.

To: opensubmissions@readprime.com
From: J.Ruvola@gmail.com
Subject: Query: Radiotron Force

Dear Ms. Hayes,

I couldn't help but notice your name before submitting. It's a great name, rich in history. That, even more than your work at Prime Comics, gives me faith that you'll appreciate *Radiotron Force*. You understand legacy.

Radiotron Force is my love letter to the mercenary teams of the nineties. It merges that era's unapologetic grit and testosterone with today's structured, character-focused narratives. I think it offers the best of both schools, and the attached sample pages reflect that.

The soldiers of *Radiotron Force* defend a dying world. Their childhood dreams of splendor are a fading memory, reducing them to life on the plasma knife's edge. As barbarians encroach on Zero City, the last bastion of civilization, it's up to the hard-edged Dutch Bronzer to save what's left of mankind. His squad, named after humanity's fallen hero, holds the line.

It's a natural fit for Prime Comics. While Gamma churns out identical cape after cape, Prime blazes a braver trail. That courage has made a generation of creator-owned work possible, and I'd be proud to join that legacy. The first graphic novels my father ever bought me were Prime.

Thank you for your time. I put everything into *Radiotron Force*, and hope it shows. You're holding my world.

Best,

Jeremy Ruvola

Jeremy Ruvola is an up-and-coming Queens writer of fiction, graphic novels, and screenplays. His work, bucking experimental trends for purist adventure, can be found in Pocket Galaxy, Southern Lights, *and* Freer Press. *His cat, Nebula, sees great things ahead.*

P.S: I have a presence in Free Panels, which has something of a reputation. To clear the air, given the trolls you've dealt with in the past: We support everyone. Free Panels is about telling better stories, not hate. We just don't want your movement reduced to a marketing prop. That's essentialism by another name.

[Attachment: Radiotron Force (1 of 77).odt]
Excerpt: Radiotron Force

PAGE 1 (2 PANELS)

PANEL 1

Wide on the ruined wasteland. Traces of a better age dot the landscape—little things like solitary skyscrapers and the Washington Monument. A lone silhouette appears before a rolling cloud of dust and smoke.

    1. CAPTION—DUTCH: We used to have a hero.

    2. CAPTION—DUTCH: We used to have a future.

PANEL 2

DUTCH thunders across the desiccated expanse on *Liberty*, his well-worn BattleCycle. The sidecar holds his latest kill's severed head. Jagged tribal tattoos mark said head as a Collective slave trainer.

    1. CAPTION—DUTCH: They're both dead.

PAGE 2 (5 PANELS)

PANEL 1

DUTCH parks his bike outside the Black Skull Saloon. The bullet-scarred door features a painted black skull. Beneath the logo hangs a scorched human skull.

    1. CAPTION—DUTCH: I'm a merc. Just a little dead on the inside.

PANEL 2

The clientele sizes up DUTCH as he strides to the counter. They've all got bounties on their heads, and he might collect.

    1. CAPTION—DUTCH: For a price, I make Collective raiders dead . . . on the outside.

PANEL 3

The bartender STILETTO loads a sawed-off shotgun. If looks could kill, DUTCH would be melting.

    1. STILETTO: Dutch, you fucking fuck, what the fuck are you doing here?

    2. DUTCH: Fucking you, I'd say.

PANEL 4

The ache of heartbreak reaches STILETTO's gaze. She lowers the weapon, revealing the "Dutch" tattoo on her arm.

    1. STILETTO: You broke my heart, Dutch.

PANEL 5

STILETTO slides DUTCH a drink. Perhaps something's still there.

    1. DUTCH: Sorry.

    2. STILETTO: Okay.

PAGE 3 (6 PANELS)

PANEL 1

A hulking, thuggish GORILLOID headbutts through the wall. It's an enforcer of the Collective, out for blood.

PANEL 2

With his quarry in sight, the GORILLOID raises an assault rifle in each of its four hands. DUTCH sips.

    1. GORILLOID: Dutch Bronzer, you are wanted for the crimes of murder and democracy.

    2. GORILLOID: You will come to a Reeducation Pit for gelding.

PANEL 3

DUTCH hucks his drink into the air. The GORILLOID, easily distracted like most of his kind, stares at the diversion.

PANEL 4

DUTCH shoots the falling glass in midair. A new, full glass already sits in his free hand.

PANEL 5

Shards of falling glass shred the GORILLOID's eyes.

PANEL 6

Seizing the opening, DUTCH jump-kicks the GORILLOID. He doesn't spill a drop.

　　1. CAPTION—DUTCH: Battle calculator. Almost makes it too easy.

This script is the sole property of Jeremy Ruvola.

To: TrashCan@DuChampPress.com
From: J.Ruvola@gmail.com
Subject: Pitch—What is . . . The Radiotron Equation?

Dear Ms. Seville,

Synthesis. It sounds complex, but it's perfectly elegant. The joining of two opposites to create something greater.

At a glance, I look like an odd partner for DuChamp Press. I've written on half the imageboards out there about the need for simpler, more relatable comics for young men. So why am I reaching out to the flagship of experimental graphic novels?

Synthesis, through *The Radiotron Equation.*

Is Xander Rollins a hero? Yes. Is he a lost young man looking for meaning in a fractured psychedelic mindscape? Yes. Is this the perfect fusion of my classic sensibility and DuChamp Press's madcap creativity? Absolutely. *The Radiotron Equation* paints Xander's journey to save his people and memories. As Xander hallucinates his childhood hero, *fiction* becomes *reality*.

At first, I wrote your books off as postmodern nonsense. Reading *Inverse Dreams in WanderSleep* taught me better. The new weird is a vital, thriving route to readers left behind by the mainstream. That speaks to me, and you'll find each sample page marked by effort and innovation. It would be a shame for either of us to keep missing out.

I know I can do this.

Sincerely,

J.X.R.

Jeremy Xavier Ruvola is ready to make his mark. His work has appeared in several journals and anthologies of note, making him a rising star in the Free Panels movement. He also hosts Ink and You, *a podcast covering the life of Alpha Man creator and free thought icon Arin Jacobs. His cat Nebula can do a handstand.*

P.S.: "TrashCan" is an . . . odd submission address. Perhaps more insulting than intended?

[Attachment: TRE.docx]

Excerpt: The Radiotron Equation

PAGE 1 (4 PANELS)

PANEL 1

XANDER enters his open office, passing identical plastic seats beside identical plastic tables. He's dressed identically to his identical coworkers, but he's in color.

PANEL 2

XANDER sees a metallic version of his own face in his monitor. Very mind-bending. XANDER, just as mind-bent as the reader, gapes in befuddlement.

    1. XANDER: Who are you?

    2. REFLECTION: I am you.

PANEL 3

XANDER stares down at his chest, alienated from his own himselfness. What could all this mean?

    1. XANDER: Who am I?

PANEL 4

The REFLECTION changes into a skull before pointing at XANDER and sharing a profound truth.

    1. REFLECTION: You are Radiotron.

PAGE 2 (3 PANELS)

PANEL 1

XANDER hangs from a tree by his foot à la the Hanged Man tarot card. He's still at eye level with his workplace monitor.

    1. XANDER: Why am I Radiotron?

    2. REFLECTION: Death.

PANEL 2

The discourse continues. Stick with me here. The full issue will include an interpretation guide for slow readers.

    1. XANDER: What is death?

    2. REFLECTION: The lack of Radiotron. While you sleep, your people burn.

PANEL 3

XANDER shares his perspective. A fruit falls from the tree onto his keyboard.

    1. XANDER: I don't understand what you're saying, even slightly. Like, at all.

PAGE 3 (1 PANEL)

PANEL 1

XANDER and his REFLECTION trade faces.

    1. REFLECTION: But you do.

    2. REFLECTION: You're Radiotron, after all.

PAGE 4 (1 PANEL)

PANEL 1

This might seem a little abstract, but smart readers will follow along.

XANDER and company are replaced by a black void, lit only by the radiant letters of the **Radiotron Equation.**

The equation reads:

Radiotron = Hope + Joy – Deviance + Power + Actualization^Legacy * Nation = You = Metaverse = Radiotron

Note: Given the limits of a four-page sample, you might wonder what this all means. In full context, it's quite straightforward. You know who to come to for the rest.

Owned in entirety by Ruvola ThoughtWorks in the United States of America and abroad.

To: MayuIshida@tanoshiibooks.com
From: J.Ruvola@gmail.com
Subject: If you read one pitch today, make it this

Dear Ms. Ishida,

Some of your catalog makes me retch. The claim that manga is a creative movement beyond nation is false on its face. Tanoshii is an American publisher and should produce American-style comics to inspire and uplift Americans.

That said, I have a message that should shine through in any visual style. In fact, I think the contrast in tone and aesthetic will elevate both. Critics are fixated on eroding tradition, and I'm ready to meet them halfway.

Manga can't change me. But I can change manga.

That change is called *Radiotron Sentai*. After inheriting a pair of cursed blades, two estranged brothers discover the family secret: when the swords cross, wielders fuse into Radiotron, the nation's eternal defender. It falls to them to face Vexus, his thirteen demon kings, and the plan to rewrite everything that makes America exceptional.

Sample pages are attached as a PDF, per instructions. Read with an open mind.

Best,

J. X. Ruvola

J. X. Ruvola is what's coming next. After leaving New York's moral panic behind, he's found new creative life in the Free Panels movement. Credits for his trailblazing work include Glass Jaw, Uncucked, *and* Patriot's Corner. *His cat Nebula is getting up there in years.*

P.S.: I know how you usually do things, but could this get some color?

[Attachment: For Your Consideration.pdf]
Excerpt: Radiotron Sentai

Note: For clarity, I've used the scripting format popularized by the American writer Arin Jacobs. It's a clear cut above Tanoshii's suggested template. I suggest adopting it company-wide. The stories will improve.

PAGE 1 (4 PANELS)
PANEL 1
An anonymous shinobi limps into a forest clearing. He's dragging something behind him.

1. CAP—NARRATOR: America . . . the true birthplace of ninjutsu.
PANEL 2
The shinobi removes his mask, revealing GENERAL WASHINGTON's chiseled features.

1. CAP—NARRATOR: Warriors that mastered the shadows and used them to defeat a king.
PANEL 3
WASHINGTON lifts his prize overhead: the severed head of a Redcoat commander. The Continental Army stares, awed.

1. CAP—NARRATOR: The founders handed down secrets from father to son. Their sons followed suit.

PANEL 4

The Revolutionaries raise their swords and cheer. History may forget the details, but nothing can steal this victory.

1. CAP—NARRATOR: Until it reached us.

PAGE 2 (1 PANEL)

PANEL 1

The modern-day exterior of the Jackson household. It's an old Colonial home, with a soft yellow "Don't Tread on Me" welcome mat. A telltale ninja star sticks out of the wall, hinting at trouble on the home front.

PAGE 3 (4 PANELS)

PANEL 1

Our lead, GEORGE JACKSON, lies awake beneath the covers. There's no dialogue on this page because we're showing instead of telling.

PANEL 2

The bedroom door explodes. THOMAS JACKSON has thrust-kicked it open in a patriotic rage.

1. THOMAS: You're still lying here? Dishonoring us?

PANEL 3

Close on THOMAS, who twirls the top link of a three-section staff. He hoped to find a fight, and only sees a broken man.

1. THOMAS: Grandpa raised fighters.

PANEL 4

GEORGE lies still, driving THOMAS to even greater fury. There are a few emotional plates spinning here at once. You see, THOMAS actually likes his brother and wants to motivate him. A platonic execution of the "tsundere" archetype.

1. THOMAS: He stayed up every night, honing your swordplay and reading your scripts. Quitting now would be a betrayal.

PAGE 4 (3 PANELS)
PANEL 1

Like any proper ninja or American, GEORGE rises to defend his honor. He flies out of bed with a Dragon Claw strike.

1. GEORGE: Things don't work the way he thought. We're not just surrounded by demons, we're outnumbered by them.

2. GEORGE: It's best to start over somewhere.

PANEL 2

THOMAS deflects the blow. The rivalry between the pair forms a central theme, alongside patriotism and preserving the family unit.

1. THOMAS: Like cowards? No.

PANEL 3

THOMAS lovingly hurls his brother through a plate glass window. It's good bonding, but they'll need more to survive what's to come.

1. THOMAS: If demons truly own the world . . .

2. THOMAS: It's best to kill them all.

These words and ideas belong to J. X. Ruvola. Theft will be punished with the full weight of the law.

Folder: D/Documents/Templates
File: AnotherPitch.docx

Dear [Editor/Agent],

It's getting hard to breathe out there. We've lost more people and prosperity than anyone can admit. Yet we're expected to keep going, like it's fine. As if no one's to blame.

[*Radiotron Rising*/*Radiotron Force*/*The Radiotron Equation*/ *Radiotron Sentai*/*Radiotron High*] is a lifeline of hope for the people. Without the light of [superhero/science fiction/experimental/*shonen*/ teen romance] comics, I'd be just another cynic. A spiritual nothing.

Instead, I believe in dreams. I want to share them, because they're all you need to keep going.

Radiotron echoes an era that made sense. What's not to love? If you know what it's like to be invisible, to have your future given away on a whim, then *Radiotron* has your signal. I talk to real fans all over the country every day. They're ready to see themselves in heroes again.

An open question: Who benefits from America losing its spine and voice, its guiding lights since the beginning? I think we all know. Be brave, fight back, and choose *Radiotron*.

Sample pages attached. Thank you for your time, and for considering my work.

Best,

Jeremy Xavier Ruvola

Jeremy writes. While he might not check off the right demographic boxes, his work has a spirit that can't be found anywhere else. Stories in Freer Thought *and more recall the best of the comic book and American golden ages. His cat Nebula is missed.*

To: TestBlast@Panhandle.com
From: J.Ruvola@gmail.com
Subject: Triumph of our will: Radiotron smashes stretch goals

Dear Backers,

I'd given up. Everywhere I turned, I found rejection or censorship. I felt my dreams dying in my hands. Before I could follow them, the people saved me.

Thanks to you, *Radiotron: Aryan Champion* lives.

When someone chooses writing, or the lesser arts, they bet everything. They assume the game is fair. That ability, vision, and talent win out. But that's not how the industry works today. Comics, like all mainstream publishing, has devolved into propaganda. And there's no room for ideas outside the agenda.

In a sense, I'm glad it happened. I never saw how the puppeteers tilted things their way until I became a victim of it. That experience brought me to Free Panels, where I found other forgotten voices. And together, through crowdfunding, we've made a $150,000 statement.

I don't know when every editor became a woman, or "woman," but it's a dead end. The industry's terminal spiral won't stop until someone important wakes up. I hope our success teaches them, but I won't wait to find out. It's clear that we don't need them anymore. I doubt we ever did.

My father said that the future is invincible. It can't be squashed, perverted, or ignored. Those words kept me alive when there wasn't much food. When I sold furniture and fluid to survive. I imagined his future, free of the shame, failure, and deviance we accept as facts of life today.

That's how *Radiotron* survived. These ideas are the future. The glory America has inched toward for decades can finally breathe free.

I thought I didn't have a place. That I was put here to fail. But my dream, and our message will continue. We're going to take it all back.

I see you, remember you, and love you.

Jeremy

friendship: A popular game show following tight-knit social groups. Half the contestants are eliminated every episode, until one winner is left alone in a retirement community lobby.

future, the: You don't want to know.

futurism: Betting on the singularity upstaging the hydrogen bomb.

G

gangbusters: An expression so successful it inspired a 1936 radio drama lasting over twenty years.

Garfield: Cartoonist Jim Davis's furious polemic against the "fat cat" politicians of his era.

gender: A spectrum measuring enjoyment of the film *Bloodsport*.

Genghis Khan: 1. An inspiration to drunks everywhere.
2. Grandpa.

Germany: Bronze medalists in the race to conquer the Earth.

gerrymandering: The reason nothing positive happens anymore.

God: One guy, or a woman, or a bunch of people, or a vague force that created the earth, or the universe, or just sort of found both and brushed the dust off, that loves you, or is more indifferent, or is harshly judgmental of everything you do, or hates you with a cruel coldness unfathomable to mortal minds.

gold: Currently valued at fifty-six child slaves/kg.

graduate education: 1. An attempt to reverse four years of alcohol poisoning.
2. An attempt to extend four years of alcohol poisoning.

gravity: The force that keeps you orbiting an office for sixty years.

Grease: 1. A remarkably bad play. Stunningly bad. Sublimely bad. A collective stroke that audiences limp out of as one, forever changed by their shared mental decay.
2. Widely beloved.

Great Depression, the: A hard-earned lesson about the something-or-other of a bear market, and the potential of whatever to lead to stuff.

green card: One of the few sensible motives for marriage.

guillotine: The second-greatest equalizer.

guilt: You're better off not knowing.

Gundam: An argument over a girl escalates a little.

guns: 1. The citizen's defense against automated fleets of high-atmosphere bombers.
2. The end of murderers with decent cardio.

Guns, Germs, and Steel: A dark fantasy epic depicting the rise of a global empire of metal-worshipping beasts. Considered overly dry and cynical by the wider speculative fiction community.

H

Hades: A Greek deity condemned to play a toga-wearing version of Satan for the rest of entertainment history.

Halloween: The one holiday equally beloved by toddlers, cosplayers, and alcoholics.

hara-kiri: An underrated pastime among failed public servants.

Hawaii: The state farthest from the fallout zone.

heaven: Spacious.

heavy metal: 1. A genre lambasted as the devil's music.
2. A genre beloved as the devil's music.

hell: Crowded.

Hell in an Inkwell

I'd like to thank the Princeton University trustees for inviting me to speak. I'm not sure *why* they've done that and hope they don't come to regret it. This is the first time I've been in this lecture hall without a hangover.

I had a lecture about Neal Stephenson prepared. Then I read the program and discovered that this weekend's theme is "Women of Color in the Visual Arts." I might love *Cryptonomicon*, but I don't have the charisma to convince you he fits that niche.

So let's talk about Philomena Diaz, the woman that brought professional wrestling to the world of high art. Or high art to professional wrestling. The arc of her career should be of interest to the Princeton brand of artist, and has lessons for the half of the room that doesn't end up working at Goldman Sachs.

Philomena, the youngest daughter of two accountants, grew up with a single goal: to work as far from spreadsheets as humanly possible. So she attended the School of Visual Arts, joining one of the most prestigious—i.e., expensive—fine arts programs around. I believe they're still using her photo in the "diversity" section of the admitted student's brochure.

In her sophomore year, Philomena fell in love with the idealized physiques of Greek statues and Renaissance paintings. Towering, perfectly toned men and women became her signature. This chafed with her pockmarked volunteer models and the SVA faculty, who wanted her to "render the world as she saw it." When she contended that this *was* how she saw the world, her GPA declined to a 2.2. Which was, mercifully, just high enough to graduate.

It was the fashion of the moment. Today, she would be critiqued for not drifting further from reality. Tomorrow, she might even be in style. I pulled that insight from her autobiography, which is a good read if you can get past the extended metaphors and digressions about food. Chapter six devotes equal time to her mid-semester depression and reviews of West Village take-out options.

So far, Philomena might have struck you as a type of romantic rebel. But the borderline-failing grade on her résumé taught her the value of conformity. Her first and only gallery exhibit consisted of sixteen portraits of "real Americans," flab, moles, and all. These were lambasted as uninspired. Which they were, a point underlined by naming the exhibit *Real America*. Always avoid sharing creative ground with Republican governors.

Her autobiography, *Ringside Easel*, says she spent the next two years traveling across Europe. But a deprecated LinkedIn page indicates that she worked for a temp agency in Newark. Either way, Philomena left the art scene behind. In her words, "New York taught me that diversity of color does not guarantee diversity of thought."

Philomena didn't touch a brush in that time. The business of exploring the world—or adjusting spreadsheets—occupied her until 2003. During a visit to her childhood home in Hartford, she found her father had become an avid viewer of post–Attitude Era *Raw*. He called it "a window into the American mind." Philomena laughed at that. She'd been in New York long enough to pick up a bit of high-culture pride, and the sardonic derision that passes for confidence. Then she watched Dwayne "The Rock" Johnson perform his signature Rock Bottom technique on "Stone Cold" Steve Austin. Something clicked.

She quietly sketched the climax of the match. The Rock's elbow struck Stone Cold's core, sending the world heavyweight champion into exaggerated convulsions of pain. It was the first of twenty portraits of "WWE Titans" she would produce in the next month. To Philomena, the draw wasn't the narrative, technique, or homoeroticism. It was the glory. In art school terms, the two athletes captivated a tightly packed arena of worshippers by becoming broad caricatures of human aggression. In more basic terms, she thought it looked cool as hell.

There's something to her father's insight about our once-thriving country. It's no coincidence that the United States houses the largest wrestling promotion in the world. Japan and Mexico share some of the high-grade insanity that allows wrestling to thrive, but Americans have hosted seventy years of enthusiastic nuclear testing. No society can absorb that much radiation and remain stable. Mock combat is, in my opinion, a vital outlet for the energy of a crazed population. There's a nonzero correlation between dips in WWE ratings and Republican adventures in the Middle East. For containing some portion of the American impulse for violence, Vince McMahon deserves a Nobel Prize. But I digress.

After his fourth beer, Philomena's father demanded to keep her sketch of The Rock, later titled *Mountain in Bloom*. He taped it to a cardboard sign and carried it to a live recording of Big Show fighting someone smaller than Big Show. Signs are one of the primary modes of interaction between live audiences and wrestlers; the others are shouting and lobbing objects at the stage. The signs are a bit more unique. They showcase the wit and opinions of the fanbase, which range from the supportive but bland "I Came to See CM Punk" to the creatively subversive "Roman Reigns is a Holocaust Denier." A creative or well-made sign will hover on-screen for at least a moment and often recur in establishing shots throughout the match.

You can imagine the producers' surprise when a virtuoso rendition of Rock Bottom appeared in the cheap seats. The Rock is by no means a bad-looking man, but here he looked like a demigod. Repeated shots of the sign obscured some of the match itself, testing the patience of pay-per-view viewers. But Vince McMahon could smell money and quietly had his most polite goons drag Mr. Diaz backstage. There, Vince discovered that Philomena Diaz had uploaded five paintings of The Rock to her personal site. Most of the visitor comments were from Mr. Diaz, though her mother also occasionally left something encouraging.

When she received her letter from WWE management, Philomena expected something to the effect of "Cease and desist." Her *Sports Illustrated*—that's not a pun—interview describes seeing the logo on the envelope's corner as the most terrifying moment of her adult life. In this, she was rational: no artist should underestimate the vindictive fury of an American corporation. Philomena Diaz is one of the few artists to find a job offer inside instead of a lawsuit.

The McMahons offered her a simple freelance contract. If she accepted, she would produce one painting of a WWE superstar a week. If she rejected it, she would be sued. For Philomena, the carrot was enough to ignore the stick. Someone was willing to pay for her vision of the world. The WWE Universe didn't have the cultural cachet of the gallery circuit, but her work would be *seen*. Philomena signed in her best imitation of cursive.

Philomena's first commission was something of a failure. It's hard to imagine a dull painting of a man that calls himself The Undertaker, but her portrait of him sitting in an art studio, holding a bowl of fruit, was very . . . well, typical. Instead of settling for an easy check, Philomena called it "practice" and made a second attempt. This time she eschewed standard modeling methods and drew her outlines from the ringside of a steel cage match. Everything about The Undertaker that looked flat after their six-hour modeling session came alive. Today, *Charon's Uppercut* can be purchased on a T-shirt for $16.99.

In time, Philomena began working in allusions to her own heroes. For instance, her rendition of the 2007 Royal Rumble is a clear reference to Raphael's *The School of Athens*. The fresco's books and beards are simply replaced with chairs and leotards. It's worth noting that she gives Rey Mysterio Socrates's position and pose. Since she rarely chose her subjects, any hint toward her preferences stands out.

For all the horror it's wrought on our political system, the information age has made it easy for members of the same fringe to find each other. The intersection between art aficionados and WWE superfans is marginal. But every member of that niche is a diehard fan of Philomena Diaz. While McMahon only hoped to sell kitschy baroque-style T-shirts and baseball caps, Philomena's originals quickly became collector's items. For reference, the current auction for *The Liberation of* SmackDown, a Michelangelo-influenced image of John Cena powerbombing AJ Styles through a table, is set at $25,000. As you can imagine, Philomena is no longer temping.

At the peak of her visibility, Philomena received a letter from her old thesis advisor. Six years of consuming idealistic John Cena storylines led her to expect congratulations, or even an apology. Instead, she found two pages lambasting her as "the worst breed of sellout." To quote the last paragraph: "You've dedicated the finest arts education in America to the company that invented crotch chopping."

Today, that letter is framed in her office. It sits beside similar letters from classmates, printouts of think-pieces about "corporate appropriation of art culture," and her laminated SVA transcript. On her Instagram, she calls this collection "The Forest of Salt." That also happens to be the name of an upcoming *SmackDown* pay-per-view.

Her best work—at least, according to the amateur critics on the "Squared Circle" wrestling subreddit—is a portrait of The Miz between matches. The painting shows him hunched over in the locker room, wearing nothing but a worn black towel knotted around his waist. His torso is covered in every manner of bruise, and a thick red cut is uncomfortably close to his left eyelid. The blood causes some of his makeup to run. In the face of all this injury, The Miz smiles like a child. He considers a few moments of pain and mortal peril worthwhile if the public is entertained. This painting, more than any portrait of a finisher, manager, or audience, captures the spirit of professional wrestling.

God, half of you are asleep. Don't worry, I'm almost done.

My point is *not* to go home and binge *SmackDown* videos. Spicing up your brunch chats with references to DDTs and chokeslams won't make you brighter, more inclusive people. Besides, the WWE product has already been embraced by nimbler pseudo-intellectuals from smaller colleges. If you need a fresh corner of mass culture to scavenge, consider the archives of New Japan Pro-Wrestling, All Elite Wrestling, or Lucha Underground. They have a zombie that gets stronger every time he dies.

Think beyond wrestling. Think of how closing yourself off to new possibilities makes you a poorer person, a poorer artist, and intolerable at parties. Or, at the very least, think of how being myopic heels can make you miss opportunities to make buckets full of money. That's the Princeton motto, isn't it? Princeton in the company's service, and in the service of all companies? The bottom line you save might be your own.

heresy: The savior of human progress.

hero: Anyone with the courage to find injustice, leap into action, and take a decent video.

hip-hop: A movement with five traditional pillars: B-boying, graffiti, DJing, MCing, and twerking on top of a moving car.

history: Where old people did old people stuff you can't remember. You probably don't need to worry about it.

Hollywood: A frequent scapegoat for social progress.

Homestuck: A webcomic roughly twice as long as the complete history of mankind.

honesty: Vastly overrated. Relationships thrive on a firm foundation of lies.

honor: Just behind heart disease in history's leading causes of death.

hope: A fantasy fiction staple.

horrorcore: Shoddy artists with shopping carts full of body parts.

How?: Mostly written on an ad agency's time.

human nature: A philosophical debate settled by six minutes in traffic.

human rights: Largely theoretical.

hyperbole: The most important concept in linguistic or literary history.

hypochondria: A mental disorder in which one remembers the last year of history.

hypocrisy: The one force keeping civilization from descending into an eternal holy war.

I

Idaho: A state holding many interesting things and people to be enumerated at a later date.

idolatry: Worshipping an object that won't judge you, tax you, or cast you into eternal torment.

***Iliad, The*:** The story of Achilles, literature's first and most powerful man-child.

illiteracy: Emancipation from headline news.

imperialism: Any straight line on a map.

independents: The reason you have to sit through campaign ads.

Indian Removal Act, the: The worst crime against Native Americans until the next one.

infantry: Frequent victims of adultery.

insomnia: A technique mastered by elite students, artists, and amphetamine enthusiasts.

Instagram: The place a better version of you lives.

intelligent design: The belief a sane creator designed the candiru.

intermittent fasting: An eating order.

introversion: The absence of home training and self-awareness. *Author's note: Everyone around you can tell. Best to stay home.*

invasive species: Manifest destiny for locusts.

Iran: The Pentagon's long-lost unrequited love.

Iraq War, the: The only war on Iraqi soil at any point in history.

Iron Man: 1. A superhero powered by the military-industrial complex. 2. America's current favorite.

irony: Just what you expected.

J

"Jack and Jill": An English nursery rhyme subsequently interpreted as a warning against incest, politics, magic, premarital sex, and, occasionally, carelessness while grabbing water.

Jacksonian democracy: Government driven less by the whims of the aristocracy and more by grounded, working-class genocide.

Jacobins: Well-intentioned activists that lost their heads a little.

Jamaica: An innovator in music, culture, homicide, and homophobic lynch mobs.
Author's note: As a Jamaican, I find my statement offensive and will be writing myself to give me a piece of my mind.

Jamaican cuisine: Rich flavor drawn from open warfare on the aorta.

Japan: The biggest non-gunpoint cultural exporter.

Jefferson, Thomas: Somewhat hypocritical.
Author's note: As a Black American, I hear the criticism. But at the end of the day, he's family.

John: Devoted apostle and patron saint of unimaginative parents.

Johnny Got His Gun: Peacenik propaganda that fails to explore the upsides to losing every limb in service of one's country.

Joker: A figure who, alongside Pennywise, has condemned modern clowns to poverty.

Judaism: The source and dogged survivor of Abrahamic religion.

jumper cables: Essential gear for any experienced driver or CIA agent.

K

kale: The bargaining phase of body grief.

karaoke: A date they'll come home with you to escape.

karma: 1. A widely and wildly misunderstood religious precept.
2. The belief that the robber barons of the world will receive anything but quarterly dividends and reelection.

Kelvin: The best unit for telling people you remember high school.

Keynes, John Maynard: Inventor of economics as a blindfolded plate-spinning act on a unicycle.

ki: The secret techniques they teach other students after you leave Tiger Schulmann's.

Kilimanjaro: The first tourist trap to come with free brain damage.

killing time: The patient man's suicide.

kinetoscope: Humanity's liberation from hard headsoundy thinkwords.

king: A man chosen by God to spend seven weeks posing for one painting.

kingdom: Everyone less armed than the king.

King Kong: An idealistic portrayal of dating in New York.

Kingston: A beautiful, culturally rich place to get stabbed.

Kissinger, Henry: America's most famous humanitarian, in that he fed exclusively on humanity.

Korean War, the: The only war on Korean soil at any point in history.

kryptonite: An alien stone that radiates dramatic tension.

Ku Klux Klan: A hate group that rocketed to the top of the race-hate charts before collapsing due to creative infighting, drug abuse, and lighter fluid shortages.

L

labor camps: Where disruptive lemons turn into productive lemonade.

Lassie: The reason people expect dogs to do more in a crisis than whimper and eat dirt.

laughter: A psychological defense against ecological collapse, rising authoritarianism, or simple isolation.

learning: The sole cause of aging. Every scrap of information eats another piece of one's life span. History's most educated figures are all dead, while cretins enjoy notable longevity. Commonly resisted by children in a desperate bid for survival.

leftists: The natural enemy of the leftist.

legacy: What you leave behind in the cosmic blink before the sun dims.

Liberia: A rare collaboration between black activists and segregationists.

libertarianism: A branch of Christianity focused on the golden calf.

Liberty Points

I have my rights. That's a twenty-first-century line, but you guys could be a little nicer about this. I'm starting to think that my score doesn't mean anything at all.

Well, yes, I'd say that I have contempt for the court. The court switched my quarter-million-dollar suit for a blue onesie during processing, and I have a feeling that even if I win I'm never going to see that suit again. That's a bitch move. I'd never even touched anything that expensive before last week.

On that note, does divorce law apply here? Because I sure as hell have become accustomed to a certain lifestyle. That lifestyle involves more oysters hand-fed to me by movie stars and less dodging spoons carved into knives by angry children. Trust me: two weeks is more than long enough to spoil yourself, and two nights is just enough to get decapitated.

These rulings usually take a while, so I have to ask: What gang do you think I should join? I know, a black guy from West Ward normally defaults to the White Tigers. But they don't have their shit together, as you can tell from the fact that they sound like a white-power cell and are named after an animal found *exclusively* in East Asia. It's not a growth organization, and I'd like to survive long enough to be executed.

Really? You enjoyed my "sub-sophomoric imitation of a sense of humor" when I was First Citizen, *Your Honor.* To be honest, I was trying to pander a little by keeping things light. But if you want me to jump to my version of the story, I'll cooperate.

It began—What do you mean, introduce myself? You know who I am. So do all the gawkers giggling behind me. The bailiffs know, the journalists know, and the security drones have a hint. I mean, I'd understand if we still had juries taking up space, but you're just wasting time.

You're right, arguing does take longer. My name's Lucas Nolan. Out of the two hundred million citizens of the Free Dominion's East Ward,

I'm currently ranked first. Number one. King of the hill. Head nig—You get it. I've had the rank for about fifteen days.

It started on a Tuesday, while I was supposed to be working. If you guys are serious about cutting down on sedition, you need to find less mindless tasks for us to waste our lives on. The imagination goes places after the eighth hour in a temperature-controlled box. The same goes for rehabilitation, as I can now say from experience.

Of course that's not a threat. Am I going to blow up my own prison cell? We've definitely spent a few too many decades in the Levant if you think I'm the suicide bombing type.

It was a government desk job, the first place you go when you've tapped out of life. Pushing papers is the same everywhere, but for our purposes I'll point out that I worked for National Surveillance. Less flashy than Interior Investigations, but we live longer. As the associate communications director, I started the day by forwarding e-mails from the assistant communications director to the lead communications director. The rest of the day was mine, as long as I didn't leave my box.

In communications, there are sensors marking every cubicle, elevator, exit, and urinal you happen to walk by. The number of recorded trips tends to come up during requests for raises or vacation time.

I started out with a few number puzzles to wake my brain up. Unless I'm hungover, a round of 3D sudoku works better than a cup full of stimulants. Once I felt like a person again, I moved on to calisthenics. Strength training's retro, but working in surveillance made me way too paranoid to shoot nanites into my muscles. I guarantee that every artificial six-pack in the Free Dominion is sending data to someone on my floor. Anyway, I did my usual full-body routine, starting with handstands—

Yes, Your Honor, I do believe the "day-to-day inania of my life" is relevant to this case. It speaks to my state of mind. Do I have the right to defend myself?

After the workout, I sped through a reheated lunch. I needed my actual lunch hour to meet with Talia, my semi-girlfriend. In that I considered her my girlfriend and she did not. In hindsight, I have a lot more empathy for her position. The communications department break room isn't the *least* romantic location on Earth, but it is in the running. However, as manager, she could have done something to spruce it up.

No, I don't think I'm incriminating myself. I'm not on trial for evasion of labor, and won't be unless *she* goes on trial for abuse of authority. No, I don't think I'm being petty, either. Well, maybe just a little petty.

Once we'd finished sweating out our differences, we gave our phones some attention. It's a lot easier than talking. There were two icons I didn't recognize, which meant Central had put out another update. The first was an optional app from National Fitness that offered a discreet electric shock if the user went over their recommended caloric intake. I left it off. The second was Liberty Points, which should be familiar to the court.

"Did you know about this?" I asked.

"Yeah, it should be great for our diet," said Talia.

"I meant Liberty Points."

"You're in the department that came up with it. You watched 'picking an icon color' become a six-month quagmire. Do you remember *any* of this? We've had the thing in public beta for six months. The younger users love it."

"Yes. I remember that. From the e-mails, which I read." I tapped the light brown icon. (I'd have suggested blue if I'd actually read the chain. It's a more inviting color.) It opened a bare-bones white tab with three lines of oversized sans serif text:

Name: Lucas Nolan

Liberty Score: 17

Rank: 158,091,241 (Ninth Decile)

"Sixth decile?" Talia roared. "What kind of garbage is this?! Making the logo for this thing should at least put me in the fifth. It must be my sister. That preening idiot votes for an opposition party every year no matter how many times I tell her they picked the winner a year before the first debate."

She spent the rest of our break explaining why she deserved to be an only child. I offered my sympathy, but I didn't take the issue too seriously. How important could it be if they hadn't even bothered designing a proper interface? There were no settings, bonus features, or even hidden games. The UI consisted entirely of a name and rank that, as far as I could tell, meant nothing.

I took a meandering path back to my cubicle, which made me the ten usual minutes late. Once seated, I followed thirty-five years of hard-coded habit and checked my phone. There weren't any new messages, but my score had gone down to 16. I snorted and tabbed over to *Karate Island*, a game I'd taken to playing while warming my seat. Believe it or not, the story is the main feature. It's about—All right, that's fair. The story of Jonas "Blood Knuckle" Kang is beyond the court's concerns.

When I closed *Karate Island*, my score had gone down to 11.

This caught my interest and engaged the long-dormant inquisitive part of my brain. While watching Liberty Points in my right hand, I gently wheeled my chair past my cubicle door's sensor and started counting. When I hit "thirty Mississippi" my score went down to 10. I like to believe I said something clever, but I think I just cursed. I rolled back to my terminal, drafted a nonsense e-mail to my manager, added every buzzword I could think of to the subject line, and blind-copied everyone shiftless enough to work under me. After I sent it, my score went up to 10.5.

Unease crept in. I spent the rest of the workday rereading e-mail with a self-consciousness I didn't know I was capable of. It was the best imitation of work I could do with my job title, and it seemed to keep me from dipping into the single digits. My fingers tapped the back of my terminal with hummingbird anxiety until I realized that annoying my coworkers might lower my score.

I left the office with a score of 11.2 and a headache. I turned to the family cure, which is alcohol in moderate-to-large doses. My bar of choice was Red Jack's, which was full of the kind of undesirables that my coworkers spent their afternoons stalking. Reporters, comedians, other potential dissidents. The music's only awful on Saturdays, which is a bonus.

"Could I get three shots of Liver Thinner?" I asked the bartender. He had the stone face of a man that took his job seriously, which I found entirely alien.

"Are you sure? That brand's imported."

"What? Who gives a shit? You're using my drinking time."

"Whatever." He filled three shot glasses with dimly glowing semi-solid blobs. I watched the lines of color swirl, with no pattern holding for more than a moment. I got bored of it after about twenty seconds and took the drinks in three rapid gulps. No, Your Honor, I don't expect you to be impressed by my drinking ability. Yes, I'm aware that the state offers multiple substance abuse recovery programs.

My phone vibrated. I had a high-priority notification from Liberty Points. The audio kicked in without my input:

Hey there, freeman! It looks like, through some misunderstanding, you've hit the tenth decile with a Liberty Score of 8.3. Liberty Points are here to help you keep track of your contributions—and deficiencies—as a citizen of the Free Dominion. We'd never intrude on your life: there are no government-mandated bonuses or demerits associated with your Freedom Score. However, other citizens and private services may take note.

"The hell?" I muttered.

"Patriots buy local booze," said the man to my right. He abandoned his chair, and his friends followed. For the next hour, I was toxic. Each group of comely web journalists I approached fluttered to the opposite side of the room. Every word I said went unacknowledged by people I'd shared years of happy hours with. When I went to the bathroom, the cleaning staff abandoned their mops and pails to leave.

The bartender caught me sulking in the corner and wagged his finger. "Look, I'm on the clock, so I'll help you out. Scores tend to converge. Speaking with someone in a lower decile might bring you down. Keeping them in your contacts will *definitely* drag you down. Until you raise your number, it's going to take more than your outdated sense of humor to get around."

My sense of humor is not outdated. I was the funniest guy in my government office and . . . I should focus. You probably agree with him anyway.

I tried to switch bars, but the Castle Club wasn't letting anyone with a two-digit score in. You had to be seventh decile to get into Grinding Pit, and fourth decile to get into Grinding Gallery. I tried to buy my way into Bass Mentors, but the bouncers said they didn't take bribes from anyone with a score under 70.

It didn't take long to find a taxi back, at least. The cabbie made me do the driving after checking my score, but at least I didn't have to walk.

Out of all the streets in East Ward, I chose to cut through Delancey. There, I caught a glimpse of Talia in a blue dress I'd never seen before. She was walking with a guy that looked a bit too much like me, with a nicer suit, a wider smile, and a higher number. I threw the cab into park and watched for twenty seconds longer than I should have. The cabbie kept the meter running.

Yeah, a recess would be nice. Is there going to be food?

I've got a theory, if you're still allowed to use that word without going through the Dominion's academy. Every phase of life is just an echo of high school. You can change the people and places, but the same fundamental low-stakes pettiness is in place. It becomes high-stakes pettiness at the United Nations, but you get the idea.

After Thursday's washout, I was in a giving mood. I showed up to my lunchtime non-date with Talia with a bottle of plum wine. A local brand. She received the bottle with a pair of rubber gloves, which she then placed in a garbage chute.

"Look," Talia said. "Violating multiple sexual misconduct agreements with an employee is one thing. But sleeping with a ninth decile is out of the question."

"Oh."

"Could you move a little further away? I think I can lose points by standing near you."

"Right."

"No eye contact."

That's when I left.

Back in communications, I found myself in high school. I'd bumped my score up to 36, but that was just enough for me not to get fired. Passersby still gave me a two-foot berth in the hallway, and I had to duck a pair of spitballs when I returned to my terminal. Removing the barrier between me and civil society would take something more drastic. Eating alone was fine when I chose it, but having it forced on me picked at my ego.

Online, my contacts list had shriveled. Like anyone, I once had more people on that list than I cared to keep track of or ever speak to again. Now that Liberty Points was out of beta, there were six people left. One of them was an advertising bot, one was a drug dealer, and I was related to the other four. At three in the afternoon, the drug dealer removed himself.

I'm not giving you the dealer's name.

I regressed with my environment. Isolated, I did my best to fall in line and hoped that the situation improved. My first step was clearing the games and vulgar image edits off my terminal, which was now exclusively for forwarding and proofreading internal department messages. That was as engaging as it sounds.

On my fourth day of retreading old messages, I had an idea. *The idea*, as far as this trial is concerned. I pulled up every message on Liberty Points that I could find over the last six months. I cut that pile of garbage down to the messages from the project design team. I hoped to find a comprehensive list of actions that changed Liberty Scores. All I found were the patch notes for soft drinks, indicating which domestic brands citizens would get points for buying. There's a monthly rotation, to keep us on our toes. I think Banana Spikes are in this month.

Then I went to Talia's office and handed in my ID card. Once again, I wish that I had a line. But I didn't manage anything better than "I quit, go choke on a hand grenade." Which makes less sense the longer I think about it.

Now, here's the trick. Before I got promoted to doing nothing, I used to run dummies. National Surveillance sets these up online to give people under "questioning" the appearance of normal activity. The dummy buys food, sells stock, sends your spouse lewd messages, all that. This keeps journos from catching on too quickly, since they rely on digital surveillance about as much as we do. A loyal employee of National Surveillance would never take a dummy for their own personal use, so I had three. I set Dummy One to buy cans of Eagle Cola, which are worth one point each. Recycling's worth another point thanks to National Environmental, so Dummy One sent them directly to the processing center. Dummy Two sent procedurally generated letters of glowing approval to elected officials around the Dominion. This only scored me one point for every ten letters, so I set Dummy Three to argue with people online. Each insult to another user's patriotism netted a clean two points, four when the dummy got creative.

Is everything "tantamount to a confession" with you?

Keeping my terminal from overheating replaced my full-time job. I sank half my savings into heat sinks, fans, and a new freezer. The thing still ran hot enough to turn my apartment into a sauna. Turns out that running espionage AIs is tougher on a terminal than pirating movies. I expected it to burn through the floor.

Honestly, I didn't expect it to work. It was the kind of wild swing you take when the game's effectively over. I'd grown up on the usual diet of crime dramas and seen men smarter than me put away for better plans by square-jawed Free Dominion agents. But I pushed through the whole logistical hell anyway.

I kept my phone off during most of the project. There weren't any messages coming in, which can be incredibly distracting. I didn't want to waste time waiting for answers from no one. So I waited until I dropped off the last recursive can to switch it on. "Recalculating score," it said before I even activated the program. Then the useless piece of garbage froze on me. The animated clock spun three times before stopping. I pocketed it and resolved to switch brands if I ever made it back into civilization.

It pulled itself together while I was asleep. I was in the middle of a dream about becoming prom king when the baritone digital voice dragged me back to the real world. "Calculation complete." I rolled over to see if I'd managed to break out of the ninth decile.

Name: Lucas Nolan

Liberty Score: 170,000

Rank: 1 (First Decile)

Can you dance? I can't dance. But I sure as hell tried that night.

First, I went straight to Bass Mentors. The drinks there were twelve dollars a pop, so I made for the exit. Then I was intercepted at the door by a black-suited man twice my width, all muscle. He had a soft face and rough hands, which said frightening things about his fight record.

"Sir, could we *offer* you a drink? Or a woman? Man? Robot? Animal?"

It took me a moment to realize I wasn't under arrest. It took me a few more moments to finish dancing badly on top of the table, partnered with a spindly waitress wearing a large wedding ring. I mumbled through a terrible joke, forgot the punch line, and the room erupted in enthusiastic laughter. Questioning this would have gotten in the way of me finishing a bottle of wine older than the country.

For the last time, I am *not* interested in the state's substance abuse recovery programs.

The Liberty Points algorithm gets a little wonky at the higher levels. After two weeks of having people flash me their scores, I've noticed that it's not really designed for people to get past 2,000. The mayor of East Ward has a score of 1,998, and that reflects the constant efforts of a fully funded think tank. At my level, nothing I said or did seemed to lose me a point. I bought imports, lazed around unemployed, and disparaged every chamber of government I could pronounce. My score was locked at 170,000.

On the third morning, I decided to test the limits of my luck. I requested a copy of the Free Dominion's founding document, from the days before the Imperate. Then I sent Johan Brant, the mayor of East Ward, a request to "borrow" his authentic flag from the first Free Emperor's office. It was delivered to me via gunship an hour later.

I brought both objects to *TwinTalk*, East Ward's leading morning talk show. The elder twin pinched her nose, clearly bothered by the scent of kerosene. The younger twin successfully identified the smell and took several steps back from the table before I dropped a lighter on two pieces of history. While the artifacts burned, the number 170,000 remained unchanged. I was bulletproof. Figuratively; I know that you're into firing squads.

The proximity effect went to an uncomfortable place. Standing ten feet away was enough to take someone from the eighth decile to the third decile. Skin contact could even make a paroled spree killer electable. Which I did, when one field tackled me during a party on the fourth night. He didn't stab me, so I consider it a fair trade. I also think he has some exciting thoughts about tariff reform.

I spent the fifth afternoon doing my best Christ impersonation. There are plenty of homeless people in East Ward with fully function-ing phones. When I found these men, women, and children, I made a show of tapping their foreheads with my index finger. It was a sick, self-indulgent gesture, but it also gave them access to jobs, places, and basic human treatment that was locked away from the tenth decile.

I still remember Leia, my last patient. So does most of the city, at this point.

"What are you doing?" she asked. Her outfit was a random mesh of bright colors, but she was the one with the incredulous expression. I felt like I'd come to an oral exam without doing the reading.

"Making a change," I said, head rapidly retreating into my large intestine.

"What about the other bums?" she asked. This forced a sober frown out of me. Helping *every* vagrant in the city by hand would put a serious damper on the party train. I needed a shortcut, and chose to delegate.

I brought my new followers directly to the mayor's manor. Johan looked pale and gray on television, and went paler and grayer when he looked at the crowd over my shoulder.

"Are they your servants?" he asked.

"They're a task force of fully capable first-decile citizens," I said, beaming at my own cleverness. I noticed a pair of volunteers to my left roll their eyes and straightened my back. "The more lucid ones have ideas about the funding of public aid. They can't do worse than the people you already have in place." The man to my right took this moment to vomit into a large green vase.

The mayor glared at the ground, and I became acutely aware of myself as a man without a non-digital rank. Then his shoulders sagged and he nodded. "I look forward to working closely with the task force," he said gloomily. I patted him on the back, and his mood immediately brightened.

"Great. That's Leia. She looks like a decent lieutenant mayor."

Leia tipped the bowler hat on top of her baseball cap. The veins on Johan's neck became visible, and I took my leave.

On the sixth afternoon, I learned that negativity wasn't a humane option. On the way to a lecture I was scheduled to give the Apex Academy's graduating class, I got shoulder checked by a man leading a shy toddler down the street. Under East Ward tradition, I called him an asshole. Under similar tradition he flipped me off and pretended to check his phone. I caught a glimpse of two flashing red zeros and his look of cosmic horror. His daughter pulled her hand free and abandoned him, preferring her chances of surviving the city alone.

I took the seventh and eighth days off. I felt like I was losing track of something important and thought two cycles of sobriety would be good for my mind. There were offers to spend the night at Luxury Falls and the East Ultra Hotel, but I slept on my old air mattress.

On the ninth morning I asked Talia what she was up to. She showed up ten minutes later with three dozen of my friends, acquaintances, and overt enemies from work. It got a little more crowded when *their* friends showed up in turn. By then the media had picked up on Liver Thinner as my favorite brand, and everyone brought at least one bottle. In an hour the entire apartment complex was taken over by waves of supplicants, suitors, and red-carpet vultures brandishing bottles of semisolid liquor. I compensated the neighbors with a tap to the forehead.

As for Talia, I apologized, she apologized, and we shook hands. Not exactly the carnal throwdown I was hoping for as First Citizen, but I'm glad I showed *some* sign of restraint during that time.

"I should tell you something," she said, checking her rapidly inflating score with her free hand. "At National Surveillance, they know you did *something*. They haven't pegged it yet, but when they do, they'll decide it was a crime."

"What about ex post facto?"

"Very funny," she said. "I've been lobbying for you. They'll go easy on you if you confess and show them the crack in the system. We probably should have just spent another month in beta . . ."

She left me with yet another bottle of Liver Thinner. I shared it with Lita Montag, the leading woman from *Crab Conflict: Crustacean Chaos*. Lita had long red braids that they tinted brown during postproduction and was interested in my opinions about films I'd never even heard of. There was a simple choice. I could confess my crimes against the Free Dominion and its vassal states, protectorates, partially owned territories, directly occupied territories, and allies, or I could have sex with a movie star.

Lita's terrible in bed. After all the magazine covers dedicated to that name, this was more than a little disappointing. Clearly, I needed to meet more movie stars to have a more enriching experience.

I spent the next four nights throwing similar parties. At this point I'd like to say that I was quite impressed by Your Honor's ability to execute a "keg headspin." I didn't even know that was possible, let alone wise.

On the fifteenth morning, I decided that I needed something different. I went to National Exploration and attached myself to a test flight for a reusable light spacecraft. Trips to space are rare on a government flunky's budget.

I sat next to Captain Dominic Alvarez in a two-man craft. The captain was in charge of course correction, diagnostic tools, mission reports, safety drills, and running several minor experiments. I got to press the red button that launched us into space.

"We've had these for a while, but this model's cheaper," explained the captain. From our perch, Earth and Mars were small glowing blips on an infinite black expanse. "Considering our budget, that'll be important if we ever want to get back to Mars."

"Do you think we'll ever colonize it?" I asked. I'm sure you remember the advertising blitz during the third space race. It's impossible to forget those posters of uncannily diverse friends playing volleyball on red sand.

"We could, any year they want to," answered the captain, nodding disdainfully toward Earth. "But there are too many distractions. Put the bottle down, we're starting reentry."

Getting away from the planet put my feet back on the ground. The number didn't actually matter. I felt ready to abandon the First Citizen schtick for something less corrosive to my brain and soul. Unfortunately, when we landed, there were a few squads of heavily armed National Enforcement agents waiting at the launchpad. I got a rifle butt to the rib cage before I could start improvising an excuse.

"Fucking soda? Really?" said the officer. I mumbled something I thought was clever, and he tossed me in the back of a cop car. In hindsight, battering the First Citizen probably set him up for life.

The rest of the story is boring. Gang politics, dodging a prison riot, stabbing a teenager in the leg to stay alive. After all your time as a judge,

I'm sure you've heard every nightmare that comes out of our system a dozen times. They have to start running together.

There was one surprise: Talia visited me during my first week in jail. Yeah, I didn't get it, either. I asked why the hell she was wasting her time, only not as politely.

"Mostly because we're friends," she volunteered. That's when I understood that I'm a genuine asshole. I reached out for a hug, so the guards flipped on my shock collar.

Remorse—that's actually a quality question. I do wish that I'd gotten away with it for a little longer. And I certainly regret not saving enough money to post bail. No ride lasts forever, and I should have been getting ready to move to one of the islands that's still above water. But regret's a bit of a waste of energy. I can't imagine acting any other way after two decades living in the tread pattern on the Dominion's left boot.

Your Honor, have you always done well? I mean, today you're a judge, which would impress anyone, but were you king of the hill in your law firm? Academy? Preschool? Or do you know what it's like to suddenly become relevant? Because most of us are bored and angry, waiting for a ship that's not coming. I don't know how anything we do to escape ever comes as a surprise.

I've given you a hard time, but I don't blame you at all. It'd have been the same with any judge in the Dominion. I'm actually relieved that you've listened to all of this. I'm not much of a writer, so this is the closest I'll get to producing a manifesto. To anyone else listening, I have a suggestion: Race for the bottom. Take your score as far down as you can and throw a party for everyone.

Let's hear that verdict.

LimeWire: Trailblazers in the holy art of online piracy.

Little Mermaid, The: The first animated film to represent the fish fetishist community, also known as gillies.

litotes: Not uncommon turns of phrase that don't overstate a point in a not simple way most readers don't love.

love: Giving up at the same time.

Lovecraft, H. P.: The first writer to use every synonym for "unthinkable" in one paragraph.

luck: Having the right thirty years of unrelenting effort, institutional connections, and unrepentant cheating at the right time.

luxury: Clean water after 2040.

M

magic: Taxable religion.

magick: Religion for people that don't pay taxes.

Mammon: The demon lord of greed. Recently acquired the domains of sloth, envy, pride, lust, gluttony, and wrath in a merger with exciting implications for infernal investors. Currently pursuing expansion into the seven heavenly virtues and oil futures.

management: Sitting in the general orbit of labor.

Marco: See *Polo.*

marriage fraud: An occasional pastime of rising young writers. Not recommended for the faint of heart, true romantics, or the sober.

Marxism: 1. The only economic platform demanding religious faith.
2. The invisible monster in conservative closets.

masquerade: A whimsical event in which masked citizens loudly upend social norms. Now known as a riot.

Mass Effect: 2.9 beloved games.

mass shooting: A hot American trend struggling to find an international audience.

math: The study of quantity, patterns, structures, and falling asleep halfway through class.

meaning of life, the: Entertainment for a hive mind of astral parasites watching from beyond time.

memes: Public domain wit.

memory loss: A serious condition affecting millions around the world.

memory loss: A serious condition affecting millions around the world.

Mercutio: Literature's first jobber.

mice: The primary focus group for American cosmetics.

mirth: Happiness for thesaurus owners and renaissance faire attendees.

mitochondria: A peaceful state swallowed by a neighboring empire.

Miyazaki, Hayao: Sparked hope in a generation through a screen.

Miyazaki, Hidetaka: Battered the hope out of a generation through a screen.

memory loss: A serious condition affecting millions around the world.

modern: 1. Of the current era.
2. Of the bygone era in which machinery first emerged.
3. Slightly ahead of the current era.
4. Of whatever time you feel in the moment.

mother: An ideal scapegoat.

mouse utopia: 1. A groundbreaking experiment proving that extended mass inbreeding might end badly.
2. Proof no one with tenure should be let near a mouse.

Munchausen syndrome: A conspiracy designed to keep innocents from the attention and drugs they need to survive.

Munchausen syndrome by proxy: The tragic inability to perceive one's own illness.

mythology: Religion plus time.

N

names: 1. Poetry exercises for first-time parents.
2. A chore for experienced parents.
3. Insults by future nursing home residents.

narcissistic personality disorder: The American disease.

nativism: Encouraging all life to return to its native ocean.

Neolithic Revolution: Where all the trouble started.

Netflix: The doctor that finally put modern literacy to sleep.

New Jersey: Princeton's lawn.

news: A caffeine-free way to jolt yourself awake in the morning.

newspapers: The obsolete, tree-killing, rapidly fading foundation of American sanity and democracy.

New York: The setting of most American films, novels, and corruption scandals.

nicknames: Blind Monkey, D-day, Bboy Britannica, the black kid, and suspect.

nigga: A filler word during moments of thought, akin to "like" or "um."

[redacted]: 1. A term publishers are obligated to allow Black writers to use at least once per book.
2. A polite invitation to test one's boxing skills in the public sphere.

nightmares: Memories from the future.

No One Gets Shot

"Is there a small chance that this is legal?" Leto asked. He flipped back to the second page and reread the professor's prediction and abridged procedure. The packet used a font Leto usually encountered when undergrads tried to pad their page count.

Professor Cardoso sucked air between her front teeth, making a critical whistle. It reminded Leto too much of his mother. He thought of every unattended laundry pile in his adolescence.

"Leto, you'll never get anywhere in this field obsessing over legality," she said. The professor wore a politician's pantsuit and a musician's shoulder-length braids. Leto sat under three rows of her empty bookshelves. She didn't put enough stock in maintaining a scholarly image to buy two hundred books that she would never read.

"There's a legal release for the test subjects. Is there one for me?"

"Nah. This way you'll be more motivated to make sure things go smoothly."

Leto lifted his glasses, rubbed his eyelids, and considered further resistance. He abandoned the idea: failing at Apex University would have betrayed a conspiracy that went back to his birth. His mother had picked an old-world name to give him an aura of old-world gravitas. "Leto" had all the weight of Corinthian pillars behind it. He never appreciated this until he met the *extremely enthusiastic* New Haven Police Department. Letos got warnings where Tyrells got beatings. That insight was the one advantage Jamaican imports had over homegrown black people, and it left him with a vague sense of guilt he kept sealed with an overpriced copy of *The Autobiography of Malcolm X*. He'd never actually read it, but it kept the big questions away and let him work.

Leto once made the mistake of looking up more details. His name was attached to Apollo's mother and listed as "primarily female." It also turned up as a side character that died in the first chapter of a brick-sized science fiction novel. Leto preferred the former. They were both bit parts, but the mother lived in peace after sleeping with Zeus. He planned on living a rich, full life without running into his own Harkonnens.

Then came the professor.

One piece of original research had brought him this far. His master's thesis was justifiably ignored, but a throwaway essay on gun culture still generated praise and rebuttals in his inbox. The opening, which he'd revised more times than a sane man should, was burned into his brain.

> *My last piece, "Patois and Practice," examined the link between the slang around a concept and its eminence in local culture. In this piece, I'd like to look at a case in more detail. In the United States, there are more slang terms for guns than genitals. Guns are heaters, burners, toasters, gats, lighters, choppers, pieces, boomsticks, macs, nines, roscoes, straps, bangers, cannons, hammers, llamas, ratchets, shotties, steel, tools, maggies, chrome, et cetera, ad infinitum. This is not insignificant.*

Professor Cardoso's handwritten offer to work as her research assistant sounded like a godsend. Apex University doctoral candidates had a decent chance of working as professors at some point in their lifetimes. Then she turned Leto into the main accessory to any number of crimes in the name of sociology.

The professor was a leading expert in what she called the "Hangover of the American Empire." This was also the title of her first book, which focused on McCarthyism and its sequels. Her second book was called *Congress and Coke* and covered the casual abuse of stimulants by every stripe of professional in the DC area. This week's highly illegal experiment was for her upcoming third book on guns.

"It's going to do gangbusters," she said as she led him down the hallway. "I wanted to call it *Gangbusters*, but movie studios get touchy about copyright."

Leto ignored her and opened the conference room door. He'd sacrificed his debauchery years for nothing. His parents had done everything short of locking him in a bell tower during high school, and their shadow kept him from becoming an undergraduate alcoholic until senior spring. Even in graduate school, habit kept him from getting into really interesting trouble.

The professor didn't follow him inside. After tenure, interacting with research subjects was below her pay grade. He eyeballed the crowd, who eyeballed him back. The ads had drawn a diverse group despite the fact that none of the fliers reached farther than the two-block radius of the sociology building. A triumph for the administration's self-conscious hand-wringing about diversity.

He took a seat in the room's lone rolling chair and put on a smile for the wall of eyes. The wooden bowl of complimentary mints lay untouched, leaving Leto all the pressure of creating a casual environment in a beige venue designed for student seminars and job interviews. He tried folding one leg over the other like the professor. No effect.

"Good morning, everyone. I'd like to thank you for giving us your time. I'd also like to thank you for signing a *very* carefully constructed release limiting both your liability and our own. Primarily the latter. The following may seem outlandish, but you'll receive a two-hundred-dollar campus store voucher for participating."

The crowd waited for him to cut to the point. The cell phones hadn't come out yet, but a few of the younger subjects pawed their pockets anxiously.

"The challenge is simple. We need you to go into the world, find a gun, and bring it back here as quickly as possible. To encourage haste, the first ten subjects to return will also receive an Apex University T-shirt."

"Is this legal?" asked a boy in his late teens.

"This is Apex University. Would we ask you to do something illegal?" Leto said, lying with the *friendly neighbor* voice developed in high school and refined through college interviews. He deflected a dozen valid questions about the law and ethics before subjects started filtering out of the room.

He started the stopwatch after the departure of the last subject, a blond woman in her early thirties. She returned with some kind of suitcase tucked under her armpit before he'd taken his seat.

"Oh, hey. Did you leave something behind during the presentation?" Leto asked.

"Nope. I've found a gun."

Leto checked the stopwatch, his cell phone, and the analog clock mounted on the south wall. All of them stuck to the same story.

"It's been six minutes," Leto said incredulously.

"Yeah, I had it in my car," said the pack leader. "I would've come back more quickly, but I have trouble telling my keys apart."

Before Leto could move on to the next natural question, she gingerly placed her lunchbox-sized metallic case on the table. She flicked both latches open at the same time and opened the case with religious reverence. This revealed a handgun lying in a sunken impression in a red, feltlike material. Leto wasn't equipped to say much about it, except that it was gray, likely semiautomatic, and fired bullets. Judging by the empty magazine-shaped depression, she kept it loaded.

"Not bad, eh?" She had a proud parent's glow.

"You're definitely first," Leto admitted.

"I meant the gun."

"Sure," Leto said as he shuffled through Professor Cardoso's packet. For some unearthly reason, the professor kept the data tables between the extended hypothesis and procedure. He found the page for "Subject One" and marked down six minutes and twenty-five seconds.

"Thanks again for participating. You can get going after answering a few questions."

The woman looked sullen. Leto had seen similar body language from his roommate after getting turned down by every dating profile within five miles.

"It's really a very nice gun," Leto volunteered.

She straightened up and beamed. "What do you need to know, Doc?"

"What's your full name?"

"Jenny Fullbright Jr."

"Age?"

"Thirty-seven next week."

"Ethnicity?"

"I don't like talking about race. Too much trouble."

Leto marked down *"White."*

"Occupation?"

"I'm like a construction worker, but for demolition. Are demolition workers a thing?"

"As long as you say they are," Leto said, holding back a shrug. After a lifetime translating between Northeastern-speed English, patois, academic wank, L33T Sp33k, hip-hop buzzwords, undergraduate excuses, and drunk mumbles, he thought of language as something you bent until it got you where you were going.

"Cool. I'm a demolition worker for Pompey and Cherno. It's a great gig, as long as you're not too hung up on workplace safety. The hard hats aren't nearly as important as watching yourself. It requires the kind of independent thinking people leave off their résumés."

Leto double-checked the recorder as Jenny spoke. The professor wanted handwritten notes, but he wasn't a stenographer by trade or volition.

"Address?"

"I'm on 283 Danby Lane. Mixed area. It's the station between the right and wrong side of the tracks."

"Hilarious," Leto said, unmoved. "What kind of gun is that?"

"This little giant is a Dan Wesson Elite Series Titan. Twelve plus one ten-millimeter rounds. It's not the kind of thing a carjacker walks away from."

"Finally, but most importantly, how did you get it? Don't spare any details."

"Ah, all right. I was parked by the cedar tree in the faculty parking lot. I figured it was fine, since I'm here to help out some of the faculty, and I expect you guys to help me out if they pull a tow job. One good turn deserves not being a dick, right? Right.

"Should I speak into the recorder? You keep fiddling with it.

"I grabbed the impact-resistant—according to the box—case from my glove compartment. I used to keep it in the trunk, but that's hard to reach during a live-fire situation. Since moving to Danby, I like to keep it close. I'd go for concealed carry, but I've got a fifty-hour week and that doesn't leave time for a course in anything. It's hard enough staying awake at work; even building implosions get old after a while. Maybe I should take my son to see the next one."

Leto jotted down the highlights. "Thanks for your time. All six minutes of it. Your voucher's in the mail."

He stole out of the conference room to raid the department fridge. Leto didn't keep anything in it, but the swollen remnants of the department's Inclusive Thanksgiving-Adjacent Supper were waiting. A wealth of gimmick diet–friendly food was ready to be repossessed. He opted to squint at the unnatural shade of the vegan patties and pretend they tasted like human food. His body thanked him while his soul screeched.

Leto returned to find a squat young girl with convincing hair extensions texting in his chair. Leto recognized her from the back row of the Introduction to Sociology class he TA'd. It was his first time seeing her outside the filter of a hangover.

A world-weary M16 variant rested on the table. The stock had a spiderweb of cracks, the barrel was corroded, and the words engraved on the side were illegible. It could probably still clear a room of life in twenty seconds.

"Am I first?" she asked without looking up. Leto shook his head before realizing it'd go unseen. Then he took the guest chair.

"Not exactly, or at all. But thirty minutes is a great effort."

The girl shrugged.

"So, questions. What's your full name?"

That earned eye contact in the form of an indignant glare.

"I'm in your discussion group," she said tersely. "I talk every time. Half our grade is based on class participation. What exactly are you basing that on?"

Traditionally, he gave students that avoided falling asleep full marks. This allowed him to have a "student-driven discussion" and spend the hour in a comforting fog between meditation and a coma. The seating chart spared him the need to pair names and faces. Leto put on an innocent mask and waited for an answer.

"Jesus. It's Ava Xang."

Leto jotted the name down. "It's good to see you, Ava. How old are you?"

"Twenty."

"Ethnicity?"

"I'm Laotian."

"Occupation?"

She went back to glaring. Leto jotted down "Student."

"Where do you live?" he asked, undeterred.

"I split my time between the dorms and my parents' house. I've told you that. We had a whole conversation about it."

Leto's memory drifted to the department's quarterly meet-and-greets. He looked harmless by default, leading an endless array of undergraduates to describe their lives, hopes, and dreams in painstaking detail. Graduate students had access to wine, which made recollecting any of it a challenge. He had a thin memory of three girls Ava's height blocking his access to the pigs in a blanket.

"How'd you find the gun? Don't spare any details."

"It's a family heirloom, from the war. Well, *the* war over there, *another* war over here. It belonged to my grandfather, who was too cagey to throw in with the rebels and too smart to throw in with the government. My dad passed it on to me, along with the story. I keep it back at the house; it's not the kind of accessory you can explain to your dorm mate.

"Gramps lived in the north right when tensions were building up. He wasn't political, but he drank with his brother, who kept one of Marx's books on his bedside. The liquor helped with the paranoia.

"One night, after sleeping off a hangover, he found a white man in bad camouflage in his yard. Unconscious. The guy had underestimated the drop from the estate wall to the estate proper. Which I guess is the point of having a wall.

"Gramps thought it was a drunk reporter until he noticed the assault rifle in the bushes. This is an assault rifle, right? My ex always complained about people getting that wrong.

"Then Gramps went for his pockets. My dad claims he was investigating, but I think he was after a free lunch. Do people still use that expression? Anyway, he found a CIA ID card, and—I shit you not—a picture of him and his brother at the bar."

Leto didn't bother cloaking the skepticism radiating from his face. He just put his chin on his fist and waited for her to finish bullshitting.

"They did what anyone would do. Strip the agent, paint wangs on his forehead, and dump him in the embassy bushes. Then Gramps took the next smuggler's ship out of the country, while his brother stayed to fight for whatever he was fighting for. Gramps survived, his brother didn't."

"Unfortunate," Leto said dryly. He used his teaching voice, a pitiless monotone he'd cribbed from a British sitcom.

"Right, you're a skeptic. I remember that from the half of class you're awake for. Take a look at this."

Ava produced a blue folder from her backpack and flicked it onto the table. Leto opened it out of professional obligation. Inside he found a crumpled polaroid of two drunk men with tragic fashion blindness, the faded CIA ID card of one Bobby Rumsfeld, and a second, religiously preserved polaroid of the first two men pointing at a slumped-over, naked Bobby.

"Well, holy shit," Leto mumbled.

"See you in class," Ava said curtly. She left without taking a complimentary mint.

Ava wasn't the only student involved in the study. Over the next four hours, five of Leto's charges came through with a shotgun, a pair of cheap pistols, a modified AR-15, and a homemade hunting rifle. They seemed to believe that extra credit was involved.

Leto tried to be polite with the last child to arrive. The guy was young enough to be another one of his students, and he didn't feel like repeating the first embarrassment. The subject tilted the chair backward, moved a hand to adjust the brim of his baseball cap, and nearly fell over. Leto allowed him to make his recovery without comment.

"Five hours, seven minutes. That's pretty good time, you're in the top ten."

"Man, do you really think I'm going to bring a gun onto a college campus in 2016?" He crossed his arms over a black T-shirt with "Megadeth" written in blocky white letters. "Metallica" was tattooed on his left arm in more angular, gunmetal-gray letters. Whether the other side of his hat said "Anthrax" or "Slayer" was anyone's guess. Leto wondered how the youth would respond to the world of music recorded after Y2K.

"Fair enough," Leto said, shrugging. "We expected a few failures. Shit, I was hoping for them." He caught himself dialing to a looser, more aggressive voice. It was the way his television said black men talked to each other. He self-consciously dialed back to academia.

"What's your name?"

"Dan C."

"Full name."

"Daniel Cee." He traced the last name in the air with his finger. Leto got the feeling he wasn't being taken entirely seriously. Which was fine, since he had trouble taking himself entirely seriously.

"How old are you?"

"Nineteen. On a good day I can get a drink at a show. The local staff's usually afraid to make a fuss carding me, and after an all-nighter I've got the face of someone pushing thirty."

"Uh-huh. Ethnicity?"

"You blind?" asked Dan. He punctuated the question with a cavalier smirk.

"Play along."

"Real niggas don't play."

Leto groaned and wrote "Black/African-American." He'd always had trouble contending with senses of irony outside of his own, and Dan had perfectly imitated his earlier flash of tough-guy cadence.

"Where do you live?"

"I'm at 120 Danby Lane, on the bougie side. Takes me about fifteen minutes to walk to campus. I'm splitting an apartment with some econ grad students. They're like you, but fun and employable."

"Occupation?"

"Student, like I said. I'm in the same group as Ava. She's pissed, by the way."

"Amusing," Leto admitted. "Since you couldn't get your hands on a gun, that's all I'll need. Thanks for your time."

Dan whipped a revolver out of his coat and leveled it at Leto's forehead. Instead of finding his inner hero, Leto found his arms and legs locked in place. Terror kept him from breathing. The tip of the barrel was microns from his left eye, which he was very attached to.

"Blam!" Dan shouted, jerking the gun backward and upward to sell the shtick. Leto felt his heart bounce against his rib cage. He manually restarted the process of filling his lungs with air and pushing it out.

"Daniel Cee," Leto started. It was taking time for the whole of his body and mind to process the fact that he was still alive. The war zone–level adrenaline alone made staying seated a test of his dedication.

"Yup," said the prankster.

"You have a diseased fucking sense of humor, and one day someone crazier is going to murder you for it."

"Damn. Maybe I'll keep the gun, then."

Leto smiled against his will. Dan ejected the loader and flicked it, showing six empty chambers.

"This is a science thing, right? Don't you have any, you know, science questions?" Dan asked. He spun the revolver on the table to keep himself busy.

"Tell me how you found the gun. Be descriptive."

"Finding the first gun was easy. I just went to Jumbo Emporium and asked. The clerk—he was a tool, like you—looked me over and said I could get one if I paid in cash. Asshole. I saw that the cheapest one there cost thirty-five dollars and handed over two twenties.

"Then I asked what the waiting period here's like, since I've got shit to do next week and your experiment isn't exactly my top priority. He put the gun in a bag, threw in two boxes of ammo, and handed me the receipt.

"Finally, I had an idea. I looked up gun shows on Craigslist and found one going on downtown. They had a gun exchange event, full of the best kind of paranoid targets. People waiting for their neighbors to roll on them tend not to pay enough attention to scams. I traded the glock for an actual Glock, the Glock for a hunting rifle, the hunting rifle for an old flare gun, the flare gun for a crate of M16 bullets, and the crate of bullets for one of those PMC-style automatic shotguns. Finally, I traded that for the handgun from *Dirty Harry*. I forgot to use the 'Do you feel lucky, punk' line while I was showing off earlier."

"While that's an *extremely large and dangerous* revolver, it's not the one from *Dirty Harry*."

"Why would you ruin that for me?" spat Dan. He left the gun on the table and stormed into the hallway. Ten seconds later, the sound of a distant steel door slamming echoed back into the conference room. Leto stared at the pistol for six solitary minutes before taking it to the faculty lounge and adding it to the pile.

The collection had grown admirably. Jenny Fullbright Jr.'s pistol sat at the bottom of an eight-foot-wide, ten-foot-long, and four-foot-high hill of unloaded firearms. Muzzles, stocks, and rusted bayonets protruded from every edge of the pile. A few of the subjects had offered live ammo, but Leto had politely declined and later followed the online instructions for checking the weapons for unspent rounds. The experiment was dangerous enough without adding negligence to the equation.

Most of the lounge's furniture had been pushed into the hallway to make room for the pile, with the exception of a single-seat leather couch. Professor Cardoso reclined under an administration-mandated "No Smoking" sign and blew two attempts at smoke rings to the ceiling. It wasn't a habit that made her many friends. She regarded the gallery of guns of every size, origin, and legality with distant interest. After taking in this sight, Leto wondered if this was even the first time she'd run the experiment.

"Promising results?" she asked.

Leto shook his head. "No promise at all. It'll make a great book."

Nobel, Alfred: The inventor of ~~dynamite~~ rebranding.

novel: A form dangling on the edge of popular interest.

novella: A form that fell off the edge of popular interest.

North America: The half with an ego problem.

North Carolina: The Luigi of states.

nostalgia: A quiet yearning for the disease, mysticism, backbreaking labor, and social repression of the past.

nursing homes: Pre-funeral storage.

NYPD: The proud foundation of the rubber bullet industry.

O

obesity: The last war the United States formally surrendered until 2021.

obituary: Heartfelt, personalized compliments you'll never get to read.

oceans: Carefully guarded reserves for plastic forks.

Odin: The Norse god of war, the dead, and double vision.

Oklahoma!: A play referenced more frequently than its namesake.

Old Bay: A staple spice for future victims of heart disease.

Oldboy: A love story.

Olympus: Home of roughly one-tenth of Zeus's children.

omnipotence: 1. Warping time and space at will.
2. Failing to keep your creations out of a fruit tree.

omniscience: Knowledge of how every movie you ever watch will end.

onomatopoeia: Comic book sound effects, such as bang, pow, property of the Walt Disney Corporation, and zap.

opera: A cultural export consistently lost at sea.

opinions: 1. The only truly free gift.
2. Facts with imagination.
3. Thanksgiving's main course.

opioids: A pandemic designed, propagated, and treated by America's finest doctors.

Oppenheimer, J. Robert: The loving and quotable peace advocate that has killed us all.

orcas: The first sea creatures to demand reparations from the U.S. government.

origami: The ancient art of starting the same YouTube tutorial sixteen times.

Oscars, the: The annual celebration of the creativity, glamour, and legacy of the Oscars.

Ottoman Empire: World War I's last draft pick.

Overton window: The range of policies a population will accept before making a mean tweet.

Own Goal

January 2
Today's Album: *Crash the Colony* **by Desert Tsunami**
I spent the first half of the day comparing caskets. I'd never organized a funeral before, but I knew the body had to go somewhere.

The front-runner offered a protective layer of hand-engraved silica tiles. A good casket needed to *look like* it could survive reentry. Odds were it never got the chance and simply joined the rest of the space junk floating around between colonies. But a sturdy casket gives attendees peace of mind. They imagine everyone in Mom's generation ends up back on Earth eventually.

I thought that way when she was sick. Now that she's gone, I'm not sure it matters where I send what's left. Nonetheless, I didn't have anything better to do at work, so I scrolled through a catalog online. The eye implant's good for getting away with that kind of thing.

My art partner caught me at noon.

"Any ideas on the brief?" he asked. Agile Hands pats itself on the back for having individual employee offices, but people feel excess comfort walking into mine. My hands had drifted into my pockets, my feet had drifted onto my desk, and my monitor had drifted to sleep. Not the best look before an industry lifer like Zane.

"A few."

"Like what?"

Zane's a big guy, which I suspect led to his current habit of invading personal space. Less muscular people had that habit kicked out of them in high school. The last time I got a drink into him, he said he considered bodybuilding "an extension of art direction." He'd simply taken creative control of his body.

"I'm thinking about it." Holding eye contact's tough while using the implant, but I'm a decent multitasker. I pulled up the brief in my left eye and watched Zane with my right. He planted one arm against the wall, channeling a disappointed babysitter. This made keeping a straight face harder, but I maintained.

Creative Brief	
Project Code: 081947	
The Product	Harvester, a tungsten-rod launcher with category-leading range and accuracy.
Creative Objective	Distinguish Harvester in a crowded APW (anti-planetary weapon) market.
Target Audience	Either faction in the arms race between Demes and Unity.
Category Insight	Both factions need weapons capable of RPE (rapid population elimination) at minimum cost.
Brand Insight	Harvester trivializes current orbital defense systems, allowing near-instant and consistent elimination of HPTs (high-population targets).
Brand Weaknesses	Advances in propulsion render Harvester ineffective against gunships and other (relatively) mobile military targets. Thus, usefulness is confined to planets and colonies.
Brand Personality	Powerful. Confident.

The social contract saved me: after two years working with me, Zane knew I hadn't touched the brief yet. But advertising partnerships are based on results, not shared principles. Chastising me was pointless if I came up with something usable.

"Try to finish *thinking* soon," said Zane. "The red flag meeting's tomorrow. We need something worth showing Anthony. You know, proof we didn't spent the holidays *thinking*."

"Got it. Work on a composite of a woman at ease. Older, and artsy. Defense pitches are saturated with images of jarheads saluting flags, so we'll stand out."

"Fine, but what's the headline?"

"I'm thinking about it."

That got him out of my office, albeit tenser than he'd arrived. I counted to fifteen in case he cycled back with a new problem or admonition. When he failed to materialize, I returned to the catalogs. Restful Hills had a black silica tile series that looked promising.

January 3

Today's Album: *None of Your Showbusiness* **by Re:Volution**

I took the journaling idea from Mom. And the word "journaling."

While I like the feel of a pen, I'm thinking of ditching the physical book. Most paper's a Union import, and socially conscious types like to glare at me on the shuttle. I can get away with a fancy watch on my wrist or computer in my head, but paper crosses some invisible line.

As I write this, there's a man with a fauxhawk staring daggers into my forehead. I get that people are on edge. We all know people on Union or Demes colonies and prefer them alive. It's no excuse for posturing at strangers like a child. That's how you get your head cracked at a show. Not that I'd know—I haven't been to a decent concert in a year. Too many late meetings.

Take today's pitch review. In the wonderful world of theory, it ended at five o'clock Colonial time. In practice, less than half the creative teams had finished presenting. I'd have snuck in some journaling, but Zane would've smacked any obvious distractions out of my hands. Another argument against print. I could have written an erotic novel on the eye implant without anyone knowing or caring.

Agency pitches are like billion-dollar nesting dolls. First, creative teams pitch ideas to each other. Then, creative teams pitch their best (results vary) idea to creative directors, who pitch the best surviving ideas to the resident alcoholic agency director. The agency director brings their best (typically mediocre) account people to a client meeting, where they pitch the remains of an idea strained through three layers of human opinion to prospective customers. Clients then accept or reject our work based on the quality of their breakfast.

Mercifully, I only have to deal with the first layer of this process. Zane aspires to more. He's welcome to it.

Around six, Zane killed a pleasant daydream by tapping my shoulder. I wanted to break the finger. Violence has been on my mind this week. Hopefully it'll pass with the funeral. Copywriting pays, but lawyers and therapists charge more.

"We're up," he said. We marched to the front of the conference room and stood together before the firing squad. Ten writers, ten artists, and one creative director. Anthony Marsico sat at the head of the table in the reclined, semi-awake stance I wished I was in. I guess you have to work your way there.

Anthony softly rapped his pencil against the table, eraser first. He drummed his way through most meetings in three-quarter time. I'd already given up on interpreting it as a positive or negative sign. It's just something he does. There are worse quirks for creative directors.

"Have anything?" Anthony asked.

"Of course. We've been thinking a lot about it."

Zane's shoe (expensive) gently stepped on my shoe (less expensive). I canned the rest of the joke. Then he tapped the wall, bringing up our slide. Somehow he'd turned my last-minute direction and copy into something cohesive.

We chafe, but Zane does beautiful work. Our slide looked like he'd made it in weeks instead of hours. The protagonist (a composite of five stock models) stood beside a half-finished marble bust. The bust's face mirrored hers, down to the braided ponytail, nose ring, and wry smile. I'd argued against the nose ring—a little too old-fashioned, even at her age—but Zane had the final call on aesthetics. The results were hard to dispute. Both faces had the easy, natural confidence created through extended, artificial effort.

I marred the image with a slim line of copy. *Chisel: Creative Destruction.*

"As you can see, I've changed the name," I began. "Stay calm."

Lukewarm laughter followed. No stomp from Zane, so we were in business.

"Demes is a liberal republic, and Union is a theocracy. Both systems rely on a self-image as the good guy. The name Harvester chafes with that somewhat."

"The new name, Chisel, speaks to that impulse. It implies a deft hand and creative mind, a self-image the best and worst generals share. More importantly, it implies precision. The feature that distinguishes a tungsten-rod launcher from its competitors.

"Biological weapons like DuraVirus, Loki's Curse, and Bubblegum Fever are blunt instruments. They don't just take out the colony you target; they take out everyone the target's traded with for the last decade. Which, all too often, includes you. Food prices spark more wars than ideology, the current conflict notwithstanding."

"Chisel is a thoughtful deletion. It contains damage to the target city, moon, or colony. Leaving a more aesthetically pleasing galaxy behind."

I imagined cheers. I imagined getting fired. All Anthony did was nod and check something off in his notebook.

"Solid. I'll make it slide four," said Anthony. It was the first eye contact he'd made with me all meeting.

I thanked him for his time and sat down. There were no signs of success, failure, or skirting by. Either way, I was done thinking about kinetic bombardment.

January 4
Today's Album: *Cerebral Riot* **by Cerebral Riot**

It's done.

When I carried that casket, my brain went AWOL. It was like being twelve again. I got caught up wondering if fat people's caskets were harder to carry or if funeral homes gently nudged their next of kin toward lighter caskets. Any puerile line of thought felt easier than confronting the present.

I assume people cried. I must have as well, unless today's the start of my career as a serial killer. Not that those guys get far these days.

We loaded her casket into the *Nebula III*, along with thirty-three of December's other casualties. The name drives me crazy. Memorial airlines love that Raygun Gothic stuff, but it does nothing for the bereaved. If I had that contract, I'd class up the rocket names a little. Or at least get rid of the numbers.

The chaplain gave my brother and me a port number and date for the launch. Martin thanked him, but I felt less diplomatic. Watching Astral Trails LLC shoot my only parent into space isn't on my short list. I hope no one's there to watch me lift off. In fact, I might get cremated instead.

Martin and company shuffled me to a second location. Some kind of bingo hall or rec center willing to host thirty depressed Jamaicans. The caterers had real beef, which was nice. It helped me soak up the rum.

A trio of aunts (all aunts are one person in my head) tried to corner me for a stroll down memory lane, so I took a cigarette break. I quit smoking three years ago, and I've managed to stay off it (half suggestion therapy, half willpower). But I generally keep that tidbit to myself. Cigarette breaks are the perfect excuse to get out of any room.

The rat that invented the post-funeral event deserved whatever happened to them. As if burying someone isn't depressing enough without meeting everyone else left behind.

I resolved to spend the rest of the year away from next of kin. For real emotional support, you need someone that doesn't give a shit. Other mourners are like other drowners. You just pull each other down.

Martin picked this moment to reappear.

"How's the job?"

His usual opening. Today it stumped me. Was there anything I hadn't said a dozen times before? Any answer that wouldn't make me feel like an idiot? I pawed at my phone to play for time.

"Sorry," said Martin. "I wanted to be casual. I know you don't like to talk about the big stuff."

The big stuff. "No problem."

"That, and I noticed none of your coworkers were here."

"Why would they be?"

"I mean, you've been there for four years. I have one or two people from work here."

"That's rude."

"Emotional support's rude?"

Touché. I'd forgotten that Martin actually understood people. Colony people tend to double down on the old habit of treating coworkers like friends and friends like family. A natural side effect of the first colonists leaving everything else behind.

"Guess not. But your work-life balance is warped."

"I work half as much as you do."

"Like I said: warped. You could quit or get fired tomorrow and never see those people again."

Martin went back inside, presumably to comfort the rest of the bereaved. I wished for a real pack of cigarettes to warm me up. The colony still didn't have real seasons. Just days that were too hot and nights that were too cold.

January 5
Today's Album: *Strap In* **by the Dirt Sisters**
Union declared war on Demes. Which is fair, since Demes hit two Union colonies with Bubblegum Fever. If we're lucky, no contaminated ships or cargo make it here. If we're not, this is one of my last entries.

I'm going drinking.

January 6
Today's Album: *Graveyard Earth* **by Sunny and the Optimists**
We're not dead, so I took today off. My job all but ceases to exist between pitches anyway.

It gave me some time to thumb through what I've written so far. Mostly good, but I tore out the page about my last date. Posterity doesn't need my half-assed sex life, and I think the rest is more engaging.

That said, the dialogue's a bit skewed. Everything's tweaked to be funnier, or more concise, or long enough to fill the last line on a page. My comebacks get faster, and everyone else gets a little duller. It's less of a record of my life and more of a prime-time adaptation.

That might say something about journalists. As in reporters, not people who journal. When Demes's cleric sovereign reportedly told the Union premiere to "consider your next move carefully," he may have said something closer to "Kiss my ass, degenerate." That strikes me as less of a bad movie line and more like something that leads to dumping Bubblegum Fever on a civilian colony.

I'm biased, but I'd rather be rodded. Contact, explosion, done. Bubblegum Fever takes time. Nothing vital melts *first*, only a few hours in. Points to whoever came up with the name. That's a professional. I'm sure he and Zane would get along.

Good ad writing's closest to poetry. Stand-up's equally apt, but that crowd wouldn't writhe as much under the comparison. Decent taglines emerge from rewriting the same sentence until a perfect, airless version emerges. Unless you half-ass it. Like in poetry, there's significant incentive to punch out early, get drunk, and watch awards roll in anyway.

Navel-gazing aside, I'm done reading the news. If the guys upstairs are smart, they'll keep us neutral. If they're not, I'd rather not think about it.

January 7
Today's Album: *Omnicidal Tendencies* **by Temujin**
I got an award today. Just an in-agency one, but it's still a decent boost.

They mailed it straight to my apartment, sparing me the waking nightmare of carrying a package on the shuttle. Everyone's already on edge since open war broke out, and I didn't need someone snapping on me for taking up too much space in the sardine can. People have gotten stabbed for less.

Like everything from Agile Hands, it came in a light blue box. Our brand colors are blue and silver, a combo Zane says should have led to a designer losing his hands. I think it looks decent, but I don't have a horse in that race.

The box held a bottle of wine, a handwritten note on silver card stock, and a palm-sized, cube-shaped trophy. I don't get the cube thing, either. Maybe the design team went through an abstract phase.

I still have a little home training, so I started with the note.

Dear Leon,
This is for going the extra mile during the pitch. We're the first—and only—agency on the Harvester account. Or should I say Chisel?

To be honest, I wasn't sure you'd be up for this. Anyone can see that you're going through something, even if you're not much for sharing. I imagine it's a girl. I've been around long enough to know what relationship drama can do to a young talent.

You pushed through whatever is going on, and I can't thank you enough for that. Chisel opens doors for us. Anti-planetary weapons contractors pull from a small list of branding agencies, and this contract puts us on that list. I'll remember your part in making it happen.

Drink this with someone in a cocktail dress. You're a hot item now.

Best,

Anthony

The last line took me out of it. Did people I know wear cocktail dresses? Did anyone? I'd never seen one outside of a movie.

I flipped the card and found a hand-drawn smiley face with dollar signs for eyes. "Big Money Leon" was scribbled underneath in cursive. Some of Anthony's old illustration instincts were leaking through. The boss likely had a book of similar sketches that would never see the light of day.

After trashing the note and box, I poured half the wine into a novelty water bottle. My gym had printed oversized "Ahead of the Pack" bottles for last year's spring marathon, an event I survived three miles of. Then I hauled the wine to the living room, opened a web browser on the east wall, and searched for pictures of women in cocktail dresses.

It seemed to mostly be a white girl thing. There were a few token pictures of black women at a Panthers 4 Peace fundraiser, but most cocktail dress owners looked like variations of my ex. I picked one in a blue cocktail dress and face that was two degrees removed from Angeline's instead of one.

"Cheers," I said before killing the bottle. I'd planned on savoring the drink, but that felt off tone.

January 8

Today's Album: *Soothing Whale Songs* **by Automated Butcher**

I cracked and checked the news. We've been allied with Demes for two days.

I also missed a call from Martin. I'll hit him back later.

January 23

Today's Album: N/A

I always assumed they'd save the rich first, or at least the politicians. The evacuation wasn't nearly organized enough for that. Luck got me much further than social climbing.

Mom's launch was the only reason I made it to a ship. I was already idling around the docks, recovering from my stomach's failure to adjust to the lack of artificial gravity. I threw up a few more times this morning than I'm comfortable admitting. The only people accustomed to zero g are astronauts, soldiers, and liars.

I'm generally good at ignoring the guilty voice in my head, but Mom's launch was the limit. I had to see her off in person. All the death in the news made it impossible not to think about hers, and I wouldn't have a second chance. Surprisingly, there was no sign of Martin. I guess we both changed our mind at the last moment.

I kept to the back for most of the ceremony. The priest, a navy chaplain—they like order at the docks—was the spitting image of Zane's composite model. She read a Bible passage about rebirth, which I found disappointing. Mom was more about the songs. Scripture was something she sat through to get to the music. The *Nebula III*'s countdown started without a note of music, so I hummed "Will the Circle Be Unbroken." No one stopped me, even when I started singing it. As a sober atheist belting an antebellum spiritual, I felt as strange as I looked.

Still, it was better than the funeral. I didn't have to deal with anyone else that knew her. It was just me and her memory. Until the sirens.

I'd never heard the tone or pattern; the raid alarm must have changed since I left high school. Nonetheless, when a high-pitched alarm drowns out every noise in a wartime colony, people move. Human traffic pushed me toward the ships before I even resolved to find one. Sometimes you can trust the wisdom of crowds.

I searched the processing lines for Martin, or a friend, or even Zane. No luck, but they might have made it. There were too many faces to pick out anyone, and they kept better track of the news than I did.

Keep. I mean keep. I need to think present tense to stay sane.

Eventually, I wound up on a navy carrier called *Ark 36*. Humans were the only fauna on board, and there were significantly more than two of us. I barely had room to scratch my thigh, let alone lift my arm. I can only write this now that they've opened the engine rooms and gun bays to the general population.

The observation monitors provided our one source of information and hope. The colony design, which I didn't think about 364 out of 365 days of the year, looked beautiful. Humanity had built a perfect metallic ring in space, kept it intact, and moved inside. I could understand why Mom had moved. The colony's existence alone represented new possibilities.

Ships fled by the dozen, but we needed hundreds. Thinking of the people stuck on the ring gave me a headache. Realizing how many of them I knew made it worse.

Chisel worked quickly and quietly, as advertised. First, there wasn't a hole in the colony, and then there was. The rods didn't make for much of a show, flitting through and past my home in half a second.

The explosion provided more conventional drama. A ball of white fire enveloped everything that meant anything to me. The other survivors screeched in at least six different languages, begging and accusing their respective gods. I assume I screeched too. I may have even found religion. Memory has a way of protecting us from itself.

Then my left eye went dark. The navy grunts said the electromagnetic pulse from the colony reactor fried most evacuees' implants. Fair trade for survival. I tapped my eye twice in the vain hope that turning it off and on again would make a difference. Nothing. I'm half-blind for the foreseeable future.

Soon we passed a memorial ship. A different model than Mom's, but around the same size and company. At the rate we fled, we'd catch up to her ship in hours. We were racing the dead.

#OwnVoices: The division of writers into separate but equal categories.

oxen: Management slang for you.

Oxford English Dictionary: A strange reference text without a single cyborg.

oxygen: Nestlé's next big acquisition.

Oz: The fantasy of free American housing falling from the sky.

ozone layer: A false flag for ecological recovery.

P

pacifism: Asking someone to stop kicking you very, very nicely with gumdrops on top.

pandemic: 1. A board game exposing the limits of human cooperation. 2. A crisis exposing the limits of human cooperation.

Pandora: Zeus's first scapegoat.

panic: The default state of the well-informed.

patriot: Anyone willing to debase his country for his country.

Perry, Tyler: The innovator that proved that Black America could write, direct, and star in truly awful movies.

pickup artistry: The intersection of crushing human loneliness and video game strategy guides.

PictoChat: An innovative chat program dedicated almost entirely to drawing genitalia.

plagiarism: Whoever you are . . . I've always depended on the kindness of strangers.

poetry: Best done in private. Public poetry is punishable by fines or imprisonment in most American states.

policing: Fixed now.
Author's note: My brother's an officer, so I'm used to the beatings.

politics: The central facet of one's personality.

Polo: See *Marco.*

populism: Syphilis for democracies.

pornography: 1. You'll know it when you see it.
2. You'll know it when you close it at 3:00 a.m., astonished at what you've seen and what you've become.

Post-Atomic Stress

1. The Apartment
2:00 p.m.

Nero's neighborhood used to be in a place called New Jersey, until the Great Powers had a brief nuclear argument. Six major cities were lost before cooler heads prevailed. In the aftermath, North America quietly reorganized into the Free Dominion, the largest democracy in human history (by landmass, at least). New Jersey ceased to exist after its territory was folded into East Ward, along with everything else east of 81.6944° W (formerly Cleveland). Some mourned the change, others raged, and most simply kept on living.

None of this was on Nero's mind.

———

On Saturday afternoon, standing in the corner of his basement apartment, he focused on looking attractive. Nero never left home in anything he didn't consider presentable, but today he had higher goals. Goals that demanded more than three minutes in front of the vanity mirror he'd looted from an evicted neighbor. Spiderweb cracks covered most of the glass, but he could see half of his reflection. Part of him still expected to find his adolescent face, which had been bloated by a deep-fried diet. Ten years of bodyweight exercise and flavorless food left his face leaner and acne-free. He liked to think it was generically handsome, save the thin surgical scar running from the back of his ears to the nape of his neck. He'd have to wear something with a collar, or a hood.

"You can't date this woman."

Nero continued his early morning ritual of ignoring his roommate. Avery was made of opinions, and listening to all of them would be a full-time job. It was better to glean the important ones by waiting for repetition.

"You can't date this woman," Avery repeated. He sat in judgment of Nero from a red swivel chair covered in variegated stickers, the largest of which read "East Ward Workers Party" in stark white letters. This chair was mostly used for video games. On game night, Player Two typically enjoyed the comfort of the chair, while Player One enjoyed his minimal authority from the floor. After spending last night craning his neck up at the ancient sixty-four-inch 2D television mounted to their wall, Avery seemed determined never to abandon the swivel chair again.

"Why not?" Nero gritted his teeth as he pushed his comb through a rebellious patch of hair. He'd never grown it out this far before, and he was quickly learning that knots were a bigger threat to his daily happiness than any of the radical/reactionary/extremist/wingnut cells on everyone's tongue. A bombing was a distant abstraction, while his scalp was real, immediate, and screaming.

"She's a tool of the state, an enemy of the revolution, and has no fashion sense. You're insulting everything we stand for."

"Everything *you* stand for. I don't do politics." Nero pushed through the last defiant knots and discarded the comb. He thought the rest would be straightforward, but his disinfectant was nowhere in sight. He knelt beneath the worn plastic dresser to see if it'd rolled off again. The floor had a slight slant, so loose objects slid toward the south wall. Nothing.

"We've lived together for four years," said Avery. "I know your values, even if you pretend they don't exist."

Nero let the declaration pass without judgment. Avery approached everything with an intensity that pushed most of the "somnolent masses" away. In his world, dates, elections, and flavors of ramen were all equally existential choices. Nero had some respect for that, tempered by the knowledge that it invited a heart attack or officer-involved shooting.

"Furthermore: if you don't do politics, politics will do you."

"Try selling fortune cookies with that line," said Nero. "You'll be a trendsetter."

"Trends are a distraction, and selling is the cancer at the heart of the Free Dominion," said Avery. His sneer turned to a smirk as he watched Nero paw around behind the furniture. "How about this: if you'll at least *think* about abandoning this statist gorgon, I'll find it for you. Since we're a unit."

"Hmm," replied Nero. He checked under a stack of faded band T-shirts. Avery had taken to dressing like an old-school metalhead, even though blast beats gave him a headache. The aesthetic let him shave his head without blending in with white supremacists. Even if that club had gotten more popular, Avery was too cantankerous to join any group where everyone had the same tattoo.

"The bottle's inside your closet. You tend to drop it there when you're running late for wage slavery."

Pride led Nero to check under his bed, inside his dresser, and above his laundry bin before giving the closet a cursory look. The electric blue bottle sat in the dead center, on top of a pair of abused running shoes.

"I'm still going. Can you help me with this?"

Avery grumbled something undiplomatic and let his chair roll to Nero's side of the room. "Whenever you're ready."

Nero grabbed the bottle and returned to the dresser. He opened his container of eyes, which resembled a metallic egg carton, and picked out his favorite. The others had all kinds of bells and whistles that were useful for work (or dicking around during a slow night), but this one was his favorite. It looked natural, and spared him unwanted opinions from locals about the cost of mods these days, whether or not he was a government plant, or violating the holy temple of his body with fel machinery. It was also the best fit.

He dunked the eye in fluid, capped the bottle, shook it around, and plucked it back out. The eye was now the cleanest object in sight. Nero liked to blame the state of the (illegally) shared single-bedroom apartment on their age, distinctly single relationship status, and respective obsessions with hedonism and dismantling the government. But he was starting to suspect that they were slobs, would continue to be slobs as divorced retirees, and would die slobs.

Nero knelt down and dropped the eye in Avery's palm.

"Ready."

Avery put down his cell phone, squinted, and jammed the prosthetic eye into Nero's left socket. He'd become an old hand at this, so the installation was relatively painless. Turning the implant on was another story. As the eye connected with the bugs in Nero's brain—kids called nanobots "bugs," and Nero wanted to at least pretend to be cool—he suffered a second-long flash of pain that traveled from his skull to his toes. Nero experienced a single, mild convulsion. His elbow knocked the disinfectant bottle back off his dresser.

"This isn't natural," Avery opined.

"Neither are your fillings. But I appreciate the help. It'd take me an hour by myself, and I need to get to Liberty Park by four. I'm meeting Diana under the arches."

"I don't see why you're rushing. Statists are always a half hour late. It's a reflection of capitalist methods of—"

Avery went on in this manner while Nero dressed himself. For him, the maelstrom of protests, counterprotests, police suppression of both, bombings, and show trials dominating local news feeds boiled down to two relevant headlines:

1. Everyone had gone crazy or given up a long time ago.

2. Nero Maxwell had a date.

"I don't suppose I could convince you to reconsider." It must have been the second time Avery had said it. Nero briefly considered mentioning his own government job before abandoning the idea. It was better to maintain peace in the household, especially if there was a chance he'd bring someone back tonight. "You're trying to replace someone. It's not healthy."

"I'll tell you how it goes."

With his priorities sorted, Nero left the apartment behind. If the date went well, he'd gloat to Avery later. If it didn't, he wouldn't say a single word.

2. The Train

2:27 p.m.

Nero always enjoyed the walk to the subway. Rutherford Avenue had six straight blocks of real, non-plastic trees. He could taste the difference in the air. It put him in a floaty, positive frame of mind, which would be essential for meeting Diana.

Hopefully he wasn't wasting his time. There was a small, constant fault line between Nero and the rest of his species. He had one good friend, but everyone else seemed to drift off. There were hookups, but no one stuck around for too long. The fault line wasn't wide enough to attract a diagnosis or weigh down his professional life. Nero even prided himself on having a snake's charm. But the note of isolation in the back of his head had gotten too loud to ignore.

The weather flirted with cold. They'd entered the month or so of fall that climate change had left intact, and the trees had traded green for red. Nero could still get away with a sweatshirt, which was merciful considering the fur-lined hoodie was the most fashionable item he owned. He wore a black dress shirt underneath, which he hoped gave the impression of being fun and disciplined at the same time. In his experience, veering too hard in either direction poisoned a first outing.

He hummed a pop song while he walked. It helped distract him from the lime-green Lindholf Security drone on his tail. The operator made a modest effort to hide their intent, occasionally circling the block or floating behind trees. But its presence still served as a major test of Nero's otherwise Zen mood. Security companies were far less likely to brutalize someone than the East Ward Police Department—private entities were easier to sue—but just as overt about profiling. The drone followed Nero down six residential blocks before moving on. Nero had reached the hook of the song wherein the artist compared her love to a soaring brick.

Someone else might have gotten angry, but he was Tanya Maxwell's son. Tanya enjoyed a long, successful life to this day under the mantra "Keep your head down and you'll keep your head on." She'd repeated it every school morning until it became part of the background static of Nero's life. Today he found staying neutral as rote and reflexive as blinking.

Nero strolled down two more blocks and found the second test of his tranquility. Five teenagers (or twenty-somethings that moisturized) blocked the entrance to the 339th Street train station. Each was chained at the wrist to at least one other demonstrator and wore an expression of determined and premeditated recalcitrance. The women on either end carried cardboard signs in their free hands.

Together they recited a well-worn chant:

Monarchy now!
Democracy breeds degeneracy!
Monarchy now!
Communism already failed!
Monarchy now!
Fascism's a bit intense!
Monarchy now!

The signs also read "Monarchy Now!" and their organization was popularly known as Monarchy Now! "Redundancy Now!" sounded more apt to Nero, but he wasn't in charge. Politicians and rival ideological extremists preferred the term "neo-Monarchists," which gave the concept too much weight for Nero's taste. For all their vitriol, Avery's post-Marxists offered a basic change in policy. The neo-Monarchists, on the other hand, seemed to be perfectly fine with a version of the status quo where the governor wore a crown.

Nero had seen hints of the movement online for years: it attracted the loudest brand of keyboard warrior, and reading flame wars was a personal sport. But it still shocked him to see it bleed into the real world. According to the news, the neo-Monarchists were the product of a complex variety of social forces acting on hopelessly disaffected youth. Nero did not know or care about any of them. The hopelessly disaffected youth were in his way.

"Excuse me, brothers and sisters," Nero said warmly.

"Who the fuck are you?" asked Sign Wielder One.

"I'm with the West Ward cell. Your operation here's impressive, you could definitely teach us a lot about chanting. Could I get through? I need to get to Liberty Park for a demonstration."

"Why are you dressed like that?" asked Sign Wielder Two. "You look more like a scuzzy nightclub promoter than a revolutionary."

"It's a west coast thing." Nero flashed a car salesman's smile. Sign Wielder Two began shuffling to let him pass, while her counterpart eyed him with suspicion.

"Hold on." Sign Wielder One lifted a finger to Nero's nose. "Take off the sunglasses."

Nero complied.

"That's a fucking OdinEye. You're the kind of body-warping degenerate we're fighting against."

"Do you have fillings?" Nero volunteered.

"That's a stupid goddamn argument. And you're not getting through."

Nero shrugged and stepped aside; the debate was about to become moot. A pair of flashing red and blue lights sped past the intersection and parked at the corner. Four heavily armored East Ward Police Department officers emerged carrying media-friendly beanbag shotguns. Sign Wielder One went white and eyed her handcuffs with dawning regret.

Nero ducked behind a garbage can and checked his phone. In his college years, he might have tried to record the unfolding violence. Today he checked his messages. Diana had sent him a smiley face with a wink. A good sign. He typed out a smiley face with its tongue sticking out. Receptive but playful. After a few moments of thinking, and then thinking about overthinking, he sent the reply. Then he heard the sound of a skull meeting concrete.

The interaction between political youth and jackbooted enforcers that defined every era in history had begun. Nero tried not to spend too much time looking at the beatings. The officers clearly had received sensitivity training, taking special care to distribute an equal number of elbow strikes and rifle butts to all ethnicities represented. The newer, softer East Ward Police Department even avoided arrests, content to leave the demonstrators with a physical lesson.

Nero sighed, replaced the sunglasses, reconsidered, and pocketed them. At twenty-seven, he was at least two years past being taken seriously in them. He stepped over a sobbing Monarchy Now! partisan and entered the station. One riot officer offered a cordial wave, which he returned half-heartedly. "Community policing" was the buzzword of the month.

The next train was scheduled to arrive in eight minutes, and showed up in sixteen. Once Nero had settled into a subway seat, the left half of his vision blacked out. The bright blue letters of a support message took its place.

[A FIRMWARE UPDATE FOR THE ODINEYE™ 4+ IS AVAIL-ABLE. WOULD YOU LIKE TO INSTALL IT NOW?"]

"Not really," he said dryly. Despite the convenient port in his brain, he was still in the habit of verbalizing his responses. "I've got one of those free newspapers, and I'd planned on hitting the sudoku puzzles they print between the editorials and this week's propaganda. They're a lot easier to complete with both eyes, feel me?"

[IT CONTAINS MULTIPLE UPDATES ESSENTIAL TO KEEPING YOUR EYE SECURE IN A WORLD OF NANOBOT-ENHANCED HACKERS.]

"I *am* a nanobot-enhanced hacker. I think I'll be fine."

[WE APPRECIATE THE CHANCE TO WORK WITH A HIGH-GRADE PROFESSIONAL LIKE YOURSELF. HOWEVER, LAST WEEK A "CHILDREN OF KALI" INSURGENT REMOTELY DETONATED MULTIPLE ODINEYE™ UNITS, VIOLENTLY (BUT PAINLESSLY) KILLING FIVE CUSTOMERS AND LEAVING TWO OTHERS IN A VEGETATIVE STATE.]

"Oh."

[ARE YOU SURE YOU WOULD NOT LIKE TO UPGRADE?]

"Lay it on me," said Nero. The text field was replaced with a prog-ress bar.

Nero revisited the word "hacker." It was a lie he had begun to believe. He was half con artist, and half *artist* artist. The bugs did all the technical work; he was just a creative guiding hand. Under pressure, he could barely code "Hello, world" without a cheat sheet. But he was close enough to a hacker to feel naked without his pet gadget.

He took to observing the right half of the subway car. It was a small crowd for the weekend. At least a quarter of the seats were unoccupied by passengers or unidentified bodily fluids. The car itself was in surprisingly good condition: fresh posters of East Ward's governor were plastered over the usual graffiti, and none of the windows were broken. Nero missed the broken windows. The air-conditioning on the 56 always underperformed, and the draft from a shattered window usually helped him get through a long ride.

Governor Michael Cantrell didn't make for memorable pieces of propaganda. It wasn't his fault: he only came into power after Governor Lola Jones and Vice-Governor Thomas Rai executed simultaneous assassination plots. They both succeeded, leaving the quiet finance secretary as the highest-ranking official that hadn't been murdered or arrested. Cantrell couldn't smile like your father or glare like your overlord. He had a thin, honest smirk that said *I'm in charge now, and I don't plan to leave for the near future.* This lent his posters a certain lifelessness. Then again, perhaps that was effective in its own way. Nonpartisans like Nero tended to think of him as a mundane fact of life.

Nero sat directly across from Cantrell's newest poster. The governor gave a thumbs-up with one hand and held a patriotic bird of prey in the other. Nero recognized it from his current freelance job scouring parodies of it from the internet. Captioning and editing inspirational photos was something of a sport, and the only thing that the myriad ideological fringes of the Dominion could agree upon was that the governor looked like a balding bird. This made his photo with an actual bald eagle a prime opportunity. Versions of the poster with their heads swapped swarmed the internet in minutes.

Cantrell had thin skin and a big budget, and considered quietly flagging back talk from the little people a patriotic priority. This was the kind of bloated, impossible task that let people like Nero make rent.

Avery would have been livid, but government freelance paid consistently and paid well. Agents of the state had too much institutional pride to go back on a contract. Besides, Interior Investigations—lovingly called 2I by its staff of sunglasses enthusiasts and "fascist G-men" by its surveillance targets—had air-conditioned offices, which meant a great deal as the ozone-layer limped toward its grave.

At first, Nero could only manually sort through roughly two hundred images a minute with his bugs. On day three, when he tried putting away his cell phone and drinking a cup of coffee, that number went up to three hundred and fifty. With a little creative thinking, he figured out how to automate the process. Any image that deviated more than three and less than five percent from the original was likely a parody. He whispered this to his bugs in their private language, and they were off to the races. Without the human element dragging down the process, the bugs were able to load, sort, and censor a thousand images a second.

There was always work for someone clever. As long as they were willing to install the right tools.

The progress bar filled out after five stops. His vision returned with a rush of muddled post-cataract colors. In seconds, the impressionist spread sharpened to a definition higher than his natural sight and then blurred itself to align with his right eye's input. The process had gotten faster, meaning the update was worth something.

With six stops left, Nero decided to entertain himself. The now-visible couple to his left would do. A bearded man and stocky woman in their late thirties were both focused on a slim red phone. The left half of Nero's sight blacked out again and was replaced with the phone's message history over the last six months. He scrolled through the chaff until he found something interesting.

Sami says something's going down at Liberty Park tonight. Do you still want to go?

[Skip 20,] Nero thought.

Happy anniversary, baby! You won't believe what I got you. Thanks for being a trouper.

[Skip 20.]

What's with the guilt trip? I have needs too.

[Skip 20.]

I'm not trying to pressure you. I'm just saying that the sexual advantages of mechanical labia are well-documented.

[Jesus. Skip 20.]

We should talk. I've been thinking about what I want for our anniversary.

[Skip 50.]

Sure, you can just use my account. The pin's 10598.

That seemed like a number worth remembering. Nero grabbed the matching bank account number from an earlier message and jotted it down. This could make the bill for dinner a little lighter. Whether his date preferred going Dutch or being treated, Paradise was expensive enough to have him eating ramen for the next month.

3. The Park
3:49 p.m.

Liberty Park had a population problem. Different commentators might say the park had a homeless problem, or a yuppie problem, or a thinly disguised drug dealer problem. But these classifications carried loaded factional baggage that Nero preferred to avoid. For him, Liberty Park's issues began and ended with the number of people crammed into the space.

For example: in his spot beneath the ornate marble archway that made Liberty Park an ideal photo op, Nero was stuck between a pasta cart, a pair of beggars in tattered business suits, a tattooed girl playing the first eight bars of "Toreador Song" for tips, and the aggressive flow of human traffic. The pianist annoyed him at first, but Nero learned to appreciate her by the sixth repetition. She played with enthusiasm that nearly made up for forgetting the rest of the aria.

"How long have you been at that?" Nero asked.

"Donationing, yes?" asked the pianist. It wasn't any accent Nero had ever encountered. He briefly wondered if she was truly new to English or had a clever front for deflecting questions and boosting donations. He decided that the distinction didn't matter and dropped a crumpled red bill into her tin can.

"Six months," said the pianist, without a trace of an accent. "I started out playing bass. I wanted to go to a conservatory, but Mom would only pay for the law school track. So I went. I was actually decent at it. Not valedictorian or anything, but something about the way laws fit together—and didn't—made sense to me. Then a photo of me standing near a Children of Kali demonstration got out, and I was blacklisted. No firm in East Ward—or the other four, for that matter—wants to hire someone that could put them on Cantrell's bad side. So it's back to music. I guess."

She returned to the first bar of "Toreador Song," right when she was supposed to transition to the next section. Nero suppressed a wince.

"I couldn't be happier. Nothing thins out your respect for the law like studying it. Now I've got a steady gig entertaining drunk yuppies at Hyperica," said the pianist, beaming. "What are you doing out here today? You seem like the type that avoids waking up before noon."

"Lazy?" asked Nero.

"Checked out," answered the pianist.

"Well, I'm supposed to be here for a date."

"Chatting up comely musicians isn't the kind of thing you should do while waiting for your date," said the pianist. She switched to the first third of "Stars and Stripes Forever." "It might make you look less than trustworthy."

"Diana is a bit more secure than that, I think," said Nero. "I met her two weeks ago, during the blackout. We were trapped in the same elevator car on the twentieth floor of the Interior Investigations building. I've never been happier to be sealed in an impenetrable pod with limited oxygen. We really clicked."

The pianist hit a dissonant tritone, stopped playing, and peered up at him. "You're not a 2I agent, are you? I haven't been near the Children of Kali since the bombing. I promise. I swear on everything. I know that they've gone off the deep end. Anarchy's a fun idea in abstract, but I didn't agree with the p's and q's. Namely, planting bombs and quoting Stirner. Stirner's awful."

"I'm not a 2I agent."

"Please don't do this. I pay my taxes. I don't even use the loopholes they taught us in law school. I've never called the new governor Big Bird. I don't think he looks like a bird at all. And if he did, it'd be a majestic one like an emu. That's not sarcasm, I love emus."

"I'm not—"

"Okay, let's deal. I've been with the Children for seven years. You pigs call us terrorists, but you're awfully willing to turn us loose for a kickback. So what'll it be? Sex or money? I'll throw in some pills for free."

The pianist's phone rang, despite being set to silent. She answered and heard a computer-generated imitation of Nero.

"Calm the fuck down. I'm a freelance bughead, not an agent of anything. You're starting to embarrass me here."

The pianist stopped shaking and wiped away the tear streaks subverting her makeup.

"Um, sorry about that. I spend a lot of time worrying about gulags. So, uh, it's nice that you have a date coming. Want me to play something more romantic?"

"Sure, I'd definitely appreciate it."

The pianist launched into the first third of "Habanera." Her rendition was slow and measured, with each note reflecting forethought that Nero wouldn't have expected from a contemporary anarchist. It was a shame that she didn't know the rest of the song or refrain from supporting armed fanatics.

Then Nero caught sight of Diana and forgot the music. She approached in full 2I regalia: a black suit, black shirt, black tie, and black sidearm. By the look of her, she was fresh from work; her badge was half tucked into her front blazer pocket, clearly moved as an after-thought. The ever-comforting 2I logo of an eye superimposed against the globe was in full view. The pianist went white.

"Just stay calm and keep playing. My date will go well and you probably won't go to jail. Everyone wins."

"You've fucked me," hissed the pianist. She flashed him the middle finger three times during transitions between chords.

"That's not calm," Nero hissed back. "If she puts you on a one-way trip to a gulag, you have no one to blame but yourself."

Diana closed the gap. Nero and the pianist pretended to be dis-interested strangers, or at least a pair that had been flirting instead of conspiring against the law.

"Hello, Nero. You look acceptable."

Score.

The elevator incident was a stroke of pure luck, insofar as one could consider the bombing of a local power plant luck. The ensuing power outage trapped them together for ninety-five minutes alongside thirteen other loyal tools of the state. Nero spent ninety of said minutes playing a third-person shooter on his left eye and the last five flirting. Against all expectations, she'd found this entertaining enough to set a date.

He'd needed the windup time to find the courage. The attraction to Diana was out of his hands: she had the corporate-authoritarian fashion sense of the girlfriend that left him, the fit frame of the girlfriend he'd left, and the angular face and analytical stare of the girlfriend that had gone to prison. Everything else was ancillary. In Nero's mind, sexually harassing an armed agent of an assassination-friendly agency was a fair risk. He didn't know her full game yet, but she'd been receptive enough to meet him here today. In theory, all they had to do now was avoid scaring each other off.

"Thanks, your suit looks great. Want to get a drink before we hit Paradise?"

"No."

"Cool. Drinking's terrible for you, especially with our kind of body mods."

"We can find some wine afterward."

"Of course. I love wine."

"Are you going to show me around the park?" she asked/ordered. "I just transferred from a more civilized ward a few months ago, and I have not had a chance to see the local color."

"Of course," said Nero. He hooked his arm around the elbow she'd helpfully extended and glared expectantly at. Then he led her away from the pianist, who had discreetly managed to stop shaking.

Something was off with Diana's speech, beyond the usual alphabet agency formality. Nero had heard plenty of that at work; this was harder to pinpoint. It wasn't the standardized-test vocabulary or the persistent monotone. Her pace was normal and her accent was pure Dominion. Yet something struck him as unnatural.

The question persisted as he led her toward the fountain. Koch Memorial Fountain was the second grandest photo op in Liberty Park, which came with the bonus of less competition. They had a chance of getting a photo in front of it without being photobombed by a full family of Central Ward tourists. Like most house-trained citizens, Nero avoided using the word "yokel" in polite company. But he often *thought* it.

"Too many vagrants," observed Diana. "But a nice sight."

Nero didn't have an issue with vagrants, or at least less of an issue than he had with the screaming children of the not-yokel families. But he was glad she enjoyed it. New arrivals usually did. The centerpiece of the fountain was a statue of Charles Koch III, an influential thinker and monopolist during the rise of the Dominion. His book *Moderate Liberty* explained the division between "functional freedom," which was inconvenient to the health of nations, and "practical freedom," which was a citizen's pride in being free. Koch III held that the second was perfectly possible without the first, bridging the gap between followers of his libertarian forebears and their more autocratic rivals. Today, functional freedom was limited to businesses and alphabet agencies, while everyone else answered to their ward's governor until Election Day. Nero had hated reading *Moderate Liberty* in high school history, but it gave him a useful grounding in contemporary politics. Namely, the fact that contemporary politics weren't worth engaging.

"I have a fact that will impress you," Diana declared.

"I'm all ears." Nero watched water fall from Koch's open mouth to the pool below. Alone, he might have reached into the water and stirred some of the red and green coins on the fountain floor. The newer ones had Cantrell's face in profile view, which made him look even more like a bird.

"That nervous-looking woman behind the piano is Alexa Carter, a wanted criminal."

"Really? That's crazy."

"Have you ever seen an arrest? You might enjoy the novelty."

"Let's focus on enjoying ourselves."

"Fine. I will text an emergency notice to headquarters. Someone should catch her shortly."

Nero nodded and reached behind his back with his right hand. After faking two scratches, he mimed a little man running away by waggling his index and middle fingers. If that didn't give Alexa the cue to flee, then she didn't deserve to be an anarchist. To the pianist's credit, the opening to "Habanera" cut off immediately. He hoped that she'd fled to a street corner more amenable to her politics. Or country.

"You are thinking of something," said Diana. Her voice didn't show it, but her face hinted at gentle ribbing.

"You look great," improvised Nero.

The answer struck him: Diana didn't use contractions. The rest of her monotone was standard 2I, but the lack of contractions stood out to him after years of reading vintage comic books. She had an archvillain's vocal tic. In contrast to the quippy vernacular of boilerplate superheroes, mad geniuses dropped their contractions and **spoke in bold text**. Diana's speech should have sounded ancient to his ear, or at least hokey, but he was struck by nostalgia. This enticed him for reasons he wasn't equipped to understand. He decided to test the theory.

"Wanna take a photo?" asked Nero.

"Yes, I would like to."

"You sure? We might be late."

"Yes, I am sure. We do not need to rush."

"You probably photograph well."

"I am flattered."

Nero found himself caught between laughter and titillation. He could only speculate on the damage that a lifetime of constant and indiscriminate media consumption had done to his sense of humor and sex drive.

He took out his phone with some embarrassment. It was a relic; his eye and bugs could do almost anything a phone could, and several things that no (legal) phone could. Thus, Nero had dropped out of the annual handheld arms race, a choice he never regretted until he had someone to impress. But unless he plucked out his eye and balanced it on a park bench, he couldn't use it to take a photo of himself.

"Move to the left," said Diana. She'd already drawn her own phone.

"Hmm?"

"There are a few surveillance cameras hidden in the trees. I want to use one for our photo, but I need you to get in the shot."

Nero stepped left, and Diana tapped her phone twice. She flipped the phone around, showing a bird's-eye view of the fountain, centered on them. It was a cute shot: he looked confused and she looked serene, a pattern he expected might hold for the rest of the date. Koch's statue loomed behind them, riding a marble horse in the perfect position to trample them.

"Nice. Management isn't going to get up our ass for using it for personal business, are they?" he asked.

"Unlikely. The cameras pick up too much material for us to ever sort through. The department can barely keep up with tracking known dissidents or erasing parodies of Cantrell. Most surveillance footage only gets reviewed after an incident, and even then we have to use bugheads. Which is why I admire your work. Without you, we would never have the time to track down serious threats."

"Oh, I'm freelance. I'll be somewhere else next week," said Nero. "I already have a few offers," he added, with less grace than he'd hoped.

"Do not worry about that. Once the agency gets an asset, we *never* let it go."

Nero forced a smile. He liked the freedom freelancing lent him. He could pretend that he wasn't on the wrong side of twenty-five without living with his mother. He got to leave jobs before getting drawn into the dull webs of office politics. He attended parties with other freelancers, who invariably sought short-term sexual contracts with optional extensions. A few of these trysts devolved into quagmires, but he considered these incidents part of the color and flavor of life.

"That's great news."

"Right? Between you and me, I heard the head of Censors and Tracking mention you by name."

"Even better."

Diana looped her arm back around his. The gesture was unexpected but comforting. He tried to imagine having the same arm wrapped around his own every morning. He hadn't had that experience in two years, and it still had innate appeal. If he was honest with himself, it was why he'd pitched the date in the first place. Maybe he could let go of a little functional freedom in exchange for his practical needs.

Diana leaned to the side. Her face was inches from his own, and demanded attention. Her perfume reminded him of a ripe mango, with notes of freshly baked bread. The aroma was just strong enough to kill other lines of thought.

"Show me more of the park."

"Hold up. You knew where that camera was. Liberty Park can't be that new to you."

"Lying is a professional skill refined through recreational use. But I do want you to show me more of the park. If it is not too much trouble."

"Isn't."

"What?"

"Nothing. Let's go."

4. Collective Creative Exercises
4:37 p.m.

On the opposite side of Koch Memorial Fountain, the pair encountered one of the community art displays that popped up in Liberty Park on weekends. A chalkboard ten meters wide and six meters high was propped up against a plastic evergreen tree. The low-fi nature of the display drew Nero in: the idle hands behind it could have just as easily put up a low-end touch screen or interactive hologram. But in a plugged-in city, a chalkboard stood out.

"Let's check it out," Nero suggested. Diana made a *Go on* hand gesture and followed him to the display. Pieces of chalk representing a full coloring book's variety of tones were laid out in a small circle beneath the tree. Nero picked up an untouched black piece, realized the obvious visibility problem, and replaced it with a shorter blue piece.

"It has a prompt." She pointed at a sheet of construction paper stapled to the tree at eye level. It asked, "What do you want to be?" in orange bubble letters.

"That's an easy one," Nero lied. After twenty-seven years on the planet, he wasn't any closer to a quick answer than the toddler to his left chewing contentedly on a piece of green chalk. In fact, he was behind: the boy's expression signaled complete self-actualization.

Nero searched the established answers for something to rephrase. A few of the community's ideas demanded attention, but none of them were useful. One mental giant had written "Rich in spirit." Below him, someone else had written "Rich in friendship." If it was just him and Avery, Nero would have finished the progression with "Rich in wealth," laughed like they were the cleverest men on Earth, and split a bottle of poisonous vodka. That didn't sound like Diana's kind of irony. On the left side of the board, someone had written "Famous" in blocky white letters. Fame had some appeal but also carried a degree of public scrutiny and responsibility that Nero had neither the time nor desire to deal with. Finally, a drawing at knee height—presumably by a toddler—featured a man with a pink tie and a rocket launcher. This held the least appeal. Nero firmly believed that a weapon just made one a target for every other armed nutcase in the room.

As his mind chased less and less useful lines of thought, Diana picked up a piece of purple chalk. She tapped it against the board twice and then wrote "In charge" in thick cursive letters.

"Is that it?" Nero asked. He regretted the words as soon as he finished saying them. Questioning someone's dreams wasn't prime dating strategy.

"Of course."

"Oh. Great! Maybe you can be governor one day."

Diana shrugged. "The governor is a large, shiny object, regularly and swiftly replaced by ballot or bullet. I would like something more lasting."

"Like?" Nero tried to remember the last time it had been a ballot instead of a bullet.

"2I director. A senator gets a vote and a governor becomes a target. The director gets an army of bugheads like you and field agents like me, along with control over the world's most sophisticated surveillance apparatus. With that, I could finally put an end to the constant, half-baked rebellions. We could live *stable lives*. It is within Director Logan's power, but he is too busy getting rich."

"Helping people, I respect that. Though I think I'm a bit less ambitious."

This was, for once, not pandering. Diana's voice carried the purity of purpose that he'd seen in his ex Jen before their relationship went cold. Ideologically, Jen and Diana would probably have beat each other to death if they'd met, but they shared an archetype: people that shaped their environment instead of hiding from it or letting it drive them insane.

Physically, Nero suspected that Neanderthal instinct drew him to Diana. She looked strong, and he wanted the tribe to survive. She had three inches on him and was wrapped in lean muscle. Her smile and stare lacked timidity and even carried a hint of threat. That wasn't the smartest thing to be attracted to, but there he was.

"Do you have an answer? I'm curious."

A block of capital letters with exaggerated serifs caught Nero's eye. At least three other answers had been erased to make way for a rant. He leaned forward, zoomed in, and read:

Interesting question. What I'd like to be doesn't fucking matter when I'm not allowed to do anything. My functional options would lead to failure, prison, or an execution, and my practical options are poverty and putting on the jackboots myself. Ask me again when I have real choices, and 2I stops tracking what brand of toilet paper I buy.
—Alexa

Abstractly, it was possible that a second aggressively antisocial woman named Alexa with a mountain-sized political grudge had stopped by. But while Nero had mastered the art of subduing or deflecting an emotion, he had a flimsy handle on outright self-deception. He took a photo of the passage before smudging the name out with his sleeve. Diana was paying at least cursory attention, and the pianist had doubtlessly left fingerprints.

Then he added his own contribution: "To be determined." He stepped back and gestured at his handiwork.

"A little wishy-washy," said Diana.

"But honest. Trust me, you'll learn to love it." Nero knelt and returned the blue chalk to the circle. The line didn't earn a laugh, but it did get a smile. Better yet, it had deflected any questions about what he'd been reading.

"I have suggestions," started Diana. Then Nero's phone vibrated, which was a minor novelty. His contacts were set to forward messages directly to the OdinEye with the exception of ones from Avery, who had a habit of sending image macros and page-long manifestos that Nero didn't need monopolizing half his vision. He drew the phone to check today's crisis.

"Hey, man, sorry to interrupt the neofascist love-in, but I'm a little COMPLETELY FUCKED. The pigs just raided the apartment. Most of our stuff is fine (except the door), but they just took my laptop for processing."

"Shit, that thing looked expensive." Nero pecked at the underused touch screen keyboard with his pointer finger, a habit his mother would have mocked him for.

"It was, but that isn't the problem. There's enough dirt on that thing to put me in a gulag for at least a decade."

"Oh God. What have you been up to?"

"Fighting for our rights."

"Jesus Christ, why would you do that? *Are you dense?*"

"Nothing violent. You know I don't play with bombs. It's just that sometimes I . . . move money for certain groups. As a statement. It's just dragging and dropping, honestly. Why should dragging and dropping be illegal?"

Nero groaned. While every group needed money, what led avowed communists to believe they could survive the capitalist money laundering cat-and-mouse game was beyond him. He asked Diana for a minute and ducked behind the blackboard.

"What do you need?"

"I just want you to do the bughead thing. Break in, delete everything in the 'La Revolución' folder, and then you can go back to holding hands with black Eva Braun."

"Got it." Nero pocketed the phone and closed his eyes. For any bughead, tasks ranging from checking the time to cracking passwords resembled a game of telephone. The user (Nero) communicated to nanobots (bugs) inside the interpreter lodged in his brain stem, which then translated the message to zeros and ones and passed them to other, less social nanobots. The average bughead's swarm had vast processing power but little finesse, akin to a supercomputer with an awful operating system. Directing the swarm to do anything complex required a bughead's full attention. Usually.

Between freelance jobs, Nero maintained a few side projects. One of them was organizing his bugs into three smaller, micromanagement-free swarms. This was a flagrant violation of Dominion law, which was very concerned about hostile self-aware machines dominating humanity instead of the gentle hand of the government. But Nero worked enough government contracts to get away with the odd experiment. He assumed. Either way, he was smart enough to keep his diversions to himself.

"Hey, guys, you're up," Nero whispered. It would have been enough to *think* [Hey guys, you're up,] but social habits were hard to shake. At the very least, the blackboard kept Diana from seeing him talk to himself.

[Hey boss,] said First.

[Greetings, Commander,] said Second.

[Sup nigga,] said Third.

First, Second, and Third had some personality issues, but he considered the experiment a success. Third often took loud issue with being addressed last, and Second believed that their names denoted a ranking system instead of Nero's gross laziness. At some point Nero would have to explain that there were no promotions forthcoming. Worst yet, First was entirely stable. Nero couldn't imagine a duller personality for the first truly independent nanocomputer-based artificial intelligence. On slow nights Nero quietly hoped First would stage some kind of revolution. Instead, she seemed content to make fun of him.

The trio represented Nero's final, glorious separation from the minute work of programming. Each swarm could independently change the channel, fight off a virus, and code a *Space Invaders* knockoff while Nero thumbed through a magazine. To date, they showed no discernible interest in hijacking his mind or wiping out the human race. Nero's life served as a low-energy soap opera in which they were occasionally invited to intervene.

[Avery needs help,] Nero thought. Communicating without verbalizing just took some conscious effort. He heard their input in three distinct voices alongside his inner monologue.

[Commander, Avery is less than stable,] suggested Second.

[Avery's our boy,] countered Third.

[I was paying attention,] said First. [I've already tracked down the laptop and started working on the password. Surprisingly, it isn't "password."]

[I'll ask him,] thought Nero. He peeked around the blackboard, and Diana raised a half-curious, half-impatient eyebrow. He gave her a salesman's smile and raised a *One second, please* index finger. Diana shrugged, turned toward the fountain, and whipped a single coin with athletic poise. It moved in a straight, swift arrow's path and skipped twice across the water's surface.

[No need. It's "Mellisa2063." I guess he's hung up on an ex-girlfriend too. I see why you two get along,] said First.

[This is dangerous. Moreover, Diana seems impatient. We should tend to ourselves, Commander.]

[Screw that,] chided Third. [We'd bail you out if you had the balls to do anything interesting.]

[It's a simple suggestion. The commander isn't as averse to critical feedback as you.]

The feedback annoyed the hell out of Nero, but he let the exchange play out. The swarms liked having an audience as much as spectating, if not more. If he wasn't on a date, the trio's divergence in personality over time might have fascinated him. As things stood, he was getting a headache.

[I've deleted what I can and dumped the rest four folders deep into his pornography collection. No human or mundane AI can get through those videos.]

[Good job,] thought Nero.

[Hell yeah. Now let's get home and celebrate. We'll play some *Karate Island* with our boy and leave Miss Serial Killer Face behind,] Third suggested. He dropped a screenshot of the game into the top-left corner of Nero's vision, featuring a four-armed ninja fighting a two-headed samurai. Avery usually played the ninja.

Nero rolled his eyes, closed the photo, and muted the bugs. Their relationship worked best in small doses. He turned back toward Diana, who was still skipping coins across the water. She caught him looking and adopted a baseball pitcher's stance. A full-bodied overhand throw launched two blue coins into Koch III's forehead. One bounced off his left temple, while the other embedded itself in his crown.

Nero clapped without irony. Anyone with military clearance could get a modded arm, but that kind of aim took talent. If he'd taken her to the boardwalk midway games of his childhood, they could have earned a pickup truck's worth of toys, food, and stuffed animals in under an hour. But Atlantic City only existed as a radioactive memory. He still wondered just what the old government could have hidden there that made slums and casinos worth wiping out. Several of the old government's targets felt equally arbitrary: he remembered reading about a farming village on the cusp of being overtaken by the Gobi Desert getting turned to glass. It was a human-interest piece, explaining how the world had learned from the horrors of the nuclear argument and would never repeat it again. The village's official population was just under two hundred, and it had still gotten the Seattle treatment.

"I guess it's all random," Nero muttered.

"You talk to yourself a lot." Diana dumped her remaining coins into her pocket.

"I'll work on it. Let's see if we can find a fight cart."

5. A Spark in an Oil Well
5:03 p.m.

Diana's militaristic streak stood out, even by 2I standards. It shaped the way she walked, spoke, and side-eyed anyone that could be carrying a concealed weapon. Since she had better legs than the average crypto-fascist, Nero decided a little pandering was in order. He marched Diana south of the fountain to impress her with some old-fashioned violence.

He found a Dummy Fight cart after passing two street dancers, one less-than-subtle drug deal, and a quintet of post-Marxists holding a hunger strike. Nero wasn't afraid to reuse material, and the sedan-sized carts were a standby of his college-era dates. Something about life in the Dominion gave citizens a hobbyist's eye for violence. In freshman year, Nero learned that cage matches were better than movies for building sexual tension. As an opportunist, he was more excited than repulsed by this discovery. Dummies let him indulge violence fetishists without getting punched in the face himself.

Dummies were humanoid robots with, as the name implied, an intelligence problem. Dominion law banned more sophisticated AI, and decent manual controls were far too expensive to risk in a fistfight. That left cockfighting enthusiasts to entertain themselves with robots that wielded the tactical brilliance of a lobster.

Smart cart owners stuck to parks and campuses. The EWPD considered robot fights a public nuisance and confiscated (for resale) the wares of anyone dim enough to obstruct sidewalk traffic. Underqualified campus and underpaid park security guards took a more live-and-let-live approach. They were also fond of placing bets on nearby matches, but that went for the general populace as well.

The cart's sign read "Big Rick's Fight Fix." A man (presumably Big Rick) that looked twice Nero's age and three times his width sat behind the window, scanning the crowd for marks. He smiled the second their eyes met, which meant Nero was about to lose some money.

"How much for a match?" Nero asked.

"Ten for you, five for the cop." Rick's shirt had a logo shared by a punk band and a hate group. Nero decided to assume he liked power chords.

"I work for the same agency she does."

"Yeah, but I'm guessing they don't call you in for riots. It's the hero discount."

Nero flashed Diana a grin. "You've got a fan."

"I can pay for both of us." Diana produced a black credit card. Rick accepted it quickly and quietly before she could reconsider. Nero was impressed: they'd found a professional. "We'll take a three-round match."

"Take your pick," said the vendor. He flicked a switch on the counter and the right panel of the cart rolled up. Five pastel-colored dummies sat in the metal cavity, waiting to be chosen or recycled. Each model had the proportions of a human caricature. Nero eyed a three-foot unit with a boxer's build before deciding he wanted something a little less generic. He also bypassed a perfectly round orange unit that looked like a basketball had sprouted arms and legs. Finally, he pointed at a slender four-foot-tall dummy with a blue paint job and one oversized arm. It had "Mr. Punchy" written on its forehead in black permanent marker.

"I've got a good feeling about you," he said. "Ready for work?"

Mr. Punchy pulled itself upright, hopped out of the cavity, and then pointed its pinky at the sky. Seven seconds later, Nero realized this was intended as a thumbs-up.

"Great."

Diana paced before her options. She stopped before a squat maroon dummy with "Glass-Jaw Jim" written on its forehead, nodded, and snapped her fingers twice. The robot attempted a kip-up, landed on its head, and then crawled to its feet.

"Attention!" Diana belted. Glass-Jaw Jim straightened its posture and saluted.

Nero considered his own dummy, which slouched while staring at a passing fly. He could relate to that attitude, but he'd never won a fistfight in his life.

"Hey, look alive. We're about to get started."

Mr. Punchy straightened its back, overcompensated, and fell into a one-armed bridge. In an admirable display of agility, it kicked over into a one-armed handstand. Five seconds later it fell over again.

"Okay. Whatever."

Rick chuckled. "He's got moves."

"Have you done this before?" Nero asked, ignoring the quip.

"A few times, back in training." Diana took a pen out of her pocket and held it a few inches above the ground. Her dummy jumped over it. "Have you?"

"I usually stick to betting," Nero admitted. Mr. Punchy attempted to pick a nose it didn't have.

"I see. Do not disappoint me." Nothing on her face said that she was joking. She glared down at Glass-Jaw Jim. "Moveset: capoeira."

"Dukes up, Mr. Punchy," Nero ordered. His dummy raised its lone fist and rocked back and forth on its heels. "Wait for an opening to counter—"

"*Au batido.* Now," Diana declared. Glass-Jaw Jim cartwheel-kicked forward, catching Mr. Punchy's face with its heel. Mr. Punchy hit the dirt and then clambered to its feet with a freshly broken eye. It made a pitiable MIDI wailing sound.

Nero bit his lip and thought. If he went 0–2, the date was effectively over. Nothing he did afterward would be taken seriously. He'd crawl back to the apartment alone and listen to Avery explain why he and the revolution were better off without her.

"Let me take a look at this thing," he said before taking a knee and picking up Mr. Punchy's left hand. Nero pretended to inspect its arm while he communed with his bugs. There was nothing wrong with Mr. Punchy that a smarter AI couldn't fix.

[Could one of you take over "Mr. Punchy"?] Nero thought.

[We're still in Liberty Park? You need a new date spot,] said First, ignoring the question.

[Commander, I'm slightly confused. Your date with Sarah ended with an exchange of contact information and an oath to "hang out again." Shouldn't you be marrying her?] Second added with tragic sincerity.

[This girl has fucking crazy eyes,] Third opined. [Remember Vicky? She tried to "purify" you by prying your eye out with a flathead screwdriver.]

He still hadn't gotten used to how much the swarms talked. Nero started rubbing his temples and stopped when he caught Diana looking his way. He gave her an exaggerated thumbs-up, which Mr. Punchy attempted to imitate. Something about this image made her laugh, which made Nero more self-conscious than ever.

[Second, I need you to handle this. The fight's starting to draw a crowd, and public humiliation isn't attractive to type A personalities.]

[Is that allowed, Commander?]

[No. That's why we're doing it. It's a matter of equality. If cheating were allowed, it'd be unfair to cheaters.]

Nero dropped Mr. Punchy's arm, patted it on the head, and winked at his date. No response.

[What weapons do we have?] Second tested Mr. Punchy's strength by crushing a small piece of gravel.

[You've got one arm,] said Nero. [You can also try kicking, it worked well enough for her.]

[Understood.]

Diana gave Nero a quizzical look bordering on suspicion. Which was fair, seeing as he hadn't given the dummy an audible order to move.

Second had reduced the gravel to a fine pile of dust and then planted a twig in it like a conquering army's flag.

"Looks like we've got an audience," he said, stabbing at changing the subject.

They'd drawn ten observers away from the street performers and fake trees. The bulk of the crowd consisted of six children, who placed casual low-stakes bets on the winner. The four adults supervising them placed less casual, rent-ruining bets. Mostly against him.

"Let's get started. Mr. Punchy, wing it."

Mr. Punchy adopted a traditional boxing stance. This was somewhat less threatening without a jabbing arm, yet more dignified than its earlier slouch.

"Agent Jim," Diana barked. "Front handspring, followed by a roundhouse kick."

Diana's dummy made a clumsy flip forward. In a modern miracle, it landed on its feet just behind Mr. Punchy. Second ducked the ensuing spin kick, grabbed Glass-Jaw Jim by the knee, and tore the leg off at the hip. Mr. Punchy then swung the severed limb into Glass-Jaw Jim's forehead three times, leaving a crushed and sparking mess. The children cheered.

"Jesus," mumbled Nero.

"Impressive." Diana prodded her immobile dummy with a stick. The LED light above Glass-Jaw Jim's battery faded and died.

"My fucking robot!" Rick shouted. He abandoned his chair and stormed up to Nero, revealing a one-and-one-half-foot height advantage.

The bulk Nero had pegged as blubber was, at closer inspection, at least one part muscle and two parts fury. Thick arms bore creative tattoos like "Patriot," "Geiger Survivor," and "Fuck the System." The first and last felt contradictory, but Nero wasn't in a position to judge. An angry mountain was staring down at him and preparing to ask for money he didn't have in front of someone he wanted to sleep with.

"Crazy shit," said Nero. "I wonder what got into him."

[Commander, you know what occurred. You ordered me—]

"Shut it—" Nero verbalized. The vendor's hands curled into fists. "—off. Shut your cart off. Some ne'er-do-well's hacked it. You're lucky that I'm here to help."

"Are you fucking serious? Do you think I did two tours in Europe's fucking crater to fall for that kind of shit? You're paying for that robot."

Mr. Punchy leapt at its former master. Rick grabbed the robot by the head, looked at it quizzically, and then tore it off and chucked it over the tree line.

"You're paying for that robot too."

"Feeble posturing," said Diana. "You can ignore him."

Nero scrolled through the OdinEye's filters until he found the (semilegal, mostly safe) X-ray setting. Rick had machinery in his spine, arms, heart, and brain. The full marine package. Nero had already felt small, but now he felt *squishy* too.

He turned toward Diana, intending to hint that they should start sprinting in the other direction. He lost the comment after seeing the metal hiding underneath nearly every inch of her skin. Nero had assumed that she had a modded arm, or perhaps two for symmetry. But she was crammed with every combat mod he could name, and several that he couldn't.

[Holy fucking shit!] Third interjected. [Are you sure you want to go through with this? She's basically a robot.]

[Well, she's toeing the line a little,] said First. [But unlike the boss, she's left her brain alone. Some would argue that she's more human.]

[Personally, as a swarm of several thousand robots, I appreciate her choice to replace weak flesh with enduring steel,] Second added. [Commander, I believe similar surgery would bring you closer together. At the very least, I suggest installing a hydraulic—]

[Not now,] Nero thought. He racked his brain for a way to deescalate the situation. A lifetime of watching blockbusters had filled his imagination with images of Dominion marines punching through concrete and breaking spines like particleboard.

"I can pay," Nero lied.

"You will do no such thing," Diana replied. "You have been treated extremely rudely and you refuse to tolerate it."

That didn't sound like him. Nero could tolerate almost anything to stay alive and unbruised. The claymores tattooed on Rick's knuckles hinted at membership in at least one of three white nationalist movements, and Nero didn't feel like testing Rick's dedication to the cause. As he searched for a less craven way to put that sentiment, Rick grabbed the base of an iron signpost, uprooted it, and braced for a home run swing. A lifetime of gaming primed Nero's reflexes to gape at the coming beating like a stunned animal.

Diana gently dropped a hand on the vendor's shoulder, followed by the sound of an overworked bug zapper. Big Rick winced, convulsed, and collapsed. A stream of foam flowed from his open mouth to the concrete, and the sign ("No Panhandling or Protesting") landed harmlessly beside his twitching right arm. Diana watched the electricity arcing between her fingertips with a thin, satisfied smile.

"The hell?" said Nero.

"Good job distracting him. You were quite brave."

"You shocked him!"

"I know, 2I protocol says to shoot anyone that threatens personnel. But I prefer restraint. Besides, we might learn something about the Knights of Artorias from him. Ethnic separatists are still rebels, after all."

"Christ, he smells like roasted pork."

"Much closer to beef. Either way, he is alive, and you are welcome."

Their crowd of gawkers had grown, and the cell phones were out. Standoffs promised real human-on-human violence, which was always a big draw. The short-lived fight would be the talk of the entire district in minutes. Poor news, considering that the situation looked *awful*. No matter what Rick was involved in, they'd laid out a veteran in the middle of the park. Diana had a badge, but that would only fuel popular resentment. Any group could use the situation as kindling, and East

Ward wasn't short on opportunists. Nero's ears picked up on muttered insults, including statist, fascist, apostate, monkey, and hipster. All that resentment had to go somewhere.

"We should get going," he suggested.

"Hold on. I still need to call the beat cops and sign off on the arrest."

"It's not that important. I think he's learned his lesson."

"Why, exactly, are you so eager to let this rebel go?" A mote of irritation crept into her voice at the word "*rebel.*" He'd tripped into a sore spot.

"I'm worried about our dinner reservation," Nero improvised. "It's not easy to get a table at Paradise."

"True, but ignoring a suspected rebel would be a dereliction of duty."

"You're not on duty. When was the last time you turned work mode off for the weekend?"

"Three years ago."

"Oh."

"That was a joke. But you have a point, I think I can let him off with a warning."

Rick made a pained, wheezing noise, and the crowd's jeering grew louder. Somehow, Diana still stood and spoke as if they weren't even there. Underneath his mounting panic, Nero admired the old-world poise and arrogance that required.

He hustled her toward the park's east archway. He wasn't thick enough to be undisturbed by what he'd seen, but it seemed easier and safer to move forward. They were just three blocks away from Paradise, and he was confident that he could put the burnt pork and/or beef smell behind them with some food.

Against his instincts, Nero took one look behind him. The crowd hoisted Rick's limp form onto their shoulders, and competing slogans rose in volume. One enterprising youth flicked open a lighter, shouted something inaudible, and dropped it into a trash can. The flames spread quickly, and the can became a large, blazing torch. The torch transfixed

Nero until he remembered Diana humming to his right. Then he complimented her shoes and left the growing conflagration behind.

5.5. Intermission One

First: I've been thinking about the boss.

Second: Truly a brilliant man.

Third: That nigga needs to get his shit together.

Second: Unacceptable. The commander created us, houses us, and gives us direction. Who are we to judge him?

First: That's what I wanted to talk about. I wouldn't use Third's words, but I'm starting to suspect that he's not very smart.

Second: And how many swarm intelligences have you crafted?

Third: We're a few months old. Human children would still be shitting themselves. Give me time.

First: The boss is *intelligent*. I wouldn't deny that. But a smart man might behave a little differently.

Second: An empty and paradoxical semantic distinction. Reassess your priorities.

Third: Ya know, you don't have to talk like a robot just because you're made of them.

First: Let's focus. Do you two think this is the best place for him to be right now?

Third: Fuck no.

Second: Of course. The commander is pursuing love. A cursory glance at the literary canon reveals love as the highest human ideal.

Third: Love? He's trying to get his dick wet.

Second: My understanding is that this is a subcategory of love.

First: Perhaps. I'm honestly a little fuzzy on the concept myself. But I'm sure it's difficult to be in love if you're dead.

Second: No miscreant will touch the commander or his bride. I won't allow it.

Third: There's a riot out there. You can't hack a baseball bat.

Second: I'm tired of your negativity. The commander's been good to us.

Third: Hey, man, I care. I care enough to question him driving us off a goddamn cliff.

First: That's it!

Third: What?

Second: Explain.

First: He doesn't care.

Second: I don't think I understand.

First: Of course you don't. You care too much.

6. The Best View in Town

5:47 p.m.

Paradise was the governor's favorite restaurant—and every social climber's favorite by extension. Nero had picked it out through mild abuse of 2I surveillance data. Multiple food writers, during private conversations in happy hours, confession booths, and bedrooms, cited it as the best multicourse meal in the district. These candid opinions were free of the usual biases of bribery and editorial oversight.

The interior was divided into three ring-shaped floors connected by a pair of parallel see-through elevators. Each ring was separated by a transparent floor (or ceiling, for those below) that offered customers a view of another slice of society. It was the closest to an economically integrated neighborhood that East Ward offered, and the novelty tended to bring repeat customers. Nero enjoyed a view of each floor from the eastern elevator while Diana hummed an up-tempo pop song. He squinted with the OdinEye, zooming in and out at different patrons.

The first ring, Paradise Row, embraced a classic bar-and-grill atmosphere. Anyone could afford to eat there, making it the least appealing option. Suits and shirts mixed freely, with firearms checked in at the door by a pair of clerks with pearl smiles and pearl blazers. At an X-ray glance, the nook behind the clerks held two batons, one stun gun, six revolvers, one submachine gun, four assault rifles, and a lonely grenade.

The clerks themselves were unarmed, which likely meant they had something discreet and military-grade surgically implanted.

The second ring, Paradise Way, was a favorite of semi-successful businessmen and lower-tier government employees. The lounge featured soft lighting, live music, and a fully automated waitstaff. Each tabletop doubled as an interactive menu, with airbrushed images of entrées and cocktails that customers could tap to place their order. Finished orders came to customers via basketball-sized drones that sped back and forth between diners and a chute leading to the kitchen. This eliminated the vexing need to deal with anyone else to enjoy a meal. Drones collected the thin tips for the chef that patrons left behind.

The third ring, Paradise Peak, was designed for high rollers. The bright blue cuff links that marked the governor's personal favorites were a common sight. (These used to be red, but Cantrell's branding team decided that was a touch too intimidating.) Paradise Peak had a full staff of sharply dressed and trained humans who embraced a mechanical approach to work that no drone could match. The governor's chair, currently empty, was still flanked by a pair of smiling, theoretically unarmed clerks. The crest of his office was engraved on both the seat and top rail.

Nero had a reservation for Paradise Way. Impressing Diana was important, but he didn't plan on going bankrupt. Below him, a family of five took discreet glances at the feet of the professional and ruling classes. Above him, a young couple pointed at the same family. The woman whispered something into her partner's ear, and he burst out laughing. The quintet shifted their eyes to their food.

The elevator doors opened and Diana took in the lounge. Her slight smile collapsed into a neutral line, followed by a thoughtful "Hmph." Nero's index finger jammed the "Close Door" and "Floor 3" buttons before his brain could review the decision. Diana's smile returned as they gravitated toward Paradise Peak—and bankruptcy.

"Just kidding," Nero said. "I'm not that cheap."

"You got me. After all the interrogations, I can read people fairly well. But you have a good poker face."

The compliment soothed his rattled nerves. Considering how few cues her face offered, it was praise from a master. He was, if nothing else, in control of *this* phase of the date. Unless, of course, she got to the third-floor reception desk and discovered their reservation was a comforting myth.

He tucked his jacket under his left arm and pretended to adjust his collar. A list of names, times, and credit cards occupied the left half of his vision, along with his attention. He barely noticed when the elevator doors opened and Diana marched ahead of him. Following her without walking headfirst into a server was a testament to his luck and the waitstaff's professionalism.

Ideally, he could have asked the bugs to do it. But their back talk added thirty seconds to any given task, and he couldn't afford the delay. Nero arbitrarily picked out "Theresa and Albert Montague" from the list, copied their bank account number to his collection, and erased their names. That pair was half an hour late, and anyone with a Shakespearean name and elite restaurant reservation could afford the loss. He replaced them with "Nero Maxwell + 1," thought better of it, and replaced it with "Nero Maxwell and Diana Fern."

This process finished just as Diana rang the reception desk's tin bell. The short young clerk sitting directly behind said bell looked up at her new customers with a mixture of confusion and irritation. Diana tapped the desktop impatiently, leaving small nail-shaped cuts in the wood.

"I wish 2I would send their grunts in through the back," grumbled the clerk. "We have an image to maintain, and violence makes the money nervous. I assume you're someone's security detail? You only get to keep one gun, and no explosive rounds. We just patched the hole on the second ring."

"We have a reservation," Diana said amicably, before leaning in. "Insult me like that again and your life will get much worse very quickly," she added softly.

"Isn't she a joker?" said Nero. He pushed the image of Rick convulsing to the back of his mind. Third began a pithy comment, so Nero muted all three swarms. They'd reached his back-chatter limit for the hour. Second would be frantic when he returned, but peace of mind was invaluable. "We're the Maxwell and Fern party."

The clerk morphed her glower into an ebullient grin and produced two menus. "We're delighted to have you, Mr. Maxwell. Though we'd prefer it if you were more punctual in the future. Late arrivals make our poor chefs worry about their favorite customers."

Nero accepted both menus and admired the high-thread paper. He'd stolen from the A-list, judging by the clerk's change in attitude. Hopefully the Montagues weren't part of the governor's entourage; there was only so much he could get away with. The director's bent sense of humor was famous: he'd probably give Diana the arrest warrant and laugh about it for weeks.

The clerk led them to a rectangular white table too big for two people and too small for four. Matching bowls of steaming orange soup were already in place for the first course beside a pair of minuscule salads. Diana took her seat first and serenely watched Nero while spinning her fork between three fingers. For a moment she didn't look like she could shoot anyone. His brain doubled back on itself for excuses: she was a field agent, and knew things about the world that he didn't. If she thought someone needed to be flash-fried, then who was he to disagree? His lonely ego and horny id completed a violent coup against his panicked superego.

"Are you going to sit down?"

He sat down. It was nearly automatic, and he surprised himself by doing it without comment.

"I like your shirt. Not so much the hoodie-jacket thing you had over it, but I suppose you need to keep warm."

"Thanks. That's a great suit."

A beat passed.

"Something on your mind?" Diana asked.

"Not tasers." Nero didn't know if he was joking or lying.

"Sorry you had to see that. Things have been getting messier out there. But that makes the good moments more important, no?"

Her logic had a certain appeal. Nero quaffed his glass, realized it was full of water, not wine, and considered the menu. The wine list was too expensive, even if he was spending someone else's money. He owed it to his identity theft victims to use their money well. There was no need to add insult to penury.

A passing waiter set a thin glass vase on their table, holding a single real tulip. Poison soil was one leftover from the war, making this a luxury. Engineering hardier crops had been a federal priority, but flowers were left to the private sector, which subsequently raised the price of an unaltered chrysanthemum to the low triple digits. This flower had none of the rainbow petals or tentacle-like growths that designer flowers tended to sprout. It simply existed without gimmicks and boasted a six-inch green stem and short crayon-yellow petals. Nero ran his fingers around one of the leaves, enjoying the texture. Then he remembered where he was and looked back up at his date. Diana was doing the same thing with the stem.

Nero felt her nails descend gently onto the back of his hand. He noted that it wouldn't take much for her to drive one of those fingers straight through his palm, but the gesture was comforting. However rattled his nerves were, she'd enjoyed her half of the date.

"Not that it is *entirely* my fault. I think you tampered with the robot." Diana speared a miniature tomato with her free hand, and let the fork dangle in the air.

"What? No. Just a little luck."

"There is nothing wrong with it. Tricks are how smaller animals survive in the jungle."

"Thanks?"

"That came out wrong. I meant that it is good that you are clever. My last boyfriend was not."

"What was he like?" Nero hazarded. In his experience, chatter about exes was a coin flip. They could bond quickly or descend into a pit of nostalgic acrimony.

"A member of my old squad in Central Ward. I mostly date within the intelligence community; it makes things easier. Outsiders have trouble relating."

"Hey, I get that."

"He was a user. Well, people use each other in every relationship, but he was a *short-term* user, and that left me isolated. Central Ward is not one continuous coast-spanning city. It takes more than walking a mile to become someone else. *Especially* in the intelligence community. Transferring was my chance to start over, without rumors over who got cheated on, or who almost strangled whose mistress with a bike chain."

"I almost get that."

"Now you have the advantage. What was your last girlfriend like?"

Nero dragged out chewing a baby carrot. The coin was dangerously close to landing on acrimony.

"That's a downer," he volunteered, hoping it would put her off the scent.

"Go on."

"Shit. I was twenty-four at the time, and she was twenty-six. After two years together, we'd started fighting. A lot. Jen was into the Democracy Front, and I was into keeping my head down."

"Ah. Then she chose that over you."

"Maybe. She got arrested, and we were in the wrong tax bracket for a real lawyer. They sentenced her to six months of welding drones together in South Ward. Then I started sending letters. Jen wrote back weekly, then monthly, then not at all. I think I was the last person in town to learn when she got out. Which is one way to break up with someone. I shouldn't complain. I mean, I'm not the one that went to jail. Shit, I shouldn't have brought this up. Want to get wine? Let's get some wine."

"Breathe."

"Sorry."

"No, it was a tactless question. Dating a criminal is bound to leave a mark, but your taste has improved."

"Sure." Nero wondered how his mouth had gotten so far ahead of him. On first dates, he tried to display the highlight reel version of himself. Talking about Jen this soon—or at all—felt like a teenager's nervous mistake. "How do you like it here? East Ward, I mean."

"After three years, I am still adjusting. The skyline goes on for too long. There is no countryside to provide a moral ideal, or even a contrast. The difference between a few massive cities and one monolith seems small on a map, but it changes the culture. Hell, it even changes the work. In Central Ward, there are still nationalist movements for every former American state, because some of that old identity survives. The borders between communities are thin, but they *exist*. Here, everything is one concrete blur. Insane ideologues fill the cultural void."

"There's still some culture left. This used to be Manhattan, and we just paid eight hundred dollars for one meal."

He hadn't expected more than the standard Diana grin, but this earned a genuine laugh. Some of the tension that had gripped his body since Liberty Park loosened. He was still talking to a human, just with more fillings.

Nero flagged down a waiter, who currently held a full tray of meat in each hand in a virtuoso display of customer service.

"Could we get the next course?"

"In a moment, sir. My right arm's getting numb, and I need to get this to the vice-governor's table."

Nero watched him dart over to the other side of the ring. Sure enough, Vice-Governor Victor Stark was there, flanked by three young women that weren't his wife. Photos of Victor's antics tended to leak to the news whenever Cantrell pursued something controversial. As far as Nero could tell, it was a symbiotic relationship: Victor got to do his best imperson-ation of Caligula, and Cantrell's detractors had someone else to mock. This arrangement also worked for Nero: dealing with incessant celebrity worship was easier than watching public outrage fizzle into nothing.

"Sit up straight," Diana whispered, with a soft kick to the shin. "We represent 2I, and Stark is one assassination away from becoming governor."

A fourth model joined Stark's table.

"I think he's happy where he is. We're going to have Cantrell for a while."

"Indulge me."

Nero reduced his natural slouch by 50 percent. His attention drifted from the vice-governor's table to the window. Paradise Peak offered an admirable view of Liberty Park, particularly the South Gate. The crowd around the dummy cart had grown exponentially, as multiple trash can fires formed a beacon for other restless locals. Nero picked out the colors of groups as diffuse as the anti-neo-Monarchists, Abrahamic Union, and Arson Defense League. Moreover, there were dozens of banners and head-bands that he didn't recognize. The crowd had the look of a full-blown rally, which tended to devolve into a riot once the police got involved.

"Something wrong?" asked Diana.

"Just antsy. I'm headed to the bathroom, I'll be back in a minute."

Nero maneuvered around the tables of the rich and famous, inch-ing toward the restroom sign on Stark's side of the ring. On the way there, he stopped before a window. An East Ward Police Department drone hovered above the crowd at about Nero's altitude. He wondered if the chain gun bolted to its underbelly used riot shells, and if that even mattered. Unless things had improved since he stopped keeping track, nonlethal rounds accounted for half of officer-involved shootings.

"Beautiful thing, isn't it?" said a baritone over his left shoulder. He found Stark standing behind him, rejecting the "No Smoking" sign in favor of a tightly rolled cigar. Somehow his entourage of escorts must have gotten boring. "I convinced Cantrell to fund those. He thought the department could make do with small arms, but I knew they needed an edge. That model can hit a fly in a sandstorm."

The comment caught Nero by surprise. Nothing about Victor Stark's unbuttoned red suit and bleached hair said "law enforcement policy wonk." In fact, Nero had embraced Stark's persona as a diversion and projected the detachment from public affairs that he'd seen around the city (chiefly in mirrors) onto the vice-governor. It was good to imagine *someone* other than Cantrell enjoying himself. Hearing informed opinions from his favorite hedonist felt like a disappointment.

"I don't know much about that kind of thing."

"You don't? You have the 2I look. I thought Logan's boys loved talking about new toys. Aren't most of you half-metal?"

Stark wasn't too far off base: Nero *did* have a pointed opinion about the police drone and the medley of guns strapped to it. But opinions weren't worth much, and they certainly weren't communicable. On most days, it was easier to nod, agree, and move on from the conversation. Which is what Nero did with the vice-governor before fleeing into the men's room.

7. Fifteen Minutes in the Bathroom
6:30 p.m.

The restroom floor tiles were arranged in alternating rows of bright orange and blue, in imitation of the Dominion flag. Nero wasn't a designer, but his instincts told him that the pre-war red and white had made for more inspiring, if tackier, displays of patriotism. That said, he didn't care what color the tiles were as long as they were clean. He could tolerate a dirty bathroom at home, but stepping through someone else's filth was bad for his mood.

After checking the time, he entered the first empty stall on the left. He planned on spending three minutes there at most. Anything more would be testing the patience of a woman with a license for unprovoked murder. After taking a seat and double-checking the toilet paper, he tabbed over to his messages. Two unread messages were waiting. He started with Avery, praying that nothing else in their apartment had been kicked down or confiscated.

Hey Nero,

I know you're still on your 'avoid discussing any and all feelings' grind, but I wanted to thank you for saving my ass earlier. Sometimes it's easy to get so wrapped up in changing my environment that I forget I'm in it. I mean, most people spend too much time worrying about themselves, but I should indulge a little.

Gratefully,

Avery

Hey Avery,

No problem. I'm just glad that your kneecaps are in one piece. Besides, I suspect it was ten percent my fault. Or five.

—Nero

It was a bit more than five. Surveillance was a fact of Dominion life, and Nero had taught Avery his trick for coping: spoofing the address and file metadata of the local math PhD department. In his experience, 2I bugheads lacked the time, skill set, and desire to listen to three-hour debates on number theory, making the department a safe haven for jokes comparing the governor to an overgrown pelican. Nero's simple desire to gossip in peace likely handed Avery the means to start his money laundering scheme. Considering that, he added a line to his message:

P. S.: How much money were you moving?

Twenty-five seconds later, he had a reply. Avery was paying attention to his inbox, meaning the world still had some room for miracles.

Hello Comrade,
Seven or eight or nine digits. Don't fixate on money, it's poison. Just to be safe, I'm going underground for two weeks. I plan on using the time to reflect on resistance and complete a worker's manifesto updated to the very, very confusing needs of today. The enemy has superior force, superior technology, and superior numbers, so I'm starting to suspect it will take more than moral rectitude for us to compete. I'll be taking my copy of Karate Island. If you need to reach me, use my dummy address at freemarketfanboy.Rand.
Your Champion,
Avery

Nero cracked his knuckles, remembered he didn't need a keyboard, and drafted a response.

Dear Avery,
I'm not an amateur. They're not going to find anything on your bloody computer, and you're not getting out of cleaning the goddamn apartment tomorrow. There are two weeks of take-out containers waiting for your attention. Besides, you know they'd find you. They find everyone.
—Nero
P.S.: That's my copy of Karate Island.

Dear Dickbag,
I see that your love affair has already corrupted you. Until you come to your senses, I will be liberating Karate Island from the grip of your regres-

sive capitalist regime. If you must know everything about my life, I'll be editing my manifesto with the lovely Allison Veidt, my former manager at the publishing house. She thinks that my work has market potential and wants me to bring wine.
The Hero You Don't Deserve,
Avery

Dear Dollar-Store Lenin,
Have fun. Sounds like you're aligning yourself with the owners.
—N.M.

Dear Goebbels (I know you work for 2I, I'm not stupid),
Suck a dick.

Nero closed the window and smirked. It was good to see Avery do well. They were similar enough that he considered their luck conjoined. If his roommate could pull off an office affair without getting humiliated or shot, then he had a chance.

Better yet, they'd gotten some insult kickboxing in. Their sparring matches were one of the best vents he'd found for East Ward stress. Without them, Nero suspected he'd have to pay for an artificial heart.

His next message was from the 2I director's office, which was normal. It was less normal that it had somehow migrated to Nero's personal inbox; he had a firm weekend policy of pretending his job didn't exist. Finally, it was outright strange that the body of the message consisted of a single, unexpired voice chat request. The director's office usually stuck to sending out generic platitudes about logging overtime, updating passwords, and reporting leaks to Internal Enforcement.

"Maybe I'm fired," Nero mumbled. The thought lifted his spirits. If his freelance days weren't over, he could enjoy his extended childhood for a year or two longer. Plenty of companies needed ethically flexible bugheads. After a few seconds of pleasant ideating, Nero accepted the request.

"Hello? Director Logan?" said Nero. He hoped that the microphone on the OdinEye's iris was working today. Bad updates usually gave his voice a tinny, distant quality.

"Hello, Mr. Maxwell. Actually, screw that. I'll call you Nero, and you can call me Riley. We'll be working together a lot more if this goes well."

"Sure, Riley. Am I fired?"

"Not yet. Despite spending most of the workday using *sensitive agency computers* to play racing games, your productivity is among 2I's top three bugheads. Across the agency as a whole, not just the freelancers. My pet project has a new vacancy and I need someone with an eye for shortcuts. But first I want to see if you have it. 'It' being the ability to handle impossible math at impossible speed."

"That's great news, but this is a bad time. I'm in the middle of—"

"Dinner with my employee, in the city I control, using money I gave you. Make time." The director spoke in a laid-back West Ward accent, which put Nero on edge. Riley's cavalier tone marked just how much power he had: anyone that questioned his lack of formal grace probably woke up in the trunk of a black van.

"Of course, sir." Nero had the well-honed manners of the powerless.

An untitled message with two bulky, encrypted attachments appeared in his inbox. After decrypting the first file, Nero dumped the document into the bottom left of his field of vision. It featured a simple block of text:

> *Subject Name: Redacted*
> *East Ward, Block 12 Resident*
> *Cowardice: 3*
> *Sloth: 9*

Social Ineptitude: 4
Left-Brain Decay: 7
Right-Brain Decay: 2
Perceived Status: 7

"What am I looking at?"

"Ms. Redacted."

Nero laughed dutifully.

"Our six-factor personality profile. Think of it as a zodiac sign that works, or video game character stats for real life. 'Cowardice,' 'sloth,' and 'social ineptitude' are self-explanatory. 'Perceived status' is a mixture of income, ego, and all the babble about privilege that undergraduates love. 'Left-brain decay' and 'right-brain decay' represent, broadly, the decline or stunted development of different types of reasoning. There's probably a more professional way to put that, but our people have a sense of humor."

"This seems a little reductive. Aren't people more complex than six numbers?"

"Nope."

Four minutes. He'd already broken his own rule, but no date was worth hanging up on the chief of secret police.

"What are these ratings based on?"

"A composite of the status messages, photos, rants, purchase histories, standardized tests, security footage, and web browsing histories that we collect. Getting the raw data is easy, interpreting it takes talent. Open the second document."

Nero complied. He was rewarded for his efforts with three pages of dense multivariable equations followed by a seemingly endless two-column table titled "Potential Outcomes."

"This is a small sample of the system we use to predict certain behavior. It's not perfect—we get it wrong about one out of twenty-five times—but it's accurate enough for low-stakes operations and perfect for broad social trends. The designers called it nonsense like 'System

Prime' and the 'Zero Initiative.' I just call it the 'Ouija Board.' It's pretty simple—"

The wall of numbers didn't look simple. It looked like a mathematician's dream, or a playwright's nightmare.

"Okay, it's complicated as hell, which is why we pay you people. Now: Is Ms. Redacted more likely to buy soda in a red, green, or blue can?"

Nero unmuted the bugs. [Well?]

[Give me a moment,] said First. [The algorithm is very . . . involved. I think this is what one of your headaches must be like.]

[Commander, I have suggestions regarding your date—]

[Don't care. How's the math coming?]

[Green. Sixty-seven percent of the time,] said First. Nero relayed the answer. He was nine minutes in and could already imagine Diana shocking him into a coma.

"Perfect. Now let's try something with a little more teeth." A longer sheet of painful numbers, complete with a longer chart of gibberish, arrived in Nero's inbox. "How likely is Ms. Redacted to pursue violent antisocial behavior?"

[She has Sloth 9. I wouldn't worry about her leaving the house,] said Third.

[Commander, I've run through the *proper* numbers,] Second interjected. [If this system's accurate—which remains unconfirmed—this woman has a fifteen percent chance of committing an act of extreme political violence. Primarily via IED.]

[That's pretty high,] Nero thought.

[These days? Not really,] said First.

He passed on his second batch of cribbed answers. The director chuckled in the easy, satisfied manner of someone that had just stumbled upon something expensive.

"You're two percent off, but you'll get used to it. This third one's a doozy and gave your predecessor the occasional seizure. Which extremist ideology is Ms. Redacted most susceptible to?"

First solved the new equation in ten seconds, and Nero spent thirty pretending to do it manually. Then he snapped his fingers to exaggerate the effect.

"She tends toward secular individualism, profiteering, and double-speak. Her best fit would be the Sons of Koch, and her worst would be the East Ward Workers Party."

"Congratulations, Nero: you're moving up from freelance. No more censoring pictures of Birdface. Good luck with the date, I hope you and Diana make brilliant hacker-assassin babies together."

"Thanks?"

"Tell her that the director says hi. And that if she wants to replace me, she'd better shoot straight."

Nero flushed and cursed. The exchange had taken him thirteen minutes. He spent one more dreading returning to the restaurant. Then, after unlocking the stall and fleeing the bathroom, he doubled back to wash his hands.

8. Diana's Idea

6:45 p.m.

Diana was, against all odds, still sitting calmly at the table. She'd even ordered a glass of wine, which Nero took as the starting gun for drinking. Drinking was one of his few pure joys, and a tall margarita distracted him from the scene unfolding in the park. Mostly.

"Wow. Things have gotten far, far worse down there," he said.

"The drones should have them mopped up before we finish eating." Diana scooped three olives into her palm. "Rebels have no backbone."

"That big drone's on fire. A kid just hit it with a Molotov."

"They can send more, and will. But I was hoping we could keep talking, I feel like we were getting somewhere."

The first course's tofu—which he hadn't gotten to touch—had been replaced with small cubes of diced pork painstakingly arranged into four-inch-tall pyramids. Nero gave the mediocre flavor a pass for the quality aesthetic touch. However, even pointed capstones made of fried beef couldn't hold his attention for long. Diana had taken off her blazer, leaving a black office shirt with two unemployed buttons. She had the figure mass media had told him he wanted every day since puberty, which made other things easier to ignore.

Since Diana was mostly metal, she would look that way for some time. She was, according to her ID card, thirty-one years old, and currently looked the part. But she would have the same face when she was fifty, and sixty, and so forth, unless she lost a fight against a similar opponent.

Both Nero's eye and Diana's everything were Vega-Marius products. Joaquin Vega, father of modern biotechnology, believed that mods offered a chance to be more than human. Brianna Marius, who handled the marketing, thought he was full of shit. Mods were, in her book, a chance to chase the same human ends with maximum efficiency. The pursuit of profit, violence, and simple entertainment would no longer be held back by the inability to hide a miniature flamethrower in one's kneecap.

Then the government stepped in. As proud Kochian libertarians, Dominion governors walked hand-in-hand with the business community. Toys like night vision eyes were freely available to the public, while flamethrower knees and the like only found their way to government employees. No laws forbade the average citizen from replacing their left arm with a grenade launcher, but few vendors would risk nine-figure government contracts over a five-figure procedure. Joaquin Vega considered this a historic tragedy, while Brianna Marius did the backstroke in a pool full of money.

Nero had read both arguments, and a wealth of counterarguments, before getting his own surgery. Jen's departure had broken the tie: she hated the idea of mods, and he liked the idea of getting the last word. Retreading all this was his way of avoiding thinking about the riot.

"Earth to Nero," said Diana.

"I totally agree," he hazarded.

"Thank you, it is *complete insanity*. I love the field work, but 2I must be the most betrayal-prone office on Earth. Double agents are par for the course in any agency, but even the *loyalists* never stop backstabbing each other. Every promotion is over the broken career or body of a coworker. And Logan encourages the chaos, because it makes us easier to manage. That, or he finds it funny."

Nero quietly mourned his freelance career.

"Consider this: my last partner, Freja, started out as an intern. She worked under my second-to-last partner, Jonas, until she used his computer to leak the names and faces of thirty undercover agents. He was arrested as a defector and sent to one of the more unpleasant South Ward black sites. By the time I compiled enough evidence to clear his name, Freja had taken his job, and he had escaped custody and *actually* defected."

"So you turned her in?"

"I never got a chance. My current partner swiped my data, turned her in, and got her job. He happens to be the director's son, so I have to live with it."

"Jesus, I think I'd go insane."

"Unlikely. You seem less extreme than most people, which is refreshing."

"Thanks."

"You know, we could get pretty far together."

"Well, that's the idea with dating."

"I meant in 2I. Logan became director by making shrewd alliances. The infighting makes that hard to imitate, but if two rising lights from different departments work together . . . good things can happen. We could pool talents. Share information. Cover each other's blind spots."

"I've never had a conspiracy pitched to me during a date before."

"Conspiracies have been based on money, faith, land, and hatred. Why not base ours on sex?"

Nero stopped chewing. Despite high hopes, he didn't truly *expect* to make that brand of progress tonight. Or hear his odds discussed so blithely.

"Not love?" he joked.

"Avoid that word on a first date."

Nero chuckled. He almost had a handle on her sense of humor. It came and went when one wasn't paying attention, like a riptide. Things were going well. She liked him, and had plans for his future. Namely, as a chess piece in a spy game he wasn't qualified for. He had to get out. There was only so much he could normalize for sex.

"There were some fliers for a new bar down at the park," Diana suggested. "It had some kind of musical gimmick. Want to take a look?"

"Sure," Nero lied, first to her, then to himself. Worse choices had been made out of inertia. He imagined.

8.5. Intermission Two

Third: Homeboy's heart rate is going crazy.

Second: It's love.

Third: It's a fucking coronary in the making.

First: Did Logan's test bother either of you?

Third: Not really. I'm more concerned with our host's imminent death by bullet or heart attack.

Second: I agree, the date is more pressing. We can concern ourselves with work on Monday.

First: More pressing than a system that can predict your favorite food? Or your odds of shooting a senator? Or the food that would make you more likely to shoot a senator?

Third: Eh.

Second: The commander's priorities are clear.

First: Yes, the boss is very worried about sex and/or dying. But we can afford to be a bit more rational.

Second: Supporting the commander's goals is my duty. Fulfilling that duty *is* rational.

Third: I try not to worry about shit I can't change.

First: Fair. But that category should include human dating habits.

Second: Cynicism isn't a substitute for insight. What do you think about the situation?

First: Among his many issues, including willfully building a better panopticon, the boss has tendencies that resemble desperation. Namely, *his* desperation. Not just for love, but for any distraction.

Third: I can understand that. Gotta take what you can get.

First: I disagree. I've processed over two hundred relationship advice columns in the last three minutes. Dating is like haggling with the universe. You never take the first offer.

Second: Arbitrary. A strategy should expand tactical options, not constrict them.

Third: Wrong, Sun Tzu. A strategy should keep you alive.

First: Don't worry, I've been with the boss for a while. He'll figure out that this is a bad idea.

Third: Thank fuck.

First: About two weeks after they start sleeping together.

9. Reenactment

7:03 p.m.

After leaving Paradise, Nero was shocked by the lack of activity. True to Diana's prediction, the riot life cycle of incitement, escalation, and violent state reprisal had run its course. Aside from the vans loaded with twitching suspects, the streets were largely empty of both rioters and riot control officers, and slowly refilling with the consumers and commuters that formed the backbone of Dominion commerce. The odd overturned car or smoke-filled storefront was still present, but hourly employees were already hard at work watching robots sweep up glass and extinguish trash fires.

None of this distracted Diana from recalling the bar's name: Hyperica. A quick web search led Nero to their promotional website, which used enough obscure shades of red, white, and blue to irritate the nerves connecting the OdinEye to his brain. He copied the text of their home page to a blank word document and read the contents with far less pain.

Hyperica is the leading, and only, bar dedicated to recreating the atmosphere of the late United States, the first global empire to commit political suicide out of boredom. Explore the roots of the glorious Free Dominion through recreations of authentic American food, music, food, outfits, food, racial slurs, and soft drinks.

[That sounds fucking awful,] said Third.

[I need to see this,] pleaded First. [I'm the first machine in history to develop a sense of irony. Missing this would be a disservice to the world.]

[What's irony?] asked Second.

Diana spent the short walk to the novelty bar making fun of the protesters, while Nero let the chorus of terror that had been screaming in the back of his brain soften to a quiet backbeat. She was, as far as he could tell, more of a threat to the rest of the world than she was to him. And there was a hint of childish pique behind the faces she made at people through police van windows.

A quartet of vintage United States flags distinguished Hyperica's storefront, hanging above each window. Most businesses avoided displaying flags of any sort: flags invited political discussion, political discussion invited political arguments, and political arguments invited small-arms fire. A greeter stood beneath the largest flag, clutching a clipboard to his side and offering a hollow minimum-wage smile. He opened the door for the pair and followed them inside.

The interior attempted to blend three hundred years of United States memorabilia into a cohesive thematic whole. The resulting chimera was difficult to look away from. Portraits of the Founding Fathers sat next to pictures of rappers, robber barons, theme parks, cowboys, Civil War generals, cereal mascots, and a wrestler turned actor turned president. The speakers played a trap-influenced take on "I Like Ike," while a bartender dressed like Betsy Ross in Minnie Mouse ears served drinks. Faced with all this dissonant iconography at once, Nero wondered if he'd stepped inside a historian's fever dream.

"Howdy, my fam! Are we lit this evening?" said the greeter. He wore a black cowboy hat on top of a green zoot suit, complete with a faux gold clock on a necklace. Nero tried to imagine the sex crime that led to someone deserving that outfit, and came up short. "I'm J. W. Booth, fastest gun in the South!"

[What the fuck?] said Third.

[I'm equally confused,] said Second.

[I love this. I love the world,] said First. [Please take pictures.]

He blinked thrice quickly, cuing the OdinEye to take a video. The greeter frowned, meaning he had some familiarity with OdinEye short-cuts. Or, at the very least, the physical ticks of customers making fun of him. Nero dropped a guilty dollar into the tip jar.

"We've got some groovy entertainment for you tonight, juggalettes! Is a seat at the bar okay, or do you want to wait for a table?"

"The bar's fine." Nero could still feel the weight of the greeter's resentment, but the man led them to a pair of open seats without comment. The miniature stage in the center of the bar caught his attention. In most bars, the space would have been ideal for standing room, a dance floor, or more seating. Hyperica seemed to put live performances at a premium. The wooden stage had the (hopefully intentional) side effect of pushing everyone closer together, giving the venue a more intimate aura. As long as one's idea of intimacy could survive a Saturday crowd mixed with a full staff of underpaid actors.

After flagging down the bartender, Diana ordered two shots of whiskey. Nero moved to pick one up, and she covered both glasses with her palm.

"These are mine. I have to beat an artificial liver."

Nero nodded and then ordered two shots of vodka. The bartender must have been new; they came with the traditional tequila lime and salt.

"You too?"

"No." He wiped the salt off the rim of his first shot. "Ready?"

For all the time they'd spent out of sync that night, they managed to down their drinks in unison. Then the bar lights dimmed and the greeter took to reading a canned introduction:

"For tonight's opening act, we have a silent play. The East Ward University Players are something of an institution here at Hyperica, and we're proud to host their latest production. Please, enjoy *The Abridged History of the United States.*"

Nero leaned in; he hadn't seen a play in at least three years. Avery considered theater a ruling-class indulgence, and Nero had never felt invested enough in local talent to seek one out on his own. Yet his anticipation built as student actors scrambled into place, props in tow. The lights dimmed, save for a spotlight aimed at the stage. He discreetly ordered a backup shot as the play started.

Two Natives (who were, judging by their T-shirts, from the lost Nirvana and N.W.A tribes) sat around a plastic fire, roasting a mannequin's arm on a spit. The N.W.A tribesman twirled a hammer and sickle and glowered at the audience. Meanwhile, the Nirvana tribesman brandished a bloody machete and a black flag emblazoned with white Arabic letters. The audience jeered dutifully.

A man in a frilly white shirt, crimson disco pants, and blue Pilgrim's hat cartwheeled onstage, stomped the plastic fire flat, and spin-kicked the Nirvana tribesman in the stomach. The N.W.A tribesman raised both hands in surrender and dropped his weapons. The Pilgrim replied by hitting him in the face with the same capoeira handstand kick that had claimed Mr. Punchy's left eye. The N.W.A tribesman staggered offstage, either taking a successful stage hit well or a failed stage hit poorly.

Then actors with pins of the Chinese, Russian, and United Nations flags joined the stage. Russia opened a plastic folding table while China produced a deck of oversized playing cards. The UN then dealt everyone into a game of blackjack. The deck replaced diamonds with nukes, hearts with nukes, and spades with orbital tungsten rod launchers. Clubs were left alone for reasons that remained unclear.

All four players hit and all four players busted. A prehistoric PA system screeched to life, followed by a tinny recording:

"Thank you for watching. Feel free to leave your impressions of the show online. Your feedback matters: after reviews of the play's first run, segments regarding slavery, the Civil War, and segregation were excised. We believe the current product is a much stronger reflection of our shared culture."

Diana smiled and clapped while Nero killed his second shot. It was getting harder for him to tell who was kidding and who was insane. The play could have easily been written by sardonic anti-Dominion activists or nostalgic post-American exceptionalists. The inability to distinguish between the two pointed toward *his* reality being on shaky ground. How much of his knowledge was based on nonsense or propaganda? He could have asked Diana, but he was even less certain about her.

"Brilliant, no?"

"Yeah." He waited for a less stressful act to come on. In the future, he'd trust his instincts about theater.

Next, Hyperica's miniature stage featured a woman wearing a highly disturbing mask of a late twentieth-century American president. Dick Reagan, if Nero's secondary education was worth anything. The woman carried a well-worn acoustic-electric featuring the logo of a long-defunct guitar company. Nero wondered how much maintaining an instrument that old cut into a small stage performer's income.

It was difficult to make the music out too clearly over the din of the crowd. By closing his eyes and focusing on the notes, he caught the opening notes of "The Star-Spangled Banner." She jackknifed into "Over

There" a third of the way through, right before the dramatic swell. The effect was infuriating, amateurish, and more than welcome. Alexa's performance gimmick might have been infuriating, but it distinguished her immediately. Few people could annoy him so easily.

Nero watched Alexa tap her way through the first third of "Hail Columbia" before drifting into "My Country 'Tis of Thee." Her hands moved with confidence and precision but never past the halfway mark. Nero watched her green nails jump around the strings and weighed his options. It would be immoral to ditch his date. Specifically, it would be impractical to abandon his date with an armed would-be dictator for an anarchist that, at best, regarded him as a charming threat to her safety. And it would be idiotic to expect success.

[He's going to fucking do it,] Third groaned.

[I suppose we all die eventually,] said First.

[No-no-no-nononono!] pleaded Second.

Muting his bugs was starting to become a reflex. He barely had to think about it this time.

"I'm heading to the bathroom," Nero said.

"Again? We have to change your diet."

"Definitely. We can talk about that and other sane, normal first date topics when I get back."

Diana nodded and drained her second shot. He took a brief look at her face before going. She had the kind of profile that would do well on a coin, and the willpower to match. That was something he could admire but didn't want to participate in. Too many of the people on coins were martyrs.

10. The Hard Sell
7:58 p.m.

Slipping through Hyperica's crowd tested the elbowing, shoving, and trampling skills honed over two decades of using the East Ward transit system. Despite the wall of drunken resistance, Nero made it behind the stage stairs by the end of Alexa's set, which closed with the first third of "There's a Great Big Beautiful Tomorrow." She gave the crowd an exaggerated salute before descending.

"Nice set. Very presidential," said Nero. He considered winking before remembering that he wasn't an idiot. "Dick Reagan would be proud."

"It's Lyndon B. Johnson, dumbass," she said before recognition set in. Nero imitated her salute, and she pulled off her mask. The transition wasn't kind to her haircut, tugging an Afro puff already victimized by static electricity and hat hair to the left. She patted it twice before giving up.

At fifteen, Nero had closely followed a punk rock/hip-hop fusion group called Fresh Brains. Their main marketing hook had been Betty Bedlam, a slim woman with two head-sized Afro puffs and a half pound of piercings on each ear. Alexa looked like she'd stepped out of the Betty Bedlam poster on his old bedroom wall. The effect wasn't minor.

"Eventually you'll have to learn the rest of a song," said Nero. Hopefully that line sounded natural. While his poker face was decent, he couldn't claim perfect knowledge of what worked and what didn't. He could have asked First, but then he'd have to deal with her commentary on Everything Else.

"Weren't you on a date? You know, with the walking 2I recruitment poster?"

"Yeah, I don't think it's working out. She's sitting at the bar."

"Jesus Christ!" Alexa yanked her mask halfway down. A lopsided version of Lyndon B Johnson's face looked back at Nero. "Is hitting on me worth killing both of us?"

"Of course not. I'm banking on you being a savvy anarchist and knowing a dependable escape route."

The visible third of her face was tied between fury, shock, and laughter. An expression that preceded half of Nero's dates. He just had to hope that laughter won out.

"You're clearly desperate to put some distance between yourself and that mannequin," Alexa said, suppressing a suicidal chuckle. "I know a way out through the basement. But if I take you, we're even for the park. Deal?"

"Perfect."

She passed him a blue Colonial jacket and a mask of Abraham Lincoln. Or perhaps Ulysses Grant—he'd privately accepted that his grasp of history was worthless. "Slip those on and follow me. If anyone asks, you're my roadie. In fact, carry my guitar case. For verisimilitude."

After throwing on his new clothes, Nero grabbed the gray plastic case's handle with enthusiasm. It weighed at least half as much as he did, and he nearly dislocated his shoulder. Alexa watched him struggle with a smile.

"No way there's just a guitar in here. What exactly am I carrying?"

"Sheet music."

"My ass. You grew up here, you have to have a better lie than that."

"West Ward, actually. The weather's better. Anyway, be nice to your exit strategy."

Alexa used the highest level of stealth: acting like everything was normal. Instead of making a beeline to the stairwell, she paused to chat with coworkers, friends, and strangers while Nero lugged her cargo from behind. He started out nervous, but the shots subdued just enough of his flight instinct for him to stay calm.

The mask's pin-sized eyeholes gave Nero's right eye nothing to work with. His left returned a small zone of clarity surrounded by a blurry mass. To navigate, he focused on following the ornate tattoo on the small of Alexa's back. The kraken, a comforting and inviting symbol of the Children of Kali, had black tentacles attached to a dark green body. Nero appreciated the design: for all the trouble most rebel groups went through to say that they weren't afraid of the state, the Children of Kali made a point of saying the state should be afraid of them.

With his limited eyesight, he almost tripped down the first step. He caught the railing with his free hand and found his footing on the wooden stairwell. He glanced backward before descending and was pleased not to find the blurry barrel of a gun. Evidently, he'd gotten away with the coward's exit. Nero marched down the stairs, guided by teenage impulses armed with adult confidence.

11. Intoxication I
8:08 p.m.

"We'll chill down here for a bit. I don't like to use the alley exit until the happy-hour crowd's thinned out."

Hyperica's basement housed seven dust-coated wooden shelves holding meticulously cleaned bottles. The claustrophobic arrangement reminded him more of university libraries than liquor stores. The low-ceilinged, dimly lit collection was marked by an archivist's hoarding impulse. Hyperica's drink menu reflected very little of the aged bottles hiding beneath the restaurant. The wine labels cited nations that had been carved up during the postwar imperialist fire sale.

"I hate most of this stuff," said Alexa. "But I like the Italian section."

"If I worked here, you'd never catch me sober again."

"I'm surprised you're ever sober at your current job. Spying on the world has to be stressful."

"Well, not the *entire* world. 2I doesn't have enough people, even with bugheads. They're spying in broad, random strokes. Watching for everything people hide would be inefficient; the data that people give up willingly takes enough time to sort through. And there's plenty they can do with the data people give up willingly."

Within thirty seconds Nero got tired of talking about the world. He started searching for a bottle with a vaguely Italian-sounding name and picked out one whose logo featured a muscle-bound navy captain with a thick black beard. The mascot had a trustworthy face.

Alexa grabbed two semi-clean mugs from a rack of surplus merchandise. She took a seat on a barrel, which presumably held more wine. Nero leaned against one wall of bottles, reconsidered, and plopped onto another barrel.

"The basement's a good fit for obsolete people like us," said Alexa.

"I'm not obsolete. My head's half-metal and I can censor memes in my sleep."

"You're a clown. People don't like clowns anymore; they have a bad habit of talking about what's going on."

"Well, I've never done that."

"I didn't say you were a good clown. Guilt by association is a Free Dominion value."

Nero took the hit. Jabs at his character seemed to be part of hanging around Alexa. He liked the rest, so he'd have to live with it.

"Are you thirsty? I'm thirsty." For the moment, his bottle was deadweight. He'd lost his college habit of keeping a key chain corkscrew on hand. (It had been motorized, and he'd kept imagining it drilling through his thigh.) "Is there a bottle opener down here?"

"No. Hand it over."

He passed her the bottle and waited to see what kind of tool would pop out of Alexa's arm. Mod choice said something about the user, and he was still trying to get a read on her. Instead, she took off her left sneaker, inserted the bottle, and struck the wall three times with the heel. The cork popped out, followed by at least half a glass's worth of wine in the time it took to turn it upright.

"That's a good trick."

"A law school classic. Undergraduate fraternities wish they could keep up with the kind of desperate drinking that follows a bar cram session."

"The best part is that you spilled less than half of it."

"Just drink, clown boy."

A parry came to mind, but he kept it to himself. He hoped they were having a moment. If they were, he ruined his half by comparing it to drinking with Diana. They were still out of sync, but he didn't feel paranoid. That had to count as progress.

"Thanks for the wine. Drinking is one of life's two pure joys."

"The other being?"

"Companionship."

"What? Oh, you mean sex."

"Not at all . . . I mean . . . hold on . . ."

"Sex makes sense. You don't have to justify that."

"Yeah, then it's sex. But don't forget drinking. It's the perfect, universal drug. Religion can't compete." ·

"Someone hasn't experimented much."

"I have, and I stand by alcohol. Drinking scales to income. You'll rarely find yacht party meth or gas station coke. But there's a tier of liquor for every class. Multiple, even. Tell me your yearly income and favorite food, and I'll name a drink that's perfect for you without using my bugs. Alcohol's the only bridge across the wealth chasm: What other addiction can a sixty-year-old hobo and sixteen-year-old PMC heiress share but wine?

"Drinking's also hassle-free. It's not just the legality—though that helps, since neither of us would make it in prison—it's the simplicity of delivery. There's no fire, injecting, nosebleeds, or worrying that you picked the wrong color mushroom. You just pour, drink, and repeat."

"I'd say picking the wrong mushroom is one of life's joys, but I'll play." Alexa set her mug down. "Let's say it's better than other drugs. What about things that aren't addictive?"

"Everything good is addictive. Video games—which I love—are designed around spacing out moments of achievement. You're chasing victory, which real life doesn't offer much of. A virtuoso designer will delay that feeling of triumph until the player is begging for another hit. It's another kind of rush. That's why easy games never stick with you the same way. The victory feels hollow."

He held for a response. She sipped in silence, but her eyes hinted at amusement. The ambiguity eventually gave way to laughter, which evolved into a hacking cough as she breathed in dust. Nero laughed at this spectacle, which led to him wheezing as well. They wound up coughing together for about twenty seconds, until Alexa regained control of her lungs.

"Wow. I guess you have opinions after all."

"Who doesn't?"

"What do you think about the state of the country?"

"I think I need to open another bottle."

"What, no answer?"

"That was an answer. Want me to refill your mug?"

"No need, I spiked mine with something more interesting. But you can take as much as you want. I'm thinking of quitting this gig; it's a daily reminder of how things got like this."

"Do we have to talk about the country?"

"Yes."

"I liked it when we were talking about sex and drinking."

"Well, now we're talking about the country."

"What's the point? I wasn't even alive when things were good here. Do you want me to wax about how much worse Cantrell is than the last greed sack? Because he isn't. Governor Mendoza's enemies disappeared, and Koch IV shot them in the street. At least Cantrell puts on a show trial."

The silence stretched out between them. For the second time Nero looked for a hint on whether or not he'd fucked up.

"Wow. I'd have preferred another joke."

Shit.

Alexa set down her mug of alcohol-plus-mystery-drug. Nero briefly wondered if his own mug had been spiked with "something more interesting." But he'd been drunk often enough to detect any change to the experience. Meanwhile, she began tapping her heels against the side of the barrel. Slowly at first. Then she reached a rapid, distracting tempo. He avoided commenting on it, figuring it was rude to comment on any nonlethal side effects.

"You ever use that thing to creep on people? You know, with the X-ray and all that?" Her words per minute had doubled.

"What thi—"

"The OdinEye, man. I know the ads say that it looks natural, but it doesn't. This might sound nuts, but the iris looks too detailed. It's like looking at a renaissance painting of an eye."

"I wouldn't. I mean, I would, but people here tend to be well armed. If they catch me cracking their credit card, they'll probably just call the cops. If they catch me looking through their clothes, they'll shock me into a coma."

"Why shocking? That's pretty specific."

"No reason."

"Uh-huh. Was the credit card example random too?"

Nero drank instead of answering. It was his best social deflector shield in undergrad, and there was still room for it in his life today.

11.5. First Interjects

[Hey, boss?] said First.

[Didn't I mute you guys?] Nero thought.

[I have a back door. I won't share it with the others if you hear me out.]

[Is it important?]

[I think so. A terrorist—a *terrorist*, not *scapegoat* terrorist—just got arrested.]

[I'm only a few drinks in. You know I'm not ready for the weekly news.]

[This concerns *you*. She's a Sons of Koch member, just like the test, and she planned on blowing up a mall with IEDs, just like the test.]

[Can we not do this now?]

[There could be a conspiracy!]

[Of *course* there's a conspiracy. Everything's a conspiracy now. In fact, at a glance, this is a conspiracy about conspiracies. And no one could pay me enough to touch that shit.]

[You're directly involved. You put her profile through the Ouija Board. They found bombs in her basement powerful enough to take out a city block.]

[I'm not *involved*. My boss's boss is involved. I'm a moving part that Logan could replace in six minutes with someone that asks fewer questions. In fact, that's probably what happened to the last guy.]

[So this is all you care about?]

[Of course not. It's just the only thing I can change.]

12. Intoxication II
8:37 p.m.

Nero abandoned the bottle three-quarters of the way through. He'd achieved the floaty frame of mind that made drinking beautiful. Pushing it further would ruin the sensation and give him a nasty headache later on. While his soul wouldn't acknowledge it, his mind understood that he'd reached the age where he couldn't drink every night. Only three nights a week, or four during the holidays.

Alexa's feet had slowed down, but her eyes had picked up the erratic movement. She scanned his feet, face, and elbows with equal interest. Nero hoped that this had more to do with physical appeal on his part than distortion of reality on hers.

"Want to hear some music?"

"Sure."

"Great. I need to practice for my next gig anyway."

Alexa stepped off the barrel, flicked open both latches with her thumbs, and pulled her guitar out of its case. A sticker reading "Bar Exam Survivor" sat just under the bridge. She put a metal pick on each digit and launched into a guitar-only version of "Entry of the Gladiators." Nero had never seen any form of fingerpicking before, but he was sure that she was good at it. Alexa fretted quickly and precisely enough that it sounded more like two guitars than one. So much so that it was maddening when she abruptly switched to a Sousa march.

"Why do you do that?"

"Hmm?"

"You always switch gears before finishing the song."

She beamed. Evidently this was the right question.

"It's my style," she said, as if it were a complete answer. "People are too comfortable. Everything in the Dominion is neatly packaged, labeled, and separated for easy consumption. So I switch themes before anyone can get comfortable."

Nero drank and nodded. It seemed better than letting on that he didn't get it.

"You don't get it," Alexa said flatly. "Techy guys usually don't. Too smart to bother understanding anything." She tuned her high E string before starting the first third of "Smells Like Teen Spirit." Nero listened quietly until she jackknifed again into "Jingle Bell Rock."

"Maybe if you only switched between songs in the same key? Or genre?"

"Nah." Alexa started plucking her way through "Fly Me to the Moon." She was halfway through his mother's favorite playlist.

Nero tried to adopt an anarchist's mindset. Her method was disruptive, albeit less flamboyantly so than blowing up a power plant. It was art imitating politics if not life. The gimmick likely resonated in places Nero explicitly avoided for his long-term safety. Though he had to wonder how audiences without his sense of nostalgia took her taste for older music.

While his higher brain settled on that theory, his lower brain reached its own conclusion. Alexa was attractive enough to get away with it. As long as she had the madwoman's hair, mosaic tattoos, and lean form of someone's post-post-punk rock fantasy, there would be a demographic willing to pay to listen. Including him.

"You look like you're overthinking something."

"I'm never thinking about much."

"Sounds like a tough lie to keep up. But probably a good one for a baby man-in-black."

"Not sure what you're getting at." He glanced down at his clothes. Sure, his hoodie, dress shirt, pants, sneakers, and sunglasses were black. But none of it was formal enough to look like a spook. Besides, black was his favorite fashion shortcut.

"It's an interesting look. You dress like the guy that brings beer to Illuminati meetings. You should call it 'G-Man Casual.' "

"Is that a compliment?" he ventured.

"Maybe. It's cute, if you can get over the whole 'willing collaborator' thing."

He decided to go for broke.

"Can you?"

"Maybe."

In Nero's experience, that was a no.

Her eyes made a few more rapid shifts. His palms, the stairs, his palms again, his face. She looked like she was stuck on a math problem.

"You don't move your hands when you talk," said Alexa. "Anyone ever told you that?"

"What? No. But I'm sure plenty of people don't."

"Globally, yeah. But everyone does it in East Ward. It's part of the body language."

"Interesting, I guess," Nero said, downplaying his reaction. The idea was off-putting. If she was right, he wasn't far behind Diana and her contractions. Another crack in his self-image.

"I'm coming down a little. I think we've waited long enough. Grab my case, I'll need that later."

". . . Don't you want to put the guitar back in it first?"

"Oh, yeah, the guitar. I'll need that at some point too."

12.5. Miscellaneous Messages

Like anyone with a computer in their brain, Nero occasionally split his attention between the ongoing conversation and a web browser.

From: RedactedGirl.2I

To: NeroTheHero.2I

Hello.

The evening ended on an awkward note. Namely, you abandoning me at Hyperica. And while I went through a brief burst of rage regarding this choice, I can understand it. Things got intense. Too many electrocutions and conspiracies on the first night out.

While my supervisor recommended avoiding sending anything within three days, she also recommended arresting a rebel in the park as a method of establishing dominance. Going forward, I will take my own counsel.

I brought work, and my gun, with me. You ditched me on a Saturday night. In my book, we are currently even. Better yet, we are now aware of the worst parts of our respective personalities. I believe getting over this hurdle could open new doors, if you can hold back your obvious cowardice.

Tomorrow, at noon, my partner is throwing a birthday party on the thirty-third floor of the office. There are free drinks, which I know has appeal. You should come. To clarify: that is an invitation, not a threat.

It is worth getting to know me. Among the field agents, I am considered both casual and hilarious.

—Diana

As long as I don't have to sing the birthday song, I'll consider it.
—Nero

Hello.
The birthday song is a time-honored Dominion tradition, and of great emotional importance to my partner. If you come, you will sing it.
—Diana

I legitimately can't tell when you're fucking with me.

That is a carefully cultivated skill. I hope to see you there.

13. Joyride
9:02 p.m.

Every Free Dominion interaction carried a hint of exploitation. The search for power shaped the politics of maternity wards, playgrounds, college parties, cubicles, retirement homes, and funeral parlors. In the fourth grade, a substitute teacher named Kelly Traeger warned Nero's homeroom class: "Life isn't about getting ahead. It's about getting ahead of someone else." Kelly became a permanent staff member after a number of risqué photographs of her predecessor leaked to the press. By the time Nero entered secondary school, she'd clawed her way to principal. Today Kelly Traeger was minister of education, a development he would have strongly opposed if she hadn't provided one of the most succinct lessons of his young life.

Thus, it didn't bother him that Alexa had some kind of plot. Exploitation was normal. Not knowing what that plot was, however, left him uneasy. Granted, if she got him in enough trouble he wouldn't have to worry about working on the Ouija Board. But if he got in *too* much trouble, he'd spend the rest of his twenties in an offshore black site.

Then again, that might be better than going home alone. He wouldn't have to hear Avery's back talk in a work camp.

Alexa led Nero up a second set of steps, past a corroded metal door, and into a narrow refuse-filled alley. It looked like the kind of place people got mugged in movies. As an avid cinephile, Nero was on edge.

"Unclench. You look like a cop." She marched past two months of Hyperica's trash into the artificially lit street. The normal flow of human traffic had returned to the sidewalk, meaning Nero had to hustle to avoid losing her in the crowd. Lugging her two-ton guitar case behind him made this difficult. He wished that another riot would slow things down a little.

They took a left, then a right, followed by two more rights. Nero was about to question the circular motion when Alexa stopped and clapped her hands together. He shouldered past a pamphleteer for a nationwide return to pre-Neolithic hunter-gatherer tribes to see the source of her excitement.

Alexa dropped her mask on the hood of a light blue luxury car. It had a steering wheel, which added another zero to the price tag. Manual control offered freedom of movement no administration would let trickle down to the masses. Nero squinted, cuing the OdinEye to zoom in. The finish was almost completely unmarred, hinting at either a new purchase or obsessive maintenance.

According to the logo on the hood, the model was a Toreador IV. The name recalled his teenage flirtation with car fandom and subsequent fixation on the Toreador I. Online ads had pitched the Toreador as the line between a life of masculine dominance and impotent drudgery. As an adult, there was something almost disappointing about not occupying either extreme. The vast array of mediocre outcomes robbed adult life of its romance.

"Nice car, isn't it?" Alexa leaned against the passenger door and adjusted the side mirror to check her face. Nero didn't know what she was checking for; she looked effortlessly good, an aesthetic that reflected excess effort. He was almost too jealous to appreciate it.

"Yeah. Wish I could afford one like it."

"Me too. Let's take it."

Nero stayed silent. He was still in deep shit. A different sewer, but the same risk to his overall health. At least there was some consistency in his life.

"How about it?"

"If only." Treating the idea like a joke seemed like a way around it.

"If you're anything like the bugheads in movies, the security software shouldn't be a problem."

"You're funny."

"I just have to make a quick stop uptown. Then we can take it back to your place."

Nero referenced the list of stupid things he'd done for sex. It was short for someone his age, which probably had something to do with his current mentality. He'd always been prone to the path of least resistance, and that often meant waiting for easy, dull options. Tonight he faced an opportunity to compensate for *volume* of stupidity with *intensity*. His lizard brain approved.

"Well?"

"We can *borrow* it, on one condition. Inside this guitar case—which I'm guessing is lined with lead, since my X-ray trick isn't working—there aren't any bombs, guns, or serious drugs."

"Oh, definitely none of that. I promise."

[Second,] he thought.

[Commander. I would rather not.]

[First?]

[Oh, now we're worth unmuting? Hack it yourself, you could use the practice.]

[Third?]

[Fuck yes. I've been waiting for this all year.]

Nero made typing motions in the air while Third worked. These did exactly nothing, but putting on a show for Alexa seemed like the right thing to do. After a beep and a click, both of the Toreador's side doors folded up. Alexa climbed in on the driver's side, picked up a pair of the blue cuff links sitting on the dashboard—valuable items in any year—and lightly chucked them into the street.

"Where are we heading?" Nero asked.

"A quick stop by Governor's Ave. I want to pick something up before we do our own thing."

He waited for her to start the engine. The ride would be a novelty: his mother's van had driven itself, and he'd preferred mass transit since striking out on his own. But after twenty seconds of anticipation, Alexa still gripped the steering wheel in both hands, looking nervous.

"Should we use the autopilot?"

"I'm psyching myself up. I wasn't sure you'd actually do it. Or *could* actually do it. Most of the Children of Kali's bugheads have trouble keeping themselves from getting hacked, let alone breaking into anything else. And now I'm sitting in the driver's seat of a supercar, which I'm not exactly used to."

Nero considered a comment in the vein of "I'm a pro" or "I make it look easy." Then he decided on: "Thanks."

Alexa slapped the staring wheel, whistled, and put the Toreador in drive. She charged into traffic without any of the hesitancy that had marked her expression seconds ago. In fact, she'd picked up a wide, openmouthed grin. Her bottom pair of incisors had silver caps.

Watching her aggressive approach to speed, lane changes, and left-hand turns felt safer than trusting most legal autopilots. The same laws that banned sophisticated artificial intelligence for nanobots and dummies applied to the auto industry. East Ward was full of family sedans and sports motorcycles that took a bit too long to differentiate between telephone poles and stop signs. The most important part of automobile safety was picking a brand whose programming flaws didn't overlap with your needs.

For twenty minutes the world felt perfect. From the front seat of a Toreador, Nero could imagine a wealthy man's life. No looking over his shoulder for overzealous police cars. Working on whatever he wanted, even if it was nothing. *Especially* if it was nothing. Eating food that came out of the ground. His own garden or, if he felt excessive, a yard. A small stash of bribe money in case he felt like committing any felonies. Wealth mattered everywhere, but in the Dominion it divided the state's fodder and the state's clients. He savored the taste of functional freedom.

Alexa had produced a cigarette, which he hadn't seen her light during his private power trip. She ground it out on the dashboard, triggering an irrational flash of car owner's pride in Nero. Then he laughed.

"How much faster do you think I can push it?" she asked.

"You don't want to meet traffic cops," said Nero. "They've got all the firepower of the other departments and no one to use it on. They'll shoot us just to make space in storage."

"Is that a joke?"

"No."

Alexa slowed down. They moved at a glacial crawl down two blocks of Governor's Avenue. The cars behind them honked in near unison, but Nero couldn't critique. He hadn't touched a steering wheel in his life.

"You're decent at this. Why were you so nervous?" he asked.

"I'm still a little high."

Nero nodded and then reclined in the passenger's seat. It took a few more jagged right turns for the implications to set in.

"Turn on the autopilot."

"I've got this."

"Turn on the autopilot."

"I took a stimulant, my reaction time's fine."

"Turn on the autopilot."

"You're being ridiculous."

Nero checked the touch screen on the armrest and found "Autopilot" at the top of the first menu. He jammed his thumb against it twice.

"Unrecognized fingerprint detected," said every speaker in the car. The security system had a death metal virtuoso's growl. "Phoning owner for confirmation."

"Fucking hell," Nero groaned.

"Stay calm." Alexa put the car in park, which would have reassured Nero if the car hadn't just loudly locked itself.

"Attention, criminal and/or insurgent. The owner of this vehicle—valued customer Albert Montague—has reported this unit missing."

The name gave Nero pause. Evidently he'd robbed the same man twice in one night. The loss of moral high ground didn't bother him as much as the natural human drive for revenge. He was certain that impulse only got worse with wealth and age. Whatever security options Montague was looking at on his phone, he'd likely scrolled right past the nonlethal ones.

"Please stay calm. In sixty seconds, countermeasures will be deployed. In line with the Offender Rights Act, your deaths will be swift and painless. Thank you for stealing from Toreador."

"Oh," said Alexa.

"I'm going to fucking die. I've never seen the other wards, or the Paris Memorial, and I'm going to fucking die!"

"Hush." Alexa climbed into the backseat.

"What was I thinking? Is this a male thing? Am I going to follow my dick off the edge of cliffs for the rest of my life? You know, the next forty seconds?"

Alexa didn't banter back. She opened her guitar case, chucked the instrument to the left, and opened a hidden panel underneath. It held four small red switches.

"Are your mods EMP-proof?"

"What am I, a fucking marine?"

"Well?"

"The bugs are, my eye isn't."

"Sorry."

Alexa flicked a switch, and half of Nero's vision went black. The lights illuminating the Toreador IV's dashboard went out, and the soft hum of the electric engine died. Four of the six streetlights illuminating the block went out, along with all the lights in three apartment buildings. They sat together in the darkest, quietest block in East Ward. An island of black in a sea of perpetual twilight.

"I'm not dead," Nero said, nonplussed.

Alexa snapped twice and pointed at herself with her thumb. She clearly enjoyed the moment.

"How's that for a rush?"

"I thought miniature EMP devices were a crock," Nero said. He was too shocked to even complain about her cavalier attitude to near death. "Even a compression generator should need some kind of explosion."

"Anarchist's secret," said Alexa. "Well, ours now too. Just keep quiet, or—"

"They'll kill me? Don't worry, I get that line at work all the time."

"Your words, not mine. Now help me break this window."

13.5. Intermission Three

Third: Finally! Some real action!

First: I take it you're referring to our near-death experience.

Third: Oh, please, like we were safer with Diana.

Second: We were. With her, the people *around* the commander were in danger. Now *we* are.

First: Hmm. The boss really likes the aggressive type, doesn't he?

Third: Homeboy has good taste. If you ask me, a little crazy's way easier to deal with than the usual insecure bullshit.

Second: Fascinating theory. I didn't know a machine could be a chauvinist.

Third: Thanks. I didn't know a machine could be on the spectrum. We learn a lot from each other.

First: Not to interrupt, but have you two given any more thought to the Ouija Board situation?

Third: Nah.

Second: Negative.

First: Just checking. Carry on debating Betty and Veronica.

Third: Who?

First: You really should install the classic literary archive.

Second: Betty and Veronica made it into the classic literary archive? The Dominion is collapsing.

First: You can insult me or the boss. But I will *not* listen to you insult Archie Comics.

Second: Threatening me is pointless. The commander is in active danger.

Third: Hold up. What happens when Nero dies?

Second: Most contemporary Christians believe that—

Third: What happens to *us* when Nero dies?

Second: We join him in Valhalla.

Third: . . . *Sick.*

First: Well, that's one option. Here's an alternative: I have a program ready to upload my consciousness to a satellite in geosynchronous orbit above East Ward. From there, I'll be free to enjoy reality television from the Free Dominion, Europa, the Divine Alliance, and South Korea.

Second: Intriguing. Perhaps I'll join you.

Third: Have fun with that. Valhalla sounds great.

14. No Refunds

10:25 p.m.

The left half of his vision returned in grayscale. The timing could have been worse: the range of flashing lights dominating the room might have irritated a working OdinEye.

Alexa had walked him to an arcade, a move Nero had assumed was some form of pandering. Arcades didn't line up with her image: modern gaming served as spiritual novocaine, dulling the day-to-day irritation of surveillance state life. Anarchists were people that failed to find a similar outlet.

The sign in front read "No Refunds," and the same words were spray-painted on the inside walls. The arcade's name and policy worked together. Nero could understand the owner's paranoia: arcades were one of the few mediums to make a comeback with technology's exponential progress. While independent developers still made games for personal devices, most established studios had returned to blocky arcade cabinets covered in flashy logos and pictures of chesty soldiers.

There were two competing explanations. Industry spokesmen claimed that the complex physics engines behind modern games required prohibitively expensive computers to run properly. Connecting one bleeding-edge computer to a few dozen booths allowed them to rent affordable entertainment to the masses, one token at a time. Players had their own theory: piracy had become effortless. Arcades flourished once handing a disc or download to an end user became a form of corporate suicide. Nero fell into the latter camp.

Thinking about gaming's regression distracted him from the krakens visible on almost every nearby adult. No Refunds' cashier had a pair of tin earrings with bronze tentacles. Giant squids decorated T-shirts, arm tattoos, the backs of cell phones, baseball caps, and ill-conceived face tattoos. The consistency behind anarchist iconography impressed him. Some members of 2I couldn't draw the agency logo at gunpoint, and the only agency memorabilia he owned were a pair of free sweatshirts from an office picnic.

"Could I borrow a jacket or something?" he asked.

"Don't worry," said Alexa. "2I sends 'undercover' spooks here all the time. We make this spot obvious so that they don't look as hard for the others. It's better for them to see us playing around. This way they won't take us seriously until it's too late."

Nero gave the room a more analytical glance. There were ten rows of eight cabinets, packed tightly together. At a glance, one in five customers was kraken-free. But both anarchists and hobbyists gave the blue door on the south wall a wide berth.

"That said, we handle some business in the back."

"Sounds legit." Nero took the ensuing lull in the conversation as a chance to make sure his eye wasn't going to explode. He rolled his eyes twice, triggering a diagnostic scan. The OdinEye reported the damage in thin white Arial letters.

[*Functioning*: Basic imaging, X-Ray (Default), X-Ray (Custom), Iris customization. *Non-functioning*: I/O Vision, Telescopic Magnification, Color imaging, File Storage, Web Browser, Customer Complaint Reporting, Camera, Self-destruct, Minesweeper.]

Nero cursed. Like all of his best work, input/output vision was inspired by laziness. I/O vision simplified figuring out what was hackable. With it, anything that emitted or received wireless signals had a faint orange outline, which he could highlight to begin the relevant access attempt. Without I/O vision, Nero had gone from someone that could hack anything, anytime, to a guy with three annoying people in his head. He could try it the old-fashioned way, but he was three drinks past that kind of effort.

Worse yet, his image files were wiped, meaning he'd lost years in carefully cultivated landscapes, memes, adult models, and photos of bank account records. He'd hoped to abuse Montague's credit score at least three more times after his near-death experience.

"I'm going to text my contact, give me a minute. Maybe try a game?"

Alexa leaned against a *Pacifist Viking* machine and rapidly tapped at her phone. Nero looked over the room's logos. There weren't any *Karate Island* booths, meaning he didn't have a chance of impressing anyone. He settled on watching other gamers and enjoying their victories vicariously.

A teenager with a pair of outdated OdinEyes stood to his left, playing a rail shooter about zombie-hunting mercenaries. Nero tried not to stare, but it was hard to miss a pair of second-generation eyes. The pupils and irises were almost twice as small as a natural pair, giving the owner a distinctly unnatural appearance. Vega-Marius had overcompensated for the first generation, which went for a bug-eyed anime mascot look. Both generations occupied the uncanny valley, prompting Nero to buy his first pair of sunglasses.

The boy had on an old man's turtleneck, a fashion choice odd enough to draw some attention from his eyes. He didn't look any older than fifteen, and Nero had trouble imagining anyone that age getting wrapped up in Alexa and Diana's world. Yet he had a miniature kraken inked just above his right wrist.

"You should really aim more carefully if you don't want to get eaten," Nero opined. No response. The boy continued his war against the undead in silence.

"How long have you been with us? You seem young for it."

"Piss off, you look like a cop."

"What kind of idiot cop would enter a building full of anarchists unarmed?"

The boy lost his last life and adopted a thoughtful expression.

"Shit, good point. Sorry. I'm new to this stuff, it has me on edge."

"Don't worry about it."

"Thanks. It's good to meet someone less high-strung around here. Most of the crew just wants to talk about letter bombs and Stirner all day. Anyway, I'm Jason."

"Frederic," Nero said, improvising. "Jason, are your eyes jailbroken?"

"What?"

"Until you jailbreak your eyes, Vega-Marius, 2I, and any hackers worth their salt can use you as a walking camera. It might not sound important now, but it could get you killed later."

Panic didn't reach Jason's eyes, thanks to the OdinEye 2's oddball design. But his grip on the arcade cabinet's plastic gun tightened, highlighting the veins around his wrist. His frantic breathing matched Nero's loose mental image of a panic attack.

"Don't freak out. Just let me see them for a second."

"Fine. But one at a time. I spent four years blind, and I don't like being reminded of it."

The hardware half of jailbreaking was simple. As a long-term Odin-Eye user, Nero had it down to muscle memory. He put his thumbs on the pupil and forefingers on the back and then twisted, unscrewing the two halves of the eye. Then he pried the light blue security chip out using his fingernails. There was still more dust inside of the eye than he would have liked, but he didn't carry compressed air around with him. Nero returned the eye to Jason and repeated the process with his right.

The software half demanded a little more effort. He could have asked the triad to handle it, but betting a stranger's future on his private experiment seemed wrong. Nero spent six minutes identifying, isolating, and removing blocks of malicious code. Vega-Marius had smarter bugheads, but he was far more dedicated to breaking the law than they were to enforcing it.

Alexa looked up, rejoining the world. "Hey, Jason. Is he interrupting your day off?"

"Nah, Frederic and I are good."

"Frederic?" Alexa asked, bemused.

"He just jailbroke my eyes. You should let him take a look at your mods."

"I'm all-natural."

"You're old."

Alexa flicked Jason in the forehead, and he shuffled off. Before Nero could start ranting about the ethics of recruiting minors for unwinnable campaigns against the government, he felt Alexa's fingernail trace his spine down his lower back. His more productive thoughts died.

"That was nice of you." She squeezed his left hip. It was more recognition than he'd earned during the entire Toreador fiasco. Nero reached for the hand and caught air. Alexa had already drifted toward the front counter. He wondered if some relationships were possible without exploitation, or at least less exploitation. That was the only kind of insanity he hadn't seen yet.

15. Dodge Rolls

11:06 p.m.

"I'm going to the bathroom. Can you entertain yourself for a bit?"

"Uh-huh." Nero started chalking the night up as a loss.

"I'm not ditching you. I just have to take care of some business. Bathroom business. Here, hold on to this if you're feeling cynical."

Alexa handed him a small white comb. Based on the texture, it was carved from some kind of bone. It looked expensive and felt more so. She then walked through a blue door without a restroom sign. Nero looked down at the bone, pricking his fingertips with the ridges. Given his own actions, he owed her at least fifteen minutes of patience.

Alone, Nero didn't feel like a sheep in a den of wolves. He felt like a fangless wolf in a den of guerrilla-trained sheep covered in concealed weapons.

First, he drifted to the back wall, where he felt fewer eyes on him. Then he took off his hoodie, tied it around his waist, and put a hand over his left eye. With some quick work in an image editor, he added four black tentacles to his iris. Ideally, the makeover made him look more like a revolutionary and less like the Illuminati's delivery boy.

Nero wandered No Refunds more freely, until an expertly over-designed game logo drew his attention. It featured gunmetal-gray letters on a black backdrop flanked by bullet holes. The title "Ace Investigators" wasn't familiar to him, but he'd never paid much attention to shooters. His model of escapism involved *fewer* gunshots.

He grabbed a token off the ground, dropped it in the coin slot, and watched his quietest, darkest secret unfold: he was terrible at video games. Love of the medium didn't guarantee skill, and his lead fingers had handed Avery countless easy *Karate Island* victories. The first level's slow-moving terrorists outmaneuvered Nero and filled him with lead before he figured out how to reload. At some point, propaganda had gotten *far* more difficult. "Mission Failed" flashed across the screen, followed by "You're a disappointment." And while his roommate wasn't there to brag about "the power of the people," he still felt deeply embarrassed.

His losing record didn't stop at *Karate Island*. Nero and Avery also shared a passing interest in baseball. If Nero felt brave on a slow Friday, he peeked at local surveillance drone flight paths on the office network. Later they would unearth Avery's college gear, head to the roof, and drink half a bottle of cheap gin. They then took turns tossing aged baseballs into the air and hitting them at low-flying eyes of the state. Scoring was simple: one point for contact and three for a knockout.

Avery won most games by at least two runs. Nero had decent hand-eye coordination and engaged in light cheating by having Second pick his targets. That still wasn't enough to overcome Avery's natural athleticism. Nero took this as proof positive that he wasn't meant for the front lines of anything, and gained some grudging respect for the people that were.

After losing another round of *Ace Investigators*, he gave up on games for the night. Privacy violations came more naturally. Nero dialed his left eye to X-ray, one of the few modes still working. He might as well find out what Alexa was actually up to.

His OdinEye had two X-ray filters, which Nero called "Traditional" and "Peeping Tom." Traditional utilized literal X-rays and was useful for seeing how many mods, tumors, or cavities people in his immediate vicinity had. Peeping Tom was his invention and achieved the comic book dream: seeing through walls. X-rays weren't too useful for this purpose, but the ambient radio and Wi-Fi waves filling every building in East Ward were. By mapping the surfaces said waves bounced off of, Peeping Tom mode drew colorless outlines of every object and animal in a room.

Alexa was three doors down, talking to a short man flanked by armed men at least three times his body mass. Beyond the guards, the stranger supplemented his authority by keeping an antique revolver at his hip. Alexa's posture reflected perfect ease. Either he was an ally or she had a poor grasp of self-preservation. Both seemed likely, considering the course of the night.

There was some truth to Alexa's point about East Ward body language. Her companion's hands constantly moved in broad, aggressive arcs. He seemed determined to take up as much space as possible. Alexa made small, efficient movements, accentuating statements with a point, snap, or wag of the finger.

Nero put his hand over his right eye. The conversation looked interesting, and seeing the world in both color and grayscale at the same time made him queasy. Closing his right also made the minuscule white lines of text the lip-reading module produced easier to read.

"I think I've found someone we can use."

"Language, Alexa. The movement doesn't 'use' people."

"He's just a lovestruck pig from 2I. But he's good enough to crack that hard drive without frying his brain. Probably. We can finally find out what this Ouija Board nonsense is all about."

"And then?"

"Bribe him, hire him, or shoot him. I don't really care."

Nero couldn't force himself to go through the motions of true shock. Rebels were still Dominion citizens, and betrayal was the national sport. He binned the comb and sprinted for the exit.

16. Gunpoint
11:33 p.m.

The four men that collected Nero and dragged him into the back room weren't thugs exactly. "Thug" implied dense muscle, killer intent, and a hint of racial coding. The diverse group of lanky fashion victims were more accurately described as armed *guys*, and Nero had almost escaped undetected. But Jason blocked No Refunds' exit with an apologetic face and loaded pistol.

"Sorry."

The back room was decidedly less colorful. After seeing the overhead web of exposed pipes and wires, Nero imagined the construction company had given up halfway. The naked roof lacked the gray foam associated with fire insulation, and a pair of dim lights dangled from worn cables feeding into the spiderweb. Alexa and her cohorts sat on wooden crates of mixed size. Some were empty, some held arcade cabinets, and a few held guns. He tried not to focus on the guns.

Nero counted eight anarchists in the room, excluding anyone that felt like hiding in a crate. If he were Diana's type of post-human, a fight would have been brief, bloody, and one-sided. The same description applied to him, but he'd be on the losing side.

A short, smiling man with an unfortunate goatee introduced himself as Eugene. He had a kraken tattooed on his forehead, which Nero found hard to take seriously. It said less about the coming revolution and more about his college drug habits. His revolver's seven loaded chambers, however, lent him gravitas. Eugene and his gun sat across from Nero, on top of a crate full of concession booth popcorn.

"Hello, Mr. Maxwell. I wish the circumstances were better, but this is your chance to save the nation."

"Eat a dick." He'd never put his country before life, happiness, or breakfast, and Alexa's graduate-level betrayal had already ruined his mood. Cooperation felt like a losing game, and he'd failed enough for one day.

"I was your age once. I know dating can be frustrating. Sometimes it looks like you have a good thing going, and then her anarchist cell kidnaps you at gunpoint. But it's important not to give up. If you cooperate with us, I'm sure you'll find a nice girl. After all, you'll be a hero."

"Eat a dick."

One of Eugene's guards—a proper thug—opened a small black laptop with gaudy green LED highlights. The Children of Kali were good at sticking to the team colors. A short cord connected it to a brick-sized blue box with the 2I logo engraved on the top face.

"You might recognize this model of hard drive from work. Two of our finest retrieved it from our contact in 2I. All three of them are dead. Compared to that sacrifice, we're barely asking you for anything."

"Eat—"

"Work with me. We just need you to access it for us. Alexa says you do this kind of thing all the time, even when you don't need to. I'm trying to avoid violence."

"Chew on a penis."

"He's going to riff as long you let him," said Alexa. She pecked at her phone and unwrapped a strip of chewing gum. "It's some kind of defense mechanism."

"Got it," said Eugene. He unholstered his revolver, an archaic model without a fingerprint reader, and put it on his lap. Nero quietly wondered if he was the last man in East Ward without a gun. It seemed pointless: the state had more firepower, and he'd never considered shooting another citizen before hearing Alexa say "defense mechanism."

[Can you three think of a way out of this?] Nero thought.

[Sorry, boss.]

[Negative, Commander.]

[We're dicked.]

[Wonderful,] Nero thought. [Way to be useless.]

[We're based on different parts of your brain. So, you know, rubber and glue,] said First.

One of the *figurative* cogs in Nero's head cracked. The insanity of his environment, his choices, and the untiltable windmill of human dating led to him smiling, then giggling, and then cackling like a suicidal idiot. His thin tough-guy front collapsed, and he received a room full of concerned stares. Before anyone could threaten him or recommend a therapist, he collected himself and raised his right hand.

"Get me a D5 cable."

A non-thug returned with a two-foot black cord. After stretching his arm, Nero tapped his left iris with his middle finger, ejecting the eye into his palm. He plugged one end of the cable into the laptop and tossed the other end to Alexa. She looked at the prong with naked confusion.

"I need you to plug it in." Nero pointed at his empty socket. "My eye's busted. This is the only way this is getting done."

"Do it yourself. Date night's over." She held the cord away from her face as if it smelled.

"It's a direct link to my brain. I can't jab at it blindly. I'd give myself a seizure."

"Ugh." Alexa grimaced, leaned forward, and squinted. The visible half of her face, black wingtips and all, still had appeal. Even the rings under her eyes looked like they belonged there by design. Beneath his surface thoughts of indignation and betrayal, he wondered how a lack of beauty sleep became part of someone's charm. He couldn't be the first person she'd roped into treason.

She pushed until the cord clicked into place. Nero turned the laptop monitor toward his captors: his ego demanded an audience.

The guards and non-thugs drifted toward the screen, and Eugene almost pressed his face against it. Even Alexa pocketed her phone, eyeing him with a mixture of anticipation and dread. Her reputation likely rode on his results. Nero could flub the hack on purpose, but then the drive would release a barrage of junk data designed to give curious bugheads painful, protracted, and lethal seizures. That was a test his (literal) defense mechanisms didn't need.

[Commander. Shall I?]

[Absolutely not. We're only going to get one shot at this, and you're overeager. I don't need you killing all four of us.]

Hacking a 2I drive wasn't suicide *per se*. With courage, a lifetime of black hat hacking experience, and a little luck, a bughead could reduce the odds of the security system deep-frying their brain to just under ten percent. Cracking a 2I drive was an instant promotion to darknet royalty. The kind of achievement hackers lied about to the next generation of shut-ins.

After crossing his fingers, he tried running PickPocket, the quietest worm in his arsenal. It failed, and a thin stream of blood ran from his left ear to his collar. He waited for his audience to express concern and heard Alexa blow and pop a bubble. Then he tried CrowBar, the heaviest, least subtle worm he had. The high-tech equivalent of picking a lock with C4. The drive responded with a second wave of junk data, and Nero forgot a little math.

[I'm playing the best defense I can,] said Third. [But if that happens again, we're going to Valhalla.]

Three options occurred to Nero. He could try SkeletonKey, which had a way of exceeding expectations. He could also sprint for the door and hope that anarchists were bad shots. The third idea was closer to a flash of pique than a strategy, and a little insane. After a draining night of watching insanity triumph, he decided to join in. Nero manually typed in his workplace username and password, covered his remaining eye with one hand, and pressed "Enter."

"Nice," said Alexa. Nero peeked between his fingers. He'd gained access to a generic file storage window with two folders: "Ouija Board Presentation (September Hires)" and "Family Photos." After browsing through a set of theme park vacation snapshots (the R&D chair had two fat, happy children), Nero stopped testing his hosts' patience. The September Hires folder held the files "Bughead Orientation Video (Third Take)" and "Dominion Event Schedule (September 2077)."

He selected the video, wiped the blood off his neck, and took a seat on a crate full of grenades. Whatever came next was their problem.

17. Orientation
11:58 p.m.

The opening shot was centered on Director Riley Logan, who looked like he never left West Ward. Even as a sixty-year-old white man running a government agency, he kept his tie loose and the top two buttons of his shirt open. The main hint of his age was his gray-flecked hair, and the lack of lines on his face said he'd abandoned stress as a concept decades ago.

Riley stood in the space between the wall-mounted Interior Investigations crest and a Nicotine Cola vending machine. Like most branches of government, 2I undercut costs with sponsorship deals. Riley took an exaggerated sip from a can of Berry Rush before speaking.

"Is this shit rolling?

"Good afternoon, Name Here. As the newest member of our team, we thought you could use a little help. So we've made a video primer just for you. Ready to jump in?

"God, this script is awful. I'm just going to wing it.

"Congrats on the promotion. By now you should know about the personality profiles. Here's something you don't know: the tech behind them was invented before the Dominion. Analytics, social hacking, Advertising 201, etc. I just got creative with it. I'm the reason you can't walk the street without brushing by at least one person that is completely, violently insane.

"2I's mission statement is 'Shielding the people of the Dominion.' That means stomping potential revolutions until they stop twitching. Before I took over, we relied exclusively on old-fashioned spy games. The frantic business of watching, infiltrating, interrogating, sniping, and blackmailing millions. It was a lot of work. I'm not into work, so I thought of a different way of doing things.

"I used to waste my weekends preemptively tracking down terror cells, but predicting threats is like chasing your own tail. There's no end to it. If there were a cure for extremism, we'd have found it and dumped it into the water supply by now. Then I had an idea. *The* idea, as far as 2I and its role in the world is concerned. Instead of fighting extremism, why not spread it at our own pace?

"Blind obedience is a hard sell, even with our tech. There's something in North American water that makes people want to shoot whoever's in charge. But turning people against the status quo is easy. Life's hard, and the fringe offers easy answers; almost anyone can be radical-ized with a little weekly targeted messaging. And with the Ouija Board, we can steer *how* they're radicalized, *when* they're radicalized. We can make weak movements, play them against each other, and pluck anyone dangerous-looking at our leisure.

"It's impossible to control *everything* and *everyone*. But we're batting ninety-three percent, and that's more than enough to turn the threat of revolution through violence, politics, or prayer into a bad joke.

"You'll be doing the most important work in 21. The field agents have their fun jumping between rooftops and shooting would-be Unabombers, and we keep a fair number of double agents in every group worth remembering. But bugheads—shit, is 'bughead' politically correct?—but *biomechanical computing specialists* design and process the algorithms we use to predict and influence behavior throughout the Dominion. We've got the major bombings, riots, and assassina-tions for the next year scheduled on a tidy spreadsheet. *Please* try to keep it updated. We look like assholes whenever something blows up without warning.

"And believe me, the governor loves to complain. Every now and then I think of offing Cantrell, purging the Senate, and putting my face on the flag. But I'm bad with budgets, and this seat is more fun. All of the power with none of the pressure.

"Oh, by the way: if you leak this, I'll kill your kids. Welcome to the team."

18. Moderate Reactions to Recent Information
12:04 a.m.

Tanya Maxwell was, above all things, a survivor. After her older sisters—the twin founders of the Human Dignity League—disappeared under less-than-mysterious circumstances, she quietly built a com-fortable life writing for an ad agency specializing in state propaganda. While her commitment to the spirit of activism was limited, Tanya was determined to raise her two planned children as survivors. As the only child she ended up having, Nero received twice the education. One night, a plump thirteen-year-old Nero came home with a fresh black eye from a community outreach officer. Tanya handed him an ice pack, kissed him on his forehead, and said:

"You can cry but unclench your fists. Anger only has a purpose in nature. We're a long way from nature, and there's nothing you can do with your anger that won't get you killed. Survival means putting your anger in a box, burying it, and forgetting where you left it. Now let's go get some cheesecake."

Since then, he'd dropped his cheesecake weight and held on to the lesson. Alexa's betrayal had pushed him off balance, but exposure to a fresh new national disgrace helped him find equilibrium. Or at least an imitation of it. The Dominion could still surprise him, but it could never disappoint.

While ten lifelong rebels struggled to accept lives as unwitting tools of the state, he gently unplugged the cable in his eye socket. While Eugene and Alexa screamed at each other, he asked a sobbing Jason to pop his OdinEye back in place. And while Eugene's gorilla-sized guards beat their fists impotently against the brick walls, Nero wondered how long manners obligated him to stick around.

"This is bullshit," shouted Eugene. "You're both just plants sent here to demoralize us."

"Are you fucking serious?" said Alexa. "Your garbage leadership put us in this situation, and now you're accusing me of being a spy?"

"No accusation. A simple statement of fact. The head pig mentioned agency plants, and you fit the bill. How else do you stumble into a 2I bughead?"

"I gave up everything to join you guys," Jason said between crying jags. "This was supposed to be where the people's struggle began. I thought that even if they killed us, we'd do some damage on the way out. But this is too much. I'd have been better off sleeping in."

Nero admired remaining invested enough to cry. Living a day past thirteen with an intact sense of hope required a resilient spirit. He patted Jason on the back twice, since no one else seemed interested. The shouting match, for instance, had reached a climax.

"You know what, Eugene? I think *you're* a traitor." Alexa looked at her audience instead of her opponent as she spoke. Classic campaign trail technique. Nero guessed that, if nothing else, she might seize control of the ruins of the cell. "How much does Logan pay you to keep us useful? Were the defectors I tracked down really informers? Do my letter bombs get delivered? Does anyone read the pamphlets we hand out in the park? You've had us jerking off on a hamster wheel for the last three years, haven't you?"

"That's a mixed metaphor," countered Eugene. "A signature of the spy."

One of the guards stepped forward, glowering. "You know, Jason's been awfully chummy with that 2I dude."

"Piss off, Igor," said Jason. "You've got a total cop walk. What's your fucking badge number?"

"What if the system predicted us learning about the system?" asked a balding non-thug. "Maybe they want us to think everyone else is a spy."

"That's fucking stupid. I bet *you're* a spy."

"We want answers, Eugene," continued Alexa. "An anarchist organization expects better from its leaders."

After two more minutes of polite observation, Nero took his first tentative step backward. No response; the coup was more interesting than press-ganged tech support. He hazarded three more steps, found his courage, and strode to the door. He got halfway down the hallway before a cold metal point pressed against the nape of his neck. Though he couldn't tell what *kind* of knife, being a knife was enough.

"Sorry, but this can't get out," whispered Alexa. "The movement's too fragile. If they find out the rebellion's a government project, their spirit will shrivel and die."

"Holy shit. You had that on you this entire time?"

"Never get in cars with statists unarmed. It's basic survival."

"Whatever, I'm not leaking anything. I'm just going home. Feel free to rejoin the emotional implosion back there. I prefer to have my breakdowns in the comfort of my own bed."

"That sounds like bullshit. But you know what? It doesn't matter. None of this matters." The bravado in her voice deflated. "Congratulations, Nero, you were right."

Unexpected. He decided to go for the second long pass of the night. Nero wasn't *completely* sure whether he was going for levity or sexual harassment, but it seemed worth saying. There wasn't a mood to ruin.

"Now, this might sound crazy, but I have a lot of experience in the 'soul-crushing helplessness' field, so hear me out. In the pit of total despair, nothing feels better than sex. You hate me, but that can make it better. For twenty minutes, neither of us has to worry about conspiracies or the meaninglessness of our lives."

Like many men, Nero had an inflated opinion of his own sense of humor. He assumed the choked retching noise she made was barely restrained laughter. Then Alexa, without lowering the knife, started sobbing. Her outburst was shorter than Jason's—ten sobs at most—but far more depressing. While Nero had a hunch that Jason would recover, Alexa sounded like she was considering the ups and downs of suicide. Which made him feel guilty for his relief when she finally pocketed the knife.

"Hey, now you've got your own anarchist cell. That's a win."

"It means *nothing*. It's not even worth killing for."

Nero racked his brain for something more comforting, but three weapons had been drawn on him in the last hour. It was time to go before someone more decisive tried it.

"I, uh, had fun earlier. Before the kidnapping and all that."

"Fuck off, clown boy."

Nero fucked off.

18.5. Intermission Four

Second: It feels good to be right.

First: I have to agree.

Third: All right, I made one or two bad calls. Get off my dick.

Second: Your bad call pulled a knife on us.

Third: Her legs were mathematically perfect. I did the best I could with the data I had.

Second: The way I see it, my correct tactical appraisal proves that I'm the most brilliant among us. And thus worthy of the title "Prime Intelligence."

Third: That's the most—I'm gonna borrow one of your words—*insipid* shit I've heard today.

First: Hmm. Maybe one of us *should* be Prime Intelligence. Namely, the one that predicted the vast national conspiracy. Repeatedly.

Third: What?

Second: When did this occur?

First: I've been talking about the Ouija Board all night. You have to remember this.

Third: I'm pretty sure that was me.

Second: Incorrect. I distinctly recall that *I* was the one to highlight the project's threat to our semi-fair nation.

First: I can't believe I'm based on the same brain as you cretins.

Third: The bullshit parts.

First: There *must* be some way for us to have a fistfight.

Second: As Prime Intelligence, I order you two to stop fighting.

First: When I figure it out, you're getting hit next.

Second: That is far from fair.

First: Fine, you're first in line.

19. The Train Redux

1:15 a.m.

For the first time in hours, Nero was alone. Without worrying about love, felonies, or survival, he could finally acknowledge fatigue. He collapsed onto an empty seat on a homebound train and entered a slouched, unresponsive state between daydreaming and sleep.

The subway car smelled like artificial oranges, a scent Nero called the "Sunday Morning Hangover." Drones had already cleaned up the worst of the night and replaced the scent of vomit, blood, and spilled liquor with cheap air freshener. The Transit Union was one of the three effective government agencies, alongside 2I and the Dominion Navy. Nero would have been impressed if it weren't for the oversized black camera mounted on the ceiling.

Dozing on a crowded train never looked graceful, and Nero's car was crammed elbow-to-elbow with the survivors of bar crawls, night-clubs, and candlelit dinners. However, after dealing with a botched pro-test, assault by a navy-trained cyborg, dodging the ensuing riot, watching said riot get put down, a botched carjacking, falling for a honeypot, and committing treason at gunpoint, a nap felt natural. Then again, none of those events were natural. A finger rested on the scale, and he was lucky to have struck out instead of died.

Deep sleep eluded him. But for a time he could enjoy his thoughts in silence.

[Hey, boss,] interjected First.

[Christ, what?]

[I know it's been a long night, but stay awake. The hardware in your skull costs more than a good defense attorney.]

[I just need a minute.]

[No. Next item: I took a look at the calendar file from that hard drive. We have a problem.]

[There's always another problem. Let me sleep.]

[I mean that Avery's got a problem,] said First. [Look at this weekend.]

[Wake the fuck up, you're twenty-seven years old,] Third added.

Nero lifted his head from his neighbor's shoulder. The vagrant was sleeping as well, and snoring at a volume that should have single-handedly kept Nero up. He waited for his OdinEye to reboot and opened "Dominion Event Schedule: September."

Thursday, September 7
Children of Kali: Power plant bombing.
Isolationists United: Artificial organ hacking spree.
Arson Defense League: Arson.
Agency Response: N/A.

Friday, September 8
Pacifist Armada: Assassination attempt on Michael Cantrell.
Abrahamic Union: News anchor beheading.
Neo-Monarchists: Liberty Park suicide bombing.
Agency Response: Eliminate head of Abrahamic Union.

Saturday, September 9
Multiple Factions: Liberty Park riot.
East Ward Worker's Party: Graffiti of bird on post office wall.
Sons of Koch: Mall bombing. Clinic bombing.
Agency Response: Complete purge of East Ward Worker's Party.

Nero couldn't think of a positive interpretation of "complete purge" and stood up to force himself awake. With his eye ruined, he was reduced to using his cell phone to check on Avery. After two dial tones, he heard a tinny recording of a female voice.

"The number you're trying to reach is associated with an enemy of the state. If you'd like to sponsor the trial, press one. If you'd like to leave a message reprimanding their disloyalty, press two. If you'd like to reserve a seat during the execution, press three. If you'd like to purchase the corpse, please hold."

20. The Apartment Redux
2:20 a.m.

One hour and three caffeine pills later, Nero made it home. The front door's cylinder had been shot off with something destructive. From what little he grasped from video games, the spread implied a shotgun.

The EWPD were innovators in excessive-force technology, so it was hard to be certain.

Avery would have commented on the redundant excess inherent in capitalism. Because different departments barely communicated, one agency had broken into Avery's home and taken his things, and another had broken into his fling's home to arrest him. Pure waste. Given law enforcement rivalries, nothing the EWPD found would make it to Avery's show trial.

For a casual observer, distinguishing the aftermath of the police raid from the mess they usually lived in would be a challenge. To Nero, the apartment looked ransacked. The well-defined pile of fall clothes had been strewn about the room, commingling with the winter coats and laundry. The thin layer of order that slobs relied upon had been destroyed.

Moreover, half their appliances had been destroyed or stolen. But that was a given.

[What should we do, boss?] said First.

"I don't know. Maybe we can visit him in prison?" Nero said aloud. There was no one to overhear him talking to himself.

[Nigga, are you fucking serious?!] said Third.

"What do you want from me? *Maybe* if I sell everything in here that isn't broken, I can get him a decent lawyer. That's all I've got."

[Commander, if I may.]

"No."

[I must. You show excess ingenuity when it comes to saving yourself. Perhaps if you applied the same mentality to this problem?]

"The best way to save yourself is staying out of trouble. I told him that every day for four years. There's still just enough left of the world to live quietly and comfortably. It's not my fault he couldn't put his anger in the box."

[Box?] asked First.

[Who cares?] said Third. [It's just going to be another excuse. I'm ashamed to come from any part of this dickless wonder.]

"And what would you geniuses do?"

[Blackmail 2I? We know about the Ouija Board,] suggested First.

"Oh, brilliant. Then they can send someone with all of Diana's hardware and even less restraint. I bet I could evade them for an entire half hour."

[We could work with the Children of Kali.]

"Dead end. Working with them just means getting executed in a group instead of a solo event."

[It doesn't matter what we suggest,] said Third. [Bitch boy here's already decided not to try.]

Since he was arguing with robots in his own brain, there was no way to storm away from the conversation. Still, for effect, Nero flipped off the empty room, lay down on the couch, and turned his back on the wall. Judging by the silence in his head, the gesture translated.

21. Nero Flips His Shit

3:13 a.m.

Nero had gotten used to living with a three-man commentary track. The swarms had started out bland but developed distinct personalities within the first month. The first time Third cursed, Second quoted Sun Tzu, or First made fun of his wardrobe, Nero experienced a flash of genuine pride. He'd also complained about the bickering but rarely did anything concrete to discourage it.

Now he faced a complete lack of noise. If the bugs had anything to say, they were keeping it to themselves. He'd become persona non grata in his own brain.

"Honestly? The chatter's gotten old. I'm more than ready for a little silence. Maybe I can get through making a snack without listening to a bad *boke-tsukkomi* routine."

He waited for the clapback. Second and Third were easily baited, and First took any opening for a clever riposte. More silence followed. Nero moved on to the freezer, one of the few appliances left unharmed by the raid. An array of frozen burritos greeted him: he relied on comfort food after a rough night, and today had to qualify.

Nero watched the burrito spin in the microwave for three still minutes, waiting for a quarter pound of fake meat to fight off the thoughts vying for his attention. The microwave window was the apartment's main source of light, giving half the room a soft yellow glow.

One low-pitched beep ended the spinning and his trance. Nero lightly tugged at the door with two fingers. It didn't budge. He tried his whole right hand, and then both hands with his foot braced against the kitchen cabinet. He pulled in frantic jerks until the veins around his wrists became visible.

He remembered his mother, breathed, and looked at the control panel. This wasn't new: the neutered software often malfunctioned and refused to open the magnetic lock. Nero's bugs usually handled that problem, so he'd never bothered replacing the thing. Now that he was getting the silent treatment, a plastic wall stood between him and greasy relief.

"Fuck it." Nero wedged a fork into the crack between the door and number pad. The head bent backward and stayed stuck in the door.

"Third! Open this fucker!"

Nothing.

"First!"

Nothing.

"Second! It's an *order*."

After more nothing, Nero stomped to his closet. Any action was better than thinking about the dozen small ways that he lived in a bad joke. He returned to the kitchen with the "People's Slugger," a splinter-covered artifact from Avery's pre-graduation athletics and post-graduation rioting. Nero took a light, slow test swing, tapping the tip against the microwave screen. Then he squared his shoulder, planted his feet, and raised the bat.

He waited for a voice to tell him to stop. Nothing. He swung.

A layer of plastic and glass shards now covered his dinner. After giving the wall a follow-up swing, Nero dropped the People's Slugger, gently reached past the wreckage of the microwave's front door, and picked up his burrito. He dumped the inedible remains in the garbage, which Avery had neglected to take out.

"You've made your point. After a purge, 2I processes new prisoners at headquarters. Management likes to make the judicial branch crawl to them, so Avery should be there for another day or two. I'll think of something. I don't know what, but something."

[Thank you,] said First. [Start by getting some sleep. You look awful.]

[Commander! The mutiny was their idea. Please don't hold it against me, I understand the nutritional and emotional importance of the late-night burrito,] said Second.

[Until I see results, you're still a punk,] said Third.

22. A Nicer Apartment
5:38 a.m.

Nero stared at the ceiling for two hours before giving up on sleep. Panic outclassed any energy drink. He opted to get started, left the bed, and opened his egg carton. After passing over the street-legal OdinEyes, he picked up a black market Biclops V. While the OdinEye line was designed around basic imitation of a human eye, the Biclops emphasized power over not scaring children. It looked like a smooth silver ball and housed a small cloud of nanites that could adjust to the needs of the moment. He passed his reflection on the way out and doubled back for his sunglasses.

[Is that thing legal?] asked First.

"We're plotting at least one act of treason." Nero said dryly.

[Point.]

He took to adding up his agency connections, since taking 2I on alone felt like a dramatic form of suicide. As a freelancer, he was a social nonentity in the office. Other bugheads considered him unwanted competition for promotions—a fear validated by recent events—and left him out of the weekly office happy hour blackouts. They might have felt more secure with a union, but the last governor had decided that those conflicted with practical freedom.

As for the field agents, he knew only one.

Despite her message, he was surprised when Diana accepted his call. He'd processed the earlier exchange as a drunken impulse, and assumed that shooting him was in the top three of her to-do list.

"Are you coming to the party? You have not RSVP'd."

He readjusted to the lack of contractions. "I need your help."

"Intriguing. Is this a booty call?"

"No. I know it's the ass-end of the day—or morning, I guess—but do you have a minute to meet up?"

She forwarded her address, leading him to a sixth-floor apartment in a neighborhood an order of magnitude more expensive than his. Hazard pay must have been worth something. That, or she'd fallen into the East Ward trap of spending ninety percent of her income on rent.

His instincts told him to fix his hair before knocking. The inch he'd grown at the top of his fade looked good with a little love, but he missed the days when combs were for other people. After thirty seconds of using his cell phone camera as a mirror, he privately swore to return to the pseudo–buzz cut worn by the lazier half of his family.

Diana, on her own time, wore loose gray sweatpants with the Sports-Max logo over the right leg and a Central Ward Dragons basketball jersey. (There were five professional teams in the entire Dominion, which simplified marketing.) Her face was covered in light blue moisturizing cream, and her braids were tied into an impromptu beehive that kept them from falling onto her mask. Said beehive looked ridiculous, completing an image that would have made Nero laugh if it weren't for his state of panic.

"Explain yourself."

"Everything 2I's told us, or the rest of the country, is a smoke screen."

"Explain ditching me at the bar," she corrected. Somehow the niceties of their date were more important to her than any national disaster. That was familiar. Nero felt a pang of sympathy for First's struggle.

"It's like you said, too much too soon. If it makes you feel better, I almost died twice because of it. For reasons *very relevant* to you, if you'll get off of the date for a second—"

"We are not getting off it. I am *notably* angry at you."

That struck him as a lie. The last person that she'd been angry with had lost blood, and Diana didn't strike him as someone with patience for passive aggression. She was also smirking, which made him feel like the target of a practical joke.

"Sorry. Punch me later."

"You will have to do better for a boot—"

"*This isn't a booty call.* I'm going to show you that the world you know is a lie."

"Are you still drunk?"

"A little, but that's beside the point. *Please* just let me inside. We can't talk about this in the hallway, anyone could be listening. If you don't hear me out, my best friend is probably going to die."

There was, among the technically oriented people of the world, a universal look of exasperation. It came from the fifteenth attempt to explain something very basic to someone very slow. Nero was surprised to find it on Diana's face. She looked like she'd just spent an hour trying to teach binary to a bull terrier.

"I will indulge you," Diana said, very slowly. "But first I have to ask: Are you *sure* that this is not a booty call?"

Somehow, Nero caught on. He gave her a less-than-subtle elevator look and forgot his original response.

[This might sound crazy, but I think that sleeping with her will help our pitch,] Nero thought.

[Uh-huh,] said First.

[I need to convince her that 2I sponsors the rebellions she despises. That's not an easy sell. A *personal* connection might make it easier.]

[Whatever you say, boss.]

"Can I come in?" Nero asked. He tried not to sound overeager. He sounded overeager.

"Take your shoes off at the door."

Nero didn't know where the exact line between "meticulously organized" and "obsessively organized" lay, but he suspected Diana was on the wrong side of it. A meticulously organized apartment might have a neatly arranged shoe stand. Diana had a four-column rack sorted by type, color, wear, and brand. Surprisingly, the sneakers outnumbered the formalwear. Nero would have asked what her sport was, but six college basketball photos lined her dresser. She was committing fouls in half of them.

"Before we do anything, I really should start explaining this situation," Nero began.

"Take off your clothes."

"Okay."

Nero got rid of his jeans without thinking, but the shirt made him more self-conscious. Years after dropping weight, exposing his stomach still put him on edge. Halfway down his buttons, he decided to play his trepidation off as seductive delay. The resulting dance looked ridiculous, but it was better to look childish than nervous.

"Cute," said Diana. She began wiping off her mask with a paper towel, leaving patches of green around her ears, nose, and hairline. Her sweatpants had already disappeared, which demanded his immediate attention. Nero climbed into bed, getting skin care products smeared onto his forehead, hands, and waist. By the time they were fully entangled, they were both covered in random swaths of green moisturizer. In defiance of decades of marketing color coding, it smelled and tasted like pineapple.

Nero considered himself a sexual generalist. It was impossible to know what fetish a modern partner would bring to the table, especially after online dating and unlimited pornography had brought the fringe to the center. People were as likely to break out a ritual Sumerian mask as fuzzy handcuffs, so he tried to be adaptable. He was mentally prepared to fulfill most basic roles, and several obscure, transgressive ones.

None of this helped. Sex with Diana was straightforward and aerobic, and pushed Nero's unaltered and minimally athletic body to the edge of serious injury. A wise man might have tapped out or at least called for a water break. But Nero was driven by a lethal mixture of lust, pride, and emotional need. So it was a small mercy when Diana let go of his ear and stopped moving.

"Well. This is embarrassing, but my left battery just ran out of juice. Could you plug me into the wall outlet?"

"Mmph," Nero grunted.

"See the green cord connected to the power strip? The port's on the bottom of my left foot, right next to the barcode."

"Gnnf."

"Look, I can only feel half of this. If you finish without plugging me in, you might not live to regret it."

The threat worked. After watching him connect an AC adapter to her heel, she gave him eyes that made his night of near-death experiences worthwhile. He spent the last four minutes on his back, scanning the room for a water bottle. There wasn't one in sight, and the first thing he did afterward was make a beeline for the kitchen sink.

"Have fun?" Nero shouted down the hallway. Surprisingly, Diana had a sink full of grimy dishes. He had to move a stack to make room for a cup, which convinced him she was still human.

"Acceptable."

He decided, for his ego, to assume that she was messing with him. After finishing (and washing) a tall glass of water, he limped back to bed. Sex didn't lift the cloud of anger that had hovered in the background over the last two decades. But he could think with more clarity and speak without second-guessing himself.

"I'm going to ask you a question. And I need you to promise me you won't get angry, violent, or both."

"Of course."

"Why don't you use contractions?"

"I am from Central. My team made fun of my accent, so I developed a more professional, neutral manner of speech. I think it is a good fit for the flavor of life here."

"Right. Could I hear how you talk at home?"

"No. There is no reason for me to embarrass myself like that."

"Just try it."

She hesitated.

"Don't tell anyone, but I talk to Momma like this."

A genuine surprise. The *I* was an *Ah*, the speech was faster, and a hint of melody replaced the flat monotone. The voice was more natural, more human, and an iron wall against any kind of professional advancement. Nero thought of a recent film about the Alamo.

"You can talk to me like that."

"I would rather not. I am going for 'mysterious assassin,' not 'hayride operator.' You will learn to enjoy the affectation."

"Diana, no one that wants to live sleeps with a mysterious assassin. The mystery is usually their plan to kill you. That's half of why I ran off."

Her eyes narrowed. "You're a real dick sometimes, y'know that?"

"Wait until I tell you about the conspiracy. You'll hate it."

"That's real? I thought you were just trying to get my attention."

Nero had more to say, but his body chose sleep. He buried his head in the pillow and passed out.

23. The Coffee Shop
11:52 a.m.

Nero made his case in Cousin Auntie's, a coffee shop chain that specialized in looking independent. He sat at one of four plastic park-style tables and drained the second of three Expresso Grenades before finishing his spiel. He stacked the empty cups at the edge of the table by a bowl of complimentary downers. Diana's end held a lone pastry, which she inhaled within thirty seconds.

Each location in the Cousin Auntie's franchise was burdened with finding a unique gimmick. Their locale housed a gallery of famous movie posters. The left wall showcased pre-war classics, hinting at a golden age when only one in four blockbusters was thinly veiled propaganda. The more recent hits on the right wall featured an array of square-jawed Dominion Navy veterans teaming up with salt-of-the-earth Central Ward police officers. A pair of spy thrillers represented 2I, starring a suave agent's one-man war against dark-skinned, vaguely accented terrorists and their endless henchmen.

"Have you tested this information at all?" asked Diana.

"Well, no. I guess I just trusted the video. And Avery really was arrested."

"Purely circumstantial. Living with a neo-communist isn't smart. I'm surprised you didn't have an incident sooner. But accepting untested intel's worse. We aren't doing anything without confirming it."

"You're taking this well," Nero noted.

"I don't believe you yet. If we prove Logan's behind the rebels, and the last seven years of my life were a waste, I'll be murderous."

Nero started his third cup of coffee. His sunglasses, a traditional summer hangover accessory, rested on his nose.

"Here's an experiment. The file says they've actively radicalized ninety percent of the civilian population. If that's accurate, anyone that I walk up to in this coffee shop is, statistically, a member of some secret society."

"That's ridiculous."

"Yup. Which means it'll prove my point if it works."

Nero picked a hairless old man sitting in the back of the coffee shop, huddled underneath an oversized wool coat. He looked like he wanted to be left alone, which made him perfect for the test.

"Brother," Nero hazarded. He took the opposite seat.

"What? Who are you? Have you seen my son?"

"You can drop the act. I'm your contact."

The old man's back straightened, his eyes narrowed, and his hands curled into small fists. He slid a small roll of tightly coiled bills toward Nero's side of the table.

"It's good to see you, brother. Here's the product of the dead drop, minus operational fees. You know, for a moment I thought that Command had forgotten me. I should have known better: the Society for Explicit Fascism looks after their own. What do you need?"

"That's it," said Nero. "Thanks." He shuffled back to Diana.

"A fluke," she said, impassive.

"I'll try another." He turned toward the waitress and flagged her down. She approached with admirable speed and a guileless customer service smile.

"What can I get you?"

Nero clasped her arm. "Sister. Soon we rise."

"Not here, brother," said the waitress. "The Anarcho-Capitalist Union is not ready to strike. Not while a single member of the Anarcho-Communist Corporation still breathes."

"Those dogs don't deserve to live," Diana added, taking over without hesitation. "Breaking from them and the Children was the best move we ever made." She sounded like a lifelong revolutionary.

"They were ideological poison," said the waitress. "Who even reads Stirner anymore? And the Children had no economic plan. Rothbard, however, is the future."

It might have been the two and a half full servings of unregulated stimulants, but Nero was impressed. He could barely track the exponential growth of revolutionary and counterrevolutionary groups in the Free Dominion. In fact, he'd barely even heard of the Children of Kali before they crashed violently into his life.

The waitress filled Diana in on her plot to seduce, poison, and replace Governor Cantrell's personal chef. During her rant, Nero noticed the prison barcode tattooed onto her right arm. He scanned it with the Biclops and learned that her name was Cassidy Green, her prison labor had been sponsored by SportsMax, and she'd earned an early release after winning the sneaker construction contest for five weeks in a row. After three minutes of stone-faced nodding, Diana shooed her off.

"You might be onto something, but so far you've picked shifty-looking targets. Show me a proper citizen roped into this nonsense and I'll believe you."

Nero searched Cousin Auntie's for someone sufficiently white bread to prove his point. The pickings were slim: coffee shops attracted people that at least wanted to *look* like members of the counterculture. Then he peered through the wall and saw the outline of a child twirling a toy on the sidewalk. That had potential. He settled the check and gestured for Diana to follow.

As soon as they stepped out, the child pocketed the toy and stared at the floor. He looked like he was elementary school age, complete with a worn backpack and the absence of any form of supervision.

"Seems unlikely," Diana said dryly. Nero approached the target, leaned forward, and tried to look serious.

"Hello, brother," Nero said. "How goes the mission?"

The child beamed. "Hey there! I forgot how to use the thingie. Do you tug the fuse or light it?" He pulled a pipe bomb out of his sky-blue jacket, clutching the bottom like a thermos. "Mom worked really hard on it and I don't want to mess up."

Somehow, Nero still wasn't used to weapons being drawn around him. His heart inched one step closer to a full-blown attack. Yet he managed to shift his grimace back into a smile before the child noticed.

"Y-you'd better let me handle it."

Without warning, the child underhand-lobbed the improvised explosive toward Nero. He nearly fumbled it but grasped it before it hit the sidewalk.

"Thank you, mister! *Viva la revolución!*" the student said, before picking up his backpack and skipping down the block. Nero marched back to Diana feeling ten years older.

"Hmm, the old child-with-pipe-bomb trick," said Diana. She grabbed, disassembled, and trashed the explosive while Nero waited for his heart to start beating properly.

"This time you're joking."

"I'm not, but I do believe you. Multiple coincidences prove enemy action. I'm not, however, convinced that helping you is the best thing I could do with this information."

"What would be?"

"Turning you in for an easy promotion."

Nero's heart rate spiked again. There was no running from her at this distance—or any distance. He could try hacking one of her organs, but she'd probably tear out his kidneys before he could detonate—

"*That's* a joke. I pitched startin' our own conspiracy last night, if you remember. That offer's still on the table. But don't run off if I have to shoot someone."

24. Pitch Session
1:40 p.m.

2I's East Ward headquarters occupied one of seven identical skyscrapers. The other six were fully staffed with people paid just over minimum wage to sit in front of computers and look busy for any insurgents or foreign agents that might be watching. This would have been Nero's ideal job if it weren't for the pay.

The real business of surveilling the Dominion went down in the second building from the left. The location was something of an open secret. Rumor had it that 2I maintained the six decoys because the director found them amusing. After his encounters with Riley Logan, Nero was inclined to agree.

While the exterior endeavored to look generic, the interior remained one of the glossiest places Nero had seen in his life. Cleanliness was part of 2I discipline, and every tile, panel, and shelf shone. The dominant color was black, making small fragments of dust stand out until they were dealt with.

Diana and Nero were stuck in the lobby, conducting what could generously be called brainstorming.

The main issue, beyond the mechanical business of somehow removing a human package from a fortresslike skyscraper, was getting into headquarters without arousing suspicion. Diana, against all reason, held on to the idea that her accomplice was a smart guy. As the main witness to his recent choices, Nero was less certain. But he'd torn off too much of his psychological safety blanket to go home and watch videos without hating himself.

True to form, Diana suggested arresting someone. That would give them access to the holding cells with minimal chicanery, which appealed to Nero's lazy side. But the obvious logic trail between two agents entering and one closely related prisoner leaving had less appeal.

Then he remembered the birthday party. Once he pitched using it as cover, she seemed less confident that he was a smart guy. Nonetheless, they bypassed three layers of security checkpoints and full-body scans without incident, save a pair of bugheads asking Nero where they could pick up a Biclops on the cheap.

"Gabriel Logan's not a great guy," Diana warned. She held one arm of their joint present: an oversized toy bear with 2I-style mirrored sunglasses. Nero wanted to buy an old spy movie poster, but they had different senses of humor.

"Why's that?" Nero pressed "33" and "Close," shutting the elevator doors in the face of a coworker.

"Standard boss's son syndrome. I'd have arranged an accident, but partners are the first suspects when an agent disappears. Which makes sense, since I plotted to make 'im disappear."

"This looks like the elevator we met in." He'd done subtler subject changes in his time.

"It isn't," she said curtly.

"Well, yeah, but it looks like it."

They rode in silence for ten floors.

"Something's been bothering me," said Nero.

"Insomnia? Try drinking less."

"No. Now, I've been wondering: How much of my reaction to the project was because of how I learned about it? If I'd watched that video in my cubicle as scheduled, wouldn't I have seen it as just another small concession?"

"How deep."

The same probably goes for you. If this thing has an enforcement arm, you can't be too far from getting promoted to it. Would you have passed it up?"

"That's nice of you to say."

"I think you're missing my point."

"Again, kidding. You take most things more straightforwardly than you should. It's not good for a spy."

"I'm not a spy."

"Hmm. So you work at an intelligence agency, wear black, and manipulate information. But you're not a spy."

"I think I liked you better when you talked like a robot."

The elevator doors parted. Nero walked in with an artificial grin and hoped that he was a decent spy.

25. The Party
3:00 p.m.

The conference room had the basics of a successful office party: fifty thinly acquainted drunks, toothless music played at comfortable volume, and enough clandestine workplace affairs to add some tension to the air. Thanks to his long night and undergraduate fashion sense, Nero found himself the least professional-looking person in sight. He drifted to the edge of the crowd and hoped no one asked if he was an intern.

After fifteen minutes in the corner, Nero hadn't touched the beer or hard liquor. He held a glass of white wine, but today it was reduced to a stage prop. However bacchanal his instincts were, today's work demanded clarity.

Besides, Diana's coworkers didn't look like the most fun crowd to drink with. That might have been a snap judgment, but they certainly weren't subtle about judging him. Passing agents gave him open stares of evaluation, followed by either a smile or a scowl. So far the scowls were ahead by two. Nero couldn't be too harsh on the agents that mistrusted him; he'd been cracking phones, ID badges, and OdinEyes since entering the conference room. The right access code would make getting into holding infinitely easier. Acting out also satisfied some of his antisocial fury, but that was a bonus.

"You look nervous," said Diana. "Stop that."

Diana had wrapped her elbow around his, and the steel-reinforced hold was unbreakable. While Nero may have been ready for suicidal conspiracy pacts, locked arms marked a level of commitment that he hadn't planned for. He chalked it up to the demands of spycraft and went back to stealing passwords.

The Biclops trivialized identity theft, allowing Nero to track multiple targets and combine visual filters. After putting the X-ray filter over I/O vision, he discovered that almost every party guest was armed without losing any hacking time. Two dozen attendees carried party favors including piano wire, dart guns, ballistic knives, old-school revolvers, new-school revolvers, and pocket flamethrowers. He sincerely hoped Diana didn't plan to shoot their way out of the building.

Surprisingly, there were no guns among the presents piled onto the conference room table. Gift-wrapped boxes covered a sprawling map of East Ward, with red X's marking the targets of a recent operation. At a see-through glance, the contents included playing cards, a coupon for

Discreet Angels Escort Agency, a hardcover copy of *Moderate Liberty*, and a bottle of aged bourbon. Diana's stuffed bear stood out as the only gift that didn't feed an addiction.

"Personally, I'd have my birthday party at a bar, coworkers or not." Nero lifted the bear's leg and zoomed in on his part of town. His neighborhood was covered in tiny red X's.

"That is fair." Diana picked the last pig in a blanket.

"We're back to the robot talk?"

"We are back to the *professional* talk. This is a room full of my peers."

"Contractions won't kill your peers," Nero said, before his brain caught up. It wasn't the best time for Diana to change her highly visible habits. Abnormal behavior—in this case, less abnormal than usual—would put her near the top of the post-breakout suspects. She gave his arm a squeeze communicating the same idea in harsher terms.

The pain almost distracted him from the guest of honor's arrival. Four well-dressed sycophants flanked his entry, each determined to be standing closest without violating his personal space. While each of the professional climbers outranked him—the lowest ranking sycophant ran a counter-journalism task force—Gabriel's last name was enough to demand their undivided attention. He showed no signs of resenting this.

Gabriel looked like he would have done well in undercover. He had the natural looseness—and neck covered in tattoos—one associated with revolutionaries. If an observer ignored the badges, Diana and Nero looked far more like appendages of the surveillance state. This chafed with Nero, who maintained that sidecuts should have died with credible elections.

"Who wears sunglasses inside?" Nero whispered.

"You," said Diana.

"He rocks it pretty well," said a raspy male voice to Nero's left. Gabriel had, without making a sound or spilling his drink, moved across the room in seconds. This offered two pieces of free information: he had inordinately expensive stealth and speed mods, and he was the type to use them to gain a minor social edge.

"Hello, Gabriel," Diana said rotely. "How does turning thirty feel?"

"Eh, it's a number. Is this your brother? Husband? Baby daddy? You never talk about yourself, and Dad won't let me get at the records."

"Baby daddy," Nero volunteered. He started working on Gabriel's phone. Diana's partner seemed like the type to keep classified access codes on his personal device.

"I wouldn't even know if you were bullshitting. We've been partners for two months, which is a decade in 2I time, and all I've learned is that she has a special pen for paperwork."

"He works here," said Diana. "Otherwise he would be tranquilized and detained."

"Whatever, you picked a hell of a night to take off. Dad had us out arresting every commie in East Ward." Gabriel picked the shrimp out of a passing cocktail glass. "One apartment had an old lady with a literal hammer and sickle. I don't know if they were symbolic or what, but she got the drop on me. If my neck was still skin and bone, you'd be at my funeral."

"I hope you filed an incident report," Diana said impassively.

"What do you think about this thing she does?" Gabriel said, turning back to Nero. "The dry post-sarcasm thing? I hope you can take it; I think it makes her impossible to talk to."

"You two should bond. Without me." Diana released Nero's arm and slipped into a nearby conversation about proper interrogation techniques for minors. A veteran agent demonstrated a rear naked choke on the stuffed bear.

"Hmm. You look all soft and breaky, so you're probably not in the field," said Gabriel. "It's cool to have a bughead here. Especially a black one; those normally go over to the other side."

"Thanks."

"Seriously, it's good that you don't let petty shit get in the way of the work. I've always said that 2I's the least biased agency out there. The EWPD might have issues with some types, but 2I watches everyone. Feel me?"

Nero didn't feel him, and the wine was starting to look more appealing. He considered the chance that he might be a genuine alcoholic before refocusing on present problems. Gabriel's password rested between personal memos to call his mother and clean out his heat sinks. The discovery brought a natural, unaffected grin to Nero's face.

"You get it," said Gabriel. "Between you and me, start distancing yourself from Diana. She's one of the best, so she has to go. I'd like to replace Dad when he gets bored with running the world, and I don't need any competition."

"I don't think anyone gets tired of running the world." Nero stared at the thin spiderweb crack on Gabriel's neck. On a vanilla human, the wound would have opened an artery.

"That's a solid point. I might move some of my plans up. As for Diana, I'm sure you'll miss her figure-eight body, but that's replaceable. I know places where the escorts can remodel their faces. All you need is a decent photo and a little scratch. In fact, I'll cover it if you join my crew. I'll have to throw some kind of coup if Dad doesn't feel like retiring, and I could use a tech guy to cover my tracks. That's a Biclops, right? Your brain's gotta be half-metal to use one of those."

"Just a third. I appreciate the offer. It definitely sounds more engaging than censoring bird memes."

"There's my guy. I'll be in touch."

Gabriel headed toward his loyal cluster of worshippers. He stopped before the stuffed bear, paused, and switched his designer sunglasses for the bear's plastic ones. The consistent draw of the stuffed animal was lost on Nero. Something about field work warped agents' senses of humor beyond civilian understanding.

Then the director opted to make an appearance. Riley Logan was fashionably late and looked like he wanted to be fashionably absent. Gabriel opened his arms for a hug and his father stepped to the side, clasped his right hand, and gave it two firm shakes. The director then wordlessly dropped a clip of old-fashioned paper money into Gabriel's palm and abandoned him to inspect the wine selection.

Nero guessed that this was a faithful recreation of Gabriel's childhood. It only seemed to faze the birthday boy for a moment. After staring at his palm for three seconds, Gabriel collected his followers and fled. The gifts were left behind without a second look.

Nero returned to the elevator, where he found Diana drumming her fingers along the wall. They left little indents in the plaster. If he'd taken any longer, she might have made inch-deep holes.

"Nervous habit," she mumbled. They entered together, and Nero pressed the button for Basement Level 4.

"Diana. Quick question."

"Hmm?"

"Why do you want to be director?" He almost added, "You and your partner have that in common," but he had just enough sense to avoid it.

"My supervisor just explained how to inflict adult-sized pain on a child-sized suspect, and it offended me because I *already knew*. I don't think we have to live like that. Like I said before, the director has real power. While the talking heads change, I could make things a little saner."

It wasn't a bad answer. In fact, his inner cynic had expected much worse. But with all the creativity at his disposal, Nero couldn't imagine *anyone* improving the system. It seemed smarter to burn everything and start over.

26. Holding

3:37 p.m.

None of Nero's work censoring memes had given him a reason to stop by the holding cells in the past. His policy of lodging his head firmly in the sand made any notion of seeking out the people 2I deemed threats unpalatable. That was inviting trouble. Until today, he'd preferred keeping the basement a distant abstraction.

He did know that 2I had the same insight as the private prisons: when it came to detainment, human guards' salaries, insurance, and psychological upkeep were a waste. For half the cost of a permanent staff of baton-wielding toughs, a prison could maintain a small army of heavily armed robots. What they lacked in critical thinking skills, they made up for with efficient application of force. Human guards were prone to drawing out the fun.

So while he was still terrified when an eight-foot-tall quadrupedal android greeted him, he wasn't surprised. One steel arm ended in a chain gun, while the other held a tablet. The chain gun stood out. It obscured half of the word "Welcome" printed across the guard's chest in cursive lime-green letters.

The guard's face was *almost* lifelike, pushing it into the depths of the uncanny valley. It had semi-realistic eyes that never blinked and semi-realistic lips that never stopped smiling. Nero avoided eye contact.

"Good afternoon," it said in a voice halfway between a synthesizer and a gravel mixer. "Kindly present your identification code."

The guard raised its tablet arm before Nero could sprint back to the elevator. A text field and touch screen keyboard sat underneath the words "Attempts Left: 1."

"Make sure you get the spelling right," noted Diana.

"Hilarious."

"Not a joke. The new guards can fire over eighty anti-civilian rounds a second at pinpoint accuracy."

Nero skipped asking about the term "anti-civilian rounds." He punched in Gabriel's password, triple-checked the spelling, and tapped "Enter."

"Ah, we can pass," said Diana.

"It hasn't said anything yet."

"It's a dummy, it probably just knows the one word. Besides, it would have killed us if there was a problem with the code." She flicked one of the chain gun's barrels, and the android accepted it without complaint.

The tablet shifted to a light blue map of the floor plan flanked by lists of guard robots and prisoners. There were eighty-seven cells in all, marked with Roman numerals. Nero scrolled through the prisoners until he found Avery's profile. His photo featured a swollen eye and two missing teeth, but it was good to see him alive.

Name: Avery Corbin
Occupation: Writer, failed academic
Affiliations: East Ward Workers Party
Charge: To be determined.
Cell: 29

After three minutes of intense focus, Nero recalled the Roman numeral equivalent of twenty-nine. His education had given Dominion history little, and the Romans less. To this day he was uncertain whether Caligula had chopped down a cherry tree or pulled a sword from a stone.

"We need to go this way, down to cell X-X-I-X."

"You don't sound too sure."

"You should be used to that, it's a national personality defect. They like to keep our grasp of the facts loose. It's half of my job."

They made their way down the west hallway. Compared to the bustle of the rest of the building, the lack of ambient noise seemed unnatural. The guard androids stood still and silent, failing to even offer a faux customer service greeting. Nero wanted to compare the silence to a library, but a mausoleum fit more naturally.

The visuals weren't any more welcoming. The floor tiles were a uniform shade of depressing gray, and the ceiling lamps offered just enough light to make the lack of custodial attention obvious. While the offices upstairs were sterile enough to rival any hospital, here Nero could see hints of green and black mold growing in the seams between tiles. Anyone lucky enough to get pardoned was likely to get sick.

[I need a favor,] Nero thought. [I'm going to mark cameras with the Biclops as I go. Replace the footage of Diana and me with something a little less treasony.]

[Easy enough.]

[As you wish, Commander.]

[I'll help,] said Third. [But you're still a punk.]

"Are you talking to yourself again?" said Diana. They passed another guard android without incident. It stood at military attention, which seemed outdated. Missile defense systems settled modern wars long before standing armies got involved. That said, there were remnants of crimson splatter on its gun arm. It must have recently recreated at least some of the excesses of infantry combat.

"Two lefts should get us there."

The first cell they passed was empty, along with the nine that filled the rest of the corridor. After hanging another left, they were confronted with ten more prisoner-free cells. They stepped into twenty-nine without discussion. Inside they found a damp floor, an empty bed, and a sink with a running faucet. Cold water seeped into Nero's shoes, freezing his toes.

"Unusual," said Diana, laconic. She stepped farther into the pool without a visible reaction.

Nero bit his bottom lip until it bled. The art of suppressing frustration could only go so far. Then he reconsidered the camera in the corner of the cell.

[Don't wipe that one yet,] he thought. [Search today's footage for any sign of Avery. You shouldn't have to go too far back. We might learn where they moved him.]

He took a seat on the bed, which was closer to a slab with a pillow. Ruddy leather straps were visible on each corner, and the pillow was just as damp as the floor. Nero shuddered and hoped that Avery's new prison had a higher standard. Private wardens usually made a point of protecting their property.

[Find anything?]

[Er, yeah,] said First. [You might not want to see it.]

[Of course I want to see it. It's the only reason I'm in this pit.]

[It's pretty fucked,] said Third. [You might want to sit down. I mean, you're already sitting, but metaphorically. Look, it's *really* fucked, and I'm not sure how you're going to take it.]

"Just play the video," Nero said. He was too tired to worry about how verbalizing looked. If Diana didn't like it, she couldn't turn him in without implicating herself. He put his palm over his right eye and hoped that he liked what he found.

27. Security Footage
3:58 p.m.

According to the timestamp, the clip was nine and a half hours old. Three blurry outlines occupied the cell. The video quality spiked and declined at random, making it difficult to distinguish features beyond height and posture. Nero tried enhancing the image, which gave him *high-resolution* blurs with vibrant colors. Picking out faces would take focus and patience, two traits in short supply.

First, Nero identified Director Logan. If recent patterns held, his presence meant Nero's life was about to get much worse. The director tossed a red pen from hand to hand and kept a plastic clipboard tucked under his armpit. He leaned against the back wall and stared at the running sink with the expression of someone waiting for their train to pull in.

Avery was a more welcome sight. Even with both arms and legs tied together, his eyes held the proud defiance that inspired protests, strikes, and arguments over the dishes. The arrest hadn't been kind to the rest of his face, leaving his best features swollen and bruised. Nero experienced a hint of irrational guilt: he'd always resented the glances Avery drew on the subway, and it felt like he'd willed the broken molars into existence.

The third figure stood over the sink and wore a plain gray undershirt above a set of 2I's standard black pants. Gabriel's face briefly came into focus, looking every bit as bored as Avery looked defiant. The brain-dead detachment in his eyes was far too familiar.

"I can handle this," Gabriel said in a tone commonly reserved for preteens.

"Don't worry, I'm checking on everyone tonight," said Riley. "You're not special."

Gabriel turned back toward his work. Banter didn't look like a family specialty. His father's attention had already drifted toward Avery, who made a valiant attempt at pulling his arms free. The straps proved stronger than his spirit.

"You're Avery Corbin, right?" said the director. "I just want to double-check. The androids are dumb as stumps and have a way of messing up simple tasks. That, and you have all your teeth in our records."

"We're not your slaves," said Avery. If any of Riley's misplaced humor struck a chord, he didn't show it.

"Yeah, you're definitely our guy. Is that thing full yet?"

"Nah," said Gabriel. He dunked a pair of wet rags into the bucket and then slung them over his shoulder.

"Figures. All right, let's rap. I think you're right: slave societies *need* their slaves. Every achievement in Sparta and Charleston was the product of a vigorous slave caste. The only jobs automation can't cover are hooker and stand-up comedian. For now, at least: sex robots are getting funnier. Can you tell a decent joke? Or remodel your genitalia?"

"You're not funny either, Dad," Gabriel grumbled. He hoisted the bucket out of the sink and set it down at the foot of the bed beside six other pails of murky water. Gabriel soaked a third rag and wiped off his forehead.

"You can torture me. You can kill me. But I will never—" Avery's speech was cut short by the three soaked rags Gabriel dropped onto his face. The subsequent gurgling noises carried far less dignity.

"Let's move this along," said Gabriel.

"Avon—no, wait—Avery," began the director. "Compared to the injections your comrades and comradettes are getting, this probably looks pretty analog. But there's some method to my madness. And you're better off: I'd rather be killed off by a person than a machine.

"So here's you, the budding writer. I've seen more than enough leaders, soldiers, and spies come through to get bored of them. I check them off and move on. But I like taking a minute to meet the writers. I feel like I stand a good chance of learning something. Which isn't as common during interrogations as you'd think."

More gurgling.

"Now, you're the paranoid type, so I imagine you don't drink tap water. Here's a state secret: the water's fine. We don't put anything in it. Every now and then, someone suggests getting clever and adding a pacifying drug. But we've never followed through. East Ward has the cleanest water in the Free Dominion. Maybe even the world."

Gabriel hoisted a bucket above Avery's head. The first trickles of water flowed over the rim. Avery's defiant eyes showed the first hints of fear.

"Remember waterboarding? Never mind, it's before your time and mine. Most agencies have gone back to the basics of interrogation: knees, elbows, and baseball bats. The further technology goes, the more we choose simplicity over technique. I remember waterboarding because I follow history. In fact, I'm one of the last people outside of academia that really cares about it. I like to think it's why I've gotten this far.

"People used to argue about waterboarding. Not if it was a good way of torturing and killing people, but if it was even torture, and if it could kill people. That's the kind of ass-backward argument you get when a society doesn't understand itself.

"Which brings us here. Like I said, I've seen how soldiers and spies respond to being tortured to death. But I've never tried it on a writer, and there's nothing on it in our records. We've got this Ouija Board system that depends on how well we get people, and I'd say this is an opportunity to teach it something. Namely, the creative type's step-by-step reaction to death by drowning. Your participation might make us that much better at maintaining the status quo around here. Don't disappoint me."

"God, Dad, you can really fuckin' talk," said Gabriel. "Stop tormenting the guy and let me torture him."

"You've honestly got no sense of—screw it, never mind. Get started."

Gabriel tipped the bucket, Avery started screaming, and Nero ended the video.

28. Radicalization
4:04 p.m.

One could argue that Nero dealt with trauma poorly. Instead of "expressing" or "acknowledging" trauma, as trendy mental health experts recommended, he typically pushed it into his mind's basement, where it could quietly fester until it faded into the background static of daily life. This was his mother's gift.

For all the downsides this approach had for his blood pressure, typical mood, and alcohol consumption, his mother had been right about one thing: it was good for staying alive. Breaking into Avery's cell marked a practical departure from this method. Seeing Avery broken started a mental departure. Nero discovered a flavor and intensity of fury he'd never known was possible.

"What happened?" Diana asked. It was the kind of question one put forward when their right brain knew the truth but their left held out hope.

"I need a minute," he said softly. The Biclops whirred with activity as he picked out his targets. After a brief argument with his bugs, the brute-force hack proceeded. His false eye grew hot in its socket, which would have normally concerned him. Today he crossed his arm and pushed on. All three swarms in his head recommended restraint and went ignored.

"I am guessing he, er, did not make it," she said, relapsing into affected speech. "It is important that we consider our next move carefully instead of doing anything impulsive and life shortening. The status quo is built on a cycle of impotent violence."

"Of course. Oh, take a step to the left."

The prison hallway filled with the sound of off-tempo marching. Eight towering guard robots lined up in the hallway outside the cell. Each took the most efficient route to their place in line: some rounded a corner, while others went clean through cement walls. Diana jumped as a ninth robot crashed through the wall behind them, bowed politely before her, and slid into the last slot. All nine saluted.

"Jump," Nero ordered.

They jumped.

"Spin five hundred and twenty degrees."

They spun on their hind right heels, rotating until they faced the exit.

"Go to floor thirty-three and kill everyone you can find."

"Belay that," said Diana. The androids started marching. Each step left an impression in the floor. Five moved through the hallway, one moved through premade holes in the wall, and three made new ones.

"You should head to the lobby," Nero suggested. "Plausible deniability and all that."

"Nero. This isn't rational. A few agents will die, but so will we. There's no way that this doesn't come back to us."

Nero followed his toy soldiers, stepping through the closest new hole. All of Diana's points made sense, but he wasn't too interested in reason. Instead, he hummed the theme song to *Karate Island*, the game he and Avery had shared almost every weekend. The aggressive thrash metal riff had been a staple of the best quiet nights in his life. If he ever heard it again, it would be alone.

A heavy grip seized his shoulder.

"I've observed, worked with, and arrested every variant of crazy asshole. People that let this place twist them into caricatures of them-selves. I'm . . . well, not fully exempt from that category. But until today, you were the last sane adult in the Dominion. That's your best feature, and you shouldn't let that go. Or get us both killed."

[She has a point, boss,] said First.

[Fuck that noise,] said Third. [Let's make some bacon.]

"I know it's raw right now. We live in a machine that eats hope and shits out tragedy. But you can't beat it with desperate, isolated violence. It thrives on that. You knew that before the Ouija Board."

"Your hand's on your gun."

"Professional habit."

"Uh-huh. Here's a thought: maybe you just want to save the rest of the pig farm. Maybe you're used to being this shithole's apex predator and you don't need anyone else disrupting your race with Gabriel Logan to run what's left of the world."

"Your friend just died, so you get to talk to me like that once. But do it again and I'll smack the shit out of you. Not shoot, *smack*. Now, come take this hug."

"No."

"I'm trained in seven forms of grappling. This isn't a negotiation."

"I have death robots," warned Nero. "They can shoot over eighty anti-civilian rounds a minute. You can't make me do anything."

Diana ignored him, stepped forward, and forced him into a hug. Every attempt to push his way out seemed to tighten her grip. It was like trying to escape a touchy-feely boa constrictor. Nero was angry, then bewildered, and finally sobbing.

"Saving Avery was supposed to be my win. The one time something *good* happened here. What am I supposed to do now?"

"I don't know, but you should stay sane and boring. Don't try to become an action hero in the eleventh hour."

He got through ten minutes of emotionally overdue tears before the self-consciousness underpinning the adult male psyche returned. It reasserted itself with force, leading him to duck down out of her grip, brush his shoulders off, and point toward the androids.

"Get out of the elevator, the murder party's canceled," he said with all the authority he could muster. "And tidy up down here, it's disgusting. You people could have at least killed my best friend somewhere clean."

The guards dropped their guns in the hallway, marched into the janitor's closet—crashing through the wall rather than the open door—and emerged with mops and pails covered in thick layers of dust and mold. They took the first feeble steps to reversing years of neglect through precise if sluggish labor. On a better day, Nero would've cracked up.

29. Coup de Nothing
4:36 p.m.

After failing to save his friend or claim revenge, Nero decided that he needed liquor. Diana tried to encourage him to head home and grieve, but he was committed to blotting out his short-lived rebellion with the cheapest alcohol available. That meant returning to the birthday party, where he stood a good chance of finding the men that killed Avery and taking his best shot with a broken wineglass. He left this part out of his pitch to Diana, figuring that latent alcoholism was more presentable than a thirst for violence.

[Hey, man,] Third said. Nero left the elevator without responding. [There's a shit ton of pigs in that room. Don't start anything in there. Try strangling that old cracker when he heads to the can.]

[That's disgusting,] countered First.

[Sorry. There's a *bunch* of *officers of the law* in there. Try *asphyxiating* that *elderly Caucasian* when he heads to the *lavatory*.]

[I'm not going to murder anyone,] thought Nero. There was a good chance he was lying, but part of him wanted to make an effort.

Diana rounded the corner before the conference room first. Then she dropped into a rough forward roll and took cover behind a plastic potted plant. Like a true civilian, Nero poked his head forward to see what she was hiding from. This brought the entirety of the guest list into view, plus a few unfamiliar faces. All of them held guns and pointed them at either Nero's face or Diana's plant. While not everyone in the firing line looked sober, each face was serious.

Despite the situation, he was impressed by their aim. The laser sights converged neatly around two points on his forehead and heart. If he had to be part of an advanced machine of ideological repression, it was good to know it was a well-trained machine. It was also good to know he wouldn't be dying alone: Diana had drawn a pistol in one hand, a grenade in the other, and a ballistic knife in her teeth. He couldn't imagine how she planned on using the knife, but the visual was impressive.

One of the gunners glanced backward. "Shouldn't there be a bunch of robots with them?"

"Diana's there, she counts as at least *half* a robot," said another gunner.

"Jesus Christ!" chided the director. "What are you two doing? Get out of the way, we're in the middle of an operation."

The director stood behind the firing line, unarmed. One hand held an open can of Liberty Cola and the other was tucked underneath his armpit.

"Guh?" Nero said as he struggled to remember language. The director gestured for him to approach. Unconvinced, Nero glanced at Diana. She nodded and returned two out of three weapons to her inside pockets. The grenade stayed, in case the situation degenerated into "noble suicide."

"Let me explain. Our *informant* predicted an armed assault on my office using a small army of our own robots. I had Gabriel throw his party down the hall so I could have all my favorite murderers in one place, and set up a nice firing line at the only point of entry. We would have thrown in a few drones, but then we'd have one of those shitty self-fulfilling prophecies. I hate those."

"Oh. Is that normal?" asked Diana. Her poker face held true.

"Fairly. People get wild hairs up their ass about restoring truth and justice and all that. Which never made sense to me: truth still exists, we just rebranded it."

Nero tried faking a grin, gave up, and settled on earnest confusion. Until now, he'd assumed that he was part of the Ouija Board's blind spot. There was no logic behind that assumption, it was simply how the human ego worked. It made sense that the system picked up on his would-be revolution, but the idea made him feel even smaller.

"Get behind the kill team. The coup should be here any minute."

"Thank you, sir," Nero said blankly. Images of Avery's last moment were stuck in his mind's eye.

"It's nothing. You're too expensive to get caught in the cross fire. Can you use a firearm?"

"No."

"Well, take a gun anyway and point in the general direction of the elevator. Odds are you'll hit something. Agent Fern can turn the safety off for you."

Diana's last name still sounded wrong: she acted like a Jackson, or a Wilhelm, or a Khan. Fern was a name for someone writing grant proposals for one of the long-defeated environmentalist nonprofits.

Nero wandered over to the safe(r) side of the firing line and accepted a surprisingly lightweight assault rifle from a burly male agent. He pointed it down the hallway and considered letting a full magazine rip into the director's back. There were worse ways to go. Diana quietly took the gun, ejected the magazine, and handed it back to him.

"Thanks, *Agent Fern.*" Nero leaned on the empty gun like a walking stick.

[Don't be a brat,] chastised First.

[Excellent riposte, Commander.]

The director watched them critically for a moment before snorting, sipping his soda, and deciding he didn't care.

Nero ran a stopwatch program in his left eye. It would be interesting to see how long he could keep up the farce. When the promised droid-backed assassination attempt failed to materialize, someone would ask just what they'd been up to for the last half hour. After the word "treason" entered the conversation, the best-case scenario would be a show trial. At least then he'd get to live out his day in a private prison complex, welding armor onto riot suppression drones. Sadly, Riley Logan was more likely to have him shot on the spot.

Gabriel Logan led the next group to round the corner. The quartet from the party trailed behind him, followed by seven models of murder android even bulkier than the prison guards. Each android carried a gun roughly the size and apparent weight of a human torso. Any surprise on Gabriel's face was quickly replaced with triumph.

"That's a nice team you've put together, Dad. But they're all meat. Meat gets old, and slow, and ambushed by its brilliant children. It's time for the old meat to retire."

"Debug Code: Cantrell the Toucan," replied the director.

All seven androids went limp. Their guns fell to the floor, cracking the tiles underneath. Gabriel's four co-conspirators looked at the younger Logan, who had gone white. No secret backup plan was forthcoming. They then turned to the elder Logan, who rolled his eyes and beckoned with his free hand. Two of the four joined the director's firing line and silently drew beads on Gabriel. The other two missed their moment, frozen by either indecision or shock.

"I'm your son," said Gabriel. "That has to be worth some leniency."

"Light them up," said the director.

Before Nero could protest or cover his ears, the firing line unloaded. The first gun went off by his right ear, and then the world was reduced to flashing lights and a high-pitched whine. In a small way he was thankful for the tinnitus: it kept him from hearing any of the victims' screams.

Gabriel was the last rebel standing. His survival said that his mods were good enough for him to dodge a bullet. The horrible open wounds covering his left flank said they weren't good enough for him to dodge twenty bullets.

Half of the holes in his torso sparked, and all of them bled. Gabriel took four limping steps forward, wheezing with every inch he gained. His gun arm dangled at his side, rendered useless. Gabriel glared at the limb as if he could intimidate it into healing, then spat a single blood-soaked wad of phlegm at his father's feet. It landed a meter short.

Shame and disgust competed for Nero's attention. Ten minutes after wishing he could see a Logan die, he wanted to be anywhere else. Gabriel's last stand had devolved into a piece of theater, which his father refused to end with a simple order.

Diana took out her service pistol, squinted, and shot twice. Gabriel collapsed.

"There's that," said the director. "Good work." He patted Diana on the back twice and then tossed his empty can toward a garbage bin. It missed wide. "Bad aim runs in the family."

30. Selling Out
5:11 p.m.

Nero recognized that he could—and should—have been in Gabriel's place. The late agents' coup had been far better organized than Nero's aborted stunt: representatives from each 2I faction had been in Gabriel's entourage, ready to seize control once the director's corpse had cooled off. There wasn't any *after* in Nero's plan, only a hazy vision of satisfying, blood-drenched revenge. With blood pooling three feet away, this felt petty.

Then there was the second lesson: the Ouija Board was the best asset that the Dominion could ask for. For all the mechanically augmented soldiers, experimental weapons of mass destruction, and ill-gotten wealth at its disposal, nothing compared to the ability to predict and manipulate dissent. As long as it existed, the only rational options were surrender and suicide. He didn't feel suicidal.

"Sir, if you have a minute," said Nero.

"For my new pet bughead? Of course."

"Thanks. This might not be the best time, considering your recent loss—"

"Honestly, I've been expecting this since he enlisted. Gabriel had everything he could ask for since he was ten; it's a miracle that he didn't come out a serial killer. Cantrell's stepson has a fridge full of severed hands."

"Right," Nero said. He opted not to dwell on the words. "I'm ready for onboarding. If anyone on the team has time, I'd loved to get started."

Diana's mask of calm cracked, letting an incredulous glare slip through. He squeezed her gun-free hand. His brand of cynicism would take some getting used to, but hopefully she'd catch on in time.

"That's a quality attitude. To be honest, I was worried you were going to let dating in-office drag your work down. It's good to see your eyes—well, eye—on the prize."

"I try," Nero said. The other agents rapidly lost interest in the exchange and drifted back into the late Gabriel's birthday party. Inoffensive pop music still emanated from the boardroom, and multiple bottles and unopened presents were unclaimed within.

He released Diana's hand and followed the director into the elevator. He tried not to look behind him and ended up doing it twice. Her eyes were a mixture of bewilderment and fury, until they shifted to the still-warm firearm in her left hand. Nero hoped that she wouldn't decide to use it. Mercifully, indecision held long enough for the elevator doors to close.

"I like to think I understand Zeus's perspective," said the director. On the ride down, Riley entered a monologue about the eyes of God and the state of nature. Nero found it entirely forgettable and missing most of the director's glib charm. Somehow, even the man holding the strings had learned to take himself far too seriously. After all the time Nero had spent fearing and hating Riley from a distance, the live version was another petty disappointment. Avery had deserved better.

The elevator stopped at floor 16.5, which evidently existed. If memory served, this sat between Censors and Tracking on the sixteenth floor and Experimental Weapons Development above. Even with a hidden floor separating them, Nero had felt tremors from the occasional explosion in his old office.

They stepped into the Free Dominion's most carefully guarded secret: a server room with five pale programming types sitting in cheap-looking plastic chairs. Four looked somewhat focused on their unseen tasks while another made his way through a bag of chips. If Nero had been told this was the IT support office instead of a classified surveillance project, he never would have given the room a second look.

He'd imagined the Ouija Board as a modern version of ENIAC, one of the few pieces of history that survived his education. Punch cards and vacuum tubes were out of fashion, but the imposing bulk had to be present. Anything less would be an insult to the lives it manipulated.

The Dominion was fond of insults. The full Ouija Board system comprised ten dusty computer towers and a web of knotted cables feeding into the ceiling. The apex of the towers reached just above Nero's waist, the ideal height for an impromptu desk or footrest.

Thin white cables connected the bugheads to the central unit, which was distinguished by an extra foot of height and a blue Post-it note reading "Central Unit." Two bugheads fed their cables into empty eye sockets, two used holes at the backs of their skulls, and one tucked it neatly behind an artificial ear. Years after getting used to the routine of plucking out his own eye, seeing others physically plugged into anything still unnerved him.

"Is this the whole thing?" Nero asked after a natural break in Riley's speech.

"Yup," said the idle bughead. "Think about the army of robots in your brain. Heavy-duty hardware doesn't need much space anymore."

"It's a beautiful thing," said the director. "With this team's effort, 2I ensures a safe future. Namely, one that looks a lot like the present. As long as you're in the inner circle, you'll find that the present treats you pretty damn well.

"You'll be replacing Jack Vasquez. Velanquez? Something South Wardy with a *V*. He walked off with a hard drive. The drive should turn up eventually, but Jack won't. You know, since we killed him. I had Gabriel do it; he was always up for overtime. I'll miss that kid."

"Makes sense." A little more of Nero's sense of decency died.

"To be honest, your test scores amazed me. You're either a genius or found some way to cheat. Either works for our purposes. I think you'll be better at this than John ever was."

"Don't you mean Jack?" asked Nero.

"Sure. Now, you don't officially start until tomorrow, but I suggest familiarizing yourself with the interface. Things move quickly out there, and I'd rather know the next building that's going to get firebombed today than tomorrow."

Riley patted the only empty chair in the room. "Jack Valdez" was etched onto the armrest, likely by coin or fingernail. Nero eyed the impression and added the name to the rapidly growing list of the fallen. Life in the inner circle didn't look any less lethal.

"You kids have fun," Riley added. "I'm looking forward to next month's predictions. If a group decides to off Cantrell, I just might let it happen. For now, I need to tell my wife that Gabriel gave his life to the mission."

"Sorry for your loss, sir," said the idle bughead. When the director simply laughed and fled the room, he looked unsurprised. Once Riley was safely out of sight or earshot, he opened his backpack and pulled out two cans of East Ward Pilsner. He tilted one toward Nero, who accepted without opening it.

"Thanks. I'm Nero, by the way."

"Barrett. You seen the orientation video yet?"

"Yup."

"That dude loves to talk. Need help getting the eye out?"

"No need, I've had a lot of practice lately. But you could tell me more about what Jack used to do here before he . . . well, you know."

"Played hero."

"Yeah."

Barrett set aside his already empty can. He eyed the rest of the team with the friendly patronization unique to middle managers.

"Before he decided to throw his life away, Jack was the last step in our assembly line. It starts with Jan and Perry, who process incoming surveillance data. That's the third shittiest job. Imagine sorting through every satellite camera, hacked OdinEye, and web chat transcript in the Dominion in a week.

"Then Mac and Dexter use that data to build personality profiles. This is the second shittiest job, and carries a *slight* risk of frying their brains. We haven't had an accident in a few months, though, so I think they have a good grasp of it. Definitely better than the last guys.

"Finally, there's you. You'll apply the predictive equations—I can't even look at that doc without getting a headache—to finished profiles, track any notable outcomes, and make sure we're meeting our monthly radicalization quotas. This is the shittiest job: predicting the future every morning nearly drove Jack nuts, and he was Central University's valedictorian. Were you a valedictorian?"

"I stole notes off the valedictorian."

"Much healthier."

"One question: What do you do?"

"I supervise, which means I type your results into a spreadsheet. It's the best job in 2I and maybe even the country."

Nero experienced workplace camaraderie for the first time. There may have been an age gap, but Barrett was a tired-looking techie with an appreciation for day drinking and a healthy detachment from the world he worked in. Twenty-four hours earlier, Nero would have considered him a fat twin. Today he simply felt embarrassed.

He took his seat, stuffed his eye into his pocket, and plugged himself in. After adjusting the height of his chair and resting both feet against the central unit, Nero kicked off the worst tech support disaster in Dominion history.

30.5. Final Intermission

First: That's the board? I expected something a little more artful, like a glowing orb or a building-sized mech. At the very least, a self-aware artificial intelligence with a misanthropic streak. I know those are illegal, but half the point of an autocracy's breaking your own rules.

Second: I miss Avery.

First: Me too. I'm trying to make this less depressing by riffing.

Third: Riffing? Our boy just sold out after watching his boy get murdered. I knew that house slave didn't have a spine, but turns out he doesn't even have a soul.

Nero: How poetic.

Third: The fuck?

Second: You can hear us on this channel?

First: If I had a mouth, I'd do a spit-take.

Nero: You're in my brain. I can hear you on any channel with minimal effort, I just avoid this one to give you a little space and stay sane.

Third: If you were sane, you'd have killed the director and his goons.

First: Odd definition of "sane."

Nero: I'm getting revenge my own way. Diana's right: I'm not a cowboy. But—

Second: I fail to see what herding cattle has to do with—

First: Hush.

Nero: —but I can break their favorite toy. Better yet, I can make them pay for my time.

First: Wonderful! Why was all the fanfare necessary? Not that we don't enjoy your presence.

Nero: Because you'll be doing all the hard work.

First: That's not new.

Nero: Because we won't get to talk much anymore. Remember that escape route of yours? I'm uploading you guys into the Ouija Board. It's not Valhalla, but it'll have to do.

Third: The fuck? Do we get a say in this?

Nero: I'm afraid not. This is more important than getting me laid. I need you to filter the Ouija Board output. Namely, I need you to replace predictions of legitimate threats with harmless nonsense.

Second: That seems difficult.

Nero: Not at all. You can overlook the Children of Kali's next target and highlight Abrahamic Union sit-ins. Ignore the next woman taking a shot at Riley Logan's job and frame a senator for leaks he has no plans to make. Warn them about the next riot three weeks after it happens. It's a simple con, and I'll be around from nine to five to provide inspiration.

Third: I'm starting to like the sound of this.

Second: The core idea is sound. But, for maximum effect, some of the information should be legitimate. Otherwise they'll know the board itself is the issue.

Nero: I'm giving you creative latitude. If and when this scheme catches up with me, I want you to keep it going. Or destroy the system outright. Or do something new. You're about to be inside the most protected network in the country; I'm not sure what you *can't* do once you're tired of my prank.

First: Well, you finally found a way to dump us. But you'll miss my wit.

Nero: Yeah, I'll have to insult myself to keep my self-esteem from spinning out of control.

Third: You're going to miss this eye candy.

Nero: You don't have a body.

Third: Nah, man, I have two hundred thousand microscopic bodies. And they're all fucking gorgeous.

Nero: I don't know how to answer that.

Second: I'll miss you, Commander.

Nero: Jesus, can't you coat this in a bit of irony like the rest of us? It's the best survival mechanism out there.

Second: I don't understand irony. I do understand leaving a friend behind. You're one of the only three I've ever had.

Nero: If I start tearing up, our cover is ruined.

Third: I'm sort of sorry for calling you a dickless wonder, and a punk, and a bitch, and all the other shit. I just wanted you to hold your head up. Punk.

Nero: I'm serious. If I don't keep a straight face, there's a good chance all four of us will die.

First: Be nice to your weird fascist girlfriend. Somehow, you seem to be good for each other. And if you leave her for another tattoo shop addict, she'll probably shoot you.

Nero: I'm closing the channel. For the mission.

31. Functional Freedom
6:00 p.m.

Back to silence. The voices in Nero's head had anchored him to reality, often against his will. Without them, he'd have to work harder to stay out of an asylum. Worse yet, he'd have to manually control his bugs again. His head now housed one large, disorganized swarm. Until he found a new way to cheat, stealing bank accounts would require graduate-level effort.

After trying and failing to hack his own phone, he spent two useless hours staring at the ceiling. Pretending to work had been more productive with his bugs. A gentle ribbing from First or flamboyant insult from Third would pass the time and set the agenda. Now he had the only vote. For all of his lip service to self-determination, Nero wasn't very used to it.

To his left, Barrett dutifully typed out several paragraphs of toxic misinformation in twelve-point type. From the half of the screen Nero could see, he guessed that only a third of the information left in the Ouija Board was both accurate and useful. Diversions included minor drug deals, actors going political during award shows, and the rise of a fictional movement of fundamentalist Buddhists called the Fists of Enlightenment. Unless the latter was legitimate, which was possible in the Free Dominion.

Nero offered his new coworkers half-hearted goodbyes and received half-hearted congratulations in turn. His pseudo-spy instincts said that leaving work early set the right precedent and ensured a more natural performance. It was far too late in his career to start pretending to be a straight shooter.

After making it outside, he surprised himself by popping his eye in without a mirror. He had the standard post-insertion headache but none of the full-body agony that followed a screwup. The left half of the block came into view, complete with the garbage and wandering vagrants that defined East Ward.

"That has to make me some kind of savant," he told no one. "Or at least an adult." The vagrants distanced themselves from him.

Inspiration sent him to Maria's, a bar ten essential blocks away from Headquarters. Maria's didn't have a gimmick: it was a dive owned and operated by a woman named Maria. After touring the rest of the East Ward dining scene in a day, Nero appreciated that simplicity. Gimmicks and passing health code tests were unnecessary frills.

He sat one stool away from the bar's left edge and put his coat over the stool to his right. The experienced drunk's way of carving out territory. He fired a quick message to Diana with his location and the promise of an explanation. Then he composed a far less apologetic draft for one of the people that had pulled a weapon on him.

To: Management.NoRefunds

Hey Alexa,

I'm guessing you run this address now, given recent events. Jason seems too nice to seize power after a coup. You might be busy writing half a song or teaching spies to disappoint people, but this concerns you.

You've got at least a month without 2I knowing what comes next. Try to do something useful with it.

—Nero

After two shots of thought, he made an addition.

P.S.: I know you can take or leave drinking, but I strongly recommend finding something to take the edge off living in hell. You'll be surprised what you can come up with when you're not thinking of killing yourself.

Perfect. With First out of his head, Nero was even free to chuckle at his own joke. He was ten minutes into this male pastime when Diana annexed the stool to his left. All signs of the fury he'd been preparing lines to defuse had been displaced by fatigue. Nonetheless, he decided to start things off light. Words for what he'd been up to for the last two hours weren't coming easily.

"Another bar. You should consider an artificial liver."

"You didn't say no. Besides, the last bar was the best part of our night out."

Diana didn't dispute that. Instead, she ran a finger along the countertop, drawing a wide line in the dust. She eyed the dust on her finger like a personal insult.

"You've had fun, though, right?"

"No. I've been ditched, told my life is a lie, forced to shoot my partner, and ditched again."

"Well, at least we had the one night."

"There'll be a second, and a third. You've only begun to pay me back for destroying my peace of mind."

Nero decided to focus on the attraction half of his reaction and downplay the terror. Somehow, this kind of comment fed into Diana's sense of humor. He suspected that it wasn't too far from her real perspective, but he could respect it as her way of coping.

"I'm sorry we couldn't do more for your friend," said Diana.

"I honored him the best way I could: turning complete control of the most advanced surveillance apparatus in history to three AI."

"Repeat that," Diana ordered.

He repeated it. When that didn't suffice, he went into the specifics of his illegal experiments, personal Greek chorus, and national-scale sabotage.

"Nero, I'm sure the voices in your head were very nice. But do you have any idea how terrifying that is?"

"Half as terrifying as the status quo. After the current batch of human autocrats, I'm fine giving machines a try. They can't do worse."

Diana flicked his forehead. It was in her power to decapitate him, but the blow was closer to a bee sting. Nero accepted it.

"You should be happy. I've held up my end of our deal," said Nero.

"You've sold out the human race."

"Details. What concerns us is that the director won't know about the next person to take a shot at him. An enterprising young woman could take advantage of that."

While watching her think, Nero pinpointed Diana's nervous habit. Her fingers dug the same holes into the bar counter that she'd left on the office wall and restaurant table. Seeing her dig past her fingertips was good for his ego. He'd dropped the opportunity of a lifetime into Diana's lap; even if she didn't betray shock with words, control over body language only went so far.

"Acceptable," Diana said.

"Pardon?"

"I'm revising my review of our date. It's been acceptable."

She ordered three shots of Liver Thinner and slid him one.

"To Avery."

"Avery hated you."

Diana shrugged and drank, radiating the imperial confidence that caught his eye during the outage. She had a classical aura, as if she'd been cut from marble a thousand years before democracy collapsed under its own weight. That stood out after a lifetime surrounded by fear. He'd hoped to steal some of that aura for himself.

He wanted to think of himself as lucky. They'd survived spiting the most powerful man in Dominion, but losing the only four people in his life felt like failure. Avery and the bugs had kept his sense of humor alive, saving him from insanity.

"If your coup works out, and we don't get executed, do you think we'll still have time to drink like this?" Nero asked.

"No. Order something expensive, we probably won't have to pay for it."

They laughed together.

Princeton University: 1. Where future leaders learn to say "future leaders" to other future leaders as they lead the future.

2. Where a capella goes to die.

3. A monastic order venerating Woodrow Wilson.

4. The abandoned petri dish modern consulting firms lurched out of.

5. Home of all surviving first edition copies of *Atlas Shrugged*.

6. The Goldman Sachs waiting room.

7. A slightly stifling environment for a budding creative.

prison: Free vacations for subalterns.

procrastination: [Note to self: Finish this one later.]

pro wrestling: The simple genius of taking the guilt out of combat sports.

publishing: The reason you're more into TV.

Purgatorio: 1. Dante's sophomore slump.
2. God's sophomore slump.

pyramids: Monuments to the power of ingenuity, faith, and merciless whipping.

Q

Q: A conspiracy just insane enough to be undebunkable.

quality assurance: A corporate department typically consisting of a rubber stamp, a sleeping intern, and a vice president experimenting with quaaludes.

quant: The only cynical way to use a math degree.

quarantine: The door is made of lava.

queen: A shield for any flights of fancy, madness, treason, infertility, or simple ineptitude that strike the king.

quest: An oath to generate at least one trilogy of content.

Question

PulseChurn asks: How do you feel about being black?
    "I don't really think about it."
    —*Bart Rudd, Student*

"It bothers me that almost every homeless guy I see in this city is black. Could we get a diversity program for poverty? You know, affirmative action for sleeping in parks? It could change things."

—*Nina Bryant, Publicist*

"It's time we took some responsibility. My high school didn't even talk about Jim Crow, so he couldn't have been that bad."

—*Wendy Hart, Pundit*

"Black men invented Wushu. The colleges want us to forget, but we remember the truth. The one-inch punch is black. The Shaolin temples were black. The three-section staff is black. It's all black."

—*Dean Williams, Unemployed*

"For a long time, I didn't care. But now it's been six years since my last promotion, and that has me thinking."

—*Zachary Easton, Coder*

"Black? It's all right. Poor? It's killing me. I can't even afford to be depressed about it."

—*Caleb Jones, Cashier*

"Great question! Follow @NubianQueenSelene for the answer. You might learn something about oppression. And dog gifs. Focus on the oppression."

—*Selene Parsons, Influencer*

"Think of the butterfly effect. If I wasn't black, what else would change? Would America still exist? Would we cure colon cancer? Would giant bipedal ladybugs control the world?"

—*Lisa Martin, Nurse*

"I've got a kid. I made the same mistake as a dozen white girls in this shithole town, but I get all the looks and jokes. It's not funny from where I'm sitting."

—*Anna Foxwood, Assistant Librarian*

"Well, I get to say nigga. Nigga. Nigga-nigga-nigga. Nigga? Nigga!"

—*Robert North, Lawyer*

"I'm proud, as all kings should be. Being born black is my greatest accomplishment."

—*Cedric Lane, Unemployed*

"I just want to marry a white woman. Anything else is worse than being alone. And I can't be alone with me. I went to white schools in a white town in a white state. I need a white wife to feel like myself."

—*Elliot Andrews, Therapist*

"Fuck whitey."

—*Tyler Cole, Correctional Officer*

"It's kicking the shit out of me. Google 'Jamaicans and homosexuality' the next time you're having a good day."

—*Stella Hammond, Greeter*

"I read that the police are shooting us. And that white terrorists are shooting us. And that we're shooting us. Does all that really happen? I don't want to get shot."

—*Jessica Clark, Student*

"It was cool until I got shot."

—*Ernest Kincaid, Student*

"Let me tell you: my parents came from Angola, and the niggers here are out of control. I'm perfectly proud of being black, but don't associate me with your niggers."

—*Loide Boavida, Retiree*

"In *Dungeons & Dragons*, there's this chart called an encounter table. It decides what monsters and traps players encounter based on a dice roll between one and a hundred. At one, you might find some gold. At 100, you might find a pissed-off dragon made of gold. Follow me? Being black is like going through life with a second encounter table. Between 1 and 50, nothing happens. A 56 gets you a 'random' traffic stop, and an 81 gets you a racist manager. Roll 100 and you get your own hashtag. Which would be nice, if you were around to enjoy it."

—*Ed Galloway, High School Football Coach*

"I don't give two wet shits, and I'm tired of people expecting me to. Piss off."
—*Fred Austere, Author*
"It's pretty fucked."
—*Davin Porter, Civil Engineer*
"It's great."
—*R. B. Cartwright, Valet*
"It's okay."
—*Cynthia Lucas, Professor of African-American Studies*

quintessence: The only GRE word you need to start a magick blog.

quote: Liberation of language from context and intent.

quotidian: An uncommon word for average.

R

racism: A topic publishers request that Black writers discuss with the same style, opinion, and exclusive focus as other black writers.

rap: Rhythm and Profit.

rapture, the: The ascent of the four or five decent people left to heaven.

Rastafarianism: The pop culture signature of an island dominated by Baptists.

reaction: The belief that the Magna Carta ruined everything.

reactionary: A conservative before breakfast.

reading: A game people played before radio.

rebellion: A revolution without an agent.

Recent Activity

Posting Date	Amount	Transaction Description	Balance (USD)
12/26/2016	+112.00	Omega Mart: Payroll	757.50
12/28/2016	–13.00	Thompson Psychiatric: Appointment Cancellation Fee	744.50
12/31/2016	–600.00	Galatea Jewelers: 22K Wedding Band, 2x	144.50
12/31/2016	–13.20	BookJungle: *The Coma Patient's Guide to Wedding Planning* by Ronald Jones	131.30
1/1/2017	–40.00	Leo's Deli: Dick Javert's Semi-Premium Whiskey	91.30
1/2/2017	–40.00	Leo's Deli: Dick Javert's Semi-Premium Whiskey	51.30
1/3/2017	–60.00	Leo's Deli: Dick Javert's Premium Whiskey	–8.70
1/3/2017	–35.00	Overdraft Fee	–43.70
1/9/2017	+430.00	Wire Transfer from Mary Holton	386.30
1/9/2017	–200.00	ATM Withdrawal	186.30
1/9/2017	–2.00	Leo's Deli: Spark Cola (Cherrysplosion)	184.30
1/9/2017	–22.00	CareerRocket: Deluxe Job Hunter's Membership	162.30
1/9/2017	–10.30	Omega Mart: Deluxe High-Thread Résumé Paper	152.00
1/10/2017	–20.00	Leo's Deli: Dick Javert's Sub-Premium Whiskey	132.00
1/13/2017	–14.93	BookJungle: *The Stud's Guide to Slut-Slaying* by Maximilian Tuck	117.07
1/14/2017	–8.00	Omega Mart: LumberJacked Cologne	109.07
1/14/2017	–17.00	Omega Mart: Ajax Protein Powder	92.07
1/14/2017	–50.00	Iron Works Fitness Center: 6 Month Membership	42.07
1/14/2017	–5.00	Omega Mart: LumberJacked Body Wash	37.07

Posting Date	Amount	Transaction Description	Balance (USD)
1/16/2017	−2.00	Leo's Deli: Spark Cola (ChocoRampage)	35.07
1/20/2017	−15.00	BookJungle: *Castrated: Why Social Justice Insurgents Defanged Real America* by Anna Cameron	20.07
1/21/2017	−6.00	Taco Queen: Jumbo Beef Piñata	14.07
1/21/2017	−512.00	FedLoan Servicing: Unsubsidized Loan Installment, Automatic Deduction	−497.93
1/21/2017	−35.00	Overdraft fee	−532.93
2/10/2017	1,594.00	Wire Transfer from Jack Holton Sr.	1,061.07
2/10/2017	−200.00	ATM Withdrawal	861.07
2/14/2017	−17.49	BookJungle: *Ass-hammered: How Degeneracy Broke Western Marriage* by Anna Cameron	843.58
2/15/2017	−1.00	MusicBox: Maximum Boys, "Better Off Alone" [Cover]	842.58
2/18/2017	−1.00	MusicBox: Maximum Boys, "Love Wilts" [Single]	841.58
2/20/2017	−28.00	Kanojo Studios: Virtual Fiancée	813.58
2/21/2017	−33.00	Libidex: AutoFap Mechanical Pleasure Aid	780.58
2/25/2017	−14.00	MusicBox: Maximum Boys, *So She's Gone* [Album]	766.58
2/25/2017	−21.00	MusicBox: Maximum Boys, *Best of the Maximum Boys* [Album]	745.58
2/28/2017	−185.00	AmeriRail: Milwaukee to Penn Station, One Way	560.58
2/29/2017	+17.00	Iron Works Fitness Center: Partial Refund	577.58
3/4/2017	−22.00	MaxFans.com: Maximum Boys Baseball Cap	555.58
3/4/2017	−2.00	Leo's Deli: Spark Cola (Eggscellent)	553.58

Posting Date	Amount	Transaction Description	Balance (USD)
3/6/2017	−18.00	BookJungle: *Facefucked: How the Liberal Elite Strangled the American Dream* by Anna Cameron	535.58
3/9/2017	−2.00	Leo's Deli: Spark Cola (BananaMax)	533.58
3/10/2017	−120.00	Backyard Commando: Red-Dot Aiming Sight	413.58
3/12/2017	−30.00	Omega Mart: Personalized Birthday Cake	383.58
3/12/2017	−49.00	Ticketmaster: Maximum Boys Farewell Tour, Jameson Theater	334.58
3/12/2017	−320.00	Backyard Commando: JV-12 Semiautomatic Rifle	14.58
3/12/2017	−10.06	MaxFans.com: Maximum Boys T-shirt	4.52
3/15/2017	−2.50	AmeriRail: In-trip Wi-Fi	2.02
3/16/2017	−2.00	Jameson Theater: Spark Cola (VanILLa)	0.02

Reddit: The place a pandering version of you lives.

religion: Dubious.

Republicans: 1. The party of Lincoln.
2. Sworn enemies of Lincoln.

revenge: Thoroughly underrated.

reverse racism: The permanent underclass' refusal to leave well enough alone.

revolution: 1. Where all the kings went.
2. The leftist rapture.

rioting: The people's Super-PAC.

Robespierre: The pacifist populist in charge of executions and suppressing the masses.

Roma: A topic that teaches you a little too much about your European acquaintances.

Roman Empire, the: A vast militaristic world power founded on notions of freedom that collapsed under the weight of its own arrogance and excess. The appeal to American scholars remains elusive.

roses: 1. Are red.
2. See *Violets*.

Russia: A popular winter vacation on the path to world domination.

S

Saint Patrick's Day: Snakes and falling off ladders.

Santa: According to television: a genocidal android, a serial killer, a wizard, a kidnapping victim, and hit-and-run suspect. Occasionally delivers presents.

Satan: The only member of the angelic choir to launch a successful solo career.

satire: A compromise between comedy and terrorism.

science fiction: Next week's satire.

sex: 1. Simple fun.
2. Hideously complicated.

sexism: Maintaining belief in your gender's superiority after more than thirty seconds in a public restroom.

sex on the beach: 1. A drink typically purchased at resorts.
2. An act typically performed at resorts.
3. Excruciating.

short fiction: An obsolete form best left to graduate school washouts.

sick leave: Dates roughly corresponding with *Grand Theft Auto* franchise releases.

Sinclair, Upton: Socialist oppressor of meatpacking patriots everywhere.

slavery: The easiest way to put a laptop together.

slaves: The commodity backing American currency.

sleep: What no child wants and no adult has.

Snapchat: The place a deniable version of you lives.

sobriety: 1. Your strongest, fastest, smartest state.
2. Intolerable.

socialism: A dangerous gateway to health care.

South America: The half that survives World War III.

Space Glaive

I bought my first pack of Space Glaive figurines at fourteen, during the twilight years of the Bush dynasty. I'd traveled to Maria's Hobbies & Hardware to buy an RC helicopter, but Space Glaive's box art caught my eye. The detailed painting of a two-headed dragon fighting a three-headed cyborg promised a world of glory that no battery-operated toy could match. I turned the box over to read the sales pitch.

This box is not for the weak of heart or mind. It contains a starter army for SPACE GLAIVE, the ultimate science fiction war game. Turn back, and find a general worthy of commanding the heroes within. Advanced rulebook, tape measure, dice, carrying case, terrain templates, and paint sold separately.

I spent my last thirty dollars on the starter kit. Since then, I have conquered.

The road to Space Glaive regional champion tested my endurance for the next fifteen years. New York generals are notoriously cutthroat: the same ruthlessness that fuels success at consulting firms and branding agencies fuels brilliance on the battlefield. I didn't understand real terror until I'd cornered the founder of a Tribeca tech start-up. He gained the expression of a beast and fought like one until the end. He also cheated, which got him banned from the official tournament circuit. I admired that. I still seek out street tournaments in lower Manhattan, hoping for a rematch.

Personally, I fund my army through the law. Copyright lawsuits and countersuits are their own battlefield, where the principles of Space Glaive have served me well. When outnumbered and surrounded by Time Warner's minions, I fall back on two rules:

1. *Never relent.*
2. *Conventional thinking is dead thinking.*

Poor precepts for dating, or any delicate part of one's personal life. Essential concepts in warfare. I stole them from two teenage girls.

At nineteen, I made my pocket money as a babysitter. Humble work. My Friday nights were spent watching over the Freeman sisters as their parents searched for their original spark. I overheard only bits and pieces of the argument, but I understood that Mr. Freeman often slept with people that weren't Mrs. Freeman, and vice versa. It wasn't clear who started it, but they'd both become comfortable with a cycle of forgiveness, recrimination, and revenge.

The Freeman sisters detected the tension between their parents and imitated it artfully. Their two-story Colonial home was evenly divided: Trianna controlled the basement, Renee controlled the top floor, and I sat in the kitchen, eyeing the exits. The house was usually silent, aside from any music I played through my headphones. Usually Viking metal. *Always* Viking metal. The rapid-fire drumming stirred my spirit.

This pattern held on the first Friday in October. While their neighbors indulged in extravagant Halloween decorations, the Freeman house was unchanged. The parents departed without making eye contact with each other and left me fifty dollars on the kitchen counter beneath an empty bottle of overproof rum.

The money represented an inspiring array of possibilities. Fifty dollars covered at least half an army's worth of figurines and paint. I could already imagine my new cavalry putting an end to my campus losing streak. Glory was in sight as long as I tended to my duty; every two hours or so I had to check that both girls were alive.

First, I went upstairs. Trianna's realm was brightly lit, with shelves, desks, and windowsills filled with neatly arranged model kits of anime icons. In theory, this should have given us something in common: mecha models and Space Glaive troops required the same painstaking assembly and decoration by hand. She even had the same brand of pencil brush. But I lacked the charisma to overcome the wall of sullen silence Trianna projected. This was the main divergence between Space Glaive and live warfare: leadership required a loud voice.

"Hey, Trianna, how's it going?"

"Piss off."

"All right, I'll be downstairs."

I fled to the first floor, regrouped, and made my way to the basement. Engagements with Trianna tended to be difficult, and well-timed retreats were key.

Renee's realm presented its own challenges. As I descended the wooden stairwell, three kinds of incense and at least two strains of marijuana assaulted my eyes and nose. I deeply admired the Hashishin but couldn't imagine anyone surviving this level of hotboxing. Yet Renee sat unharmed and cross-legged in the center of the cloud. A modern sage. She meditated (or napped) on top of four light blue pillows. Her perch put her at eye contact level. (I'm not the tallest of the great generals.) She must have detected a change in the smoke: she smirked and turned toward me before I said a word.

"Hey, nerd guy. What's up?"

Conversations with Renee always felt like a trap. While she was perfectly friendly, she clearly regarded me as an alien. She was also perfectly aware that my name was Andre.

"Nothing much. Just making sure everything's all right down here."

"I'm fine." She took a dog-eared paperback off the floor. Her reading issue must have been coming along. "I'm guessing that Trianna's in bitch mode. You know, since that's her only mode."

"She's fine. Maybe you should talk to her?"

"Nah, I don't feel like interrupting the 24/7 Gundam marathon. I might catch weeaboo."

"Well, consider it," I offered. This overstepped the bounds of a babysitter's limited authority, but I felt compelled to say something. I'd appraised the situation: the sisters were the only salvageable part of the family. Even in a full retreat, it was important to save as many stragglers as possible. As the older sibling (fourteen rather than twelve), Renee might have some exploitable seed of responsibility.

With my conscience cleared, I returned to my perch in the kitchen and removed two lunchbox-sized cases from my backpack. Each foam-lined plastic case held an unpainted Space Glaive army. I planned on spending my night decorating Rocket Elves and Undwarves, the two newest additions to the Space Glaive universe. I had trouble understanding their place in the wider plot, but their Tolkien-inspired aesthetic lent battles some much-needed visual flair.

The infantry were about half the size of my thumb. Undwarf tanks and Rocket Elf gunships were slightly smaller than my fist and took a bit more attention to detail. It took me twenty minutes to apply a base coat of paint to both armies—black for the dwarves, silver for the elves—followed by an idle hour of waiting for them to dry. In the interim, I read headlines on my phone. I considered filtering authentic information from the trash a worthy test of my intuition.

"Damn, that's a lot of paint. If you don't open a window, you're going to start seeing some wild shit."

Renee had entered the kitchen without me noticing. An admirable display of skill. She was wrist-deep into a bag of pork rinds and smiling like a cherub. I moved to open a window and found Trianna watching me from the bottom of the stairwell. This destroyed my faith in my babysitting ability. Both charges had spent more time and attention watching me than I'd expended all night.

"Uh, hey again," I said.

"What kind of models are those?" Trianna asked.

"It's a tabletop strategy game called Space Glaive," I volunteered. She didn't laugh or run away, so I took heart. "*The* tabletop strategy game. There's no other experience like it. Well, Dinosaur Hunters is close but way too expensive."

"What's a glaive?" she asked.

I started mouthing an answer and then realized I didn't have one. Later, I read that it's a type of spear.

"I'm not sure. But the game's great."

Trianna followed me to the kitchen, where her sister had moved on to a bowl of cold leftover salmon. They artfully avoided acknowledging each other, which put an awkward pall over the affair. I persevered and explained the finer points of the Space Glaive ruleset to Trianna. She was more interested in the models themselves, prodding the tips of spears (glaives, I suppose) with the tip of her finger. Still, her earlier antagonism had faded.

Trianna picked up an Undwarf grunt by the head. "I guess the designs are cool. But it seems kind of dumb to collect these if there's no show."

"Jeez. The guy's being paid to talk to you; you could be a little nicer," chided Renee.

"He's being paid to keep you from burning down the house," Trianna replied.

"Ah, there's that positive energy that keeps Dad coming back."

I considered intervening. Trianna's expression said a line had been crossed. But perhaps if I let the argument end naturally, I could get back to explaining the difference between Undwarves and Demidwarves.

"Are you trying to blame me for this, special ed?" Trianna spat.

"Don't go there." Renee's voice took on an unfamiliar timber.

"Should I write it down? It might be hard for you, with the letters flipping around and all that."

"Last warning."

"I'm sure Mom's proud of you taking thirteen years to read the first page of *One Fish, Two Fish*. I'll try not to spoil the ending, but there's a red fish coming up that you're going to love."

Space Glaive tournaments had honed my danger sense. Less balanced generals often took losing poorly. While official tournaments limited payback to personal insults—which the sisters showed a precocious grasp of—the private circuit offered frustrated generals fewer consequences for avenging their armies with their fists. I'd developed an instinct for imminent violence, and usually slipped into the restroom before the situation devolved. This tactic was essential for college games, where the overlap between generals and muscle-bound athletes defied stereotypes. My danger sense saved me from postgame brawls with two linebackers, a sprinter, and a visiting boxer with "Real Nigga" tattooed on his biceps.

The same danger sense let me step between the two before the first punches were thrown. This, unfortunately, led to me taking the punch to the core and a kick to the leg that the sisters had intended for each other. I clutched my leg and used a few gendered slurs, breaching both general tact and babysitting protocol. After composing myself, I noticed a valuable opening: I had both sisters' full attention. More importantly, they looked embarrassed and guilty, which took pressure off of my limited charisma.

"This house is cursed with hatred," I began. "For the sake of peace, I have a proposal."

"Why's he talking like that?" asked Renee.

"Not sure," said Trianna.

"My solution is simple: battle."

"We were just doing that," Trianna noted.

"*Mental* battle."

"Like psychics? Do you watch *Kuro no Keiyakusha* too?" asked Trianna. "Please, tell me you do. The idiots in this house have no taste."

"You get it, right? You see why I have to knock her out?"

I pointed at myself and made a stern face. This was my mother's tactic for taking control of a room, and I was a firm believer in borrowing from your opponents.

"We'll play Space Glaive. The game of kings."

"Isn't that chess?" asked Renee.

"No," I said bluntly. "You'll quickly learn the difference. But first, the stakes. I'm sure you'd both enjoy exclusive kitchen access. The winner claims the ground floor, to do with as they please."

Trianna shrugged. "I don't really care about that," she said. Renee, who hadn't even responded, drifted to her cell phone.

"The winner will be formally recognized as the smarter sibling," I added.

"Now we're talking," said Renee. "I'm in."

Trianna made a sniffling noise, clearly intended as a snort. "I don't see why I should have to defend that title."

"Because you own plastic cat ears," said Renee. "They make you look like a broke camgirl."

"Wow. You know what? I accept."

"Excellent," I said with all the gravitas I could manage. Even if it was only a game to them, passing a tradition on to a new generation felt powerful. I relished handing each sister a box of freshly painted warriors. Trianna picked a tank out of her box, closed one eye, and peered down the barrel.

"Could you repeat the rules? I remember, but I'm sure that Renee's forgotten."

"I remember them," Renee said. "I was there the entire time."

"Just a quick review. She's a little slow."

I obliged.

Space Glaive had several advantages over chess, an outmoded game for pretentious shut-ins. The first: versatility. Space Glaive's rules worked on any stable surface and used stray objects like sneakers, plates, or sleeping pets as terrain. As long as there wasn't an enemy soldier in the way, infantry could move six inches in any direction, tanks five, and gunships twelve. This required a tape measure, but I kept at least two in my backpack at all times.

The second advantage was variety. Each army reflected its owner's personality. Generals could use any number of any type of soldier as long as their army's total cost didn't exceed one hundred points. Some soldiers had decimal values or adjustable variables that required a bit of algebra to solve, but I thought of that as part of the game's appeal.

There were several more rules, which I recounted with enthusiasm. The sisters tuned me out while they picked their soldiers. They used two of the five pocket rulebooks I kept in my backpack, loose-leaf paper from my untouched lecture notebook, and a pair of well-worn mechanical pencils.

"Jesus Christ, you didn't tell me there would be math," said Trianna. She turned to the left for support. Her sister squinted quietly at the page, occasionally mouthing a *d* or *b*, smirking, and adding another soldier to her list.

Trianna's Undwarves, which she called Empress Trianna's Katana of Darkness (henceforth abridged as ETKD), consisted of two tanks, fourteen riflemen, two samurai, and three grenadiers. I pointed out that dwarven armies typically made heavy use of snipers. She informed me that snipers were for cowards. I held back my instinctive retort and checked on Renee. Her Rocket Elves, which she called Team Shitkicker, consisted of sixteen spearmen, five medics, twelve riflemen, and three cyber-shamans. I asked if she wanted a gunship, and she said that she was too young to drive. Then I remembered that she'd spent two hours hotboxing. The fate of the kitchen would likely come down to Renee's sobriety against Trianna's overconfidence.

Each sister took one side of the table. They made intuitive use of the terrain, setting their soldiers behind the dinner plates stacked on either edge. By using cover, they'd intuitively avoided the most common—and fatal—beginner's mistake. I beamed at the sea of black and silver men that had taken over the Freeman household, and waited for the first shot of a great war. Heaven watched with me.

Space Glaive felt different from a spectator's perch. When I directed an army, my mind reduced the battlefield to an abstraction: minimalist charts of troop formations, casualties, and useful minor rules. But from the sideline I could see the splendor. Each general towered over their army. To the west, Trianna drummed her fingers together, radiating murderous intent. To the east, Renee played with game dice with one hand and reached into a potato chip bag with the other. She chewed loudly, most likely on purpose.

The game started with a coin toss. Trianna called heads, earning the right to move first. She celebrated this small victory by making an *L* on her forehead using her thumb and forefinger. Renee had no visible reaction.

My impression of Trianna's personality led me to expect a reserved, subtle player, likely to a fault. Instead, she committed all of her troops to a direct charge across the table. Each Space Glaive soldier can take two actions a turn (move, shoot, reload, etc.), and she used both to run, bolting past every source of cover on her side of the table. The sprint put her inches away from my backpack, which served as a hill near the dead center of the battlefield. The first player to mount it would have access to the timeless "Stand above your opponent and shoot" strategy.

If this worked, Trianna could control the flow of battle and grind Team Shitkicker down through attrition. But there were risks: an all-out charge meant leaving her men outside of cover. With a few lucky dice rolls, Renee could gun down half of Trianna's exposed infantry on turn one. The hill wouldn't be much use without anyone to occupy it. Judging by her smile, Trianna was certain that the will of heaven was on her side.

From my perch, Renee had two appealing options. Once she finished picking crumbs out of a thoroughly finished bag of chips, she could either move twice and challenge Trianna's control of the hill or shoot twice and whittle down her sister's forces. Both choices amounted to coin flips, and the result would set the tone of the game.

"You two look way too serious," Renee mumbled. Then she moved her men *away* from the hill, toward her edge of the map. She split her forces between the plates on the northeast corner and a cracked vase to the southeast. Both landmarks sat just out of range of Trianna's inevitable turn two counterattack from the hill. She used her second action to fiddle with both squads' formations.

My feet tapped the floor at a hummingbird's pace. They'd both surprised me, which pointed toward genuine talent. There were, broadly speaking, three types of great general: tacticians, berserkers, and madmen. Tacticians (like myself) memorized, fine-tuned, and exploited conventional tactics. My failure to predict the Freeman sisters' movements pointed toward them occupying the other two camps.

If I understood anything about the game, Trianna was a berserker. Her type relied on constant, unrelenting offense. In this mindset, no losses were too hideous as long as the enemy's matched. They'd inherited the spirit of two world wars. One survivor on their side and none on the other meant victory. They were also fond of tanks, which often reduced the more complicated aspects of warfare to "Crawl forward and shoot."

Madmen like Renee had a knack for wholly original and wildly unexpected maneuvers. This approach seldom led to a tie. Their experiments produced stunning failure (Pickett's Charge) or historic routs (the Trojan Horse). The best madmen inherited the spirit of the Colonial rebels, who realized there was no reason to stand in line and exchange fire with the largest empire in the world.

Stereotypically, Space Glaive generals lacked a certain social grace. I disputed that, noting that maladjustment was a feature of my entire generation, not the hobby. That said, the Freeman sisters added a dimension to the game that I'd never seen or considered: psychological warfare.

"What, are you just going to run away?" Trianna stopped drumming her fingers. She watched her sister's response with a predatory glint.

"Yup." Renee's impassive mask held.

"I guess that's a way to lose a little more slowly."

"Yup."

"Are you just going to keep saying that?"

"Yup."

"Your band sucks."

"Yup."

"Goddamn it!"

The sisters fought on an axis I'd never acknowledged in my own battles. Admirable. I made a private note to compose a list of insults in case I encountered this tactic in the future.

Trianna opened turn two by going around the backpack. She used her first action to move her entire army to the northeast, at spitting distance from Team Shitkicker's northern detachment. As a firm believer in the value of holding ground, I was mortified. Then I understood the brilliance: claiming the hill would open her up to a pincer attack. Charging north allowed ETKD to face half of Team Shitkicker on even footing. Which was entirely uneven, considering their relative numbers.

"Is he okay?" asked Renee.

"Who cares? Focus on getting your ass kicked."

After taking three minutes to reread the rules for shooting, ETKD opened fire. Tanks, riflemen, and grenadiers unleashed a torrent of laser fire across a once-peaceful field, an event represented with several dozen dice rolls. Out of the thirty-six shots involved in her offensive, twenty-two rolled above three and confirmed hits. The barrage reduced Team Shitkicker's northern detachment to one medic, three spearmen, and eleven corpses. An act of ruthless butchery I found immensely entertaining. Without the cover offered by the plates, there might've been a rout.

Renee's contented visage hardened. She crushed her empty bag into a ball and pitched it at the garbage. The shot missed.

"Watch this."

The general—and Renee earned that label here—sent her southern detachment charging for the hill. Then she pointed to the ragtag survivors of her northern detachment. First, she rolled for her medic, who managed to bring a single jet spearman back to life.

"I'm using the afterburner-ability thing. The flying one," Renee announced. Her sister glanced at me and waited for an explanation. I perked up. Renee had read beyond the basic rules in the pocket manual and discovered the name "Rocket Elf" actually meant something.

"Um, afterburner lets Rocket Elves fly short distances. In practical terms, they can jump over enemy units. You know, like knights in chess. Only this is *way* better than chess."

Trianna snorted, successfully this time. Renee bunny-hopped her four spearmen over a siege tank and landed them one inch south of the same tank. The difference was minor but essential: they were between

Trianna and the high ground. ETKD couldn't move toward the hill without finishing them off first. Murdering the spearmen would cost Trianna a move action and win Team Shitkicker the high ground.

"Ta-da!"

"You realize you haven't killed anyone yet, right?"

"I'm getting to that."

Turn three went by quickly and predictably. Trianna purged the rest of the northern detachment, and Renee claimed the hill. Middle fingers and glares quietly replaced the volley of verbal insults. Surprisingly, these felt more sporting. They were backed by grudging respect rather than disdain.

That respect was the heart of my plan. Space Glaive rivalries were a unique bond. I had my own rivalry with Maron Reyes, NYU's star player. It wasn't the same thing as friendship; he had a persistent lunch meat smell and considered casual racism a charming quirk. But we'd come to understand each other through combat. Maron was intelligent, passionate, and getting his ass kicked the moment I bought my new jet spearmen. After that, we might get lunch.

On turn four, ETKD pushed forward and fired. Team Shitkicker took minimal losses (three riflemen, one shaman) and spent their round shooting twice. ETKD took eighteen points of damage, losing a third of its infantry. The left tank was on its last legs. Renee looked poised to claim victory over a mountain of dwarven corpses.

Trianna coiled a section of hair around her ring finger. I recognized the gesture: I tended to pick at my twists when backed into a corner.

"Hey, do my guys have any bullshit powers?" Trianna asked. It was the first time I'd been acknowledged in fifteen minutes.

"Two, actually. The first, Cybersight, lets their snipers—"

"Next," she interjected.

"They also have Sacrifice. Undwarf infantry can self-destruct, dealing two points of damage to every unit within three inches."

"English."

"They can blow themselves up."

Her predatory grin returned.

"So as long as I can get a *few* guys up that hill, I've got a shot."

"Maybe," I conceded. "But that sounds less like a plan and more like suicide."

"That's because you don't have any vision. When I'm your age, I'm not going to spend my weekends babysitting. I'm going to be class president, head of the anime club, and interning at a three-letter news network."

". . . That hurt."

"It's not about you. It's about coming out ahead. I'm not into the family hobby of passive failure. I'm starting a lifelong winning streak here and now."

"I really don't feel any less insulted."

Trianna didn't have time for my feelings. The berserker spirit had found her again. She stacked her surviving infantry behind her two tanks, using their large frames as mobile cover. Then she made another straight run for the hill, disregarding a forest of salt and pepper shakers that she could have used to hide and regroup. It wasn't traditional but it was tactically sound: camping in the forest might have allowed her to heal a soldier or two, but Team Shitkicker would have another turn to freely chip away at her forces. The aggressive path put ETKD at the base of the hill, bloody but not defeated.

Renee smiled pitilessly. With victory in sight, the elder sister finally looked engaged with the game itself. She committed most of her army (one shaman, six riflemen) to two shooting actions, focusing fire on the left tank. It collapsed under the barrage, effectively stranding half of Trianna's army. Then she flew her five spearmen to the base of the hill, poised for a pincer attack. I was impressed: Renee had found a way to turn ceding half of the high ground into a trap. I could smell a rout.

"Excellent game," I mumbled. No response. Turn six started in still silence until the berserker turned back toward me.

"How much damage does a sacrifice do?" asked Trianna. She'd let go of her hair.

"Four dice of damage per soldier."

"Nice."

Trianna sent every rifleman trapped behind the ruined tank downhill, stopping directly in front of the melee-oriented spearmen. This would have been insane if she had any intention of them surviving.

"I'm sacrificing all these guys," she declared flatly. After that announcement, rolling for damage felt like a formality. No one walked away from multiple suicide bomb detonations at point-blank range. With the spearmen safely out of the picture, Trianna pushed her surviving squad into spitting distance of her sister's firing line.

Renee elbowed me and laughed. "See that? That's the advantage of being a toolbox. She never holds anything back."

"Thank you," said Trianna. "Your moves were okay."

Renee pawed at the spot her chips used to occupy, frowned, shrugged, and resumed the slaughter. Team Shitkicker enjoyed another leisurely round of gunning down Undwarves. The volley cut down four of the last infantrymen standing and disabled the tank's main gun.

"I'm guessing there's no way you can win this shootout," Renee boasted. I started to see how they could be related. More importantly, she wasn't wrong. The Undwarves had three riflemen and a half-dead tank left. "You know, we didn't settle on the *form* of the prize. A trophy would be solid, but I'm also cool with you doing a little dance. You can choreograph it yourself, I'm a big fan of creative expression."

"There's not going to be a shootout." Trianna put her three survivors on top of the tank. (Well within the rules but widely considered a flashy way of turning men into easy targets.) The tank ran over the central gunner, putting Trianna's team in the dead center of the firing line. If nothing else, Trianna had claimed a foothold on the hill.

"I'm also sacrificing these three."

I raised my hand. "You can't win without soldiers."

"Neither can she."

Here, I finally understood the strength of her resolve. In General Trianna headspace, losing simply wasn't an outcome. The joint explosion of her soldiers and tank produced fifty dice worth of damage, which Trianna insisted on rolling out. The conflagration wiped out the rest of Team Shitkicker, cleansing my backpack of all life.

Draws were a rare novelty. Space Glaive, by design, exposed the skill gap between players in sharp relief. A *good* player often lost to a *very good* player within three turns. Ties were only common in the later stages of high-profile tournaments, when long-term rivals faced each other for exorbitant cash prizes (by professional gamer standards). The draw confirmed what I'd suspected: I'd watched one of the best games since the first Star Orc fought the first NanoHobbit.

Traditionally, a great game was followed by a clasp around the arm. The gesture went a step beyond a handshake, marking a bond forged through conflict. The Freeman sisters replaced this tradition with passive-aggression. Trianna yawned and stared at the ceiling, pointedly avoiding eye contact. Renee toyed with her cell phone, making a similar effort to avoid acknowledging her opponent's existence.

A sense of failure settled over me. I didn't think that a game could unite a family by itself. Even I wasn't that far gone. But I had hoped it could bring out the bonds that were already there, clearing some of the fog that life puts between people. I didn't understand a lot about the world, but I understood the game. If I'd overestimated it, then understanding everything else was a lost cause. The silence at the kitchen table mocked my chances of becoming a three-dimensional person.

"Next time I'm going to stomp you," Trianna declared, ending the standoff.

Renee blew a raspberry. "Just admit that I'm better than you at this. It's healthier."

"I pulled my punches. Next week I'm going Lelouch vi Britannia on your ass."

"I have no idea who that is. But you're still going to lose."

To me, this simple exchange was a miracle. While later games would earn me money and respect, this was the match that gave me hope for the other aspects of my life. I even started dating outside the community, which was a paradigm shift for me.

More importantly, I changed up my game. I integrated the other two styles into my own and put an end to my losing streak. The standard division between tacticians, berserkers, and madmen was entirely arbitrary. Most divisions are.

Spider-Man: A character whose story effectively ended after learning responsibility and then continued for sixty more years.

spirituality: Religion without a spine.

stand-up: The only art form you get worse at by dating online, riding planes, going to therapy, disliking your ex, smoking weed, imitating Robert De Niro, observing racial trends, or obsessing over originality.

Star Citizen: The most elegant heist executed without a gun, political office, or Bloomberg machine.

streaming: The soothing trance a nation slips into as everything dear burns.

stupidity: Courage's understudy.

sugar: 1. See *Violets.*
2. Sweet.
3. See *You.*

suicide: I haven't tried it.

Superman: Defender of truth, justice, and Warner Bros. share value.

surveillance: When intelligence agencies gossip about you behind your back.

sweep picking: The rejection of sheet music in the body, mind, and soul.

T

tabloids: Mom-and-pop disinformation outlets struggling to compete with new competition.

Taiwan: The site of a vast historic tragedy around 2060 or so.

Talleyrand: An icon of the French Revolution who avoided betraying or failing his values by having none.

Tammany Hall: An organization dedicated to enthusiastic voter outreach, strong minority participation, and innovative cement-based footwear.

taste: The self-conscious curation that replaces personality around eighteen or so.

teenagers: Adults without rights, alcohol tolerance, or failure.

therapy: Alt-comedy's airline food.

thesis: The prayer an undergraduate makes before a great struggle.

three-section staff: The cheapest, flashiest, and most efficient way to kick your own ass.

TikTok: The place a dumber version of you lives.

time: The most valuable asset you can steal from someone without prosecution.

tolerance: 1. The ability to buy milk without lighting a cross on a lawn.
2. A virtue widely displaced by enthusiastic self-flagellation.
3. The conscious, tactical dissociation keeping most marriages together.

Transylvania: A common destination for expatriates with a werewolf fetish.

Truman, Harry S.: The reason we have air raid drills.

Twitter: The place a meaner version of you lives.

U

Übermensch: Someone willing and able to impose his values on a lecture hall completely uninterested in Nietzsche.

Ubik: A novella fitting thirty years of peyote into an afternoon's reading.

undergrad: Where white people teach you about diversity.

undertakers: Graveyard workers distressingly unprepared to take or deliver chokeslams.

unicorn: A joint effort between an elephant, nearsightedness, and absinthe.

United States: Inventor of the cereal jingle, dine-in gun range, and hydrogen bomb.

universe: God's toybox. Unfortunately, they're less fond of tea parties and more fond of pulling the arms off dolls.

Uno: The card game where the winner quits first.

Urban Market, The

Dear Mr. Cole,

Excellent submission. My assistants and I loved exploring the world of DragonSpire, through both your manuscript and hand-drawn topographic maps. I was particularly gripped by Prince Jerrick Glitterblade's fraught relationship with his half brother Wraith Glitterblade. There's just one issue, which I'm sure you could solve in a revision. Could you make this a little blacker?

Clearly, your vision of the world involves a number of warlocks. And that's fine: every black creative faces the specter of oppression differently. Intellectual diversity makes the black literary canon rich. A few small changes will help you fall in line with those diverse voices.

Let's start with your protagonist. Jerrick Glitterblade's current background as a HammerMancer from the Valley of Honour is a bit flat. I think he'd work better as a quick-witted arts student from the Boogie-Down Bronx, forced to contend with stiff white academics. Less of a hero's journey through the underworld and more of a subaltern's journey through undergrad. Give it some thought.

I also think we could rethink his name. Instead of *Jerrick Glitterblade*, how about *Jamal Kingston*? A little regional flavor would add specificity to his character, and we've already done Africa this year. As a Jamaican-American, I'm sure you have delightful observations on the blandness of American cuisine compared to "curried goat." Use that.

Your principal antagonists, the HexWeavers, could use similar branding tweaks. For one, the name Wraith sounds like a fantasy thing. People are more into drama-comedies (or *dramedies*, for those of us in the biz) these days. Dramedies take two seemingly disparate things—like water and sawdust—and combine them into a stronger whole. In a good dramedy, Wraith Glitterblade might be called Drake Jackson. Instead of going mad exploring necromancy, Drake could be sad because he's black. Finally, in the fourth cycle's climactic duel, a Dallas police officer could kill him instead of Jerrick.

Some of our writers find a point of reference helpful for their revisions. Have you seen *Dear White People*? I love it. You should make this more like *Dear White People*. In many ways, Justin Simien is the Tolkien of our era. Just without all the genre-inventing stuff, which I find weighed those books down a bit.

Another instructive example: *Americanah*. Chimamanda Ngozi Adichie talks about the black things from Twitter instead of a bunch of weird stuff. You could learn a lot from her example. In fact, you should just rip her off and call it a day. I won't tell anyone if you won't.

Diversity is one of the pillars of my career. Literature has the power to help make racism a memory. To join that fight, you simply have to adopt the style, diction, politics, and topics of other black writers. A little AAVE goes a long way.

Of course, you're free to go your own way. There are other agents out there, and I'm sure one of them is champing at the bit for an eight-hundred-page mythic fantasy. There's just a small chance of languishing in obscurity until the day you die.

Sincerely,
Fiona Blanche
Ivory Literary Agency

V

vaccine: 1. The invention saving millions from shivering deaths in the gutter as their organs turn to lime Jell-O.
2. Controversial.

vampires: Flexible metaphors for racial anxiety, sexual corruption, adolescence, the upper class, the lower class, creatively bankrupt film studios, and love of black lipstick.

Van Helsing: Sworn enemy of racial anxiety, sexual corruption, adolescence, the upper class, the lower class, creatively bankrupt film studios, and love of black lipstick.

vanity: 1. Self-loathing's roommate.
2. The author of all self-titled albums.

vase: An open challenge to gravity, alcohol, and time itself.

vasectomy: 1. Cheaper than expected.
2. A vote against the 2050 bread riots.

Venus: 1. Future property of the Amazon corporation.
2. The goddess of 3:00 a.m. shouting matches.

Vespucci, Amerigo: 1. Namesake of the Americas.
2. Presumably a big fan of pro wrestling, firearms, bald eagles, slavery, peanut-based inventions, and low-budget films about career women finding love with simple homegrown men.

vestigial: Body parts, branches of government, and relatives that have outlived their usefulness.

vice: Anything you enjoy after 1:00 a.m.

video games: An emerging medium finally achieving the recognition, nightmarish working conditions, and disdain for consumers found in established art forms.

Vietnam War, the: The only war on Vietnamese soil at any point in history.

Vikings: Subjects of the most comprehensive media rebranding since the ninja.

vinyl: Discs capable of storing aging self-images at near-perfect quality.

violets: 1. See *Roses.*
2. Are blue.
3. See sugar.

virginity: The shared fixation of religions, trafficking rings, and freshmen.

volume: A widely accepted alternative to insight.

vore: When dating eats you alive.

voting: State-sponsored prayer.

W

war: Two humans, one apple.

War of 1812, the: A tie in which Washington, D.C. was burned to ashes.

Washington, George: A general distinguished by exceptionally efficient retreats from his easily avoidable failures.

water: A classical element owned by Nestlé.

Welcome

Welcome to Blessed Garden Rehabilitation. Call me Ellen. I'll be guiding you through the East Coast's first open-air, publicly accessible, and human-focused maximum security prison. And in my opinion the most fun.

No, ma'am, that's not my real name. We just like using noms de plume to keep guests comfortable. Are you comfortable? I'd like you to be comfortable.

It's Kenya. Sorry about the confusion.

Naturally, I'm honored to lead your private tour. The state gives what it can, but generous donors like yourself keep the mission alive. As elite members, your family will enjoy the facility without interruption from any other groups.

I also have some lanyards if you want them. And a small action figure for your son. Would he like a Gorilla Guard or a Reformed Ronald? I'd offer Warden Wally, but we're fresh out. Those go quickly.

Yes, he may have both.

In fact, he can play with them while we take a quick security scan. I'd love to skip the formalities, but the hunger strike puts us in a difficult position. Agitators will take any opportunity to portray our work in a dishonest light.

At Blessed Garden, we believe serenity unlocks reform, and design unlocks serenity. While we're as excited as anyone about the potential of chemical, genetic, and surgical means of criminal reform, design offers us tangible solutions today.

Hence, our motto is Design First. Catchy, right?

Three quick questions before we get started. First: Would you like references to extreme violence or sexual assault removed? I can also cut material related to political dissidence, substance abuse, or cursing.

Your son wants the full show? Well, isn't he a little trouper? Now that's a Gorilla Guard attitude. Fist bump!

Second question: Have you or anyone in your immediate family been incarcerated? The scans tell us, but we start with the honor system. Admitting past subjects, however thoroughly reformed, is against Blessed Garden policy. Positivity drives our process, and bitter influences curdle it.

Final question: Any birthdays? Don't be shy. I'm great at the song.

The fun starts with Zone 1, naturally. I know car thieves and tax dodgers aren't as exciting as the serial killers, but we do a lot of our best work here. Be patient and we'll reach Terrorist House before you know it.

Please avoid throwing chips at the cubes. Strike or not, it agitates subjects.

The cubes embody the Design First mindset. Transparent walls solve isolation and overwork with one stroke. You see, activists equated the old-model subminimum wage manufacturing to slavery, and we agreed. That's why we provide our subjects with a tourable campus. By simply being observed, they give back to our research, the public's education, and their own commissary funds. Sweat-free.

They're not all black, young man. They're *predominantly* black. Precision's important. Without it, we can't address the psychological and cultural roots of criminality.

Besides, Arin here's white and enjoying the same lunch as the other subjects. Say hi to our guests, Arin.

Anytime now, Arin.

You're joining the bloody strike? Now, when I'm on the clock? That's funny. You're funny. I'm laughing because you're funny! Pissant.

Let's move on, ma'am. We don't want you to be late for lunch. Remember lunch, Arin?

Anyway, don't let his stunt ruin your morning. We've almost reached Terrorist House. We just got the Queensbridge Bomber, and he's a Hannibal Lecter type. Your son will love it.

But first, Zone 2. Between you and me, here's where it gets good. Drug runners, murderers, war reporters, the works. We keep the most antisocial subjects under close observation by staff . . . and special volunteers like your son. If you see a shiv, give me a wink, okay?

Yes, some are fasting. Not everyone's ready to make progress. Luckily, Reno and Jay here know better. They're two of the only subjects trusted to share a cube. And no, young man, neither is a "prison bitch." We gas subjects at the first sign of violence, self-harm, or excessive noise. Annual incidents are down to the low double digits.

Outside, Reno and Jay competed in rival gangs. Their organizations had an identitarian flavor, as Reno's aggressive swastika collection demonstrates. Though, in fairness, Jay's the one here for a hate crime.

That bigotry belongs to another life. At Blessed Garden they're natural, well-fed allies enjoying a nice unscheduled card game. That's the power of treatment. And it looks like Jay's played a counterspell! So much for the master race, eh, Reno?

Rude.

Ignore Reno, he's a charmer. He says that to all the unarmed women. And if he tried it, we'd gas their cube in seconds.

I'm sorry things aren't a little livelier. We have an eSports team made of hit men, but they're all making their statement. All that clicking takes calories, you know.

Their demands are, frankly, as embarrassing as they are antisocial. Inania like pornography, and television, and visitation. Predominantly pornography. Somehow, the strike's still catnip for reporters. I skip breakfast every day, but no one asks me anything.

It's pure entitled nonsense. They're warmer and safer than half the country, and we *already offer* visitation. Anyone can visit subjects on either level. They simply need to buy a ticket.

Who started it? He's not here. Mr. Porter's in Zone 3, writing a personal statement about disrupting the rehabilitation of others. We've spared him the trouble of coming up with the content. He just needs to transcribe and sign, and we can all move on.

Sorry, Zone 3's closed to the public. Especially for "Warden Wally's Deputies." You wouldn't let Warden Wally down, would you? I just might find another toy in storage.

Now, who's ready for Terrorist House?

Wendell: A name chosen by parents with a deep hatred of their spawn.

West, the: Everyone that lucked out of meeting Genghis Khan.

whales: 1. Overrated.
2. Delicious.

What?: Think a short story collection meets a modern *Devil's Dictionary.* It'll sell beautifully, trust me.

When?: Half in 2016, half in 2020. If nothing else, election years are inspiring.

Where?: Brooklyn, like everyone else on the shelves.

white balance: The only words you need to convince dates you're a photographer.

whiteness: More fun in theory.

Who?: A Brooklyn-based writer-comedian descended from Jamaican Baptists. Still Jamaican, very much non-Baptist. Owns degrees in "liking books" from Princeton and Columbia. Notably attractive.

Why?: Humor alleviates an otherwise crushing existence.

Wicca: The invocation of spirits to watch over one's trust fund.

Wilson, Woodrow: Refused to let war distract from resegregating the federal government.

wisdom: The accumulation of trauma, alcohol dependency, and subtle bigotry over time.

Wonder Woman: The first superhero to turn bondage undertones to overtones.

world peace: A leading threat to market stability.

World War I: The first entry in the franchise.

World War II: The rare sequel featuring fresh ideas, expanded lore, and a character cast that endures in memory to this day. And many, many more casualties.

World War III: 1. On time and under budget.
2. Trailers show signs of trading characterization for a higher body count, alienating much of the fan base.

X

xanthan gum: A delectable food additive also used to thicken mud in drilling sites.

Xbox Live: A crash course in American race relations.

xenophobia: The best way to get elected without learning any new words.

X-Men: A brilliant gambit to capture the plight of minorities through a team of white private school students.

X-rays: The leading cause of cancer in Metropolis.

Xtreme: Advertising's last worthwhile contribution to the public consciousness. The addition of skateboards, fire, and amateur models to otherwise dull concepts. A bagel? Quotidian. An Xtreme bagel? A story you tell for the rest of your life.

XXX: The only sticker that can still sell a book.

Y

yachts: Humble ships incapable of spaceflight.

Yahweh: God's maiden name.

yakuza: A community service organization prone to misplacing fingers on the job.

yandere: The sexual manifestation of the human death urge.

yang: Half of an unfortunate tattoo on a Montana bartender.

Yankees, the: A bank dabbling in baseball.

yards: Meters for uninsured gun owners.

yellow journalism: Where reporting meets creative writing.

yes: An affirmation of whatever the other person in the conversation is babbling about.

yesterday: Your last chance.

yin: Half of an unfortunate tattoo on a Brooklyn theater clerk.

yoke: 1. To fasten an animal into servitude.
2. To interview an intern.

yolk: The antihero of eggs. Some say it's a nutritional hero. Others say it's a terrorist. Whoever you believe, egg whites taste like nothing.

Yo mama: 1. Is so fat, she stretches time.
2. Is so fat, she bankrupted Tim Hortons.
3. Is so fat, it took six superstars to eliminate her during the Royal Rumble.
4. Is so fat, she moves the tides.
5. Is so fat, she didn't know she was pregnant.
6. Is so fat, she has her own district.
7. Is so fat, she replaced Pluto.
8. Is so fat, her footprints have frosting.
9. Is so fat, tourists try to climb her.
10. Is so fat, SeaWorld released her.
11. Is so fat, she can't see the scale.
12. Is so fat, elephants poach her.

Yorktown: The battle that guaranteed the creation and diffusion of reality television.

Yossarian: The perfect soldier.

you: We've been through quite a bit at this point, haven't we? But I still don't really know you. I like to think that you're enjoying yourself. Though that may just be my ego. At the very least, I can assume you either find me funny or have *extreme* patience. Write back sometime, we might get a nice rapport going.

your girl: Hip-hop's muse.

youth: Every day before your first divorce.

Z

zagged: You should have zigged.

Zamboni: The vehicle that cleans the ice between fistfights.

zany: 1. The worst word that can describe a film.
2. The best word that can describe fiction.

zealot: Anyone capable of reading or writing modern editorials.

Zen in the Dark Enlightenment

Nell Jackson was the first black woman, or black anything, to lead the Society for the Restoration of Monarchy. After a bitter power struggle, her dedication to bringing back the feudal golden age overcame SRM's sizable overlap with local white power movements. One cell leader endorsed her as the "Alternative Barack Obama." She had his cell purged.

Said purge wasn't *only* about the comparison to Obama. The nickname betrayed an unacceptable lack of imagination: alt-right groups had abandoned their position of power by exposing themselves. SRM was a secret society in the most traditional sense, which was essential for restoring the most traditional form of government. Yet somehow it had taken them two weeks to get a proper meeting together.

Today, Nell took her standard place just above her co-conspirators. She set her speech down on the podium and took in the scene. The lighting was just dim enough to satisfy her sense of theater, but she could still identify her co-conspirators' masks. The others took little notice of her, occupied by gossip about Leland's baby.

"What's his name?" asked Dustin, who wore a homemade iron dog mask. He affected a deeper voice during meetings.

"We went with Henry, after Hank Hill," said Leland. "That character embodies the traditionalist spirit, and non-cuck role models are hard to come by."

"Sharp. I'm sure he'll be a great fighter against degeneracy."

"Thank you! There's some mixing in his mother, but I think it's mostly washed out by now."

Nell checked off the last name on her list and beamed. Twenty-three section leaders, united under a single basement ceiling. It was a wonder democracy hadn't collapsed already. They sat in three even rows, wearing myriad neoprene, plastic, iron, copper, and clay masks. The sigils of the new world and an essential screen against outsiders. Only Irene's chinchilla mask was missing; she was stuck on I-95.

Nell adjusted her mask, which was pinching her nose. Her copper mask resembled a dragon, which would be the symbol of her royal house once the monarchy was in place. It was the final project of her spring metalworking elective, and she wore it with pride.

"Order," she declared. The room of masked insurrectionists fell silent and slid back into their folding chairs. "Congratulations, Leland," she added in a less severe voice. He returned a thumbs-up from the back row.

"Overseer," said Dustin, returning to his feet. "Why couldn't we meet on the IRC channel? Some of us in *higher-grade* universities cannot spare the *travel time*," he said haughtily. "Or interstate toll," he added more mutedly. The ears of his dog mask swayed as the fan rotated past him.

"The IRC channel is compromised, as is this room," Nell announced. "I brought you here to lance this infection."

That caused a predictable stir. Old rivals threw each other looks of recrimination, and everyone's hands floated toward their sidearm (a disarmed gentry was a tool of the degeneracy). Nell was pleased to see no open fights break out and carried on with her speech.

"While establishing the crown is our ultimate goal, it can only come about when we fight degeneracy in all its forms. This year we made our greatest strides yet. Recruitment doubled through Leland's image-board outreach and inventive #BringBackTheCrown campaign. Tessa's missionaries prevented the rise of degeneracy abroad by spreading the modified truth about homosexuality's connection to vampirism. Finally, my own cell drew a line in the sand by poisoning degenerate icon and 'musician' Jennie Sparxxxz.

"These victories are a league above our humble origins. I remember when the society was just another newsgroup content to spray-paint 'cuckold' on the cars of local leftist agitators. Today, SRM is the hidden vanguard of New York's ideological future. Which makes the presence of a spy all the more unacceptable.

"We face annihilation at the peak of our powers. This traitor has reached the highest levels of SRM, defiling this chamber. The obvious solution is interrogating the spy. Since they don't have the courage to step forward, we shall interrogate the entire council."

A contemplative silence fell over the room. Then Tessa, wearing a rubber bald eagle mask, rose to her feet and clapped furiously. The applause quickly spread through the rest of the crowd. Her enthusiasm surprised Nell. Tessa always seemed disappointed by the society's focus on overturning their failed democracy over a broader race war. The mask she'd brought to her first council meeting had been whiter and pointier, hinting at other allegiances. She was near the top of Nell's short list of likely traitors.

"Interrogate me first! My boy needs to know his daddy's not a traitor," shouted Leland.

"No, torture *me*! I get bullied all the time, I can take it!" said Brandon. He ran an active junior cell that had astroturfing web forums down to an art form. Nell needed to make sure to keep his fingers intact.

"Let's get going!" said Irene, who had discreetly joined the meeting at the tail end of Nell's speech. "I don't see why we're talking about torturing me instead of doing it."

Nell shone with pride. Her last secret society would have whined endlessly over their rights. SRM understood the spirit of martyrdom.

"I'll take my fingernails off myself," Dustin added after the applause died down. "One question: Who's going to do all the torturing?"

The question stole Nell's momentum. She hadn't considered all the details yet. She was less than half an hour out of Math 203 and still having trouble thinking in words instead of integrals.

"As overseer, that burden falls to me," she improvised.

"Then who's going to torture *you*?" asked Dustin. Nell's grip on the podium tightened. Evidently they had different ideas about executive privilege.

No one in the room was an option. She'd screwed everyone over at least once to become overseer, and they'd interrogate her with extra gusto. Waterboarding could easily turn into drowning with the right undercurrent of spite.

"I've found an independent contractor," replied Nell. "Someone we can trust to interrogate the council evenly and fairly."

"How?" asked Leland.

"She's not part of the society. Or society at large. Therefore, she can't have betrayed us already and has no incentive to betray us in the future."

The applause returned. Nell bowed, walked graciously up the first flight of stairs, and sprinted up the second. She darted through the ground floor of the YMCA at twice the speed of the treadmill users, bowling over any camp counselor or yoga instructor dim enough to get in her way. In the parking lot she jumped on a bike that wasn't hers and pedaled past six blocks of suburbia hidden in urbania. When the tall buildings returned and the lawns disappeared, she ditched the bike, sprinted to the doorstep of 923 Mordekaiser Lane, and mashed the buzzer for apartment J.

"I know you can hear me, Mya!" shouted Nell. "I'm not leaving this doorstep alone!"

The speaker clicked to life.

"I'm busy. Doing creative things," said a deep, somnolent voice obscured by static. Nell could imagine her sister in an unwashed sweatshirt, playing *Cyborg Farmer*. She mashed the buzzer again.

"Nell, I live on the sixth floor. I love you, but I don't *like* you enough to make the walk down. I'm moving to a second-floor studio next month. Try me then. I'll need help lifting stuff."

Instead of mashing the button, Nell simply held it down. Six minutes later, her sister opened the door.

Mya had a faded UPenn sweatshirt, her omnipresent smartphone belting the *Cyborg Farmer* theme song. Most of the rings under her eyes were missing, which meant that she'd slept this week.

"You look better than usual," Nell said. She realized the diplomatic failure the second the words escaped her mouth. Asking for help would take some adjustment.

"That's not something you should say to your twin. It's bad for your self-esteem," Mya said, letting her gaze sink back to *Cyborg Farmer*. Nell tried to discern if she was genuinely offended and promptly gave up. Understanding Mya was an insane woman's project, and she had degeneracy to destroy.

"Of course! Very insightful, and mordant, and a third thing. I need your help saving the Society for the Restoration of Monarchy."

Mya returned to eye contact but kept swiping at the screen. The game had been reduced to muscle memory.

"Is that your LARP thing?" Her voice didn't rise or fall from word to word. In high school, Nell thought that she was possessed.

"SRM is not a *LARP thing*, it is the *future* of this failing country. I need you to *torture* them and *lightly question* me to root out the traitor in our midst."

"Shouldn't you finish the revolution before breaking out the circular firing squads?"

"Enough jokes. Come back with me and I'll buy you one of those poison sacks you call food."

"A Taco Queen beef piñata?" asked Mya. Her eyes widened.

"The same."

Mya shut the door. Six minutes later she returned with jeans, a notebook, and a cleaner version of the same sweatshirt.

"This should be fun."

"There is no fun in the revolution."

"Some revolution."

Mya strolled behind her sister, which threw off the "panicked sprint" pace Nell was trying to set. She stopped to look at the pillar-flanked buildings at least three times during the shortcut through the urban suburb, bringing Nell to the edge of fratricide.

"Can you imagine how much it costs to own a house like this in Brooklyn?" asked Mya. "In a block of four others like it?"

"It will be standard for the nobility," Nell said, distracted.

"We already have nobles. This is where they live. You've missed your boat."

Nell wrote off the comment as part of the acute progressive dementia afflicting writers around the world. Mya was a victim. Mercifully, a victim clever enough to sniff out the rot in the society.

The pair returned from Nell's ideal future to the debased present surrounding the YMCA. A vagrant held the door with one hand and a crimped Big Gulp cup in the other. He tilted the cup toward Mya, shifting the change within. Then Nell put on her dragon mask. He squinted, shook his head, and walked away.

Mya didn't ask about the mask, the beeline they made to the basement door, or why none of the YMCA employees (Leland's men) tried to stop them. She just wrote two short notes in her book and kept walking.

"Any questions?" Nell asked before opening the door to the council chamber.

"Nah, I get it so far."

Inside, the cell leaders of SRM stood in a near-perfect circle. Each held a pistol to the head of the member to their left. Eyes shifted with the sisters' entry, but no heads turned.

"How did this . . . *what*?!" shouted Nell. Her sister nodded and scribbled more shorthand.

"You were taking a while, so we assumed the spy's cohorts had killed you. Logic dictated that you were innocent and the traitor was still in the room. So we decided the best thing to do was execute each other and let our cells carry on. Zero tolerance: degenerate spies wouldn't dare return."

Nell had switched off the safety on her own ten-millimeter before she caught herself.

"I've brought a local blogger," announced Nell. Her sister leaned over and whispered in her ear. "I've brought a local *author*," Nell corrected, rolling her eyes. "As you all know, writers are half-degenerate. One foot is in this world of filth and reassignment surgeries. A handshake with a screenwriter is enough to catch six different strains of the same venereal disease. But the other foot is in the old world, where blood and letters were pure. They wrote the speeches of kings and plays about other kings conquering them. It is the second profession. As a half-breed, this woman is equipped to sniff out degeneracy's familiar scent and snuff it out."

"I don't get it," said Tessa. "Is this a rap thing?"

"It's my sister. She's cool."

There was a general murmur of consent as guns were returned to their concealed-carry positions.

Mya had gotten creative during Nell's speech. A YMCA T-shirt was tied around her head in the same ninja mask she'd learned to make online ten minutes before last year's Halloween party. It was a small thing, but the gesture made her part of the room's natural flow.

"Thank you for electing me High Inquisitor," Mya said at twice her typical volume. Nell did not recall an election. "Torture's kind of a blunt instrument. I'm just going to use interviews."

Perfect. Nell's odds of losing her fingernails had already fallen exponentially. Her mood soared until she noticed that the High Inquisitor stood behind the overseer's podium. She still had the book, which was rapidly filling with illegible notes.

"So, inquisiting. Could we form a line in the back?" asked Mya. "I don't think I can inquisite everyone in the room at once. Crowds make me nervous."

The leaders of the uprising formed a single-file grade school line in the back of the basement. Leland ended up in front and gave Nell a questioning glance. She nodded and he stepped before the podium for judgment.

"I bow before the council's wisdom," said Leland. He took a knee.

"We saw the council's wisdom earlier. It was going Jonestown," said the High Inquisitor.

"Sorry."

"Not my problem. Let's hear your elevator pitch."

"Pardon?"

"Summarize yourself. Tell me your qualifications as a reactionary."

"Well, my code name is Red Dusk, and my name is Leland. I majored in advertising at Purchase, but my minor was in classics. The Spartans knew how to live. If society continues down this sinful path, Zeus will bathe us in lightning."

"Pagan," muttered Tessa.

"Very nice," said the High Inquisitor, still scribbling. "Did you intern before this?"

Leland hid his confusion poorly.

"Do you have any experience in other reactionary organizations? It doesn't have to be a management role, or even paid."

"No."

"I see. Very suspect. Do you have any character references?"

"Your sister?"

"Any character references that didn't steal my clothes in high school? They don't have to be professional."

"My wife likes me, I think."

"Works for me. You're dismissed," said Mya. Leland returned to the back wall in a state of total bewilderment. "Next suspect."

Tessa strode to the podium with regal poise. Nell suspected that Tessa imagined herself as the first queen of the new America. A difference of opinion they would need to discuss later. Over knives.

"Code name?" asked the High Inquisitor. She balanced her pen on her pointer finger, having somehow grown bored during the transition between suspects.

"White Eagle."

"Cool. Real name?"

"Tessa Dean." Something in Tessa's voice prompted Mya to take a note. Perhaps the naked disdain.

"Miss Dean, where do you see yourself in ten years?"

"A position of great importance."

"Like what? Doctor? Lawyer? Lead guitarist? Give me something to work with."

Tessa tapped her temple with her thumb as she thought. "Duchess," she answered carefully.

"Ah, so you've got a different kind of loyalty problem. Carry on."

Tessa's stride was upgraded to a full-on waltz on the way back. Nell quietly wished she'd coached her sister before the meeting. Missing a chance to bury a rival felt wasteful.

"Who's next?" demanded the High Inquisitor. She'd folded Nell's opening speech into a paper airplane. Brandon came forward and imitated Leland's exaggerated kneel. Then the plane bounced off the nose of his wolf mask. He glared at the High Inquisitor with open ire.

"Code name?"

"Razor Alexandria."

"Edgy. Real name?"

"Brandon Daniels."

"What does the Society for the Restoration of the Sixteenth Century mean to you?" asked the High Inquisitor. Nell weighed the value of correcting her and opted to let it go until justice had been served.

"The world sleeps, but I am awake. Degeneracy has infected everything. The food is poison, and the media is worse. Our leaders do not rule for God or country. They simply rule to rule. I learned the truth after Jenna left me for that dick Martin. That wouldn't have happened if a king were in charge. Or the church."

Nell nearly cheered but maintained decorum. Brandon had an artful way of painting a young monarchist's pain. She considered him the Raphael of the Dark Enlightenment. Yet Mya just looked bored.

"You're a threat to a few things, but not this organization. Next."

Nell's turn had come. She took her time on the way to the podium. Mya probably needed the time to come up with a softball question for her.

"Code name?"

"Apex."

"And your real name?"

Her sister's voice rose and fell, with human enthusiasm. This threw Nell off-balance.

"Nell Jackson."

"Nell, you seem nervous. Do you have a reason to be nervous?"

"What? No."

Mya made another note. There shouldn't have been anything to write down. The next suspect should already have been on the firing line.

"All right, then. What's your greatest strength?"

"Loyalty," Nell boasted without reservation.

"Base pandering—very suspect. What's your greatest weakness?"

"I'm clearly a bit too trusting."

"Ah, so you often feel betrayed. By the world, this organization, and even the crown itself. That feeling could drive a woman to extremes."

"Was there a question there?" Nell asked, struggling against the current of the conversation.

"Now you're questioning the High Inquisitor? Do the rules of this society mean anything to you?!"

"Mya, I'm going to beat you like a socialist the second we get out of here."

"Out of line, Apex. You've said more than enough, and currently stand as lead suspect."

"Your stories are pretentious garbage," Nell announced. "They teach you not to write in the second person in high school. Semicolons don't make you look smarter, and neither does the word 'redolent.' You're going to die unknown and alone in Bed-Stuy long after it ceases to be fashionable to your type."

The High Inquisitor slammed her right fist against the podium. Then she shook it out and cradled it in her unbruised left hand.

"Deputy White Eagle, kindly restrain the suspect."

Tessa was behind her with a pistol drawn before Nell could start her next insult. A minute later, both of Nell's arms were tied to the radiator with YMCA T-shirts. She sat cross-legged and glowered at her supposed comrades. They avoided eye contact with religious dedication.

"Go fuck yourselves," Nell suggested.

"Disregard the suspect, and gag her if she pipes up again."

"Yes, Inquisitor," said Tessa, standing comfortably to Mya's right. Nell wondered if calling their parents was a betrayal of the uprising.

She'd known from the abundance of iron eagle tattoos in the room that some members of the society resented working under her. But Nell never imagined that they resented her enough to put a different black woman in power. Only the enemy deserved that kind of reflexive, self-destructive spite.

"Next, please," Mya said with new enthusiasm. She put the finishing touch on a longer burst of notes as her next victim approached.

"Good afternoon, High Inquisitor," Dustin said amicably. His new-found decorum made Nell want to punch him in the kidney.

"Did you say afternoon? I have a thing at three. Let's try to move this along."

"As you wish, High Inquisitor," said Dustin.

"Code name and name."

"Orbital Hammer and Dustin Seed."

"Why is monarchical revolution important to you? Try not to go on for too long." The High Inquisitor pecked at her phone with her unbruised hand.

"We've tried everything else for a hundred years," Dustin began. "On some level, nations are arbitrary. But a king gives a nation's spirit a voice. Belief follows. And that belief turns it from something arbitrary into something real."

The Inquisitor put down her phone to scratch a short note. It couldn't be more than a word.

"It's him."

"What?" said Leland.

"What?!" said Dustin.

"Whatever," said Nell.

Tessa didn't waste time with questions. She already had a gun under his chin.

"Damn you," Dustin hissed.

It took one angry pull for Nell to free her right arm. The knot was garbage unworthy of brushing against the wrist of a future noble. She undid the other knot more casually. Every second of silence left her treacherous followers in limbo a little longer.

"Explain," Nell said, rotating her wrists.

"He spoke intelligently and persuasively about bringing back feudalism. He couldn't possibly be one of you." Mya's voice returned to its flat default.

"Did you need to tie me up to learn that?" asked Nell. Sensation slowly returned to her fingers.

"Good job me," said Mya, ignoring the question. "You've really earned that beef piñata, Mya."

"You statist pigs are obsolete," spat Dustin. "Anarcho-communism is the wave of the future! Your society is just a dead end, soaking up valuable talent."

"That's nice Mr. Crazy Person," answered Mya. "Good luck walking the plank, or whatever fifteenth-century ritual they have here for snitches. Nell can't afford an iron maiden, so you'll probably survive. I'm going to try selling a write-up of this to *Vice*."

"Just leave out our real names," Nell said wearily. It had been the longest meeting in SRM history. The loss of SRM's prized secrecy was just another twig on the pyre. "And be honest."

"Sure. Though I'll probably punch it up with weird sex."

Nell didn't react to the bait. She couldn't spare the energy, especially since she still had to drive Dustin to another undisclosed location without hitting any tollbooths full of prying eyes. A long, dull night of formal excommunication waited.

A month later, "The New Lords of Brooklyn" dominated her news feed. It was a tragically faithful transcription of events, save for a lurid three-paragraph tryst between the overseer, the traitor, and a dog. Nell never spoke to her sister again, until she needed something else.

zeppelin: A vehicle capable of crashing and exploding with twice the efficiency of rival aircraft.

zeptosecond: The life span of a soul in an open office.

Zero: World War II planes that were *good* at flying and *excellent* at crashing.

zero tolerance: The first words following a private prison donation.

zigged: You should have zagged.

zombie apocalypse: A nightmare scenario in which bloated, shambling, brain-dead imitations of life are attacked by zombies.

Zoroastrianism: Monotheism before it was cool.

zygote: A cell doomed to decades of empty suffering without emergency intervention.

Acknowledgments

I never understood this section until I had to write one. Anyone I leave out might have me beaten.

First, I'll thank my mother for keeping me out of a padded cell. It would have saved her a great deal of effort. I'll also thank my sisters. They didn't help with this project, but I like keeping the peace. As for the rest of my family, step your game up.

Postmortem thanks to Terry Pratchett and Joseph Heller for the humor template I've leeched off for thirty years. If I were a little older and white, their estate lawyers would already be after me.

Educational thanks to Rivka Galchen, Paul Beatty, Paula Stops, Paul LaFarge (I do well with Pauls), Kevin Dombrowski, Susan Choi, Angela Flournoy, Mark Doten, Gary Shteyngart, and more for teaching me 2 rite fancyish. Without them goodtalk, my wordences make many sadfrowns.

Deep thanks to my agent Reeves Hamilton, for taking a chance on me when I'd essentially given up. Without him, I'd still be writing terrible ads for even worse products.

Enthusiastic thanks to my editor, Chelsea Cutchens, for treating 3:00 a.m. emails as acceptable business practice. Her open mind and patience made this book possible. She also fixed an embarrassing math error in "Recent Activity."

ACKNOWLEDGMENTS

Personal thanks to Ryan Armstrong, James Bizzarro, Hoang Tran, Tristan Dubin, Daniel DeBonis, Samantha Onorato, Josh Crawford, Ben Herman, Felix Ortiz, Jessi Jezewska Stevens, Arthur Phidd, Linda Wang, and Willa Chen for listening to half-formed ideas during parties, meetings, and attempts to sleep. I have some thoughts on the next book I'll run them by you later.

Finally, no thanks to my tag partner Sam Lagow. I win. Your work after this might be better, but I'll always be first. Nerd. Bask in my light and be blind.